I0738656

OPERATION AMELIORATE

A Clio Project Story

MARK S. ROBERTS

Copyright © 2020
MARK S. ROBERTS
OPERATION AMELIORATE
A Clio Project Story
All rights reserved.

No part of this publication may be reproduced, distributed, or transmitted in any form or by any means, including photocopying, recording, or other electronic or mechanical methods, without the prior written permission of the publisher, except in the case of brief quotations embodied in critical reviews and certain other non-commercial uses permitted by copyright law.

MARK S. ROBERTS

Printed in the United States of America
First Printing 2020
First Edition 2020

10 9 8 7 6 5 4 3 2 1

This book is a fictionalized portrayal of the U.S. Air Force security police, security forces, special operations, bases, and their surrounding region. It is not intended to depict actual persons, organizations, or places. All characters, names, places, and incidents are products of the author's imagination or are used fictitiously. Any resemblance to any actual persons, living or dead, events or locales, is entirely coincidental.
The author took dramatic license with some descriptions of vehicle usage and associated weaponry to simplify the narrative. In the event you use of the information in this book for yourself, which is your constitutional right, the author and publisher assume no responsibility for your actions.

DEDICATION

This book is dedicated to my parents, Don, and Joe-Ann Roberts, and to my in-laws, Gerald (Jerry) and Elizabeth (Betty) Schaff, for their unwavering love and support, and being good people.

Mom and Betty, I miss you both.

TABLE OF CONTENTS

CHAPTER 1

The five security police members arrive on base at 0400 hours. They approach a gate at Area 51, dim the headlights to the HUMVEE, and slow to a stop when one of the gate guards emerges from the darkened interior of the gate shack. He extends his hand in a gesture indicating the vehicle should stop.

"Good morning," the guard says to the driver as the window is cranked down.

"Good morning to you, and it's an early one at that. Just love coming to work at oh-dark-thirty," the driver says with a ready smile, pulling out his identification card and collecting the other passengers' cards. The driver holds the cards out so the guard can take them just as a second guard exits the same gate shack and approaches the passenger side of the Hummer. The passengers roll their windows down and say hello.

"Where you guys come from? Haven't seen you on the base before," the second guard asks while saluting the lieutenant in the front seat when he recognizes the rank.

The front passenger, 1st Lieutenant (Lt.) Derrick, smiles. "We're from Nellis, operations inspection. Orders from the Bank and MILES HQ," he explains.

"Ah, been seeing more of you MILES types here lately," is all the guard says and looks over the hood at his partner, who retreats into the gate shack for verification. The second guard turns back to the passengers. "Must have been a long ride. You all billeting or staying in the barracks?" he asks, watching each passenger with his weapon at the low ready.

The lieutenant shakes his head. "Neither. We're going straight to work, then head back out. Short assignment. We'll catch some Zs on the way back to Nellis if needed. It's not that far a drive." The lieutenant looks at the gate shack as the first guard comes back and hands the identity cards back to the driver.

"Everything is good to go. Know how to get there?" the guard asks.

"Sure do. Been there a few times before. Routine assignment," the driver tells the guard, taking the cards from him.

"All right then, have a good one, Sergeant, Lieutenant," the guard says, coming to attention and saluting. The second guard does the same, and Lt. Derrick returns the salute as the driver moves the Hummer past the guards and onto the base.

Lt. Derrick turns in his seat to look at the NCO and two airmen sitting in the back. "Everyone knows what to do, right?" he asks them.

"Yes, sir," the men and woman answer. The lieutenant looks at each team member who stare back, nods then turns back around to face forward, watching the dirt road unfold in front of him.

They drive through the desert for several minutes, cresting a hill as the base comes into view. The dirt road finally ends, and the Hummer drives onto asphalt with the sound of the tires changing from a bumpy gravel crunching sound to a smooth hum. The dust cloud that was chasing them like a ghost also dissipates when they drive onto the hard surface as if a magic spell had been cast to drive it away. They continue until they locate the building they are looking for.

The driver pulls the Hummer up to the front of the building and stops. The lieutenant grabs his briefcase and exits the vehicle with the two NCOs and two airmen doing the same. They follow the lieutenant to the door of the building. Lt. Derrick flashes his identification badge at a camera, and they hear an audible click, indicating the door is unlocked. They enter the building, and the door closes behind them, trapping them in a foyer that has another door leading into the building, a Sallyport.

"Lieutenant Derrick," a voice booms from a speaker in the small room, "you and your team need to relinquish your weapons, ammo, vests, as well as your briefcase. We will also need you to remove any metal objects larger than a button from your person and place those in the box as well."

The lieutenant un-holsters his nine-millimeter, as do the NCOs, with the airmen unslinging their M-16 rifles. They double-check the weapons to ensure them safe. The vests, ammo, pistol, ammo, and personal items are placed into a large drawer that opens along the wall to their left. The briefcase is inserted as well.

Once done, the drawer collapses into the wall. The rifles are stacked in a rotating cylinder that opens a housing rack for the weapons. Once they are inserted and secured, the cylinder rotates back so the guards can remove them.

"Now, sir, step into the screening room," the bodiless voice instructs. The lieutenant steps up into a large box, like the ones used in the courthouse for body scanning, but much more sophisticated.

"Raise your arms above your head and remain still."

Lt. Derrick does as he is told. Each member of the team recreates the same scenario and when the last person is through, they are allowed entry further into the building. The lieutenant opens the door and sees a Federal Protective Forces (ProFor) Security Police officer sitting behind a large desk, a podium, where he sits higher than the lieutenant and his personnel.

The guard issues each person a badge, which they place on their uniforms. Their weapons, equipment, and personal items are returned, as is the briefcase. They thank the security police officer at the desk and proceed down the corridor.

Much of the base security is overseen by NNSS Security Protective Force Officers, with a few USAF Security Police members assigned to stand-alone Air Force assets, such as the Clio Project. This is where the five newly arriving members proceed. They arrive at the door leading to the security police office. One of the airmen opens the door, and Lt. Derrick and the others enter. The room is spacious, and to the left is a hallway leading to offices.

Blocking access to that hallway is a desk with an SP Senior Airman (SrA) sitting behind it. She looks up when the door opens and acknowledges the team by asking for their orders. Lt. Derrick puts on a friendly smile, hands her a small, encased CD, and asks to speak with the captain in charge.

She takes the encrypted CD and places it into a slot on her computer. She types in a few strokes and fiddles with the mouse, then removes the disc, handing it back to the lieutenant. She then tells him Captain Spencer is on his way. After a few seconds, the captain arrives.

"Lieutenant Derrick, I'm Captain Spencer. What can we do for you?" he asks as the two men shake hands. "I see you are here on special assignment and I'm to cooperate in any way I can. Can't say I'm happy with this. Usually, we get a warning before anyone shows up. This is unusual even for MILES and the Bank. Didn't even know they worked together."

Lieutenant Derrick clears his throat. "Ah, Captain Spencer, we are here for a quick inspection of the Inabular Devices. The Bank is concerned after hearing some chatter that they might be the subject of a heist. Highly unlikely, but the Bank asked MILES to conduct an unannounced check, just a precaution. We need to have access to it as soon as possible, and once our assessment is completed, we can be on our way and out of your hair," he finishes with a smile.

Captain Spencer's eyebrows rise, and he sighs. "Well, okay. Let me get a couple of NCOs to go along—" He is cut off by the lieutenant.

"Sorry, sir, we are going to do this ourselves. As you can see by the orders, we have autonomy with this, and your assistance is not required, other than your cooperation, as you just stated. We're just following orders, same as you, sir," Lt. Derrick says, again with a smile.

Captain Spencer looks at the computer screen. "Yes, I see that. Well, just let me know what you need, and we'll be on it."

Lt. Derrick clasps his hands together. "That's great, sir. First, Senior Airman Willis will need access to the control room and relieve your on-duty personnel. Second, Senior Airman Franz and Staff Sergeant Milner will relieve your guards of their posts, and Master Sergeant Butler and I will conduct the inspection," he tells the captain.

Captain Spencer does not like surprises, as this is a highly classified area, and surprise inspections are not routine. Being one of the most secure facilities in the USA, they don't really have any security concerns, thus no need for surprise inspections. They are professional and self-contained, only conducting internal exercises among themselves, but as more testing of top-secret projects come along, the more need for heavier security, he surmises.

But this is different. They have never had someone come in to look at the Inabular Devices like this. He looks at the lieutenant, nods, and tells the Senior Airman at the desk to notify the others of what is transpiring. She does so immediately. The captain turns back to the lieutenant.

"Is there anything else, Lieutenant Derrick?" he asks.

"Yes, sir. We will only be here a short time, so have your troops stand by. Once we are finished, we will inform you, and they can return to their duties."

"Will you be coming back to this office?" Captain Spencer asks.

"No, sir. Once we are finished, Airman Willis will inform you, and once your people have returned to their posts, we'll be on our way. It's been a long night," and he looks at his watch, "and now day. We're anxious to get back to our base," he says with a chuckle. The captain smiles his understanding and holds out his hand, which the lieutenant takes.

"Nice to meet you, Lieutenant. Good luck. I think you'll find everything in order."

Lt. Derrick nods. "I'm sure we'll find that to be true, sir," he says, releasing the captain's grip. He turns towards his group. "Let's go, people, daylight's burning." They leave the room.

Spencer still doesn't like this and has never cared for MILES, a self-contained, seemly self- serving branch of the government that works for a small group of senators. Knowing politicians as he does, he doesn't trust them, nor their Minions. He turns and walks back to his office. Once there, he picks up his phone and dials the Bank. An automatic answering system announces he has reached a classified area, and it explains the procedures which must be followed before being allowed to speak to anyone. Captain Spencer follows protocol with preauthorized answers and is quickly put through.

"Bank. What extension?" a male voice asks.

"Bank Management," Spencer answer.

The voice on the other end doesn't say anything as he's is being transferred.

"Colonel Rhodes' office, this is Rebecca, what can I do for you?" the voice asks when the phone is answered.

"This is Captain Spencer, Branch Teller. I need to speak to the CEO. Is he in?"

"Yes, sir, he is, hold one please," the woman answers.

Spencer waits for only a few seconds before he hears the colonel come online.

"Captain Spencer, what can I do for you?"

"Sir, there's a team of security police here for a security check of device 341. They claim they are a joint operation between MILES and the Bank, at your request."

"Yes captain, that is correct. We received word someone might be looking to take the devices, and we don't want to take any chances, so I asked if MILES could help us out."

"Well, I see, sir. Okay then, sorry to bother you, just double-checking."

"That's quite alright, Captain. Good thinking on your part. Anything else?"

"Ah, no, no, sir. Again, sorry to bother you, and thank you."

"Quite alright, son. Goodbye." The line goes dead.

Spencer takes a breath and releases it. *Well,* he thinks, *I guess that's that,* and hangs up the phone. He still has a funny feeling in his gut though, and he trusts his gut.

~   ~   ~

A recreational vehicle is parked in a Crystal Spring rest stop, right off the extraterrestrial highway that leads to the tiny communities of Hiko and Rachel. The outside of the vehicle is marked with, "I Believe", "Show Me Them Aliens" and other stickers and UFO memorabilia throughout. Inside the vehicle is a whole other world. The interior is filled with multiple types of electronic equipment, used to monitor radio and telephone wavelengths. This particular vehicle is used to intercept and decode cryptic telephone messages from Area 51.

The men and woman using the equipment just finished intercepting a message from Captain Spencer. This was a telephone call they were expecting. The call was transferred to their system and mimicked the Bank's system. When Captain Spencer made his call, he thought he was talking to the Bank but, in reality, he was conversing with two MILES agents inside the RV. MILES knew someone could become suspicious and contact the Bank to ensure the MILES SP team was authorized to enter the Device Vault. Once Spencer hung up, they look at their leader, who is leaning back in his chair, sipping coffee.

"That went well. Time to move, people," he says quietly, taking another sip of coffee.

One of the male agents and the female agent move to the front of the vehicle. The male agent sits in the driver's seat and turns the ignition switch. Everyone is dressed in civilian clothes mimicking UFO enthusiasts out to visit the sights. The other agent stays at his post monitoring the radio and radar as they drive away.

~ ~ ~

As the SP group walks down the hall towards the control room, Lieutenant Derrick reaches into his briefcase and retrieves a cell phone, along with a Zippo lighter and a ballpoint pen, all of which he hands to Airman Willis. Willis takes the items and places them into his cargo pants pocket and stops in front of the control room door. He knocks once and watches the others as they continue down the corridor. After a brief wait, the door opens, and Willis relieves the control room NCO of his post.

Once the NCO leaves the room, Willis removes the items and begins dismantling them. He opens the cell phone and unscrews the pen, which contains an electronic connector for the phone. Next, he pulls the lighter apart and takes wires that contain small alligator clips on one end and small plugs on the other. He connects one end to the cell phone connector and drops down to the floor and crawls under the console.

He reaches into his ammo pouch and pulls out a weapon magazine. Unlatching the bottom of the magazine, out drops a small electric screwdriver into his hand. He begins unscrewing the bottom panel of the console. Once open, he reaches in and pulls on some wires. He finds the wires he looks for then connects the clips. Satisfied it is connected correctly, he turns on the phone and clambers up into the control room seat. Upon checking the security feed, he grins. The device is rerouting the camera footage, as well as disabling the security alarm systems. Though the alarm system more than likely won't be triggered, better safe than sorry. He has had just enough time to accomplish his task when he sees the others approaching the outer door to the Inabular Devices safe room.

Lt. Derrick approaches the first door and relieves the guard of his post, leaving Airman Franz in his place. The lieutenant looks at the camera, clearly the go-ahead signal to Willis, and hears a whining sound as the door is opened. He and the rest of the team enter the foyer, where the second guard is relieved of her post and Staff Sergeant (SSgt) Milner takes her place. The second door opens, and Lieutenant Derrick and Master Sergeant (MSgt) Butler enter the Inabular Devices Vault.

Wasting no time, the lieutenant disables the security system and opens the vault. Once open, he enters a seven-digit code, and a small box slides out of the wall revealing the object they came for, one of the Inabular Devices. MSgt Butler has already removed a section of the lieutenant's briefcase and retrieves an exact duplicate of an Inabular Device.

He hands it to the lieutenant, who exchanges it with one of the real devices, then hands the original back to Butler, who places it into a hidden compartment of the briefcase and closes it. Lt. Derrick closes the sliding box, secures the vault, and turns towards the Master Sergeant. He grins, and they leave the area.

SrA Willis watches the whole process, and when the two men exit the room, he types in a code that makes changes to the security footage. Now, when anyone watches the video, all they will see is the lieutenant and sergeant entering the room, examine the Inabular Device without touching it, then secure it, and leave the room.

Airmen Willis calls the Senior Airman at the desk and notifies her that their people can return to post. Once he finishes, he drops back down to the floor, removes the electronic device, secures the cover, returns everything to its proper place, then waits for the NCO to return.

Once all the SP personnel return to their posts, Lt. Derrick and his team begin their way back down the corridor towards the exit. They are met by Captain Spencer along the way.

"Lieutenant Derrick, I hope everything was above board."

"Sir, we did what we came here for and will report our findings, or lack of findings, to our supervisor," he says with a broad smile, hoping the captain gets the idea the inspection went well. "I'm sure he will be in contact with your commander soon. Thanks for your cooperation, sir," he says and moves around the captain to the debarkation room.

The captain eyes the team as each one passes him and says goodbye or just *sir*, as they pass. Again, all weapons, equipment, and the briefcase are placed into a separate area for screening. Once the team is in the room the captain turns towards the ProFor Officer. "I want those weapons and briefcase checked thoroughly, then checked again, got it?"

The officer acknowledges and whispers into his radio to the police force officers conducting the search and screening.

Lieutenant Derrick waits impatiently for the guards to get them their equipment and his briefcase.

What the hell is taking them so long?

He walks over to the call box on the wall. "What's the holdup, officer?" he asks, then releases the talk button.

"Sorry, sir, takes a little longer processing out than in. It shouldn't be too much longer," the voice says over the intercom.

After an agonizing wait, the team grows restless, and the lieutenant becomes more impatient. He has been through screenings before and this is taking too long. He walks back over to the intercom to inquire about the delay when the drawer opens and their weapons, gear, and the briefcase are returned. The lieutenant says thank you to the officer and everyone grabs their weapons and gear. Suiting back up, they walk to the exit door.

After another agonizing wait, they finally hear the door release mechanism *click*, and they proceed into the foyer. Once the interior door is secured, they hear the outer door unlatch, and they all calmly exit the building and get into the Hummer. Sergeant Butler starts the vehicle, backs out, and turns the vehicle towards the gate.

They stop at the gate and show their ID's to the guards. One guard contacts the main base, and when he returns, he informs the team they are free to leave. The guards salute, and the lieutenant returns the salute and wishes the two a good morning.

Once outside the perimeter of the base, each member of the team removes a clear plastic coating from their hands and fingers. The thin coating of material was applied before they entered the base to cover their hand and fingerprints so as not to leave any evidence of their presence behind in Area 51.

They are about thirty miles from Area 51 when they hear Senior Airman Willis exclaim, "Ah, shit. Ah, shit!"

MSgt. Butler glances into the rearview mirror at Willis as Lt. Derrick turns in his seat. "What's the problem Willis?" he asks, watching the airman as he pulls out magazines from his Mollie.

"Ah, shit," is all Willis keeps saying. "I can't find it."

"Find what, Airman Willis? What are you doing?" the lieutenant asks with tension in his voice.

Senior Willis places his hand on his Mollie and looks at the lieutenant, "I'm missing a magazine LT. One of the ones holding some of my tools," he finishes, tightness in his eyes while looking around the vehicle.

"Are you sure, Willis?" Lieutenant Derrick asks but is ignored by Willis.

"Airman Willis!" the lieutenant asks more forcibly.

"Are…you…sure?"

"Yes, sir. Ah, shit."

Derrick turns back around in his seat and looks at Sergeant Butler. Butler glances at the lieutenant. "Orders, sir? Want to go back?"

Lieutenant Derrick purses his lips and rubs his chin in thought. "No, too risky. If they have the magazine, they've opened it by now. Once they see what's inside, then it won't be long until they start investigating. Sooner or later, they'll figure out that one of the Inabular Devices is missing." He turns back in his seat and looks at Airman Willis.

"Willis, calm the fuck down. It doesn't matter, we're out of there, and we have the device. That was the mission, and we succeeded, so get frosty right now. We won." The lieutenant then scans the entire group. "Now, let's get to the rendezvous point while we still have time."

They continue driving the posted speed limit. With very few cars on the freeway at this time, and this portion of the state being the home of several military bases, no one pays attention to them. After about fifteen minutes of travel time, they see an Eighteen-Wheeler parked along the side of the road with a state police patrol behind it, lights flashing. The semi-trailer has the roller gate up, and a ramp is extended out the back.

MSgt Butler drives the Humvee around the cop car and stops the vehicle at the base of the ramp. The passengers get out, removing their uniforms, and Butler drives the vehicle up into the trailer. Lieutenant Derrick and Staff Sergeant Milner have state police uniforms under their military clothes and are provided with weapon belts and hats to finish the look. Master Sergeant Butler and Senior Airman Franz are dressed in jeans and faded T-shirts with a rock band name on one, and a national beer company logo on the other.

Both men grab worn baseball caps and place them on their heads. SrA Willis wears a motorcycle outfit and grabs a helmet and a motorcycle from inside the trailer. Butler and Franz jump down from the trailer, and Butler races around to the cab, climbs in, and starts the big diesel. Willis rides his bike down the ramp and stops by the rest of the team. Lieutenant Derrick walks over to him.

"Willis, be careful, and we'll see you later," the fake state trooper tells him.

Willis smiles and closes the shield on his helmet, revs the bike, and takes off, gunning the engine to raise the front tire off the road as he goes down the freeway. Lieutenant Derrick and Sergeant Milner go to the patrol car where another person dressed as a state police trooper waits. They enter the vehicle and watch as Franz closes the back of the trailer and locks it. He gives a quick wave and rushes to the passenger side of the cab and enters.

The patrol car moves onto the freeway and passes the semi-trailer just as Butler puts it into gear and moves the big rig onto the road.

CHAPTER 2

Captain Spencer watches as the ProFor and security personnel examine each item from the five-man team. When finished, the Profor team leader shakes his head.

"Everything is in order, sir."

Captain Spencer with a frustrated shake of his head informs the inspector to give the equipment back. He goes to a security monitor and watches as the Security Police members gather their belonging, exit the facility, enter their vehicle, and depart. He knows something isn't right, but he just can't put his finger on it. He turns from the monitor and proceeds down the corridor towards his office.

Staff Sergeant Becker, the control room monitor, looks around his desk to ensure everything is still in the same order before being relieved of his post. Finding nothing amiss, he sits in his chair and swivels back towards the monitors scooting the chair closer. His right boot strikes something that moves across the tile and makes a metallic sound as it strikes the console. He pushes back in his chair to look under the console desk. He sees an M-16 magazine lying on the hard floor.

He reaches down and retrieves the magazine and lays it on the countertop. He is about to call it in when the bottom of the magazine catches his attention and notices the bottom plating is hanging open with a hinge. M-16 magazines don't have hinges, they slide open.

Setting the phone back onto the cradle, he lifts the magazine and opens the plate the rest of the way. There is no spring attached to the bottom of the plating and when he looks inside, he sees there are no bullets. He turns it in his hands to look at the bullets on the top when something falls out, first onto his lap, then tumbles onto the floor. He holds the magazine up, looking at the opening, then at the small electric screwdriver that fell onto the floor. Bending over, Becker picks it up, examining it and the magazine. Then he tries to push the bullets down into the magazine but finds they won't move, they are stuck in the top row position, glued, welded, something keeping them in place. He realizes what he has and that the airman who relieved him must have dropped it. *What the hell was he doing with this?* Becker thinks, then reaches for the phone.

Captain Spencer walks towards the Senior Airman at the desk, noticing she is on the phone, and overhears her, at the same time as she raises a finger in a "Hold on" gesture.

"Hang on, Sergeant, he's right here," she says, looking up at Captain Spencer, "Sir, you might want to go down to the control room. Sergeant Becker found something he says you need to see. Says it's important."

Captain Spencer doesn't acknowledge her, he just turns and quickly walks back into the corridor. A few seconds later, he stands at the control room door, using his key card and handprint to enter. SSgt Becker stands when the door opens and turns towards the captain. He points to the magazine and screwdriver on the countertop.

"Sir, when I came in after the airman left, I found this on the floor underneath the console. The bottom was slightly open, so I finish opening it and this screwdriver fell out. Another thing is the bullets aren't real. This is a container used to transfer the screwdriver. No one would know the difference just looking at the magazine from a distance, or even picking it up, not unless they tried to remove the bullets."

Captain Spencer looks at the sergeant for a second, then walks over to examine the items more closely. He doesn't understand. He looks inside, then tries to remove a bullet to no avail.

"You're saying this—" He doesn't finish the sentence and places the magazine on the console, tells the sergeant to secure the magazine as evidence, and hurries from the room. He runs to the Inabular Device safe room where he and the sergeant on duty enter the room. Captain Spencer and the sergeant open the Inabular Device's drawer, and Spencer sighs in relief when he sees all the devices are is still in place. He relaxes a little, then both men leave the room after re-securing the devices.

Captain Spencer stands in the hallway, thinking, *Why would that team need to be here, and why would a person need a fake weapons magazine containing an electric screwdriver?*

Captain Spencer heads back to his office and calls the Officer in Charge of the **Air Force Research Laboratory (AFRL)** branch located on the installation.

"Major Douglas' office, Sergeant Phelps speaking."

"Sergeant, this is Captain Spencer of the Security Police squadron. I would like to speak to Major Nayar. It's top priority."

"Yes, sir. Hold one, please," the sergeant says and places the captain on hold.

Less than a minute passes and the phone is picked up. "Major Nayar. What can I do for you, Captain Spencer?"

"Major, we recently had an outside team of security come in and look at device 341. Checking on security systems is to be expected, but something was off about this team, and I would like some of your people to look at the devices. Just as a precaution."

"Anything particular we're be looking for?" the major asks.

"Not sure. Just want to make sure the devices weren't tampered with or damaged or whatever someone could do to them," the captain explains.

"I can have a team over there within half an hour," the major replies.

"That'll be good. Thank you, sir." The captain disconnects the call.

Captain Spencer returns to the control room and asks the sergeant to playback the video of the security teams' entry into the safe room. The sergeant complies, and they both watch as the lieutenant and sergeant from the security team enter the room, open the device drawer, and just look at the Inabular Devices. The two men just stare at the devices for a few minutes, then close the drawer and exit the room. Nothing nefarious about it, but it still doesn't sit well with the captain.

"Play it again," the captain asks.

The two men watch the video a few more times when the captain notices the two men are stone still. The timer in the lower corner of the video shows the clock running, but the men don't move a muscle, not for over a minute. He looks like he's staring at two people frozen in time then, suddenly, they move as if released from some spell.

"Sergeant Becker, can you make a copy of this?"

"Sure, sir, no problem," Becker answers.

"Good, get that to me ASAP," the captain tells him and leaves the control room.

Captain Spencer heads back to his office and calls the Office of Special Investigation (OSI) located on the base. He asks to speak with the commander and is put right through.

"Steve, what's up? Haven't heard from you in a while. Must be something going on," the colonel in charge of OSI asks.

"Colonel Gorman, sorry to bother you, but I've got a request. I had a security detail come in earlier for a visit and something just doesn't feel right. I've got a couple of things I would like you all to look at. First is a fake M-16 magazine that was used to conceal a small electric screwdriver, and second is a video of the team members entering a classified room and examining device 341." Captain Spencer explains to the colonel.

Colonel Gorman doesn't hesitate. "Anyone handle the magazine? "

Spencer is a little embarrassed, knowing evidence should have been handled with gloves and not handled at all if possible. "Yes, sir. Sorry. Sergeant Becker and I have handled the magazine as well as the screwdriver. We were the only two, except for the airman who left it in the control room. It's since been placed in an evidence bag."

"No worries, shit happens. We have everyone's prints on file, so we can eliminate you and the sergeant when scanning for further prints. Okay, when can you get the evidence here?"

"I'm on my way as soon as I get a copy of the video, which should be any minute now."

"Good. I'll have the lab boys ready for you," the colonel informs the captain.

"Thank you, sir. I'll see you in a few minutes." He hangs up. He looks up at movement in the doorway and notices a sergeant stands there with a CD in one hand, his other hand about to knock on the door frame. Spencer stands and asks if he has the video he requested, which the sergeant acknowledges he does. Spencer takes it and dismisses him. He grabs his beret moving towards the exit.

The OSI building is located at the center of the base, and it takes only a few minutes for Captain Spencer to arrive. He exits his car and walks into the building where he is met by an agent in the lobby.

"Good morning Captain Spencer, Special Agent Gibson, I'll take you to the colonel," the younger woman says and opens a secure door, allowing the captain entry, and then herself. They walk down the corridor and stop in front of Colonel Gorman's office where she knocks once and is told to enter. The colonel smiles as the captain salutes.

"Captain Spencer, not here, we're agents, don't salute us. Unless we're in uniform," the colonel says to him, rising to shake his hand. "You got something for me?"

Captain Spencer hands the evidence over to the colonel, who doesn't take it but indicates Spencer should hand it over to Agent Gibson. She takes it from him and signs a chain of custody form, then leaves the office. Spencer watches her go, then turns back to the colonel. The colonel points to a chair, and Spencer sits.

"Now, tell me, what this is all about?" the colonel asks.

Captain Spencer goes through what has transpired throughout the morning, even explaining he has personnel from the AFRL coming in to examine the Inabular Devices. As if on a cue, the captain's cell phone rings. He excuses himself and checks the number calling: it's his office.

"Sir, I need to take this, it's not private."

"No, please, go ahead."

"Thank you," he says and connects to the caller. "Captain Spencer."

The captain listens for a few seconds, then says, "Let me know the minute they have anything. Yes, I'll be here, thanks," he says and disconnects the call.

"That was my office, the AFRL personnel are in the building and are in route to the device vault for an inspection. I said I would be here if needed."

The colonel gets up to grab a cup of coffee and offers one to the captain who declines. Before the colonel can get back to his seat the captain's phone chimes again. He immediately picks it up, then listens for a few seconds before quickly standing up. "Are they sure?" he listens more. "No, contact the commander, inform the local authorities to be on the lookout for that Humvee. Send everyone pictures of the five airmen and secure the safe room and vault," the captain finishes, then faces the colonel, whose forehead is furrowed, eyes watching.

"They swapped out a device."

"What?" is all Colonel Gorman can ask?

"I knew something was up," Spencer says, looking at his watch. "They couldn't have gotten too far, and they came from Nellis. We can probably get a chopper up and sweep the area and locate them. Shouldn't be too many Hummers rolling down the freeway."

The colonel tells him to use his office and get the ball rolling.

"Playing devil's advocate here, but what if they aren't from Nellis? What if they head in a different direction? It's still a good idea to send out a Blackhawk, but I would bet they have other plans to avoid us."

Captain Spencer agrees but still wants to try. The colonel nods and informs the captain that the Bank must be notified of the situation. The colonel says he will also be flying out to the Bank to brief the commander personally. He turns and leaves his office so that Captain Spencer can do what he needs to.

Gorman walks into another agent's office and tells him to send a secured priority message to the Bank, then proceeds to spell out what he wants to say to Colonel Rhodes.

CHAPTER 3

Senior Master Sergeant Scott (SMSgt) Rees stares at the faded security police beret crest in his hand, a grin on his face. He turns it over and examines the backside for a second, noticing the metal prongs that are used to attach the crest to the beret are worn down, then back at the front where the TAC (Tactical Air Command) emblem looks worn, but still readable. He pockets the crest and looks at Senator Olsen.

"I'll see that he gets it, sir, and thank you."

"Oh, that's quite alright, Sergeant. I really just wanted you to see that in case you didn't believe who I am," the congressman says with a wry smile, then continues, "I am serious about possibly needed you and your team. I know it's a little early yet," he says and looks towards the tent where the men's remains were just removed, "but, sometime soon, I'm sure we will ask for your help."

Rees looks at the man, glancing at his assistant for a second then back to the congressman.

"Sir, I am a member of the US Air Force and follow orders when they are given. I can't speak for the others as we have not really had time to get together and discuss our futures. I'm not sure what is going to happen to us," he says as Olsen raises his hand in an indication for Rees to stop talking. Rees complies.

Olsen smiles and shakes his head. "Sergeant, you will all be allowed to make your own decision as to what you want to do. If you decide to stay in the Air Force, you will stay in. Anyone who wishes to leave may do so, with conditions of course," he adds.

"Of course," Rees replies.

Congressman Olsen continues, "As I said, my office oversees the Clio Project, which you and your men are a part of. You are pioneers, as well as Rock Stars to many of us."

Rees gives Olsen a quizzical look, raising an eyebrow. Olsen notices the look.

"Oh, yes, you all are heroes to those who know what you've accomplished."

Rees' quizzical look turns to one of anger."

"I'm sorry, Congressman Olsen, not trying to be disrespectful, but we didn't accomplish shit except to get some of my men, my friends, killed." Rees, points towards the tent, gritting his teeth and clenching his jaw. "As well as lose a portion of our lives we will never get back!"

Senator Olsen raises his hands and waves them in a calm down manner and shakes his head.

"I'm sorry, Sergeant Rees, I misspoke, something I usually try to avoid in my profession. I do apologize, and I am deeply sorry about what has happened. You must understand, it wasn't my generation who did this, and those who were responsible for the mishandling of the experiment were punished. We can't take back what happened, but we can make your lives as meaningful and productive as you would like. What I meant by accomplishments is you were able to travel in time and return as well as not screw up the timeline and have shown us how it's done," Olsen says with a smile still on his face.

"I wonder if they practice that continuous smile?" Rees asks himself, distracted, then returns to the subject, and interrupts the senator. "As far as you know, sir. We haven't had enough freedom in the outside

world to see what may have changed," he says, then feels bad for jumping in. "Sorry, sir, go on."

The congressman takes it in stride and continues.

"Those in charge of the project, the higher-ups I mean, the Council, they had no idea about what could have happened by pushing the project forward and not listening to the scientists' concerns about space-time continuum and other time constraints that could have altered the course of history."

Rees calms down and adjusts the coat he is wearing shaking water off it. Congressman Olsen gives him a second, turning away, then looks back at Rees.

"Walk with me, Sergeant, please?" he asks. Rees comes alongside the man, and they walk towards the parking lot where Rees can see a large Cadillac surrounded by men in suits. Olsen walks slowly and gives Rees a sidelong glance.

"Listen, Sergeant Rees, I am on your side. My ancestor's stories are the reason I pushed to get involved with this project after I became a senator. We will do anything to help you and your men. As I said before, anything you each decide to do will be granted. Again, within reason of course. We would hope all of you decide to stay in and stay with the program."

Rees glances at the other man as they walk. "I thought you were a congressman?" he asks.

Olsen tilts his head towards Rees with a frown, and then understands. "Ah, sorry. Yes, I am a senator, but you can call me a congressman or senator, either is correct."

"Yes, sir. Sorry, I'm not that up on what people in your position are called. I am only acquainted with what I can remember from high school," Rees tells him. "Okay, about all of us staying in. What about TJ, I mean Sergeant Shepard? He lost his leg, what about him?"

"Not a problem. We have others who are disabled who have been allowed to continue to serve. He will have the best medical treatment there is, as well as state of the art prosthetics. We will continue to teach and train each of you, to get you caught up, and to make you the best versions of yourself you can be. I believe each of you has something to offer us, and we would like you to stay. I hope I can count on you to help me get this across to the others."

Rees stops just short of the limousine and turns towards the senator.

"Senator Olsen, I hope you don't mind me calling you senator, just easier for me?"

"If that's what makes you more comfortable, please, senator it is," Olsen replies.

Rees continues, "Sir, I don't know you. You seem like a decent person, but you are a politician."

Olsen looks at Rees for a second, wondering if he is joking or not. Then he takes a gamble, hoping he is, so he laughs.

"Why yes, I am, and I know how members of the military feel about politicians."

Rees smiles, but it doesn't reach his eyes.

"Yes, sir, and you are correct. I'm sorry, but politicians put me and my team in this situation, and now you want me, them, all of us to just trust you?"

Olsen takes a deep breath and lets it out.

"Okay, fair. I know trust must be earned, and I was hoping my being here as well as being involved in your safe return would help, but I see that I will need to work a little harder for it. I will be in touch with you again sergeant. In the meantime, please talk with Colonel Black, sorry, Major Black, hasn't put it on yet, and others about me." He places a hand on Rees' shoulder in a fatherly gesture. The gesture feels genuine to Rees, not a gesture of a politician looking for a vote.

"We'll work this out, Sergeant. I do hope we can come to an agreement and work together as a team. I want this project to carry on, not stay mothballed. I believe you and your men can help us with that. All I ask is that you give me a chance. Okay?" he asks, and he releases his grip.

Rees nods. "I will try, sir."

"Good, that's all I ask. Come, let me introduce you to my wife," he adds, walking over to the limo. An aide opens the door, and Rees looks inside to see an attractive older woman who stares out at him and smiles. *Probably turned quite a few heads in her day,* the younger man thinks.

Olsen introduces her, "Sergeant Rees, this is my better half, Joyce Olsen."

Rees walks over to the open door. Joyce Olsen steps out and offers her hand, which Rees takes. Her grip is firm, something Rees didn't expect but appreciated. "Mrs. Olsen, good to meet you," he says, still in her grip. Suddenly, Rees gets a strange feeling from this woman. Nothing he can put his finger on, maybe it's just the way she looks at him, seemingly to study him.

"No, Sergeant, the pleasure is all mine. I've heard about you, and your team, of course, and I wanted the chance to meet you. See you myself," she replies with her radiant smile and she releases his hand.

"And please, call me Joyce," she insists, retracting her hand and still smiling.

"Yes, ma'am…Joyce," Rees gets out.

Senator Olsen intervenes, stepping out from under the umbrella.

"Thank you again, Sergeant Rees, and we will be seeing you soon."

Olsen then looks at the sky.

"Well, the clouds are breaking up. Good, a good sign," he finishes, giving Rees one last look, a smile, then enters his vehicle after his wife.

CHAPTER 4

Rees watches the senator leave, then looks at the sky, glad to see the rain has finally stopped and that the sun is breaking through. He takes another look at the tent and watches the crew working around it, cleaning up and putting things back as they were. He turns back to the parking lot and begins walking towards his Ford F-150. He smiles inwardly, after receiving his first check, well, direct deposit they call it, no more checks, to his bank, he was mildly surprised at the amount. Okay, he nearly shits himself when he saw the amount. He used a portion of the money to pay cash for the truck, and he got all the bells and whistles he could.

He opens the truck door and clambers in, enjoying the new car smell. He still hasn't gotten used to the computer screen and all its stations and mapping, but he has time to learn. He starts the engine and drives away, listening to a Little River Band song along the way. He looks around until he spots his escort parked discreetly away in the corner of the lot. He thinks about waving to them, then decides against it.

"They're there only doing their job," he says to himself. The government doesn't completely trust him, or any of them, quite yet. The major said it was for his safety, and that could be true, but there's only a handful of people who know about the project and of him, and the squad. Of course, all it takes is for one person to say one little thing and the whole story could get out. Loose Lip Sink Ships as the World War 2 poster used to say. There could be agents or spies out there looking to grab him and see what he knows. He guesses it is good thing he has a couple of bodyguards, as well as his personal security, a Smith & Wesson M&P 40C.

He turns onto the road and heads back towards the base. He stops at a 7-Eleven for a cold drink and a pack of peanuts. As he pays for the items, with cash, he still hasn't got used to the ATM card yet, he looks at the packs of cigarettes behind the counter. He yearns for one but really doesn't want one. One of the perks of what happened during the return from his time travel adventures. Somehow the doctor's or scientist, or whomever, were able to wean him, and the others who smoked, off tobacco. All except TJ, who said he liked to smoke, so he continued. Rees will talk with him about that. The clerk returns with Rees's change, and this brings him back to the present. He thanks the lady, grabs his items, and pockets the change. *Damn, the price of things now, wow,* he thinks and exits the store, liking the auto doors.

As he climbs into his truck, he sees his escort, again trying to be discreet, but failing miserably, parked among some other vehicles in an adjoining parking lot. Rees shakes his head, starts the truck, and pulls out of the parking lot.

He drives straight to the base, sipping his soda and munching on the peanuts. Along the way, he thinks about what the senator told him. He did seem genuine when speaking with him, but he is still a politician. Of course, he was partially responsible for getting him and his team back. He will have to speak to the major about the senator, get his opinion, which he has come to trust.

Pulling up to the main gate, he shows his identification card and is allowed entry. Rees drives to the building where he and the others are housed as well as train, study, and work. The Clio Project has its own building, set miles away from the main section of the base, and is surrounded with double-layer electric fencing, concertina wire, alarms, mines, and a guard gate.

He approaches, slows, and even though he is recognized by the guards, he is still required to identify himself before being allowed entry. The guards go through the routine, say hello to him, and he proceeds.

He parks his vehicle in his designated spot, another perk, and jumps out. Looking around, he sees that everyone else with a vehicle has returned. He walks to the main door, and using his right hand, places it on a scanner that reads his fingerprints, as well as his palmprints. After the screen scans his hand, he hears an audible *click*, indicating the door can now be opened. Still holding the soda in one hand, he uses the other to open the door and enter the facility. He feels the difference in the temperature once inside, always cooler. *Must be because of all the computer equipment stored inside*, he thinks.

He heads down a corridor and comes to yet another checkpoint. He shows the Security Forces airman his identification and uses a thumbprint on a smaller screen. Again, his identity is verified, and he can proceed to the elevator. The guard opens the doors from his desk, and Rees gives the young man (shit, not much younger than he is, relatively speaking, of course) a nod and enters the hoistway.

On the way down, he thinks about Corporal O'Toole, the young Irish cavalryman they accidentally brought back with them. He hasn't had time to speak with the man and scolds himself for not doing so. It is partially his fault he was brought to the future after placing him in the *Duck*, the armored vehicle they used in their time period, then forgetting about him during the battle between them and the Union Army. He was so engrossed in the battle that he forgot about him, and when the time travel process began, it was too late to do anything about it anyway. They didn't have time to think about anything except their survival before being transported to the future.

As the elevator doors open deep underneath the base, Rees tells himself he will go talk with O'Toole and see how he's doing.

Rees exits the car and walks down to his room. He wants to change out of his dress blues and into another uniform, then go see the major. He must inform him of the meeting with the senator. Using his identification card as his key, he enters his room.

"Lights," he says as he enters, and the room becomes lighted. Another modern development that amazes him. *Star Trek stuff everywhere,* he thinks, removing his overcoat and hanging it up.

Rees's room is a good-sized room. More of a small apartment than a room. He has his own bathroom, separate bedroom from the living room, a small office, and a separate kitchen that has all the appliances needed to keep food, as well as give him the ability to cook for himself if he decides he doesn't want to eat in the dining facility. He still calls it the chow hall and gets reamed about it constantly from the services personnel.

Fuck 'em if they can't take a joke, he thinks.

Rees finishes undressing, hanging up the uniform, and changes into his Airman Combat Uniform (ACU). He smooths down the front of his uniform and makes sure everything is in order. The new uniforms have taken a little getting used to, and as military personnel will do, he has listened to some of his men bitch and gripe about it. Nothing can be done, just get over it and get used to it. Besides, in a couple of years, they'll be changing into the Operational Camouflage Pattern (OCP) uniform currently used by the grunts, he means Army. One thing about the military, it is a living organism, always in flux, growing and changing.

That got him to thinking about when he was at his first base and they had rotated officers in and out over the years. Every officer wanted the Standard Operating Procedures (SOP's) changed, so they did. One month you'd be doing things one way, a few months later, you'd do it another way. While Rees was at one base, the SOP's changed completely around, a 360-degree process where they were doing the same procedures they had been doing four years before, but wait, they would change again in a couple of months, starting the process all over. He shook his head at the memory.

He drops his reflection of the past and just as he is ready to leave his room the computer on his desk chirps. He checks and sees that TJ is calling him. Rees answers the call, and TJ's face fills the screen.

"Christ, Sergeant Shepard, pull that ugly mug from the camera lens. Bad enough I have to look at you, I don't need a grotesque giant size face filling my screen," Rees says, a bemused smile while thinking, *More Star Trek stuff.*

"Sorry," TJ responds as his face moves back from the camera, revealing a normal size head, well almost. A person can be seen standing behind him. "Not used to these damned things. Camera's so little."

"You're fine now. What can I do for you, and hurry, got places to be," Rees says, looking at his watch like he's late for an appointment.

Shepard looks nervous and turns and looks at who's standing behind him. The person behind him smacks him on the back, urging him to talk. Rees shakes his head.

"Spit it out, Sergeant, and who is the anonymous person behind you pulling your strings?" Rees asks.

TJ laughs. "Told you he could see you."

The person behind JT leans over to reveal SSgt Tosseti.

"Of course, Tosseti. Should have known. What the hell you two scheming up?" Rees asks, chuckling inside but staying serious on the outside.

"Hi, Sergeant Rees. Hey, listen. We know it's only been a short time since everything has happened, but we were wondering when we're gonna be let off the base for real. You know, a little sightseeing, you know some things educational. Local history. You know what I'm talking about," he says in his thick Bostonian accent, looking sheepish.

"Yeah, I know what you're talking about, sightseeing. Let me guess, that's Tosseti and Shepard for bar hopping. Educational would be learning what brand of liquor and beer are at the sightseeing places and local history. Oh, that would be you two wanting to make history with the local women. Am I close?" Rees asks.

Tosseti looks at Shepard, who leans back in. "Aw shucks. Com'on, Sarge, it's been months, and we're going stir crazy. Even Tosseti is starting to look good," TJ whines.

Tosseti punches TJ. "Hey, fuck youse, you fucking peg-legged hillbilly," he says, receiving a punch back.

"How about it, sir? Can you talk with the major about it? I gotta get laid," TJ begs.

"What, five-finger-Rosy break up with you?" Tosseti asks.

"I got your five-finger Rosy right here, you sawed-off fuck," TJ spits back as he grabs his crotch.

Rees shakes his head. "Alright, knock it off. Won't you two ever grow up?" Rees admonishes them, then sighs. "I'll see what I can do. I assume you're not the only ones. The others feel the same?"

"Yes, sir, all except MSgt Bouvier. I don't think he likes girls." All the guys start laughing.

Rees again shakes his head. "I'll see what I can do, and I'll be sure to let Jack know what you think of him. Isn't he your supervisor?" Rees asks and shuts off the call before the two men can answer.

Rees checks himself, looks around the room, and heads out. "Lights," he says as he leaves, and the room goes dark. Rees knows he doesn't have to turn them off, as they do so on their own once the computer sensor system realized no one is in the room, but he just loves saying it.

He goes back to the elevator and tells the system to take him to the command level. *Even more Star Trek stuff,* he thinks as the elevator drop down a few more levels. Once it stops, the doors open, and he walks down the hall. He passes what will be his office and looks at the plaque on the door that has his rank, name, and new job title, NCOIC (Non-Commissioned Officer in Charge) Development & Deployment. He still isn't sure of his position in the squadron but is very curious and a little excited to get started, whatever it is.

He continues along the hall until he gets to a flight of stairs that lead into Major Blacks assistant's office (got to be careful not to call her a secretary, that's cause for an ass-whooping, or worse, an ass-chewing from her). Rees enters the front office where he is greeted warmly by Samantha Johnson, the major's aide.

When Sam was in the Air Force, she had worked for the major in Special Operations. When her enlistment was up the major offered her a job as his aide, which she readily accepted. Granted, she does the same things she did for him when enlisted, but now, she makes a lot more money and only answers to the major.

Rees opens the door and smiles at Sam.

"Good afternoon, Miss…shit, sorry, Ms. Johnson," he says with a lopsided grin. "I'll get used to using that more since it's deemed more appropriate."

"Good afternoon, Sergeant Rees," she says with a smile, her dark skin accentuating her perfect set of teeth. "And don't worry about the Miss thing, I know you boys have to get used to a few things, and I find it cute, not off-putting like if the others tried that."

Rees noticed she used boys and accepted the little comeback due to his mistake. Point taken.

"How was the, ah, ceremony?" she asks awkwardly. "Sorry, just don't know what to call it," she finishes sheepishly. Not something Rees has seen from her since getting to know her.

"It was fine, very moving. Not too long, and I think we can all get some closure," he tells her, placing his beret on a rack. Trying not to stay on the awkward side, he changes subjects.

"What you are packing nowadays, Ms. Johnson?" Rees asks, referring to her pistol he keeps next to her for security reasons.

She smiles. "Well, first off, if you keep calling me Miss or Ms. Johnson, we are not going to continue to be good friends. I've told you before, it's Samantha, or Sam, okay?" she asks with another smile.

Rees nods and raises his hands in surrender. "Got it, will do."

Looking down at where she keeps her weapons, she continues, "Still using a Berretta 92-F. I tried a few others, but I'm just used to this one. I might try a Glock, but for now, this will do."

"Cool. And I wouldn't want to try you with it. Being ex-Special Operations and all," Rees says, trying to keep a straight face, but failing, but also knowing she would be able to handle herself quite well.

She smiles back. "And you would be right."

"The major make it back?" Rees asks her, still smiling.

"Yes, hang on," she tells Rees as she picks up her phone.

"Sir, Senior Master Sergeant Rees is here," she says into the receiver. "Yes, sir." She hangs up.

She looks at Rees. "Go on in, Scott," she tells him, and he looks a little shocked. "And don't forget it's Samantha or Sam," she finishes and winks, causing Rees to blush slightly, which he tries to hide by hurrying onto the major's office.

Major Black stands by his desk, looking into the room housing the now mothballed Clio Project. The rooms are in the exact location they were in when built in the 1970s. Same room, just refurbished and updated with newer equipment, electronics, computers, alarms, and furniture, everything you could dream of. He was thinking about what it must have been like when his predecessor, General Richardson, stood here decades ago, watching the first men travel through time.

His thoughts are interrupted when Sam tells him SMSgt Rees is here to see him. He acknowledges her and turns to wait for Rees to enter.

Shutting the door behind him, Rees strides to the major's desk and salutes. The major returns the salute and looks at Rees quizzically, with a slight smile on his face.

"What's wrong, Sergeant? You looked a little flush. Feeling okay?" the major asks, seemingly concerned.

Rees shakes his head. "No, sir, nothing like that. I just let Sam, Ms. Johnson, your assistant..." He doesn't finish before the major understands. Raising his hand for Rees to stop talking, he chuckles.

"I get it. She has that effect on men. I can talk to her about that if you like," he says, already knowing the answer.

Rees looks aplomb. "Oh, no. No, sir. No need to do that. I can handle it. Just got to get used to the 21st Century woman, that's all."

"Good, good," the major replies, inwardly laughing. "What can I do for you?" he asks, sitting down behind his desk and pointing to a chair in front for Rees to sit in.

"A couple of things, sir. First, I want to say congratulations on your promotion to colonel," Rees says as he takes a seat.

"Thank you."

I didn't know you could jump two ranks. How'd that work if you don't mind my asking?"

The major chuckles. "Well, it seems that to oversee this project you need a colonel or higher. Since I am the son of the man who created Clio, and I am most familiar with the project, the powers that be felt I should be the one in command. That, and Senator Olsen, as well as POTUS, both seem to like me, so they bypassed the law requiring me to be a lieutenant colonel for a period of time. Kind of like a step promotion of sorts."

"I guess it pays to have friends in high places," Rees says with humor in his voice. "Well, congrats again. When do you put it on?"

"The orders should come through any day now. Sometime this week, I'm sure. Hell, it could be today for all I know. Senator Olsen said he wants to pin them on me here since we can't really have a big ceremony. Not that I mind. Really not into the dog and pony show," Black says. "And, again, thank you. What else is on your mind?"

Rees nods. "Second, I would like to see Corporal O'Toole, if possible. I haven't spoken to him since our return, and I think it might be good for us to talk."

The major nods. "That can be arranged, and I agree, you should speak with him. Not just you but those who dealt with him during and after his capture. The shrinks and historians have been hammering him relentlessly, and he'll probably like seeing someone else who won't badger him for information. He's been very insightful for everyone concerning how a 19th Century person thinks and firsthand information concerning the war, as well as everyday life in the mid-1800s."

"That's good to know, and thank you, sir."

"Anything else?"

"Yes, sir, there is. After the…the ceremony," the only thing he could think of after what Sam called it, "I was approached by Senator Olsen."

Black leans back in his chair. "Yes, he told me he wanted to speak with you and Sergeant Bouvier."

"Did he tell you what about, sir?" Rees asks.

"Something about returning an object that belonged to one of your men, and that he just wanted to meet you and Sergeant Bouvier. He wanted you to know who he was and where he stood concerning Clio and its possible use."

Rees nods. "I need to ask you what you think of him. My first impression is positive, but he is a professional politician. I assume you've known him for some time?"

Black nods. "Several years now, a good man. As I've said before, he is the one most responsible for getting Clio back up and running, then getting you all home. I've never had a reason not to trust him. Why? You have concerns?"

Rees sits straight in his chair and removes an invisible piece of lint from his trousers, then brushes his pants with his hand absentmindedly.

"Well, politicians put us in this mess…well, not mess, but where we are now. I know we work for them, but I just never trusted them. Maybe I'm being a little paranoid, but you can see where I'm coming from."

Major Black leans forward, placing his elbows on the desk and clasping his hands together, resting his chin on his thumbs. "Sergeant Rees, I can understand your reluctance in trusting him, but believe me, Senator Olsen has nothing but the best intentions for you, the men, all of us. He believes in the Clio Project and just wants what is best for the country in using it. I give him my wholehearted support and hope you will, too."

Rees gives a half-hearted smile. "Yes, sir. If you trust him, then I will also. Since being back, everyone has been great and supportive of us. I'll give it a shot."

"Good, that's good. I don't know what he has in store for you, or Clio in fact, but I'm sure we will find out. He's been pushing to get it back on track, but there are hurdles. Before using her, we have to make sure we can do it in a safe manner, and with the understanding that everything we do can change the timeline. This is a priority before the project gets up and running."

Rees again nods his understanding. "Yes, sir."

The major watches Rees for a few seconds, seeing concerns in his eyes. He stands and walks over to a cabinet that houses a small bar. He pulls downs a bottle of Woodford Reserve bourbon from the shelf, then pours a small amount into a couple of glasses. He walks over and hands one to Rees.

Rees, who is lost in thought, looks up after the major taps him on the arm with the glass. He comes out of his reverie, looks at the major, and then the glass. He turns slightly in his chair and accepts the glass.

"Uh, why thank you, sir," he manages to get out.

The major smiles and pulls out the other chair and sits across from Rees, getting out from behind the desk. Two military men having a drink and a chat.

"What else is on your mind, Scott?" Major Black asks.

Rees takes a sip of the bourbon, looks surprised. "Good stuff, sir. Have to get me some of this," he says as a way of deflection. The major says nothing, takes a sip himself, eyes never leaving Rees. Rees knows he's waiting for an answer.

"Sir, we've only been back a few months. The men haven't come to grips with what has transpired, not completely anyway. We have a lot to catch up on. Take me trying to talk with Sam for one. I don't know how to interact with a woman like her. Think what it's going to be like once we all get out into the world. Thirty-eight years is a damn long time, and adjustments may take some time. And speaking of getting out into the world, sir, we've been stuck here for quite a while now. And we do appreciate you letting us go off base, but we need to be able to interact with others, not just military personnel. The guys are getting a little antsy, nothing to worry about, but they're wanting to get back some normality in their lives."

The major grins. "You mean women?"

Rees looks at the major, serious at first, then chuckles. "Well, that would be part of it I'm sure, but I'm talking about interaction with all civilians. Going somewhere where they can talk with others, become adjusted to the outside world. Nothing big, start out letting us out for an evening somewhere close to the base. We know our escorts will keep an eye on us, and I promise the guys will behave. If not, me and Sergeant Bouvier will snatch a knot in their heads."

Major Black thinks for a few seconds. "Scott. Hmm, let me ponder that for a little while. This isn't all for me to decide. The command structure wants to make sure none of you get out into the world and make yourselves known. Let me see what I can do, okay?"

Rees nods. "Yes, sir. That's all I ask. Thank you."

The major is still silent for a few seconds, takes another sip of his drink. He leans over with his elbows on his knees and places the glass between his hands, rolling it back in forth as he stares into the golden liquid. Finally, he speaks, going back to a prior subject.

"Scott, I can't imagine what you and your men went through, and I, as well as everyone else here, won't pretend to. This section is still operational because of the senator and a few others willing to bet on Clio and to help you and the others adjust. Sure, it's going to take a while, but you have all the time you need to get up to speed and back into operational status. We are patient and are here to help."

Rees again thanks the major.

"With that being said, we do expect you to become operational. The shrinks have said that each of you have become well-adjusted, and they are surprised at how well each of you have handled the situation. Not one of you seems to have any emotional trauma or psychological damage. In fact, they say you all have adjusted faster than anyone who has come back from a war zone. No Post Traumatic Stress Syndrome whatsoever. Quite amazing.

"Each of you have gained knowledge at a phenomenal rate. You all absorb everything you read, or see, and retain that info, far superior to a lot of other people. Now, it would be a fluke if it was just one or two of you, but every member of your team. Spooky is what it is."

A slight headshake from Rees. "Don't know what to say, sir. I feel the same. Don't think I'm any smarter than I was."

The major waves his hand in a dismissive manner. "Not anything to worry about, and I'm sorry I brought it up. That's not what you were talking about anyway. We were talking about you and your men coming to grips with being in the future and losing things important to you from the past. I get that, but I was assured by the good doctors that each of you have recovered well and adjusted to the new situation. They said all of you are slowly accepting what has happened and should be able to interact with the outside world in a few months."

Rees again nods his understanding.

"Listen, Scott, I know you are a little heartbroken over Nora, again, I'm sorry—" the major begins but is interrupted by Rees.

"Oh, no, sir, it's not that. Sorry, didn't mean to interrupt you," Rees says, and the major shakes his head dismissively.

"I will get over this. It's not just about Nora or other friends who will never know I'm still alive. It's about..." Rees hesitates, thinking. "Can I be a 21st Century man, can I adapt? Hard to explain." He looks at the major and his demeanor changes. "I tell you what, sir. Don't worry about us, we will get over it. Improvise, adapt, and overcome, right?" Rees asks with a wide smile. "Didn't mean to get melancholy on you, sir. After-effects of the ceremony, I guess. Probably be this way until after the funeral service, but if we keep busy, which we will, it'll pass."

"Have you had time to talk with the others about their futures?" Black asks.

"Not in a formal manner, no, sir. We've each talk at one time or another, but like I said, it's only been a few months," Rees answers.

"That's good, keep me in the loop. I think it's better if you talk with the guys before I do about this.

"Yes, sir. I do too."

With that, Major Black stands, and Rees follows suit. Rees starts to salute, but Black reaches his hand out for a shake. Rees stops his salute, looks at the major's hand, then grasps it.

"I think we're going to become good friends, Sergeant Rees, and hopefully partners in the future of the Clio Project. Now, go see the corporal."

Smiling, Rees releases the grip. "Will do, and thank you, sir."

CHAPTER 5

SMSgt Rees exits the major's office and walks over to the stand to gather his beret. He glances at Sam out of the corner of his eye as she is busily typing some report or something on her computer with her back to him. He reaches for his beret when she speaks.

"Walking out without so much as a goodbye or a screw you?" she asks with her back still to him.

Rees is rattled and tongue-tied.

"Ah, no. It's just that you were busy working, didn't want to disturb you is all," he stammers as an excuse.

She turns in her chair to face him. For a Senior Master Sergeant, Rees is young, mid-twenties, and had been dating Nora Miller, the daughter of a retired Air Force Lieutenant Colonel, for a pretty long time before the incident. He wasn't afraid of talking with women, but this one made him act like a little boy. She was intimidating but in a playful way.

"Well, you don't get off the hook that easy. Come here," she orders him, and he walks over to her desk. She reaches out and touches his face, grinning. "My God, for a sixty-something-year-old man, you sure are cute," she tells him with a twinkle in her eye.

Rees loses it and doesn't know what to say and is afraid that if he does say something, it will be stupid. He is already embarrassed and feels his face flush. She chuckles, smiles, and knows she has him all flustered.

Satisfied in her conquest, she sits back down and turns towards the computer.

"Sergeant Rees, I have work to do. I can't sit here all day and have you flirting with me. Time for you to go, sir," she jokes.

Rees opens and closes his mouth like a smallmouth bass, not sure what has just happened. Knowing when he has been outmaneuvered, he decides his best course of action would be to retreat, or as the great poet Monty Python said in the epic poem, *Monty Python and the Holy Grail,* "Run Away! Run Away!"

Rees leaves the office and walks down the stairs still embarrassed by Sam's attention. *I'll never get used to the modern woman, not if they're all like that,* he thinks as he turns towards the elevators, deciding to go to the chow hall and get something to eat. As he enters, he looks around and sees MSgt Jack Bouvier and TSgt David Kriger sitting at a table in the corner. They see him and wave him over. Rees acknowledges them by jutting his chin up, then holds up a finger indicating they should hold one, and then points at the chow line. They both nod.

Rees walks to the line and grabs a tray.

"Good afternoon, Sergeant Rees," the airman behind the line says.

"Good afternoon to you, too, Airman Young," Rees replies, then asks, "What's good today?"

"We've got fried chicken or lasagna, or if you want, I can make you a steak. Just got some fresh in, ribeye, fillet, NY strip, whatever."

Feeling a little lightheaded from the booze, Rees realizes he's not that hungry.

"Tell you what, how about I just get a piece of apple pie, if you got it."

Looking like he lost his best friend, the airman walks over to get a slice of pie and brings it back to Rees. "Hey, Airman Young, nothing against your cooking, just not real hungry right now. I'll take you up on that steak later, though. I know you make 'em good. Thanks for the pie," Rees says, raising the plate, reassuring the young services airman.

Rees takes his tray and walks over to the beverage bar and pours himself a cup of coffee. At least they still use the same coffee urns they did in his day, only more modern. He then retreats over to the table with Bouvier and Kriger. Placing the coffee and pie down, he returns the tray to a waiting cart, then sits down.

Kriger reaches over as if to grab Rees' pie and gets a rap on his knuckles for it.

"Ouch!" he cries out, whipping his hand back and fanning it like he was really hurt. "Damn, I thought we were friends," he exclaims.

"Not when to come to my food we aren't. Basic survival mode kicks in where that's concerned, young sergeant."

"Oh, young sergeant, is it? I'm only two years younger than you, old man. What are you, twenty-four, twenty-five? About time to put you to pasture, ain't it?" Kriger says with a grin, looking at Bouvier, who has a slight smile on his face.

Bouvier looks at Rees.

"Where you been? I thought you were coming back here after the disinterment," he asks.

Rees chews his first mouthful of pie and eyes Bouvier. He wipes his mouth with a napkin and reaches for his coffee.

"Disinterment. I was calling it the ceremony. That's what Sam called it, and I couldn't think of anything else when talking with the major."

"The major? What did he want?" Kriger asks.

"Nothing, I went to see him."

"And Sam?" Kriger asks grinning like a Cheshire cat.

Rees sips his coffee and sets the cup down.

"No, David, not Sam. Jesus, I've only been away from Nora for a few months, give me a break. Besides, Sam harasses every guy who comes in there."

"Oh, I beg to differ, mon amie!" Bouvier smirks.

Rees looks at Kriger a little harder. "Enough, I was there for business, nothing else. You just love busting my balls, don't ya?" Rees asks, looking from one man to the other, then changes the subject.

"A Senator Olsen stopped by for a chat at the park right after you left."

"Olsen, Olsen? Why does that name sound familiar?" Jack asks aloud.

"Any relation to the Olsens we ran into during our little time travel trip?" Kriger asks, referring to their being sent from their timeline of 1980 to the year 1862, then returned to the year 2018 in the first-ever time travel experiment. This was done without their knowledge or consent, and it cost them the lives of some of their fellow airmen. During this trip, they interacted with the Olsens of the Town of Hendricks Hill whose family have lived and prospered in the surrounding area for generations.

Rees nods. "The same family. Decedents of young Olsen, whom you corrupted."

"Hey," Kriger snaps, "don't forget I was with you. I had nothing to do with that, and you know it. In fact, if you recall, I'm the one who took that Playboy magazine from him!" he finishes in a huff.

"Jeez, David, calm down. A joke, man," Rees says, then snorts. "Anyway, right after you leave, Jack, Olsen and an aide walk up to me, and he introduces himself. He wanted to speak with you, too, but you were already driving off. Anyway, he walks up, and…" he stops and reaches into a shirt pocket, pulling out the crest, "gives me this." Rees places the crest on the table.

Kriger picks it up, examines it, then hands it to Bouvier. Bouvier turns it over in his hand then sets it back on the table.

"Why would he do that? It's an old TAC crest, so what?" Bouvier asks.

Rees turns his attention to Kriger. "Remember when we left the Town of Hendricks Hill and were in the Duck?"

"Yeah, so what?" Kriger says.

"Tucker lost his crest," Rees says, then taps his finger on the one in front of them.

"Oh, shit, that's right. He was freaking out, and you told him it would show up. He's gonna shit when he sees this," Kriger says, picking the worn crest up and looking at it in a new light.

"Right. At first, we thought he just lost it. Now, it seems young Mr. Olsen stole it from Tucker when he wasn't looking. Boy got himself a souvenir.

Bouvier leans on the table. "So, he comes all the way out there to give you a crest? He could have given it to the major or stopped by here, or even mailed it in."

Rees shakes his head. "No, he wanted to meet us. Said he wanted us to know he was on our side and he was the one responsible for getting us back. He is the Clio Project fan club president."

Now, Bouvier shakes his head. "So, he wants us to know it was all him that got us back. He that hard up for votes?" Jack says, crossing his arms.

"No, it didn't seem like that, Jack. He really seemed genuine and sincere. I didn't trust him, either, and you know how I feel about politicians."

"You and everyone else on this team," Kriger chimes in.

Rees continues, "He told me that the team might be needed for future use in the Clio Project."

"Oh, great, just great. Couldn't kill us off the first time so they want to finish the job," Bouvier exclaims, leaning hard back into his seat, crossing his arms over his chest.

"Again, Jack, I didn't trust him when first meeting him. That is one of the reasons I went to see Major Black. The major told me Olsen was the man behind the scenes getting Clio back up and running. He got Chief Black back into the country and routed funds into the section to get the program up and running and to get us back. I trust the major," Rees explains, looking from one to the other. "Com'on, guys, they did retrieve us out of that time-zone buffer," he says, referring to the team being stuck in limbo when Clio was destroyed while they were in transit from 1862, "and they have given us the best medical treatment around, physical and mental. As well as re-education, equipment, allow us to go off base, granted with an escort and only a few miles away.

"And don't forget the damn good food and lodging!" Kiger adds.

Rees continues, "Why would they do all of that just to send us back to get killed. They could have just left us in the buffer, but they didn't. Kind of ironic now that I think about it. What if we hadn't run across young Olsen back then, or if he hadn't taken the crest?" Rees asks.

"So what?" Bouvier asks.

Rees grins, getting caught up in his theory. "Think about it. Young Olsen took the crest so he'd have proof of the men from the future. He must have shown it to his sister or father or both. No telling who else he showed it to. Anyway, apparently, no one believed him that we know of, except his family, as they told the story throughout the years, passing it down through the generations until it got to Senator Olsen. He told me he heard stories of us from his family growing up. Must have been given the crest sometime after learning about us. He became a politician and heard rumors of a secret time machine project from the 70s. He worked his way up through congress and must have dug deeper until he found out about Clio. Since then, he worked on getting the program running and getting us home."

Rees takes another sip of his coffee and grimaces at the cold bitter taste. Talking too long, it had gotten cold. He looks at Kriger and holds the cup up. Kriger holds his middle finger up, rising to refill his cup.

"Damn, Senior Master Sergeants too lazy to get their own coffee. Thought this was the 21st Century, figured there'd be robots doing this shit," he grumbles to himself, re-filling the cup.

Bouvier is still leaning back in his chair, rocking it now, with his hands on his head, fingers interlocked, watching Kriger and grinning.

"Okay, but I got to meet this man. See for myself."

"Oh, I'm quite sure we'll hear from him. Like I said, he wanted to talk with you, too."

Kriger returns with the coffee and places them on the table. Bouvier snatches Kriger's cup before his hand has barely released it,

"Damn. Thanks, David, you're going to go far looking out for your supervisors like this."

Kriger reaches for the cup but is too late. "Yeah, fuck you…sir."

"Is that disrespect I hear from you, Technical Sergeant Kriger? I am shocked. Aren't you shocked, Senior Master Sergeant Rees?"

"It's beyond apprehension, Master Sergeant Bouvier," Rees replies with a fake shocked look on his face.

"Ha-ha. See how long I take this abuse. You just wait until you need some medical help."

The men chuckle and watch Kriger return to the urn to get another cup of coffee.

Rees sips his coffee and sets the cup down and waits for Kriger to return. When he does, he leans on the table.

"Okay, on to something else. I thought we would go see Corporal O'Toole tomorrow. The major approved it, thought it might be a good idea since none of us have seen him since we got back. Major Black said he's doing well but would probably like to see someone he knew from where and when we took him. Granted he didn't know us well, but a couple of familiar faces probably wouldn't hurt."

"That's cool," Kriger says. "Would like to see how his leg's doing. I know the doctors here are great and all, but it all started with my magical medical hand touching his busted leg that started the healing process."

"Lord save us. Surprised we're not all dead. Are all you assholes from Chicago the same way?" Bouvier asks.

"What, handsome and intelligent?" Kriger replies, turning his face upwards, touching his chin in a pose.

"No, short, stupid, and always a smartass," Bouvier retorts.

Kriger looks at him and silently mouths, "Asshole."

"Oh, good comeback, David. That's always your go-to when you don't have a smartass comment to come back with. Which, I've got to say, is unusual."

"Okay, guys, that's enough…for now," Rees interjects with a smile. Let's meet up here for breakfast at 0600 and plan our next move. You got classes tomorrow, David?" Rees asks Kriger.

Kriger enrolled in advanced medical training for field duty. He said he felt the urge to continue learning medicine, and the Air Force was more than willing to oblige him with training. He is going through some of the same training as Pararescue. Some of the others were also taking advanced courses in physics, advanced combat training, history, martial arts, and a variety of courses that were made available upon request.

"Yeah, but it's a light day and in the early afternoon. No worries, I can make it to see O'Toole."

"Good. Jack?" Rees asks.

"No, I'm good. Got a late afternoon visit with Doctor Lockhart."

"What, again. You've been seeing her, like, five days a week. There's nothing wrong with you. You're insane as the rest of us," Kriger blurts out.

"Have you seen Doctor Lockhart? Really?" Bouvier returns the slam.

"David, he's got you there. Got to agree, she is easy on the eyes," Rees says. "But, Jack, she is an officer, and she can't be here forever."

"Hey, I'm going for pure medical help, and she is helping me psychologically and spiritually. Now, mind your own business. Both of ya."

Kriger shakes his head as he gets up. "Great, and you," he says, pointing at Rees, "upstairs trying to make time with Sam," then points at Bouvier, "and you with your boy crush on Captain Lockhart. And here I am stuck looking at you two ugly fuckers every day."

"Hey!" Both Rees and Bouvier say at the same time, and both stand as if to chase Kriger, who is already backing away with both hands raised in surrender.

"As they say these days… Just say'n."

CHAPTER 6

Rees sleeps fitfully, his mind trapped in the events of what transpired just a few months earlier. He wanders through a pine forest alone... No, not quite. There are soldiers running to and fro through the shadowy woods. Some running scared, others giving chase, the uniforms all from different eras and places. The doughboys of World War 1, Dogfaces of World War 2, Mexican Army from the 1830s, Centurions, Spartans, American Civil War, Samurai, men form the Boar War, Dragoons, and many others he did not recognize.

They are all around him, and he turns and watches in fascination until the actual fighting begins. A Samurai slices through the back of a Doughboy, who is bayoneting a Roman Centurion, then a French Legionnaire shoots an American Indian, who uses a tomahawk on a Vietnam era Marine. A Civil War Confederate is in hand-to-hand combat with a Zulu Warrior.

Rees is stunned as the carnage intensifies. Blood flies from all makes of wounds from various weapons. Men screaming, yelling, cursing, some crying out in pain, others begging for mercy. War cries, rebel yells, and several hollering in languages he doesn't understand. He starts to reel and doesn't understand what is happening. He just wants them to stop, and as he thinks it, they do. Stop. Stop, and then all eyes turn towards him.

He swivels his head and looks around at the warriors and soldiers, turning his body in a circle, looking at each person, not knowing what to do, but he is scared. As one, every person surrounding him slowly walks towards him as he watches in horror and fascination as they encroach closer and closer, raising weapons as if to attack.

"No, wait, no!" he implores, holding his hand out showing he is unarmed. "No, please, wait," he begs. Rees has nowhere to run, no weapons to defend himself with. They charge. A loud, hellish scream fills the air as every one of the soldiers and warriors close, with weapons being brought down upon him, and death being the only inevitable outcome.

Rees covers his head in anticipation of being beaten and stabbed, then he hears one voice that overshadows the rest. A female voice. Soft-spoken. Calling his name.

"Scott."

He thinks, *Nora?*

Then he hears it again. "Scott." But it isn't Nora's voice.

He listens to the voice, wanting to know who it belongs to, and when he looks up, the men are fading away. Rees is falling back, back through the pine trees, moving into darkness, then a hazy light approaches, and he can still hear the voice.

"Scott."

He wakes.

"Scott, it's 0400. Time to get up. Scott, it's 0400. Time to get up."

Now, he recognizes the voice. It's his computer alarm. He comes out of his nightmare and sits up in bed, rubbing his face, his bed wet from sweat.

"Okay, okay, I'm awake. Shut off," he tells the computer, and in the middle of a sentence, the computer voice goes silent, leaving him alone in the darkness with his nightmarish memories fading.

"Goddamn, I've got to stop with these dreams," he mutters to himself. He sits in the bed for a few minutes reliving the dream and trying to make sense of it. Not getting anywhere with that, he throws his legs over the side of the bed. "Lights," he says.

After a few more minutes, he rises and dresses into gym attire. Still groggy from sleep, he leaves his room and makes his way to the gym, and begins a workout. A few minutes later, more of his team come in and begin working out. He chats with a few of them and informs them he will be seeing Corporal O'Toole later. Some of the men want to go, but he tells them he already has Bouvier and Kriger coming along and that they will all get to see him later.

Finishing his workout, he returns to his room to shit, shower, and shave. He then dresses in his ACUs and makes his way to the chow hall. Once there, he gets a bowl of oatmeal and a bowl of fruit, milk, and coffee. He doesn't see Kriger or Bouvier anywhere, so he finds a table closest to the door, places his tray down, and grabs a seat.

Taking his first bite of oatmeal, he sees the two men walk in, arguing about what, he doesn't know. They don't even see him as they make their way to the chow line, still in animated conversation.

He watches them intently, sipping coffee and shaking his head. *Didn't take long for us to get back to our old selves,* he thinks, still watching his two friends argue.

Bouvier and Kriger grab their trays and look around until finally seeing Rees, who raises his coffee cup at them. Kriger says something to Bouvier and briskly walks over to the table.

Before he even gets there, he's talking to Rees, "Rees, Rees, you gotta hear this bullshit spewing from Bouvier's mouth," Kriger says as he sets his tray down on the table. Bouvier casually comes to the table shaking his head and sets his tray down also. Kriger continues, "Listen, Bouvier is spewing crap that the Eagles have had better running backs than the Bears. He's all, 'Yeah, we had Po Sanders and Montgomery,' and I can't help but laugh. Com'on, next to Gale Sayers and Walter Payton, there is no comparison."

Kriger leans his arms on the edge of the table and looks at Rees. "You tell me, who's has the better backs? Plus, the fact we kick the shit out of the Eagles every time we meet in the Super Bowl."

Bouvier is trying to sit as Kriger bends Rees' ear.

"Hey, not every time, just most of the time," Bouvier says. "Damn, sorry I brought it up."

Not going to be denied his one up on Bouvier, Kriger keeps on, "Come on now, Sergeant Rees, what do you say?"

Rees looks at both men. "Guys, I'm from Arizona. What the hell do I know about the Bears or the Eagles. I grew up a Chargers fan."

Both other men look at each other, then back to Rees. "You got to be kidding?" Kriger exclaims. Who's a Chargers fan? Why does California even have a team, or teams? That's about as bad as those damn teams in Florida. And for crying out loud, where the hell is Jacksonville? And Charlotte? Jaguars and Panthers! Next, Alaska and North Dakota will have teams! Christ, football belongs in the north. I can't believe either of you."

Rees shrugs. "What can I say. It was the closest team to my city, though I guess I will have to become a Cardinals fan now."

Kriger finally sits down and picks up his fork, then points it at Rees. "See what I mean? How the hell did the Cardinals even get to Arizona? The whole league is screwed up. And I missed my Bears winning the Super Bowl," he finishes, stabbing his fork into eggs.

Rees and Bouvier moan.

They banter about football for a little longer, enjoying one another's company and their breakfast. Once finished, Rees grabs more coffee and returns to the table.

"Okay, I guess we should go see Corporal O'Toole now," Rees says when seated.

Kriger looks at both men. "Should we bring him something?"

Bouvier leans towards Kriger, eyebrows raised. "What, like flowers?"

Rees snorts. "Jeez, Dave, I didn't know."

"Fuck you both," Kriger replies. "You know what I mean. We haven't seen the guy in months, and we don't know what he'll think about us. I don't know, maybe something they took from him. Give it back."

Rees thinks about that and looks at Bouvier. "He's got a point. I know they took everything from him, including his uniform. The major said they have kept him in the dark about where he is. I'm sure he has a million questions, and they won't answer them."

"What about us? Can we let him in on anything?" Bouvier asks.

Rees shrugs. "Actually, I don't know. I wasn't told not to. Let's just go and play it by ear. He's probably figured out some things but doesn't have any definitive proof. As far as bringing him something, I agree. Let me call the commander and see what he says," Rees says, then gets up from the table.

Kriger and Bouvier turn in their chairs and him as he goes over to a wall where an internal phone is attached. Rees picks up the handset and talks into it for a few minutes, then hangs up and walks back to the table.

"Well?" Bouvier asks.

"He wants to see us before we go. Nothing bad, just wants to give us a few dos and don'ts. You two ready?"

"Sure, let's go," Bouvier says, and they leave the dining facility.

As all three men enter Sam's office. She looks at each of them and gives them her radiant smile.

"Good morning," she says pleasantly.

"Good morning to you, too, Sam," Rees says, smiling back.

"The major is expecting you, Sergeant Rees. You all may go right in," she finishes and goes back to whatever it was she was doing before they came in.

Rees looks at her quizzically, not sure what she is doing. She doesn't give him her usual banter and seems all business-like. Shaking it off, he heads for the major's office. As all three men pass Sam's desk, with Kriger last in line, he gives Sam a lopsided grin. She catches him and winks, both knowing she is messing with Rees.

The men enter the office and report to the major. He tells them to grab chairs, which they do.

"Thanks for coming in. I should have talked to you a little more about Corporal O'Toole yesterday, Scott. My fault. Before you all go see him, I wanted to make sure you know what is going on," he says, looking at each man, who nods their understanding. "Good. O'Toole is not appreciating being here. He's cooperative enough but not adjusting to being kept locked up. I believe the man seems confused and scared, of what I'm not sure. We've been very good to him, but he seems to be fading away from us. Like he's already given up. I can understand his confusion, and we haven't told him much, and he has not been allowed out of his room. I would probably be the same. No matter how well you're treated wherever you are, if you aren't allowed freedom, it's a prison."

The three men look at each other, and Rees speaks, "Sir? Why not?"

"Why not what, Scott?" the major responds.

"Why haven't we told him where he is, what is going on? He's not going anywhere. He's not a POW. He's just a young guy who's been snatched from the 1860s and flung into the 21st Century. He probably thinks he's stuck here forever with no friends, no family. I'd be pissed off, too," Scott says, adding, "Sir. Besides, he's seen us and our vehicles, and the facility is not something they had in the 19th Century. He's not stupid. We should just let him in on what going on."

The major stares at Rees, then sighs. "Sergeant Rees, I agree. The hell with the politicians. Command said I had autonomy with this project. They don't want anyone else sticking their nose into it. I thought it might be best to keep O'Toole in the dark, but that may have been a mistake. As you said, he has had to figure some of it out. You men go ahead and fill him in. And by the way, he does have a family. Well, decedents of his sisters and brothers anyway. We ran his DNA, and his branched out with hundreds of families. Who they all are we're not sure of yet. Still running DNA sequencing."

All three men look at each other in mild surprise. Bouvier smiles,

"That's great, sir. Also," he starts and looks at Rees, "can we give him back some of his stuff?"

Rees nods. "Yes, sir. We thought giving him his things back might boost his morale a little."

The major smiles. "Why not? In for a penny, in for a pound. Go ahead," he says, then presses the intercom on his desk. "Sam?" he calls and releases the button.

"Yes, sir?" she replies.

"Contact Captain Wells and tell her that Senior Mater Sergeant Rees and company will be coming down to see Corporal O'Toole. She's to allow them access and give them any assistance they need. She is also to let them have access to all of O'Toole's belongings. If she has a problem with this, tell her to contact me, but she is not to interfere with Rees and his men."

"Got it, sir," Sam answers.

The major looks at each man. "Okay, anything else?"

The men take this as a sign the meeting is over, stand, salute, and thank the major for his time. As they head for the door, the major asks Rees to stay behind for a minute. Kriger and Bouvier tell him they will meet him at Captain Wells' office and leave. Rees turns back to the major.

"Yes, sir," Rees says.

"Thought I'd let you know. I'll be promoted to colonel on this week."

Rees breaks into a large smile. "Well, again, congratulations, sir." He holds out his hand, which the major takes.

"Thank you. Senator Olsen called and said he'd be here to pin them on. Thought you and your men might want to attend. Nothing big, just us."

"Yes, sir. It would be a privilege and an honor to attend. Thank you, sir," Rees says, still grinning.

"That's all, Sergeant. Now, go see the corporal, and good luck."

"Yes, sir," Rees replies and leaves the office.

CHAPTER 7

Corporal O'Toole sits on his bed, his chin drooping, eyes lackluster. He has been in the facility for several months and hasn't adjusted well, and it is beginning to show. The people here have all been good to him, but no one will answer his questions or tell him when he can go home. They won't tell him how the war is going or if it's over, nothing.

He's been prodded and poked, asked a thousand questions, yet gets no answers to his questions. If he's a prisoner of war, these people are sure friendly, what with feeding him, making sure he is comfortable, but nary an answer to a question concerning the war.

Sighing, he lies back and rests his head on the pillow, throwing an arm over his dull eyes. The pillow is another convenience and one like he has never had the pleasure of using, as well as the nice bed. They must think he's a general or something. Try as he might to stop doing so, his mind wanders to Mt. Airy, Maryland, his hometown.

He hopes his folks are alright and the war isn't affecting them too much. He knows his ma and pa wanted him to join the Confederates, as they are sympathizers with the south, but he felt he needed to help defend the Union and ensure the nation stayed together. His parents weren't too happy about that but took solace that his two brothers joined up with the Rebs.

Thinking back about his brothers, he smiles. He is the oldest and had no mercy on them growing up. Even when they both tried to take him in a fight, he would whoop them. He misses hunting and fishing with them and hopes that they can all get together again.

His two little sisters, Ada and Kaillie, wanted to go with him, and he laughs thinking about them little ones begging to go do their part. Only twelve and fourteen, and they were a handful. He quietly chided them and explained that they could do more for the war effort by staying home and helping on the farm. He explained that while he and his brothers were away, someone needed to help Ma and Pa, and now it was up to them. Both girls pouted and kicked the ground but relented.

Then there is Emma Kelly. The prettiest girl he ever laid eyes on. He was just beginning to court her when the war broke out. He received a few letters from her, but they had not been courting too long, and he is afraid that scoundrel Timothy Walsh will be sniffing around, what with his pretty looks and smooth talk and daddy's money. He is full of shite is what he is. Always bragging about this or that, throwing his folks status in Andy's face, as well as everyone's.

Then the war breaks out and what does Walsh do. Nothing. His father paid the $300.00 to keep him from being drafted. Andy shakes his head, clenching his fists, nostrils flaring thinking of this. Walsh always had a shining for Emma, and Andy was afraid that now that he is not around, she will forget about him and let that jack-ass Walsh sweep her off her feet.

Then his mind wonders to the eventful day that led him here. It was that hot August day when he was assigned to a patrol to scout ahead of the battalion. Sergeant Merrick was assigned as the leader with Corporal O'Toole second and privates Torney, Hearn, Fagan, and Doan along.

He remembers they were out for about two hours, not having located any enemies, and they were about to return to camp when

Sergeant Merrick finds that damned canteen. If they had only turned around just two minutes before, he would be back where he belongs.

He thinks about the two men, a white man, and a darkie, both dressed almost identical. Dark green shirts and pants with dark blue stripes and silly-looking pots on their heads. They wore other things that O'Toole did recognize and carried weapons he had ever seen.

He thought they were Rebs because both had southern accents. The white guy's was very prominent. The rest was a blur when the shooting commenced because that goddamn hotheaded Merrick reached for his pistol. O'Toole was lucky he was not shot, but not as lucky as Fagan, who got away.

O'Toole had to admit they treated him well, even fed him, and he was in awe of the equipment they had, especially the horseless metal wagon that could deflect Minnie balls and even cannon shot.

Why they didn't let him go he still didn't understand, and he knew he wasn't in Andersonville.

Damn it! He needed to get home. Even though these people were nice to him, it didn't matter. He needed to get home. His captives will not even let him know if he had any letters from home.

O'Toole was becoming despondent more and more with each passing day. He didn't know what he could do. Escape? That was a possibility. But he didn't know where he was. He wasn't allowed outside and hadn't seen the sky since being brought in here. What was he going to do?

While still lying in the bed with his arm over his eyes, he hears the door open. *Ahh, more questions for me, or more poking,* he thinks, not moving.

"Well, look at this." He hears a familiar voice, but not sure who it is. He moves his arm and looks towards the door to see one of the men who had been holding him hostage after they captured him. It's the ranking sergeant who was nice to him but wouldn't release him. He sits up, not sure what to say.

Rees steps further into the room and allows Bouvier and Kriger to enter. O'Toole recognizes these men, too, especially the one call Kriger, who took care of his leg. And as if Kriger was reading his mind, he asks, "How's the leg, Corporal?"

Still confused, he finally says, "It's fine so," then he just stares, swinging his legs off the bed onto the floor and sits.

Rees leans out of the doorway, and O'Toole hears him ask for some chairs. A few seconds later, three folding chairs are brought in. Rees hands one to the others and they all sit. O'Toole is fascinated by the chairs. Of course, he's fascinated by everything he sees.

Rees looks at him. "You remember us, Corporal O'Toole?" he asks.

"Yes, sir. You're one of the ones who captured me, and I am thinking brought me here. Your clothes are different, though."

Rees nods. "That's mostly correct, and we'll get to that later. We just wanted to come by and see how you were holding up."

"Holding up?" Andy asks.

"Sorry, it means to see how you are doing. You look well," Rees explains but notices the dullness in his eyes and the downturned facial features.

"Yes, sir. I am well and everyone here has been good to me. Well, other than they won't tell me anything about where I am, how the wars going, if'n I have any letters, when I can go home."

Rees waves his hand. "Whoa, whoa. That's the other reason we are here. We are going to take you out with us, show you around, and try to help you understand what is happening. Does that sound good to you?"

O'Toole's eyes widen, "You mean that, sir? You're going to let me go?"

Rees shakes his head. "No, not let you go, but let you out for a little while. With us and answer any questions you have. Okay?"

O'Toole stands slowly. "Yes, sir. When do we go?"

"Right now, if you want. Now, Andy, do you mind if I call you Andy?" Rees asks.

"No, sir, I don't mind. It is my name," O'Toole responds. The three sergeants chuckle.

Rees smiles. "Yes, it is. Well you can call me Scott, this is Jack," he says, pointing to Bouvier, "and the man who worked on your leg is David."

O'Toole looks at each man. "Not an Irishman amongst ya."

The three men look at each other. "I guess not. My folks were Welsh, Jacks is French, and Kriger is German. But what you must understand, Andy, is that the United States is a melting pot. Different nationalities marry and have children who repeat the process. Again, these are things we can explain more to you later. For now, let's get you outside. And don't be frightened by some of the things you will see. All will be explained," he says, then looks around, "Ready?" He walks out the door with O'Toole in tow, the others behind him.

Rees turns his head as he walks and looks at O'Toole. "Andy, I assume you sort of figured some of this out."

O'Toole shakes his head. "No, sir. I haven't made heads or tails out of what has been happening. I do not understand anything. You all dress funny, and the material of the clothing I have been given, I do not know what to make of it. It is not wool. I know some is cotton, but I am confused. The food is nothing like I have ever ate, even better than what you gave me out of those little bags."

"MREs," Bouvier answered.

"What?" O'Toole asks, squinting.

"They're called MREs. That's short for Meals Ready to Eat. It's what we carry into the field with us. It's come a long way from hardtack and pork belly."

"Ah," is all that Andy can come up with?

They turn a corner and see Captain Wells standing in the hallway in front of the elevators. Apparently, she has been waiting for them. They approach her and stop.

Rees smiles. "Captain Wells, how are you? Something we can do for you?"

She holds a clipboard across her chest, almost like a shield. "I want to make sure you take care of my patient. I don't agree with you taking him outside, much less informing him of everything."

Rees' smile doesn't falter. "Ma'am, I can understand your concern, but we all feel it's in his best interest to tell him the truth. We can't keep Corporal O'Toole locked up forever. You and your people have had ample time to conduct your tests and interviews, now it's his turn to interview us. The man needs some sunshine, fresh air. He's not going anywhere except inside the compound with us."

Wells pushes her glasses up onto her nose and sighs. "I can agree that he does need some outdoor time, but full disclosure is a mistake."

"In your opinion ma'am. I believe different and our superiors agree with me."

"I know and I am allowing this under protest. The psychological impact of what you are about to tell him, to show him could have devastating consequences for him. I just hope I'm wrong." and walks by them. "Have a pleasant day, Sergeants, Corporal."

"What the hell was that all about?" Kriger asks.

Rees walks over to the bank of elevators and places his hand on the panel. "You know doctors, always worrying about everything. It's all good," he says as the doors open. The four men step inside, and Rees thinks, *I hope.*

Once the sergeants are inside, they see O'Toole scratching his cheek, a frown on his face, apparently not wanting to enter. Rees notices.

"It's called an elevator. It's what we use to go up and down in a building. It's perfectly safe, Otis makes good elevators. Don't you have elevators in Baltimore?

"Yes, we do, but I never got into one," O'Toole replies, still examining the box.

"Don't worry, come on in."

Hesitantly, O'Toole steps inside. Rees tells the elevator to take them to ground level. A female voice comes over the speaker, "Ground level."

O'Toole looks around, eye wide. Rees smiles. "Not to worry, Andy, it's not magic. It's call technology, progress since the 1860s."

O'Toole looks apprehensive and watches the lights on the panel read each level passed. Rees and the others look grin at the childlike expression on O'Toole's face.

"This is going to be fun," Rees whispers under his breath.

The elevator comes to a stop and opens into the lobby of the ground floor. A few personnel are walking around, hurrying from one office to another. The men walk towards the exit, and the SF on duty has the NCOs sign out. He was previously informed they would be coming with O'Toole, and he didn't need to go through the exit protocol.

Once they signed out, Rees leads the group to the front exit door and the door automatically opens. O'Toole warily follows the NCOs, turning in circles and amazed at the size of the building then stops, staring at the glass doors before exiting. Once outside, he shields his eyes from the glaring sun. Rees removes his sunglasses from his pocket and puts them on. Then he removes a second pair and hands them to O'Toole.

"Sunglasses. Another invention to help when it's bright like today."

O'Toole takes them and studies them for a few seconds. He awkwardly places them on his face, then quickly removes them and stares at them. Again, the NCOs chuckle. O'Toole places them back on, then takes them off, then puts them back on. Bouvier shakes his head.

"If Corporal O'Toole does this with everything we show him, it'll take all day."

Finally, O'Toole leaves the glasses on and looks at his surroundings, taking in the sights of the chain link fence with the concertina wiring, the guard shack with the two SFs inside, the vehicles parked around the building. He turns to look at the building he just exited, again, amazed at the size.

Where are we? Looks like North or South Carolina or maybe southern Virginia. And all this?" he asks, pointing to the fence, gate shack, cars, and building.

"We're in North Carolina," Kriger answers. "Not far from where we found you."

"You mean captured me? I'm a prisoner of war, ain't I?" he asks, staring at each man.

"No, Andy, you're not. I thought maybe you might have figured some of this out. What you see is here is part of the military. We are the United States Air Force Security Forces personnel. I know that's a mouthful, but you're just going to have to listen and try to accept what we are going to explain to you. Why don't we go over there?" Rees finishes and points to a table shaded under a roof.

The men walk to the table and sit.

"Andy, when we found, er, captured you, it was August 1862. Now, this is going to be hard to hear," Rees starts and looks at the two other NCOs. "Well, Andy, it's 2019 now," he says, then watches for O'Toole's reaction, which wasn't what he expected.

"I sorta knew it," he says evenly. "I'm just a culchie, and not well educated, but mama read to us a lot.

"Sorry, what's a culchie?" Bouvier interrupts.

"Culchie? Someone from the farms," O'Toole responds, waving his hand.

"Okay, thanks. Sorry, go on."

O'Toole looks at them and continues, "She read stories from the Brothers Grimm, *The Last Man* by a lady named Mary Shelly, I think, and other fanciful tales. Oh, *A Voyage to the Moon* was another. I liked that one. I loved those stories, and even though I knew them to be made up, I always wondered what the world would be like if things like in them stories did happen."

Kriger laughs. "Well, some did," he says before Rees gives him the eye to let O'Toole go on. Kriger just shrugs.

"Go on, Andy," Rees prompts.

"Since I met you fellas, nothing is as it should be. I saw you with weapons that we do not have, and I know the graybacks do not have. Those carriages or wagon without horses, your uniforms, southern speech mixed in with northern speech, darkies, Indians, food in a metal bag, naw, noth'n was right. Then that strange feeling I got when you were fight'n the cavalry, then waking up in a room that was nicer than any room I been in, even in Baltimore. The food, the way everyone talks, those crazy people asking me questions, and others using things on me I ain't ner seen no sawbones use. I just laid there in that bed and said that I must have died and went to Hell, or I was a' dreaming constantly, or I was on the moon. But being sent to the future didn't really occur to me." He trails off and looks around.

Thinking that O'Toole is finished, Rees breaks the silence.

"Andy, I'm glad you sort of figured this out. A lot of things have changed since the 1860s, and you're not the only one who's experienced this problem."

O'Toole looks surprised. "You mean there are others like me? Others from the past who are here?" he asks in a tone they can't read. Excitement, anger? They can't be sure.

Rees nods. "Yes, in a manner. You see, we all," he points to Bouvier and Kriger, "as well as some of the others are from the year 1980."

O'Toole just stares at Rees with a blank expression. Rees continues, "We have been sent into the future as well. We were sent back in time to 1862, during the Civil War, as an experiment. The plan was for us to just stay in your time period for a short time and return to the year 1980. But the time machine used to transport all of us was destroyed. It wasn't fixed until the year 2018, and that's when we were all brought back. To include you. So, we are all fish out of the water, only you're over a hundred-fifty years from your time, and we're about forty years from ours. Do you understand what I'm saying?"

O'Toole sadly grins. "Of course, I do. I ain't no idget."

"Of course not, that's not what I meant. Listen, all I'm telling you is that we can understand what you're feeling. I'm sure you miss home, your family, and friends? Girl?" he asks with an eyebrow raised.

"Well, kinda," Andy replies, face turning slightly red. "There was a girl, Emma Kelly. I just start courting her," he continues with a smile that soon fades. "But I guess that's over. I bet she ended up with that louse Timothy Walsh," he finishes and doesn't continue.

The three sergeants all look at each other, with Rees and Kriger both sympathizing with him.

"Andy, we know how you feel. We all lost our girls, too. But we must go on, and that's why we're here. To help you adjust, and in the long run, maybe you can help us, too," Rees says, hoping to help.

O'Toole looks at him. "Sergeant, I mean Scott. I'm so homesick, all I want to do is go home. I do not belong here and do not want to be here. I'm a simple farm boy who sought glory in the army. I saw things and did things I did not think I would ever see or do. Nor do not wish to see or do them again," he says, then sits up straighter. "I will never fit in here, and I do not want to. Do me a favor and take me back to my room. I have got lots to think about and I have saw enough," he says, standing.

Kriger leans over. "Hey, Andy, come on. It'll be alright. Listen, we'll come by every day and keep you company. Each of us. You'll get to know the other men, and who knows, once you're here for a while, you might like it," Kriger says, looking at O'Toole, then decides to change course. "Hey, some of your mom's stories came true," he says, brightly causing O'Toole to look at him.

"Yeah, we put a man on the moon. Several times, in fact. Right now, there's an international space station orbiting the planet. People from different parts of the world are inside it. You can even see it sometimes," he says, pointing to the sky with O'Toole following his finger.

O'Toole stands still, then slowly releases his breath. "You pulling my leg?"

"Naw, wouldn't do that. I'll show you sometime. First, I'll show you on the computer," he says and sees the confusion in O'Toole's face.

Kriger waves his hand dismissively. "Never mind, we'll get to that. Come on, let's get you to your room, and I'll get that computer and get you educated on the 21st Century happenings."

O'Toole seems a little better, but Rees can see he's still hurting. Kriger and O'Toole get up and start to leave. Bouvier stands, but Rees stays seated.

The men turn and look at Rees.

"You coming?" Bouvier asks.

"Yeah, in a minute. Dave, you and Andy go on back. I want to have a word with Jack. We'll be down shortly," he tells them.

Kriger nods and leads O'Toole towards the door, Kriger talking a mile a minute. Bouvier takes a seat across from Rees.

"What's on your mind? Seconds thoughts about staying in?" Bouvier asks to break the solemn moment.

Rees smirks. "No, no, I'm staying. I was just thinking while O'Toole was talking."

"Okay, about what?"

Rees rubs his ear, then leans his elbows on the table. "We have a time machine," he begins before Bouvier cuts him off.

"Whoa, whoa. Un-huh. I don't know what you're thinking, but we can't be using the time machine for whatever you are scheming."

"Shut the hell up and hear me out. Damn, you and Kriger jump into every conversation without letting someone finish. Both of you two would learn a lot more if you'd just listen."

Bouvier raises his hands. "Sorry, carry on, o' great one."

"Thank you. Now, as I was saying, we have a time machine. Why don't we use it?" Rees sees Bouvier begin to open his mouth, so Rees raises his index finger, "Ah, don't interrupt, grasshopper," he interjects. "What if we can go back and take O'Toole with us? Return him to his timeline. I mean, not right now, but after we do some research. Make sure we don't pollute the timeline. We go back to a time after we left and ensure his safety until we find his unit. Then we tell them he was captured, which he technically was, escaped, ran into us, and we helped him get back to his battalion.

Bouvier shakes his head. "You're bat shit crazy, you know that? Have you really thought this through? Okay, we send him back, what if he starts talking about what he's seen, what he knows. Then what? He could change everything. Invent something that changes the timeline."

Rees shakes his head. "First off, he wouldn't be believed. Time travel, men from the future. Just another storyteller. Look at all those others who saw us in Hendricks Hill, young Olsen, and his family. Look around, has anything changed?"

Bouvier leans one arm on the table and turns his head to look outside the fence line. He turns back to look at Rees.

"We don't know. They could have done something that changed something we haven't seen yet."

Rees nods. "Possibly, but so far nothing has changed that we are aware of. Besides, what difference would it really make? I don't think anything will change, not after what we did, stomping around 1862 North Carolina, fighting Civil War soldiers, shooting a civilian in a store. Naw, I don't see it. Like I was saying, even if Andy talks, everyone will think him nuts. As far as inventing something. What? What has he seen that he could invent? Scissors? Hypodermic needles? Cotton underwear? How about a car? Come on really? The man's been locked up in a room and has only seen, well, the room. Now that he's been outside, what has he seen?"

Bouvier looks around. "Not much, I guess."

"See. Anyway, it's not our decision to make. That'll be left up to the major and the higher-ups. I just want to tell him about it, and I'm hoping you'll be on board," Rees says, tilting his head and eyeing Bouvier.

Bouvier notices. "Hey, I'm not saying I'm against it. I just want us to be careful. Even if you can talk the major into it, he's got to be able to talk the powers that be into it."

Rees slaps the table with his fingers making a *da-dum, dum, dum* sound. "Not to worry about that. I got an ace up my sleeve."

CHAPTER 8

Two days later, Rees sits in his office sipping a cup of coffee and reading regulations. He's not really enjoying this part, but he needs to be up to speed with the changes that have been made over the last thirty-nine years. He does like the fact that he can remember a lot of what he's been reading and won't have to re-read them. This will help due to the amount of source materials he and his fellow security troops must brush up on. Not only this, but he is expected to learn his new position, and how to be a senior NCO, having jumped two pay grades in a blink of an eye.

Just as he thinks of taking a break, in walks TSgts Shepard, McGuire, and SSgts Nionee and Tucker.

"Well, well, looks like a mob has intruded upon my office," Rees says with a smile. "How's it going, guys? Am I in trouble? No, wait, you think it's my birthday and you're here to take me out to dinner?"

Shepard hobbles over and plops down in a chair without being asked. "Naw, Sarge, we just wanted to see how ya'll was doin'."

"Well, have a seat why don't ya TJ," Rees says wryly, "And ya'll is doing fine, thanks."

"Why, thank you, sir, don't mind if I do," Shepard replies in a sing-song tone of voice.

"How's the leg? Looks like you're getting used to the prosthetics."

"Not bad. Still hurts like the devil, and I'm not the most graceful person who walks, but I'm getting the hang. Won't be climbing no mountains for a while."

The other NCOs move into the office to different areas and lean on the wall or stand. Ray Nionee looks at Rees.

"Osda sunalei Nugvwayusadegi."

Rees stares at him for a minute. "That's a lot for just…good day?" he finally says with a proud grin.

Nionee shakes his head. "Close enough. Anyway, we heard you, Jack, and Dave went to see O'Toole the other day. Dave said the corporal was a little out of it. Thought we'd get your side. How is he?"

Rees lets the use of first names go because it was just his team in the room and no one from the outside heard him. Nionee knows this and would use his rank if anyone else were within earshot.

"Dave is right. Man is homesick. Can you blame him? Hell, we're all homesick to a degree. Different circumstances, though. I was going to call a meeting with all of you. Dave and Jack already know what I'm going to say, and I'll get with the others after, but since you four are here, I'll fill you in on my idea. Take this as is because I have to run it through the major first." He stops and checks his watch. "Which reminds me, he is due to receive his promotion in about three hours. Are all of you ready to attend?" he asks and watches as all the men nod and acknowledge they are. "Good. Anyway, I want to take O'Toole back."

It takes a second or two for what he said to sink in, then the men all look at each other before speaking.

"Yo, Sarge! What do you mean take him back? You mean back to where we found him. Now? Then? 1862?" Tucker blurts out, looking around the room at the others. "We can't do that! Can we?"

"Why sure we can, Nate. We got a fucking time machine," McGuire says, folding his arms across his chest and leaning against the door frame. "All we gotta do is waltz right in there and tell those eggheads operating that top-secret piece of machinery that we want to take a little trip. Just for nostalgia reasons. Oh, and by the way, we're bringing along Corporal O'Toole cause he wants in on the fun, too. Not a problem that I can see," he finishes and looks to Rees straight-faced.

Rees rubs his hand over his face the entire time.

"Do you realize you guys have the same problem that Kriger and Bouvier have?" Rees asks. "You don't let me finish what I was saying before you start running off at the lip. Like I told them, if you would just shut the hell up and listen, then maybe you'd get the whole picture before blurting out useless shit." He watches to see if he can go on. "Now, what I was saying is that I need to speak with the major about this first. I have been thinking about this and have some sort of a plan, but we will need to work on it a little more. My initial plan is to go back to a time and place where we can return O'Toole back to his company. We bring him back and explain we liberated him, or he escaped from some Confederates who captured him while on his patrol. Which is what had happened when Tucker and Shepard nabbed him. The man that got away most likely said that's what happened as I'm sure he didn't have time to see a lot. Once we safely deliver him back to his unit, we return," Rees finishes and looks around the room.

"What's this *we* shit, Kemosabe?" Nionee says with a wicked grin.

"Hey, we all have to pull our weight, even you Indians," Rees retorts.

"Why, Sergeant Rees, from what I've been reading up on, that's racist. I am an American Native, by God."

"Okay, whatever," Rees responds, then continues, "I'm not saying *we* as in all of us are taking him back. I mean I am taking him back. The *we* are all of us working helping me come up with a working plan."

As soon as the words are spoken an audible intake of breath can be heard from some of the men. Others jerk their heads back, jaws going slack, and then the grumbling and yelling begins with several men jumping up from their seats as one and begin firing questions towards Rees. He listens to the gripes and the unintelligible asked questions for close to a minute. Then he raises his hands, nodding his understanding and looking at the men, remaining quiet until they all stop talking.

"Okay, I get that there is no need for everyone to go. I will go alone. You guys have done enough, and I don't feel that we need every swinging dick traipsing around possibly screwing something up that will disrupt the space-time continuum. I will escort O'Toole back to his lines, ensure everything is fine, then *bam*, I'm back. This will also give the council a look at the use of Clio and see it can be used without disrupting the timeline."

"Why can't we just send him back by himself?" McGuire asks, and the others nod in agreement.

Rees smiles. "I thought about that, too. But I think it would be better if someone went with him. Moral support. Besides," Rees stands, "I want to go back knowing what I know now. The last time was a surprise. This time, I'll be ready and prepared. I won't be too long, and this will be more of a trial run. When it works out, we may be able to pave the way for all of us to take little jaunts through time."

"Hey, you're the boss, and as you said, they might not go along with it," Tucker says.

"We'll see," Rees replies. "Now, get out of my office so I can get some work done."

The men shuffle out, and Rees yells loud enough so they can hear him down the corridor, "And don't be late for the ceremony."

CHAPTER 9

The Gulfstream G500 jet lands and taxis to base operations. Senator Olsen and his wife unsnap their seatbelts as the private jet comes to a complete stop. The inboard assistants make their final preparations, and the exit ramp is lowered. The senator thanks everyone on board for their help and makes his way out of the aircraft.

At the bottom of the stairs, there is a small reception waiting for him. The base commander, General Paxton, along with his entourage, and the chief of Security Forces, Colonel Maxwell, and a few others. There are two security force members who have taken positions at the bottom left and right side of the ramp.

The senator gives a large smile and waves and with a bounce in his step makes his way down the ramp with Joyce right behind him. When the senator reaches the bottom, handshakes are given all around, as well as pleasantries. The senator takes the time to talk to the security force member at the bottom of the ramp before following the general and his staff into base operation.

Once inside, the senator again smiles and says hello to everyone he can see and walks through the building and out into a waiting vehicle. The vehicle departs and small talk lasts just a short time before they reach their destination, the facility housing the Clio Project. The vehicle arrives at the entry checkpoint, and the guards ensure everyone is authorized entry, and the gates are opened.

The vehicles drive to the front entrance and stops. An SF member opens the door, and the senator and his wife exit, as well as the general. They are greeted by Major Black and SMSgt Rees.

"Welcome, Senator, Mrs. Olsen," Black says and shakes their hands, then turns and salutes General Paxton.

"General."

"Major," the general replies, returning the salute that is also given by Rees.

"Sergeant Rees, good to see you again," Olsen says and shakes his hand. "You remember my wife?"

"Yes, sir, I do," Rees says, smiling. "Good to see you again, ma'am."

"Oh, please, call me Joyce. Ma'am is my mother," she sweetly replies with a cool southern belle accent.

"Alright. Joyce, but you do understand my upbringing and training make that awfully hard," Rees replies with mirth in his eyes.

"Well, we'll just have to work on that," she answers back.

The major clears his throat. "Sirs, Ma'am," he starts to say and receives a warning look from Joyce Olsen. "Joyce," he says, correcting himself. "Let's go inside where it's a bit more comfortable." He leads the way inside the facility foyer, and they all follow.

After making their way through security procedures allowing them entry into the lower recesses of the facility, they make their way down to the floor where the conference room is located.

"Well, Major, a special day for you. Not only a promotion but a double one at that," Olsen says.

"Yes, sir, it is," Black replies as they approach the conference room door.

Sergeant Rees opens the door. "Room, ten hut!" he barks, holding the door open for the others to enter. The sound of scraping chairs can be heard as the military personnel come to abrupt attention. The civilians also rise, but not to attention.

The group enters the room, and the senator, general, major, and Rees all go to the front. Major Black smiles as he sees his father, retired Chief Master Sergeant Black, is in attendance, standing in the front of the room with a smile on his face.

"At ease," Rees says. "Thank you all for attending. This is a promotional ceremony for Major John A. Black to be presided over by General Paxton. In attendance are Senator Olsen with his wife Joyce and Chief Master Sergeant, retired, Joseph Black. Please, have a seat as the senator would like to say a few words. Senator."

Senator Olsen stands in front of the room and, uncharacteristically of a politician, gives a short speech concerning the major and his accomplishments. When finished, he steps back beside his wife.

Next, General Paxton comes forwards and says a few words then stands in front of the flag and turns towards Major Black, who turns to face him. "Post the orders," the general commands.

SMSgt Rees addresses the room. "Attention to Orders," he says, and the room comes to attention once more.

"The President of the United States, acting upon the recommendation of the Secretary of the Air Force, has placed special trust and confidence in the patriotism, integrity, and qualities of Major John A. Black. In view of these special qualities and his demonstrated potential to serve in a higher-grade, Major John A. Black is promoted to the permanent rank of Colonel United States Air Force on this date. By special order of the Secretary of the Air Force," Rees finishes reading the orders and looks at the crowd.

"Please, be seated while Major Black's father and Senator Olsen pins on his rank." He faces the chief and senator. "Senator, Chief, if you would stand next to the promotee," he says, and they comply, standing on each side of the major, facing him. "Master Sergeant Bouvier, please, bring the new rank and stand by for the old."

MSgt Bouvier walks up to the senator and chief and opens a small box containing the rank insignia. The two men each take one of the eagle insignias and remove the gold oak leaf clusters and hand them to Sergeant Bouvier, who takes them and moves away. The colonel rank is then placed on Black's shoulder lapels.

The rest of the ceremony consists of the newly appointed colonel reaffirming his oath to office, followed by a quick speech. The room is then dismissed, and after a few handshakes and congratulatory remarks, the conference room slowly empties except for the senator and his wife, the chief, colonel, Rees, and Bouvier. General Paxton also excuses himself as he said he is needed elsewhere.

When it is just a small group, the senator announces it is time for a celebratory drink. The newly appointed colonel agrees and makes his way to a hidden cabinet located in the wall. He presses a button, and the wall opens to reveal a small well-stocked bar. MSgt Bouvier walks over and claims that since he is the lowest ranking, it is his duty and obligation to serve the others.

"Damn, where's an airman when you need one," he says to the chuckles of the others.

As each has a drink, the talk changes from one subject to the next. After a few minutes of small talk, Joyce stands and the men stand.

"Gentlemen, as great a time as I have had with ya'lls wonderful company, I think I will excuse myself and make my way outside. I'm sure you gentlemen have some business to talk about before we leave, so I will let you get on with it. Congratulations again, Colonel, and it was nice to see you again, Sergeant Rees," she says, looking at him. "Gentlemen," she says to the rest and walks towards the door.

Senator Olsen walks with her and opens the door, where there are security force members standing by to escort her.

"Thank you, dear," the senator says, giving her a kiss on the cheek. "I won't be long." He closes the door behind her.

The senator turns back towards the group. "Gentlemen, as my lovely wife said, I'm sure we have some things to discuss since I am here." He tells the others to have a seat as he pulls his chair out. Rees and Bouvier exchange a look, and it is noticed by everyone. Colonel Black speaks first.

"Sergeant Rees, you and Sergeant Bouvier seem to have something on your minds."

"Ah, yes, sir, we do. Colonel, Senator. It is something I have been thinking about, or I should say we, meaning Sergeants Bouvier, Kriger, and myself. We spoke with Corporal O'Toole a few days ago. Seems the man is not happy and feels like a prisoner, which he kinda is, so he asked to go home," Rees says, listening as the senator whistles, the colonel harrumphs, and the chief just smiles.

"Sergeant Rees, I'm not sure we can do that," Colonel Black says. "He's been here a long time, and his knowledge of future events, well, there's no telling what he could do to screw up the timeline."

Chief Black looks at his son. "From what I have gathered, he doesn't know that much. Wouldn't you agree, Sergeant Rees?"

"Yes, sir, I would," Rees replies, thankful for the support. "Sirs, O'Toole promised he would not say anything, and I know that doesn't mean much, but he hasn't really seen anything other than his room, the halls, just what's outside, and some videos. The videos he has seen are science fiction to him. He could talk all he wants, but I don't believe anyone would believe him, and I'm sure there's nothing he has seen that he could invent. I said maybe scissors, but I think those were invented thousands of years ago, or he could invent a new type of pillow.

"But I'm getting off track. I'm no expert in psychology, of course, but I can tell when someone is hurting, and Jack and Dave both heard how O'Toole feels about being here. He misses home, and I can't blame him. I'm not sure what you had in store for him, but can we honestly say that keeping him here will do anyone any good? Haven't the historian and shrinks gotten enough out of him?" Rees asks as he looks around the room.

Chief Black speaks first, "I agree. When this project started over fifty years ago, I thought it would be used for history and scientific research, but I never intended it to bring people back from the past, and we did that double, what with Rees and his men, and then O'Toole. I say send him back."

Senator Olsen raises a finger. "Okay, but what if something did happen? Something we didn't foresee?"

Rees speaks up, "I thought about that also. I think we should have a brainstorming session with everyone. Come up with every feasible idea of messing up the timeline. Then working out what we could do to stop it or lessen any impact. Take our time, there's no hurry, and I believe just letting O'Toole know we are working on it would boost his morale."

"Okay," the colonel interjects, "how would we do this? Just throw him back to where you found him?"

"No, sir," Rees says. "I was thinking I should go back with him." This causes Bouvier to snap his head and look at Rees, but he doesn't say anything. "We go to some spot away from where everyone is fighting and bring him back to his lines. We would explain to them we escaped from Confederate troops and are returning to the unit. As I told the others, this would fit in with whatever the soldier that got away may have said. This would also give me a little time to look around and maybe gather some more information for our historians. I would have a little freedom, not being from their regiment. Just another lost trooper working his way back to his unit. Maybe have time to grab a few items, I don't know, talk some with the troops, then come home."

"So, you just walk right on in," the senator says, smiling, and Rees can tell he is being a little sarcastic.

"No, sir, actually we would ride right in. I would go in as US Cavalry, just like O'Toole, but from a different troop." This brings a laugh from the colonel and the senator, but the chief, again, just smiles.

"US Cavalry. What the hell do you know about the US Cavalry from the 1860s?" the senator asks. "I can't go along with this. We need another plan if one is needed at all. I know we want to get the Clio Project back up and running, but I think we need something more tangible as a reason to do so."

"Sir?" Rees interrupts. "We have knowledge of history on our side. I've ridden horses before, and I'm sure we can get the uniforms and gear. Hell, there are hundreds, thousands of re-enactors who do this all the time. Plus, O'Toole will be with me, and he knows the ins and outs of being a cavalryman. Isn't returning him to his timeline a tangible reason? This is doable, sirs."

The men are all silent for a few minutes, and all eyes are on the senator who looks in deep thought. Finally, he looks up and sees everyone watching him, and he chuckles. Hey, might as well. We've been wanting to have a reason to restart the Clio Project and this just might be our answer. Granted, we will have to do a feasibility study first to ensure the timeline can't be polluted, and you will need to train, of course," he says and looks at Colonel Black, who raises his hands in surrender.

"Okay, let's try this. Rees, get me an ops plan on my desk in say, what, forty-eight hours? Good enough?" Black asks.

"Shouldn't take that long, sir. Already working on it," Rees says with a bright smile.

"Of course, you are," Colonel Black says, not surprised.

Rees, still smiling, rises from his seat.

"Not so fast, Sergeant. Do you really think we should tell O'Toole? I mean, if this doesn't work out, it might make it worse on him."

Sergeant Bouvier answers, "Sir, sorry, but I think we should let him know. Tell him the truth. We will try, but we can't guarantee him anything. This should boost his morale some."

"What about the rest of your squad? They know about this?" the colonel asks.

"I haven't spoken with all of them, but the ones I did talk to understand why I'm going alone. This will be only the second time this has been tried. If it works, fine, if not, then it's only me who pays the price," Rees says, again getting a look from Bouvier that he catches but ignores.

The small group talk a bit more wrapping up their discussion about O'Toole, then cover some items concerning the Bank, then break up the meeting. Senator Olsen shakes everyone's hand and asks to be kept in the loop. He is assured he will be as he leaves the room with Bouvier going with him.

Colonel Black, Chief Black, and Sergeant Rees leave and walk down the hall. The chief stops, and Rees and the colonel do also, turning to face him.

"Dad? What is it?" Colonel Black asks.

Chief Black just stands in the hallway, thinking. He looks at Rees.

"You and I need to have a conversation. Soon," Chief Black says, then continues down the corridor.

CHAPTER 10

That evening, Sergeant Rees calls his team for a dinner meeting at 1730. He made plans with the dining facility NCOIC, a Chief Master Sergeant, for porterhouse steaks and all the fixings and informed him they were to be the only ones eating at that time. The chief said that would not be a problem, and the rest of the facility personnel could eat in the secondary dining hall.

Rees informed the chief that when everyone was done eating, that no one from the services squadron could be in the dining room, and it was to be secured for a classified meeting. The chief understood and promised it would be handled. When leaving the chief's office, Rees shakes his head. *It's still a chow hall,* he thinks.

The team members all arrive on time and really enjoy the dinner. McGuire is the first to make a statement that this feels like a last meal, and Rees jokingly ensures him that if he keeps up his smart-ass attitude, it will be. For him.

The atmosphere is relaxed, but everyone feels something is up, and they all know it concerns the Clio Project and Corporal O'Toole. After eating, everyone clears their dishes and grabs coffee, soda, or water, and returns to their seats. The facility manager ushers everyone out and informs Rees the room is his and no one will disturb them. Rees thanks the chief and lets him know they shouldn't be too long. Once the room is shut down, Rees comes back to his table as the men all watch and wait. Rees takes a sip of coffee and smiles at the group.

"I'm sure most of you know why I asked for this meeting."

"Because you haven't had one in a while, and you wanted to make sure we remember who the boss is," shouts Sergeant Shepard.

"Says the man who can't win an ass-kicking contest," Rees replies.

"Hey, that's racist, or something like that," Shepard retorts.

"Not if it's true, *Vato*," Montoya says.

This brings chuckles, and the room relaxes even more.

"Is this about O'Toole?" SrA Green asks.

Both SrA Green and SSgt Montoya returned from the time travel experiment with serious head injuries. Green from falling and striking his skull against a Jeep, and Montoya from a .58 caliber musket ball striking him in the head. Luckily for him, the ball hit at just the right enough angle that it didn't completely go through his steel pot helmet, but with enough force that it caved in the helmet and part of his skull.

They both were fortunate they returned to a time where medicine had advanced enough that they both were able to survive their injuries and able to return to duty. Both men are monitored and are constantly seeing doctors and psychologists, as well as having regular physical therapy, but can work light duty.

Green is the lowest ranking and the only airman on the team. Upon the squad's return, everyone was advanced two pay grades. Green and Airman Steele were the only two E-2s in the squad when they were transported to the Civil War. Steele was killed when a cannonball struck the Jeep he was in during an attack.

"Yes, Steve, it is," Rees replies. "I want to take him back to his time period," he says and waits for the room to erupt. To his surprise, no one says a thing.

"Well, that's not what I expected from you all. I thought there'd be a mini-riot."

"No, sir," Tucker says. "We already talked about it with the guys before you called the meeting. We worked it out amongst ourselves, and everyone is behind you."

This, again, surprises Rees and pleases him immensely.

"Guys, I really appreciate the backing. I'm sure you have questions, so go ahead. That's why we are here."

Jack stands and looks at the group, then at Scott. "We pretty much know what's going on, and I think everyone who we met with before has had most of their questions answered."

Rees nods his thanks. "Listen, guys, I do appreciate your support, and I'm sorry you won't be going."

This caused a small rumbling among the men.

Matt Tosseti speaks up in his loud New England accent, "Just as well, can you see Shepard trying to ride a horse with one leg?" He begins cackling, making the scar he bears from a saber slash make him look almost fiendish.

"Don't let me having one leg stop you, you fucking scar-faced Yankee. I don't need two legs to fuck you up," Shepard says, standing up. Tosseti starts towards him and is grabbed by Tucker and McGuire.

Rees looks down and shakes his head, then says in a loud voice, "Okay, both of you, shut the hell up right now." And everyone stops. "You two are going to be the death of me. Now, sit down and do not, and I mean, *do not* pull that bullshit again," he says, looking at both men. "Sit! Down!" And they do, glaring at each other. "No wonder I drink. It's like raising children 24/7." Which gets some chuckles from the men.

He continues, "If the colonel gives us the green light, I must be prepared. I want every one of you to come up with any thoughts of what

I may do to screw up the timeline. I need scenarios for the eggheads and upper echelon to look at so they can ensure I don't mess it up. Now, any questions? And he looks at Shepard and Tosseti. "Serious questions?"

McGuire raises his hand. "Not that it matters, but what are we calling this little trip of yours. You know how the military likes their code names." The others chuckle and agree.

Rees grins. "I was wondering if anyone was going to ask. It's called Operation Ameliorate."

"What?" Both Shepard and Tosseti ask in unison, then they flip each other off. "Why that? What's it mean?"

"Look it up," Rees tells them.

"Guys, we went through hell the last time, but we weren't prepared. This time, I will be. If you want or need anything, come see me, or Bouvier. If you don't have anything for me, that's all I've got for now. Thanks for coming," Rees finishes and sits down.

There are murmurs of conversation from the group and the scuffling of chairs being scraped along the floor as many of them stand to leave. Rees takes a sip of cold coffee and grimaces. Kriger stands by him with a fresh cup and smiles.

Bouvier looks at him. "Where's mine?"

Kriger stares at him. "Hey, I am only sucking up to the big man, go get your own."

Rees chuckles. "Thanks, Dave, you'll make a great sycophant."

To which Kriger holds the cup away from Rees. "You mean I *am* a great sycophant, don't you, old great NCOIC of whatever it is you're the NCOIC of?"

"Ah, yes, I did mean you *are* a great ass-kisser, my friend. Can I have the coffee now, before it gets cold?"

Kriger sits the cup down. "That's better. If you want me to keep sucking up, you make sure you acknowledge it, especially in the presence of others." He joins the two men.

"This is wrong, Scott," Bouvier says. "I should be going with you."

Kriger raises his hand towards Bouvier and flips it like a slap. "Fuck you. Both of us should be going."

Rees shakes his head. "Naw, like I said, if I screw this up, it's on me. If we all go, the chances are multiplied for an accident. Better this way. In and out, then we will see where the project goes from there."

"I still don't like it," Bouvier replies.

"Me neither," Kriger agrees.

Rees smiles. "I appreciate it, guys, but it's my rodeo. My decision. RHIP (Rank Has Its Privileges)."

CHAPTER 11

A few days pass before Rees hears anything about the operation. The time is spent with the squad coming up with possible scenarios that could disrupt the timeline. Finally, Rees is summoned to the colonel's office. He walks into Sam's office, and she lights up when she sees him.

"Well, good morning, Senior Master Sergeant Rees. Aren't we looking well-rested and handsome as ever?"

"Good morning to you, too, Sam," he says, ready for any banter she can throw at him.

"The colonel asked for me," he tells her.

"Yes, he did, and he's expecting you. Go right on in," she replies and goes back to work. Rees walks past and watches her, waiting for some quip, but she doesn't say a word. He knocks once on the colonel's office door, then enters, still waiting for something from Sam. *That woman is making me paranoid, and she knows it,* he thinks before entering the colonel's office.

"Good morning, sir," Rees says cheerily and is surprised to see Senator Olsen and Chief Black in the room, as well as another man Rees instantly recognizes as a Special Forces type due to the mismatched uniform, long hair, and slight beard. That and the way the man sits, like a mountain lion ready to spring at any second. Rees walks over to the desk and salutes the colonel, who returns the salute. Rees then shakes the senator's hand. "Good morning to you, too, Senator." Then he turns to the chief, shaking his hand as well. "Same to you, Chief."

"Morning," Olsen replies.

"Good to see you, Sergeant," Chief Black says.

"Sergeant Rees, I would like you to meet Captain Farnsworth, Air Force Special Operations," the colonel introduces the man, who stands and shakes Rees' hand. "I'll explain why he is here in just a moment."

The colonel indicates that Rees should take a seat, which he does, and the senator turns to face him. "I'm pleased to inform you, Sergeant Rees, that your request has been approved."

Rees smiles broadly and looks from one man to the next. "That's great news, Senator, Colonel. Thank you. When do we go?"

The colonel raises his hand. "Not so fast, young sergeant. There's going to be impact studies conducted with various agencies within the Clio Project framework before anything else."

"Yes, sir. I already have the men doing research and asked them to come up with any scenarios they can think of that may cause a timeline problem."

"That's good, but we will need time, no pun intended, before we can make this happen. I want you to think about what you need for the operation, and once the council is satisfied that you can safely make it there and back without screwing up the timeline, you will be taking the first prepared for time travel jaunt."

"Don't worry about this, Rees. I'm sure it won't be too long, and you will be on your way returning O'Toole to his command," Senator Olsen tells him.

The colonel turns his attention to the other officer in the room. "Scott, Captain Farnsworth will be joining you."

Rees' smile falters some. "Sir?"

"Captain Farnsworth is a superb horseman."

"Whoa, sir, I wouldn't say superb. Adequate," Farnsworth interrupts with a grin, then turns to Rees. "Rode a few times with some Afghan warriors."

The colonel looks at Farnsworth. "Did you fall off?"

"Ah, no, sir. I maintained my dignity," Farnsworth replies with a smirk.

The colonel looks at Farnsworth. "Okay, so in my book, that makes you a suburb horseman." Then turns his attention to Rees. So, the thought is he might be able to assist you. He has seen combat, and we feel he will be an asset to you."

Captain Farnsworth looks at Rees. "This is still your show, Sergeant. I am just here to assist. You've been back in time. I haven't, but I know a little history."

"Colonel, no offense against the captain, but I thought this was just going to be a one-man operation. I mean, if someone else is going, it should be Bouvier or even Kriger, especially Kriger since he's our MedTech. Someone who I have worked with and has traveled once before," Rees says, then looks at Farnsworth. "No offense, sir."

Farnsworth looks back at Rees, shaking his head. "None taken, Sergeant."

Senator Olsen chimes in, "It's not the colonel's fault, Sergeant Rees."

This causes Rees to pause and look at the senator.

"I'm the one who suggested it. You do need someone there to back you up, and I also thought that a military SpecOps tagging along would be better to cover your back. This is not a slight towards you, Scott. Believe me, I have nothing but the utmost confidence in you, but you will be focused on getting O'Toole back to his unit, whereas the good captain can kick some ass if needed," he says with a smile.

Rees thinks about it a minute and accepts it. He has no choice, and it might be good to have a Special Forces type with him, just in case.

"Okay, yes, sir, I see your point," he tells Olsen, then looks at Farnsworth. "But if you intend on going, I think you should be in charge," Rees replies.

Farnsworth glances over at the colonel, who nods, then back at Rees with a smile. "You have to understand, something about us special operation types, we don't really stand on formalities when in the field. We all have a job to do and must work as one unit. It is understood by everyone who the ranking person is, but everyone's opinion and ideas are shared and accepted. Everyone must understand we all have one goal and work as a team. Granted, if it comes down to a quick and final decision having to be made, it comes down to the ranking person to do so, but other than that, it's a group decision. I hope we can do that here."

"I don't see a problem with that, Captain," Rees answers. "But while we are there, formal rank will have to be used.

Farnsworth nods his understanding. "Got it."

"Good," Colonel Black says. "My father will be here as a technical consultant and will assist you in any way he can. He still knows more about Clio than anyone, so he is an invaluable member of this team."

"I'm not here to get in the way but, please, make an old retired chief feel useful and ask me a question once in a while," Joe Black says, chuckling.

Oh, I'm sure they will," the colonel says and stands. Rees and the officer also stand, knowing they are being dismissed. Colonel Black reaches out his hand for Rees, who takes it. "Congratulations, Scott. I'm glad you had this idea. It's something that we have been wanting to do, and now we have a go. I'm sure you're anxious to tell O'Toole, so have at it."

"Thank you, sir. Thank you, Senator," Rees says, smiling. He then salutes the colonel, shakes the senator and the chief's hands, then turns to the captain and asks him to meet him in his office in half an hour to go over some details. The captain agrees, and Rees leaves the colonel's office.

When he is in Sam's office, she sits there with a solicitous grin on her face.

"And just what is that shit-eating grin for, Sam?" Rees asks, standing next to her desk.

"Just that congratulations are in order, Sergeant Rees. Going on a little excursion, are you? I know that just made your day," she says with a genuine smile. "Good for you."

Rees does not show any expression when listening to Sam. This causes her a little concern. Then, without warning, Rees leans over the desk and kisses Sam square on the lips. When he straightens up, she is just staring at him, seemingly flabbergasted, mouth open as if to say something, but can't.

"Well, I'll be," Rees says to her, still not showing any emotion. "Wow, seeing the look on your face is worth it," he tells her and walks out the door with a grin on his face that she can't see, leaving Sam sitting behind her desk with a wicked smile. Rees sticks his head back inside. "Oh, by the way, can you tell my guys to meet me in the conference room in fifteen minutes? Thanks," he says and closes the door thinking, *Damn, finally got the last word in.*

~ ~ ~

Rees is in the conference room as his squad comes in one and two at a time. Once they are all inside and seated, Rees gives them a knowing smile.

"You got a go!" Bouvier says, sensing what Rees is happy about.

"That's right. Now, it won't happen like tomorrow because I will need your scenarios and any input you have for the brainiacs to go over. The sooner we get our ducks in line, the sooner O'Toole, Captain Farnsworth, and I can be on our way."

"Who?" Kriger asks.

"Captain Farnsworth? Who's Captain Farnsworth?" Bouvier asks.

"Captain Farnsworth is a SpecOps guy who has done a few tours in the Middle East and is supposed to be good with horses. Colonel Black and the senator think he should tag along in case I need some assistance."

"That's bullshit. We all have trained and studied for this. You don't need some officer telling you what to do. It's your idea, your plan and you're Ops," Bouvier argues.

"You're preaching to the choir, my friend, but orders are orders. Besides, it might be good to have someone with his experience coming along. He's got way more combat experience under his belt than I do. It'll be fine," Rees explains.

"Yeah, well, why can't we go then? I thought the whole thing was for you to do it alone, so the timeline doesn't get screwed with, or if something goes tits up, you're the only casualty. In and out, you said. Besides, you don't know this guy. He probably works for the CIA or NSA or OSI, or even that old group, what where they called?" Kriger asks.

"Oh, you're talking about MISS," Bouvier answers.

"Yeah, them. Bet they're still around wanting to get their hands on the project," Kriger finishes, his face red.

"Christ, guys, knock off the paranoia crap. He's just an Air Force officer who has the credentials to tag along. You didn't expect this to stay within our little group forever, did you? No, this is good. It'll work out. Now, I've got a meeting with the captain in my office in a few, so

I'll get in touch with you later, and we'll go see O'Toole," Rees says and departs.

Bouvier and Kriger stay behind.

"Yeah, we'll see," Kriger mumbles.

Rees goes back to his office and pours himself a cup of coffee. He takes a sip, and when he turns around, Captain Farnsworth stands in the open door.

"Oh, sorry, thought I had more time before you got here, sir. Come on in, please. Have a seat. Can I get you a cup of coffee?" Rees asks.

Captain Farnsworth is all smiles, and Rees takes note of his size, six feet one or two, about two-twenty, two-twenty-five and muscular. Longish blond hair, slight beard. Rees chuckles, and the captain stops before taking a seat and looks at Rees.

"I do something funny, Sergeant?" he asks, holding onto the chair and watching Rees.

"No. No, sir. You just remind me of a flight chief we used to have. We used to call him Captain America. Great guy. Now, I'm wondering what happened to him. Anyway, sorry, just something that flashed when you walked in," Rees explains and holds the coffee pot up.

Farnsworth shakes his head, and Rees replaces the pot, then pulls his chair out from around his desk and next to the captain.

Farnworth takes note of this action as it shows that Rees isn't intimidated by his rank and is not using his desk as a shield. It also shows that Rees thinks of themselves as equals and the captain should be aware of it. It tells the captain that Rees is going to try to work with him. Good, makes things easier.

"Sergeant Rees, please let me start this off if you don't mind. I know you asked to meet with me, but I would like to say something before we start. This is an honor for me just to have met you. I have always been fascinated by time travel and wondered what it would be like to go back to some period in time and witness it firsthand. When I was approached with this offer, I couldn't believe it. Actually, I didn't believe it until I was brought in and showed the videos of what you and your team underwent. I was in awe. You did and saw things I had only dreamt of. So, let me say, I am here for you in any capacity that you need me."

Rees just stares at the man, then takes a sip of his coffee, thinking, then sets the cup down and sits back in his chair, looking directly at the captain.

"Captain Farnsworth, thank you for that. But what you saw on the video were men scared to death, confused, and angry. We lost friends there. Yes, we saw the Civil War firsthand, but we didn't have time to study it or be inspired by it, we didn't even know what was going on. We were trying to not get killed and just wanted to find our way home. The team is still angry over this, but we have come to terms with it. I understand why command wants you along, but it doesn't mean I like it. I follow orders and will do whatever it takes to get O'Toole home. If it means taking you with me, so be it. I'm not angry at you, sir, and I'm sure we will get along fine. But having an unknown factor added to this mission just throws me off a bit. I can adapt and overcome anything, I just hope this goes as planned, and we can get in and out safely." Rees stops, then adds, "And you can get to what you were actually sent here to do." He watches the captain for a reaction.

Leaning forward, the captain looks Rees in the eyes. "No, Sergeant Rees, I get it. I have lost friends, too, but we volunteered to do what we did. You and your men didn't. That's what I admire and respect about you, about your men. You were all thrown into a situation no one could have thought possible, then to fight your way out and come back here. That's just amazing. That's all I'm saying. I do hope we get the corporal back, as I know that is the mission. I have a mission, too, and it's to help you accomplish yours. That what I have been sent to do"

Rees studies the man for a few seconds, then stands. "Fuck the coffee. Bourbon?" He reaches out his hand. Also standing, Farnsworth grasps the offered hand.

"Thought you'd never ask, good sir," Farnsworth says with a smile.

CHAPTER 12

That afternoon, Rees, Bouvier, and Kriger go see O'Toole. Rees chides himself for waiting this long to tell him the news.

"You mean it?" O'Toole asks, his voice loud. "I'm going back?"

All three NCOs smile.

"So far, so good. We have a green light," Rees says before catching himself.

"A what?" O'Toole asks.

"Sorry, a green light means yes, we have permission to take you back," Rees explains.

"Thank you so very much! My God! Thank you so very much!" O'Toole says, whooping loudly. "When do we go? Can we go right now? I am ready."

"Not so fast," Rees tells the man. "There are some things that have to be done first. It might be a few weeks. I hope not, but we just got the okay, and there are things we have to do first before we can go."

"You said we? Who is going with me?" O'Toole asks Rees.

"Me and an officer named Farnsworth," Rees answers, not wanting to say too much.

"Alright, what do you have to do?"

Rees sighs. "Listen, Andy. This is a complex thing we must do. The machine that sent us back to your time, to when we found you, was called Clio. That was the first time it was ever used to transport people back in time. When they tried to use it to bring us back to our time period of 1980, it was destroyed, and we all…" Rees indicates by pointing to everyone in the room, "were in some type of time zone, or limbo you might say. It took them thirty-eight years to build another time machine, Clio II, to finally bring us to the time period we are in now."

O'Toole looks like a deer in the headlights of an approaching car. Rees chuckles at the look on O'Toole's face and finishes.

"Some tests must be done first, and then we can go. I know you're anxious, as am I, but this is out of my hands. Don't worry, it'll be time to go before you know it."

O'Toole listens and seems downtrodden as he shakes his head, then perks right up. "Hot damn, I'm going home," he says with a grin that stretches his face to the breaking point, then he turns serious, "I hope Emma is still there. It is been so long, and I usually send her a letter as soon as I could. She has not heard from me in such a long time. I hope she does not think I am dead."

Rees grins and shakes his head. "Andy, no need to worry about that. We will actually return you to a time not too long after we left. When we get back, only a few days will have passed. It'll be all right."

Andy looks at Rees with squinted eyes. "You pulling one on me, Sergeant Rees?"

Rees shakes his head. "Not in the least."

Andy smiles. "That's good to hear, and I thank you for it.

Rees smiles back. "Once everything is cleared, we will let you know, then we'll be on our way," Rees explains. "Until then, just keep your chin up, and we'll go from there."

Andy nods, and the three NCOs stick around and listen to Andy talk excitedly about going home.

When they leave, the NCOs hear their names over the intercom and are asked to report to Resource and Development (R&D), weapons division. The three men take the elevator to R&D and make their way to the weapons area. Entering one of the rooms, they are told that Captain Epstein has asked to see them. The NCOs walked down the hallway and enter the weapons development section, where they are greeted by Captain Epstein. Captain Farnsworth is also in the room holding a rifle, an old looking rifle.

"Ah, good of you to come," Captain Epstein says, looking like a child ready to open presents on Christmas morning. "I wanted to show so what we have been working on. Please, come with me, come on," he says with an impatient voice, fast-walking to another area with the three men hurrying to catch up. Once there, they see scores of different weapons and weapon parts everywhere. Epstein quickly moves to one section of a worktable and picks up a rifle that looks to Rees like an old breach loader. The captain turns towards Rees.

"This is something we have been working on for your next trip. What I am handling is an updated and modified replica Spencer breech loader," he explains, handing it to Rees.

Rees takes the weapon and turns it over, looking to see what may have been modified, even though he's never held one in his hands before now and doesn't know what to look for.

The captain continues, pointing at a button on the butt of the rifle. "Push that there," he tells Rees, and Rees complies. The bottom of the buttstock *clicks* and comes loose. Rees pulls on it and sees that the bottom section is an ammo magazine. He holds it up for the others to see. Epstein grins and reaches for the magazine.

"The magazine holds thirty 5.56 mm rounds. The weapon has been modified to fire semi-automatic. The magazine has been made to fit in the stock when you insert the magazine," he starts to say, then reaches for the weapon. "Here, let me have it," he says and takes the weapon from Rees.

He picks up a loaded magazine and places it in the rifle. Pushing the magazine into place, they hear an audible *click*. He turns it over and shows that the bottom of the magazine matches the wood grain so no one will notice that it has been modified.

"We made it this way so you could blend in easier but still have superior firepower when needed." He then turns the weapon right side up and points to a small extraction in the butt of the stock. He pulls it out and releases it and an audible snap can be heard. "That is the charging handle, the round is now chambered," he says, and then points to the hammer. "The safety is the hammer. When it is forward, you're on safe, and once you pull it back, you are ready to fire. The weapon is slightly larger than the rifles carried at that time, but not so much as to be noticeable. It is gas-fed, just like our weapons now, and can be broken down and cleaned easily," he tells them, smiling.

"Also, it can fire single or three-round bursts. Pull the trigger, and it fires one round, pull the trigger and hold, it will fire the burst," he adds and turns and quickly walks away. "Follow me," he tells them over his shoulder and leads the men into another room where there is a shooting range. He points to a table, and there are compact earpieces.

"Those are specially built earpieces that will allow one to hear almost normally until the noise decibel reaches a point that can cause injury. They self-activate to reduce load noise that could cause hearing damage. When worn, they are almost invisible to the naked eye." He demonstrates by placing the pieces into his ears, then smiles. Each man in turn does the same.

Captain Epstein hands the rifle to Rees and points to the target downrange.

"It's ready to fire, Sergeant. Go ahead," he says, and Rees aims the rifle, pulls the hammer back, and fires three rounds that strike the target just a little low and to the right.

"That's nice, Sir. What about sight adjustments?" Rees asks, and the captain holds his hands out for the rifle. Rees gives it. The captain flip opens the front sight and shows Rees how to make an adjustment. Rees takes the weapon back, makes the correction, and fires again. This time, three rounds are dead center. Rees smiles. "That's totally bitch'n," he says, looking at the other men, with Epstein's eyebrows lifted in a questioning manner.

Farnsworth looks at Epstein and grins. "I assume that's 80's slang for meaning the weapon is awesome?"

"Sorry, yes, sir. Something you'll have to get used to," Rees answers.

Captain Epstein breaks in as if nothing occurred. "That's not all we have for you." He heads back out into the main room at a quick pace over to another workbench. Once there, he picks up what looks like a US Colt Navy pistol. He proudly shows it to the men. "This is a modified replica, of course, of a Colt Model 1862 Pocket Navy. The original weapon was a percussion cap and ball, this one is a breech-loading 9mm. It's only a six-shot pistol. We did look at possibly making it into a semi-automatic, but we couldn't find a way to make it seem like something from that era. Sorry, you'll have to do it the old-fashioned way."

The three NCOs laugh. Bouvier looks at the captain. "That shouldn't be a problem since we are used to using .38's. Do you have speed loaders for them?" he asks.

"Good question, Jack," Rees replies.

Captain Epstein's gaze clouds for an instant, then realization dawns on him. "Oh, speed loaders. No, no, we don't but give me a little while and I will. That's a good idea. Sorry I didn't think of it. Haven't had a call for those things. Ever," he says with a smile. "You want to try this out?" he asks Rees.

Before Rees can answer, Kriger jumps in, "I would!"

Rees tells them maybe later as he has a feeling the captain has more in store for them, and he does.

"This is not all, Sergeants. If you'll come with me." He leads them to another table where they can see blue clothing, which Rees assumes are Union uniforms. The captain picks up a jacket and holds it out from the men to look at.

"This was actually Captain Farnsworth's idea, and we made it happen."

Rees touches the jacket. "Very nice." He rolls his eyes.

The two captain's laugh, and Farnsworth looks at the NCOs. "No, watch this."

He takes the jacket from Captain Epstein, and they all walk back to the shooting range. Captain Farnsworth places the jacket on a mannequin and carries it downrange. When he comes back, an airman waits for him, carrying a musket. Farnsworth takes the musket from the airman.

"She ready to fire?" he asks.

"Yes, sir, good to go."

Farnsworth smiles, and then aims the musket downrange, sights in on the mannequin, and fires. The musket *claps*, and the cap ignites the powder. The *boom* is followed by a billow of smoke that is quickly sucked into the air filtration system. The men stare downrange for a few seconds, and Farnsworth hands the musket back to the airman. He then turns to the NCOs.

"Come on guys, check this out." He leads the men downrange. When they reach the mannequin, he points to the jacket where there is a small indentation but no hole.

"What the hell?" Rees says as he reaches out and touches the impression on the jacket. "Bullet resistant?" he asks.

"You got it," Farnsworth replies. "The material is something that has been used for civilian clothing, but with some military upgrade. Not only is the jacket resistant, but all the clothing, to include your boots and hat, or cap, whichever you prefer."

"Jesus Christ!" Kriger blurts and looks at Captain Epstein. "You're Q," he says, and everyone stares at him. He laughs. "Q, 007, James Bond for crying out loud. Q, the guy who makes all the cool gadgets for Bond!" he explains, seeing no one gets it. He runs his hand down his face and shakes his head. "Urgh!"

Finally getting it, Rees, Bouvier, and Farnsworth laugh with him, but Epstein just looks perplexed. "Who is James Bond?" he asks, and this causes the men to laugh harder.

After this, Epstein shows them the rest of the uniforms and demonstrates how there are hidden compartments for different items. A slot in the back of the coat for a small knife, a belt buckle that can be made into a .22 caliber pistol and hollowed-out boot heels that can contain different items. This causes Kriger to laugh again and shake his head. He looks at the other men, and Rees knows what he's going to say.

"Jim West, right?" he asks.

"You got it. This is too good," Bouvier adds.

Now, Farnsworth and Epstein both stare at the three NCOs with blank looks, and Rees sees it.

"An old TV show, *Wild, Wild West*. About two secret service agents who work for President Grant but, in reality, are secret agents who foil the plots of all sorts of evil villains, like James Bond, but in the late 1860s. Rode around in a train with secret compartments, fight the villain of the week with modern super cool gadgets. Not unlike what Captain Epstein is showing us now. Next thing you know, he'll be handing us Star Trek shit like a phaser or tricorder," he says with a chuckle.

Farnsworth and Epstein look at each other, and the smile fades from Rees' face, "What?" he asks.

"Well, now that you say that…" Epstein answers.

He then shows them the GPS tracker, built-in camera and microphones, and other devices to make their journey easier.

"Not really Star Trek, but considering the era you're from, it's close. The GPS tracker may or may not work," Epstein warns them, "It's not been tested, of course. Our theory is that we should be able to send a signal to you from our space-time, so that wherever you are, you can use it. Again, this is only a theory. If not, it's the old map and compass."

"Shouldn't be a problem. I'm sure Captain Farnsworth is well versed in map and compass, as I am. But we'll be glad to test your gadgets for you, sir," Rees tells the man. "I assume that O'Toole won't be given any of this equipment?"

"No, he won't. He'll actually be given his old uniform back. No sense making him look any different than he was when he went on patrol."

"Got it," Rees replies.

"If I come up with anything else I think might be useful, I'll let you know, and if you think of anything you could use that I don't have, let me know. I'll see what I can come up with."

"Yes, sir. Thank you. This is some impressive equipment."

"Why thank you, Sergeant. I like to think so, and if I don't see you before you leave, good luck."

CHAPTER 13

SOMEWHERE IN A WESTERN UNITED STATES DESERT

Lt. Derrick and his team arrive in a section of the almost seemingly unending Mojave Desert that is uninhabited and undisclosed to most people. At one time, the area was frequented by prospectors looking for their fortune in silver. A thriving mining town at one time, the silver ran out decades ago, and the town was abandoned, as with many others in the vast desert.

Constructing an underground facility without being seen under the watchful eye of US satellites, as well as those of other nations, was no small task. Senator Helen Hellberg made sure the facility construction was concealed, and she used significant influence to ensure its secrecy. It had taken several years to accomplish, what with having to stop production during some satellite flyovers or having to deal with lookey-loos who had to be taken care of, permanently and discreetly. The desert was a dangerous place to be wandering around in. People disappear. But in the end, she was sure it would all be worth it.

Under the cover of darkness, the motorcycle, police unit, and semi-trailer are led to a cavern that connects to the underground facility. Once the vehicles are secured, a large hydraulic door slowly retracts, covering the opening of the cavern, making it blend into the surroundings. The team gathers and walk towards the elevators, which will take them deep into a secured area of the facility. They exit the elevator and proceed to their destination.

Cedric Novell, director of the Military Intelligence, Law Enforcement & Security, MILES, waits inside his second office, the first being in Washington DC. MILES was born from the ashes of MISS (Military Intelligence Security Services), which was disbanded in 1980 after its founder, Senator Minten, was disgracefully removed from office and several agents arrested for numerous crimes to include kidnapping and murder. Novell has been waiting anxiously since he received word that the infiltration team's mission was a success and just received word they were on station. His intercom buzzes.

"Director Novell, Lieutenant Derrick, and Master Sergeant Butler are here," his secretary advises him.

"Please, send them in," Novell replies, releasing the call button and standing.

The door to his office opens seconds later, and the two men enter. Novell is on pins and needles as he stares at them, then looks to the briefcase being carried by Derrick.

"Congratulations are in order I understand," he says in a form of a greeting.

"Yes, sir, that they are," Derrick replies with a smile, holding up the briefcase. Novell waves his hand towards his desk, indicating the briefcase should be placed there. Derrick does so and steps back. Novell just stares at the case.

"It's in there?" asking a rhetorical question.

Without saying a thing, MSgt Butler walks over to the case and opens the hidden compartment and removes the Inabular Device. He places it in front of Novell and opens it. Novell is all smiles as he reaches out to stroke the mechanism,

"So, this is what all the fuss is about. The one thing we need to finish our project," he says to the men, almost seemingly hypnotized by the device. "Not such a big thing, is it?" he asks aloud.

The two men do not answer.

"Okay, get this down to the lab. I'll inform the senator that we're almost ready," Novell tells them as he closes the case, picking it up and handing it to Lt. Derrick.

"I also understand that after you left, it wasn't too long before they discovered the truth. That's unfortunate, not a problem, but unfortunate. We were just hoping they wouldn't discover it missing for some time. No worries, though. The plan is still on schedule, and I don't think there's anything they can do to stop us."

Derrick takes the device without a word spoken, then he and Butler leave the office.

Novell sits back in his chair and picks up the phone that goes directly to Senator Hellberg's office. The phone rings, and within two seconds, it is picked up.

"Tell me you got the damned thing, Cedric."

"Yes, ma'am, we do. In fact, the team is taking it down to the lab right now."

"Good work, Cedric. Your team has done an excellent job…so far. I'll be there shortly to oversee the initiation of Janus. We are about to change history, Cedric, and I for one am excited as hell. I'll see you soon," she says and hangs up without another word. Novell replaces his phone and sits back and smiles.

~　~　~

Derrick and Butler carry the Inabular Device to the laboratory and turn it over to the head technician. He takes the device gingerly like he holds a precious artifact or nitroglycerin. He moves towards a console with a slot the same size as the Inabular Device and inserts it. Other technicians sit at various stations around the room, and once the device is inserted, they all begin watching their monitors and typing on their computer keypads.

"What are you doing?" Lt. Derrick asks.

The lead technician fiddles with his computer and seems to ignore the lieutenant. Just before the lieutenant starts to ask the technician the question again, the tech turns his face towards him.

"Oh, sorry, not ignoring you, just need to concentrate while we do this. We're checking the compatibility of the device with Janus. Running tests to ensure the Inabular Device will work with our time machine. We only had so much to work with when building it. Without the Inabular Device in our hands, a lot of what we were doing was guesswork. Granted, highly intelligent guesswork, but..." he says without finishing the sentence, again becoming engrossed in his work.

Derrick and Butler watch the technicians for a few more minutes, then grow bored. Derrick turns towards Butler. "Let's let the eggheads do their jobs. Besides, I'm hungry," he tells Butler and walks to the exit. They leave the laboratory and go up a level to look for the rest of the team. He goes into a common area and finds them cleaning weapons.

"Just the kind of thing I like to see. Thought you all would be sleeping, eating, playing ping pong, but nope, you're cleaning weapons," Derrick says.

Willis pipes up, "Oh, no, sir. We were goofing off, then we figured you would be popping in, so we thought we'd look like we were actually working."

Derrick shakes his head. "From you, Willis, I would expect that," he tells the younger man, grinning. "Alright, everyone, the device is in the lab and being tested for compatibility with Janus. Stay on your toes. We could be called upon any time now. I'm sure it won't be immediately, but once the senator gets on station, then things are going to move quickly, so stay alert. If you haven't already, you might want to get some chow and rest up some," Lt. Derrick informs them. "I'm going to the cafeteria myself. You coming?" he asks Butler.

"Sure thing. Tacos are calling my name," Butler replies. The two men leave as the others continue what they were doing.

CHAPTER 14

Senator Hellberg hangs the phone up on Director Novell without a word. She leans back in her oversized leather-bound high back chair with a smirking grin on her face. She spins the chair around and looks up at the "I Love Me" wall behind her. Pictures of herself with several dignitaries from various states, as well as dignitaries from around the world. There are quite a few of her with different entertainers, actors, singers, writers.

She learned from her father you need to fit in with everyone, be a person of the people, smile, and make everyone feel as if they are the only ones in the room with you. On her desk is a photograph of her and her late husband, Captain Hellberg, who died of a coronary. Next to this is a photograph of her son in his Marine uniform, also deceased, Afghanistan, then one of her daughter at college, and a final photograph of her father.

The senator's mind wanders as she thinks of her father. He, too, was a senator. One who was sent into exile after being disgraced by those who owed him everything. His body was discovered in a lake days after they found his boat adrift. The official cause of death was ruled a suicide, but Helen never bought into it. That just wasn't her father. She vowed to avenge him and crush those who hurt him, as well as her and her family.

Senator Hellberg had served in the United States Navy before resigning her commission as a commander. She joined the Navy at the bequest of her father. He had wanted someone in the Navy to keep an eye out for any scientific advances that he could possibly acquire for his agenda. She served from 1977 until 1988 when she decided to pull the plug and start a career in politics. Even after her father's death, she stayed in, thinking she still might be able to carry on his legacy by acquiring Navy secrets and exploiting them for her gain.

It never worked out that way, so she decided another route might better suit her. Her brother also served during the same time period, except he was in the Army. He, too, was assigned the same task to uncover scientific research for his father's benefit. Both siblings served with distinction but never reached the goal their father aspired towards.

Their cousin, a captain in the United States Air Force, had been assigned to a top-secret installation working on the Clio Project. He had been killed when he tried to spill the beans about the project to a news crew. Earlier, he had been reprimanded by his commanding officer and some asshole E-9 sergeant, so he thought he would get back at them by blowing the whistle on the project. It backfired, and a secret organization, overseen by her father, terminated him, along with the news crew. It was a futile gesture on her cousin's part as the project was shut down shortly after, with her father becoming a scapegoat for the powers that be. It cost her cousin's life, as well as her father's.

Having worked her way into the fold as a senator, she, as well as her brother, were able to gather information on various projects that mostly stemmed from the USAF. The Air Force seemed to get most of the scientific projects. She guessed the government trusted the flyboys with these things ever since the Navy screwed it up with the Philadelphia Experiment back in the forties, and as for the Army, hey, they are called *grunts* for a reason, and she won't even go there about the Corps.

Oh well, now that she was a senator, and on various oversight committees, she could keep tabs on these things. But she learned a valuable lesson from her father's mistakes, don't try to take over the project, create your own. So, she did just that, building a scientific fortress in the Mojave Desert right under the noses of her own government, as well as that of the US military.

She had misappropriated funds under the guise of humanitarian projects, military testing of different weapons systems, and other sleight of hand maneuvers that, so far, have seemed aboveboard. She also had the backing of some third world countries that, thinking they would be rewarded for helping her out, would be in for a surprise when they found out they were left out in the cold when the time came to collect, and there was nothing they could do about it.

Not that it mattered anyway, if what she has planned works. Most of these third world assholes would probably not even be in the positions there are in today. She won't owe anyone. Monies were transferred to a charity set up by some of her supporters, with the money secretly being transferred to her projects. She makes sure they're thrown a bone now and then, but nothing that could be considered a conspiracy. No one would be the wiser. Again, it really doesn't matter.

She has learned, years later after being in politics for some time, that the Clio Project had been the time machine that her father was trying to take control of. When the takeover failed, and the loss of several military and government personnel, as well as the deaths of civilians, had occurred, it resulted in the project being terminated.

It took her and her brother years gathering information about what transpired, and with a stroke of luck, she discovered that several of the scientists who worked on the original project had kept schematics, blueprints, scientific journals, and all sorts of top-secret information on Clio, and some were not happy with the regime when they disbanded. Using the power of her office, as well as that of her brother's, they were able to gather most of the information needed to build their own time machine.

The one thing they didn't have was the Inabular Device, which they did not know existed until recently. They thought that Chief Master Sergeant Black, Clio's creator, had destroyed the device to keep it out of the hands of others. But, as luck would have it, her brother found out, through some brutal means, that several Inabular Devices were being kept at Area 51. Good thing, too, since none of the scientists they had working for them could figure out how to operate their time machine without it. Now that they have it, Janus would be up and running in no time.

She is deep in thought when she hears the knock on her door, then hears it open. She turns her chair around and is about to give someone an ass-chewing when she sees her twin brother leaning into the room, with one hand on the doorknob and the other on the door jam. Leaning further in, he has a shit-eating grin on his face and a twinkle in his eye. Hellberg immediately returns the look, then a smile breaks across her face. Her brother moves into the room and closes the door behind him.

Aeson Minten is Helen's fraternal twin. Where he stands six-foot-three-inches in height, she is a smaller five-foot-eleven-inches. He is muscular and lean, having been in Delta Force for years before retiring as a colonel. Helen is slimmer, though in exceptionally good shape, with an athletic figure. She resembles her father, as her brother took on more of her mother's looks. His hair is dark, with the sides turning silver, and hers blond, though she must cheat now and again to keep it that color.

Both are extremely attractive and use it to their advantage, just as their father did. One thing they do have in common is that they both seemed to think completely alike, almost as if they know each other's thoughts. They were told growing up they were almost scary, especially when one would call the other, knowing something was wrong, or more astonishingly, when something good happened. People thought them kind of freakish, so they learned to keep it among themselves. Wouldn't do to have freaks in government, not knowingly anyway.

Aeson straightens and comes into Helen's office, closing the door behind him.

"I think you have some good news for me, little sister," he says with a smile.

She shakes her head. "You know how to ruin a good surprise, don't you? And quit calling me little sister, we're twins." She gives him the side-eye, and the corner of her mouth turned up in a slight grin.

"What?" he says, feigning surprise. "Uh-uh, remember, you are my little sister. I'm ninety seconds older than you." He finishes moving around a chair in front of her desk and sits without being asked to. She just looks at him, and he returns the look. "Hey, you were going to ask me to sit," he says, tapping the side of his head. "I know these things."

She shakes her head and lightly chuckles, then her features harden somewhat.

"We got it," she finally says.

Minten claps his hands once, then quickly spreads them upwards, "Bam, I knew it!" he exclaims. "I knew the plan would work. I've got a good group of talented people for these types of operations. All those years in Special Forces and Delta Force weren't wasted. What with you being where you are and me where I am, we will be unstoppable, little—" He was cut off by Helen raising her hand to him and giving him a stern look. "I mean, Senator."

"That's better. Now, get your things together, we've got a flight to catch."

"We going to the Dragon Lair?" Aeson asks.

"Why do you insist on calling it that?" Helen asks her brother. "Why can't you call it by its proper name?"

"What? Olympus?" Aeson cries. "Come on, we've got to change that. Just because we were named after Greek gods and such doesn't mean you had to name the area housing the Janus project Olympus. Can we call it something else? It just sounds too silly."

Helen grabs some belongings as he rambles on about the name. "And Dragon Lair isn't? Damn it, just suck it up and roll with it. It's just a name, and one that is quite appropriate for us." She stops and turns towards her brother. "Listen, I used Olympus because, in twenty-four hours, we will be gods. Do you get that? Gods! We will be changing the course of history and molding it to what we want. We will be running this whole country, as well as having major influence throughout the rest of the world. With any luck, Father will be there with us, so we have more important things to worry about than the name of the project center. We've got to get going. You got what you need?"

"I'm fine as is. I've got things there, let's just get going," Aeson tells her. "I still don't like the name, though."

They stand in the middle of the room and look at each other. Helen gives him an exasperated look, then reaches out and touches his face.

"We're finally going to do this," Helen says as they both realize that they are. She drops her hand from his face, and Aeson opens the door, and they both leave the office. Tomorrow at this time, things will be different, really different.

They walk outside the building where their car and driver wait. The driver opens the door for them. Once inside, the driver climbs in the front and drives off.

"Everything ready at the airport?" Helen asks the driver.

"Yes, ma'am. The plane is fueled and stocked and will leave upon your arrival," the driver answers.

"Good, thank you," she says, remembering to be friendly to the minions, even though it grates against her skin to do so. She reaches over and raises the partition that separates them from the driver. She looks at her brother, who smirks.

"What's so funny?" she asks.

"Oh, nothing. You should see your face when you have to be nice to someone you deem below you. It's a wonderful tell."

She glares at him, knowing he right but won't give in to answering. She pulls out a folder from her briefcase and opens it. She starts to read a report when her brother interrupts.

"I know, let's call it the Citadel!"

Helen drops the report into her lap and looks at Aeson again.

"You on again about that? Listen, Olympus fits with what we're doing. You only want Citadel because you're Army. It's not a fort.

"Yes, it is. Think about it. It's almost impenetrable, deep underground, it's a fortress. So, Citadel fits."

Helen blows out her breath. "Fine, if you want to call it that, we will call it that. What is in a name anyway? We'll just have to notify every one of the name change and redo all the paperwork with the Olympus markings, not a problem," she says, reading the reports again.

Aeson looks out the window, watching the city flash by, then cuts his eyes to Hellberg. "Just kidding. Olympus is fine. I just wanted to see how long it took me to get you to change it. Was really just trying to get you thinking about something else other than Janus."

Hellberg starts to protest, but Aeson raises his hands. "I know it's important, but you need to relax a little and not worry about what's about to transpire. It's going to work, and as you said, we will be gods. Who else can change the course of history?"

Hellberg smiles and leans her head against her brother's shoulder. "We will at that, big brother." She continues to read the report.

They don't say anything for the next twenty minutes and arrive at the airport where a Bombardier Challenger 350 waits on the tarmac. A steward and crew members stand by the boarding ramp. The vehicle pulls to a stop, and the steward rushes to open the car door. He welcomes the senator and her brother and tells them everything is set, and they can leave as soon as they are seated and the luggage is stowed. Hellberg informs the steward there is no luggage, and they wish to leave immediately. The steward nods and informs the flight crew by radio.

Senator Hellberg and Aeson Minten board the aircraft and take the first forward-facing luxury seats and seatbelt themselves in. The boarding ramp closes as they do this, and the jet is already moving towards the runway. Within ten minutes, they are rumbling down the runway and are airborne soon after. Once in the air, the steward brings drinks, a fifteen-year-old, Highland Park Scotch, neat, for him and a Vodka Martini on ice for her. After serving the beverages, the steward informs them he will be in the aft compartment if needed and leaves them alone.

Hellberg takes a sip of her drink and places it in the chair's holder. She takes up the reports and starts scanning them. After finishing one report, she hands it to Aeson, who reads it for himself. It is an after-action report by the team who retrieved the Inabular Device.

"Your team did an excellent job. They are to be commended, as well as you."

"My goodness, a compliment from the senator. Why, thank you," Aeson says.

Hellberg looks up from the second report. "I mean it. Without the Inabular Device, we would be nowhere with the project. They did us a great service, and they should be rewarded as well as informed of the great job they did. Even if they did fuck up by leaving equipment behind. That could have been costly, but as is, they got the job done. We are now on our way. Once we arrive, I want to meet with the team that will be traveling. A pep talk, and I want to see how they are holding up. I don't want any screw-ups. This must run like clockwork. Or as dad used to say, 'As smoothly as the taking of Pelham, 123.'"

Aeson groans at that. "Because he always said that, I wouldn't even watch the movie. Still to this day."

"Movies. Plural," Hellberg informs him. "And a book."

"What?" Aeson asks.

"There are two movies, both based on a book. Never mind, it doesn't matter. What matters is that this must run like clockwork. Once everything is changed, we should be able to step right in where Father oversees everything, and those who did us wrong will pay. That is if they are still around."

Aeson watches his sister, then returns to the report. *Yes,* he thinks. "They did get it, but there's going to be hell to pay for fucking up and leaving equipment behind."

He finishes the report and picks up his glass of Whiskey. He downs it in one gulp and stands. "I'm going to hit the head, as you squids say, and take a nap in the back," he tells his sister, placing a hand on her shoulder, patting it. "I suggest getting some rest, too. Going to be a long one once this gets rolling."

"I will," she replies with a smile. "Sleep well."

Hellberg finishes the second report and sips her drink. She begins thinking of her father and what it will be like to see him again.

CHAPTER 15

2019

Rees sits in his room, trying to watch the TV mini-series *The Stand*, which was one of his favorite Stephen King novels. He has been trying to watch it for weeks now, but something always comes up preventing him from doing so. He finally decided he would take the evening off and watch it. He sits down with a bowl of popcorn and tries to enjoy it, but his mind keeps wandering.

First, his thoughts wander to Nora, and he feels a pang of regret. He admonishes himself about it, and then shakes it off. *Probably wouldn't have lasted, anyway,* he thinks. *I would have gotten orders or something else.*

Next, he begins wondering about the upcoming mission and how he will react when sent back to a time where he lost men under his watch. His friends. This makes him even more melancholy. He tries to shake it off, but it is too late.

He turns off the television and just sits. A few minutes later, the female voice of the computer announces he has a visitor. Rees snaps out of his slump and tells the computer to let them in without even asking who it is. The door opens, and Colonel Black walks in. Rees jumps to his feet, almost spilling the popcorn.

Colonel Black waves his hand dismissively. "No need for that, Scott. Not here on official business. Just wanted to stop and chat awhile."

"No, sir, please, come on in. Have a seat. Can I get you something to drink?"

"Yes, that would be good. Bourbon and water," he says, looking around the room, "You'll join me, of course?"

"Yes, sir, I will," Rees answers and go to the kitchen area to make the drinks.

"Hope I'm not disturbing you. I know you don't get much *me* time," Black says, studying the room.

"Not at all. Was trying to watch a movie I'd been wanting to see but just can't get into it," Rees answers, returning with the drinks. "Please, sir, have a seat."

Both men find a chair and sit. Colonel Black takes a sip of the drink and grins. Holding the glass up, he looks at the liquid. "Elijah Craig?" he asks, finding a coaster and setting the glass down.

"Yes, sir. Know your bourbons."

"What I know is that we must be paying you too much if you can afford this stuff," Black says, chuckling.

"You forget, sir, thirty-nine years back pay," Rees replies.

"Ah, yes. Forgot," Black says. "Like I said, just wanted to see how you were doing. A lot of things have to be going through your head, what with the upcoming mission and all."

"True, sir. But I believe it'll all work out."

"How are you and Captain Farnsworth getting along? Any concerns?" Black asks, watching Rees.

"No, sir. He seems like a very competent officer. We are getting along fine. Why do you ask?"

Black shakes his head. "No reason, just he's one of Olsen's picks, not mine. I ran a check on the man, and he's what he seems. A combat veteran, decorated at that, well versed in history especially Civil War history. Funny, I couldn't locate any family history, didn't ask, but I don't believe he's an orphan, but we can't locate any family members…yet.

"Might be he in the same boat as me and the guys, sir," Rees answers, referring to his entire team being without families. This is why they were picked for the first experiment.

Black nods. "I suppose." He picks up his drink and studies it in thought. "Okay, so I didn't just come here just to shoot the breeze," he finally says, sitting back up. "I need to tell you about something that happened a couple of decades ago."

Rees is now intrigued and takes a sip of his drink and sits back in his chair. Colonel Black looks at him and does the same.

"In 1997, a rogue senator got her hands on one of the Inabular Devices," Black begins. Rees looks as if he doesn't understand but doesn't interrupt. Black sees the look. "When my father came back, we made several copies of the device in case something happened to him. No one else knows how to recreate the device, so he consented to making copies. Anyway, the devices are kept in Area 51, but to make a long story short, security was bypassed, and one of the devices was stolen."

Now, Rees' look turns to one of concern, and Black shakes his head. "It's all good," he says and tells Rees the story.

CHAPTER 16

Colonel Gorman arrives at the Air Force Base and makes his way to the Bank. After going through the security procedures, he heads straight for Colonel Rhodes' office.

Douglas opens the door entering the outer office. Rhodes' assistant, Rebecca, looks up as he enters and informs Colonel Rhodes that Colonel Gorman just arrived. Gorman thanks Rebecca and walks to Colonel Rhodes' door, grimacing as he turns the knob and enters.

Colonel Rhodes stands behind his desk, finger still on the intercom button when Gorman enters. The two officers shake hands.

"Frank, thanks for coming so quickly," Colonel Rhodes says, using his hand to indicate Colonel Gorman should have a seat. While Gorman sits, Rhodes grabs the chair next to Gorman's and sits.

"What the hell happened, Frank?" Rhodes asks.

"Al, I don't know what to tell you. My team, along with ProFor and SP investigation personnel, are still looking into it. The team that infiltrated the vault knew exactly what the security procedures were and had all the necessary credentials and orders to allow them entry. There's no excuse for this, but what could they possibly want with a device. It's not any good to them, not without Clio," the colonel finishes, realizing he has made a fist while talking.

Colonel Rhodes notices it, too.

"Relax, Frank. We can't do anything right now except investigate and keep on looking for the infiltrators. I take it there is still no word on where they may have gone?" Rhodes asks.

"No, Al. They didn't have much of a head start before the SP OIC (Officer in Charge) figured out what was happening, but they had enough time that they could have gone anywhere. Apaches, Blackhawk, drones, everything we have was sent out searching for them. Not a Humvee in sight. They probably changed vehicles and hid the Humvee, something like that. We would have found them otherwise. Damn! What nerve!" Colonel Gorman exclaims.

Colonel Rhodes goes to his cabinet and reaches for a cup of coffee, then changes his mind and pours the two men a couple of fingers of something stronger. Rhodes hands one to Gorman. "Here, take the edge off."

Gorman takes the glass and raises it in salute and takes a good sip.

Colonel Rhodes moves to his desk, sipping his drink, leans on the desk watching Gorman.

"You might not think that whoever took the device can't use it, but they took it for some reason," Gorman says.

Rhodes looks down in thought. "You said they told Captain Spencer they were a joint Bank and MILES team?"

"Yeah, they claimed the Bank asked MILES to check on the Inabular Device because you were worried someone might steal it, or sabotage it, something to that effect. The team had everything to indicate it was true. They had to have some backing from a government agency to get documentation as well as vehicles, weapons, and equipment to pull this off."

Black drums his fingers, then taps the desk. "Let me get Major Down, our Clio Project overseer, in here."

Gorman looks at Rhodes in surprise. "Overseer? I thought Clio was shut down permanently. I mean, after she was rebuilt, I was under the impression she wasn't to be used, even to attempt retrieving those lost men."

"Well, technically it is, and on paper it is," Rhodes replies, "but we keep checks on it, maintenance, updating little things here and there, you know, just in case we get the go-ahead on retrieval."

Gorman shakes his head then nods. "Of course, you do. I would do the same thing. I will never understand the council's reluctance in bringing those men home. What are they afraid of?"

"I'm not sure. Maybe they worry about what the men may say or do. Maybe they're all dead, and they don't want that known. I don't know. I'm just waiting for the day we get someone with some balls in charge who can make the right decision."

"Doesn't the new Bank Council come in and inspect, and what about MILES?" he asks.

Colonel Rhodes waves him off. "Nope, the council used to check on us all the time, then seemed to stop worrying about it once they realized we weren't trying to be operational. And as for MILES, they can kiss my ass. Even POTUS won't allow them access here. That's why I'm surprised the infiltration team even mentioned a joint task force. Hell, everyone should know we won't cooperate with them."

Gorman smirks.

"Oh, one more thing," he says, "Captain Spencer said he called the Bank to verify that the team was legitimate. Went through the security procedures and said he spoke with you and that you verified the team was there because of a possible security breach and threat of the device being stolen."

Black looks up at Gorman. "Well, that's bullshit. I never spoke to Captain Spencer, much less verifying that a MILES team would be allowed access to the device. My God, we are dealing with something big here, and I want to know who they are!" he exclaims.

Gorman stands and places his empty tumbler on the cabinet. He turns back towards Black. "Well, if you don't need anything else from me, I'll be heading back to the office. I hope we can get to the bottom of this. Whoever took the device is up to no good. I can't imagine it going on the black market, but one can never tell these days. It could be as simple as that, but this smells of something else to me."

Rhodes looks Gorman in the eye. "I agree. I got a feeling we are in for some major shit. I mean, space-time continuum, paradox, and butterfly effect shit unless we can put a stop to it."

A knock on the door interrupts the men, and Major Downs enters the room. "You wanted to see me, sir?" Downs asks, walking into the room and coming to attention, then saluting.

Standing and returning the salute, Rhodes again leans against his desk. "We've got a situation here," he begins, then turns to look at the other colonel. "Frank, can you fill him in?" Rhodes asks, and Gorman tells the major the situation up to date.

The major whistles. "Sir, I don't know what to say. But I can tell you one thing, it won't do whoever took it any good."

"Why do you say that, Major?" Rhodes asks.

"Well, sir, only Chief Black can use it. Someone may have built something, but unless Black is there to use it, I can guarantee you they won't be able to make it work. The chief has to be the one operating the device, or it won't work. Not as far as I know unless someone has figured out a way to bypass his security systems."

Rhodes and Gorman exchange looks. "You positive about that, Major?" Rhodes asks.

"Yes, sir. I know the chief, and I know he put so many failsafe's into the device that it has to be him or nobody."

"Okay, Major, thank you for coming, and for the information. You can go," Rhodes tells him.

"Yes, sir," Downs replies and turns to leave.

"And, Major?" Rhodes stops him.

"Sir?"

"This information stays in this room."

"Without a doubt, sir," Down answers and leaves.

Once gone, Rhodes stands. "Well, that's partially good news, but we're not out of the rain just yet. Someone took it for a reason, and we need to find out, get it back, and hang someone's ass out to dry."

"I agree," Gorman says and stands. "I've got to get back. You need anything from me before I go?"

"No, Frank, we're good. Just get me a report as soon as you can and keep me posted on the investigation from your end. I'll be starting one here, and we'll get to the bottom of this ASAP.

"Sounds good. I'll keep in touch," Gorman says and leaves the office.

CHAPTER 17

The jet arrives at McCarren International Airport in Las Vegas and taxis to a private hanger. Once the jet stops, the engines wind down as the hanger doors begin closing. Before the sound of the engines has completely faded in the echo of the building, the plane's ramp comes down, with Senator Hellberg and Aeson Minten standing in the hatchway.

Personnel chalk the tires and refuel the tanks. The ramp completes its extension, and the two passengers disembark. Director Novell stands not too far away, waiting for them.

"Senator, good to see you again," he says, sticking out his hand. "As well as you, Colonel." Referring to Aeson's former rank, which he still uses occasionally.

"Enough with the pleasantries, Novell. Is it ready?" Hellberg asks in her form of a greeting.

"Yes, ma'am. Everything is set, and the team is standing by, waiting to see you."

"Good, then let's get this show on the road."

Novell turns and points to a Chevrolet Suburban, and they walk towards it. Beside the Suburban is a limousine with the motor running. The hanger doors begin to open, and when wide enough, the limousine drives out and heads towards the Las Vegas Strip.

Novell opens the back door of the Suburban, and Hellberg and Minten enter the vehicle. The interior of the vehicle is luxurious, complete with a bar, television, and computer. The windows are tinted, and the vehicle is painted white and is very non-descript. The only feature that makes it different is on the outside. Located on both front doors, is the logo for Clark County Utilities and a yellow emergency light bar on the roof.

The passengers sit and wait patiently for a few minutes, letting the limousine get ahead of them, hopefully leading anyone watching away from the hanger. Hellberg knows the Pentagon is keeping an eye on her and her activities, as well as others. They suspect she is up to something but have not been able to find out what.

Hellberg pours herself a Vodka and adds ice. Aeson reaches for the Bourbon and studies the brand name. Not his usual, but still good stuff. He helps himself to a couple of fingers, straight, and sits back.

After a ten-minute wait, the Suburban exits the hanger and heads towards highway 93, which is the first leg of their journey.

After a few hours of driving, they arrive at a deserted mining town. The town is not really deserted, and it's not a real town. Just the façade of the town that is the gateway to the underground labyrinth known as Olympus. The vehicle pulls up to what looks like an old livery stable, and the doors open, allowing enough room for the vehicle to enter. Once inside, the doors close and everything looks normal. The vehicle stops, everyone exits and walks toward the side of the building where an elevator waits for them. They enter, and the doors close.

"Level Janus," Novell instructs the automated elevator. The female voice repeats the request, and with just the faintest of movement, the elevator descends.

Novell clears his throat. "I thought you should know, the Bank has been sending up more drones around the area. I'm sure they're still searching for the team that took the device, but we should have nothing to worry about. They have flown over Olympus a couple of times, but our camouflage seems to be doing its job. We've been monitoring their radio traffic, and nothing stands out that would cause any alarm."

Hellberg looks straight ahead at the elevator door and doesn't say a thing. Minten looks over at Novell.

"Just make sure it stays that way. Any changes, we want to know immediately. This is about to go live, and we can't afford any interference. Make sure security is on alert, and be ready for anything."

"Yes, already in place."

"Good."

Just as Minten finishes, the elevator door opens onto the level where Janus is housed. The three people walk out and down a corridor that leads to a waiting room. Novell rushes forward and opens the door for Hellberg.

Hellberg looks straight ahead and asks, "How soon until we can launch?"

Novell, keeping stride, says, "It's ready now. You just give the word, and we can begin the startup sequence. It will take a little time to get Janus' power up and, of course, system checks once it is running. If everything is given the green light, it's a go."

"Good," Hellberg says, this time looking at Novell. "I'll let you know when I'm ready. I want a meeting with the scientific team, as well as the technicians who will be working the equipment. I want to see them, get a feel for them. See if I can trust them."

"Senator, I can assure you…" Novell begins but is silenced by Hellberg stopping mid-stride and staring daggers at him. He walks two more step, stops, and see the expression on the senator's face.

"I don't give two cents about your assurances, Director Novell. As good as you say these people are, I want to see them for myself, ask some questions, look them in the eye, then when I'm satisfied they're qualified, we will continue. Is that clear?"

Novell is used to the senator, so this doesn't faze him. He also knows about the rumor of her being able to look at someone and in just a few seconds know what type of person they are and knows if she can trust them as well as manipulate them.

"Yes, ma'am. Just say the word, and I'll have everyone assembled in the conference room."

"That will be all, Novell, thank you," she excuses him, and Novell continues along the corridor.

Hellberg turns to her brother, who is grinning.

"What's that for?" she asks.

"Nothing, dear sister, just like watching you work is all. Shall we go?" he says and walks away towards their office.

CHAPTER 18

Hellberg sits on a sofa that overlooks the Janus room. She watches as the technicians and scientists scurry about checking and rechecking systems. She is glad to see everyone so busy. It fills her with more confidence. She knows they all want this to work. Some of these people were considered quacks in their career fields by academia.

She had searched every major college around the world looking for just the right people. Those who believed in time travel, molecular transportation, nanotechnology, anyone and everyone who had an idea that others thought crazy, she found inspiring. Once she stumbled upon those who had parts of schematics of the original time machine known as Clio, she didn't waste any time gathering a group of scientific misfits to create the Janus Initiative, her version of the Clio Project.

The one thing she still worries about is being able to transport someone not only when, but where. She assumed that Chief Black had more likely than not figured it out, which he had, but her team didn't have a clue how to make it happen. Not until one of the so-called quacks from M.I.T. and another from Bombay, India, figured out how to compensate for the Heisenberg principle.

They were able to match matter transposition with the time machine, thus allowing a traveler to go from one place to another, as well as from one time to another. They haven't figured out how to make a transporter itself, but what they do have working helps immensely for this project. A transporter can wait.

She turns and looks at Aeson, who stands and watching the same thing. He, too, is filled with confidence and is anxious to get going. But, as a military man, he knows the importance of checking your equipment and knowing the plans by heart before each mission. This is no different. He feels her stare and smiles.

"Nervous?" he asks.

"Not a bit. You?"

"Just another mission," he says with a half-hearted shrug.

"Huh-huh," she replies with raised eyebrows.

Standing, she walks over to the desk and picks up the telephone, then presses the button for Director Novell's office. It is immediately answered.

"Yes, ma'am," Novell says.

"Have everyone meet us in the conference room," she tells him and hangs up before he can reply.

"You ready?" she asks Aeson.

"You bet. After you," he says, opening the door for her.

"Chauvinist," she says to him as she passes and walks out the door.

"It's pronounced *chivalrous*," he replies, walking out behind her and closing the door.

They take their time going to the conference room, allowing personnel time to be there when they arrive. The lead technicians and the scientist are crowded into the large conference room, and the talking comes to a halt when Hellberg and Minten enter.

"Good day to you all," Hellberg says with a practiced smile as she enters the room. "Thank you for coming," she continues as she takes a seat at the head of the long conference table. The senior techs and the scientist have already been seated at the table and stand when she and Aeson enter.

"Please, gentlemen, ladies, sit," she tells them. "I asked you here so I can get a feel of how well each of you and your teams feel about Janus and its ability to do the job correctly," she says, looking around the room at each person. Hellberg is pleased so far, as everyone she looks at returns the look. *Confidence,* she thinks.

"Are there any concerns, problems, anything we should be worried about? Does everyone have what they need to get the job done?" she asks, again looking everyone in the eye. Her look passes one of the lead scientists near the end of the table, and she thinks she sees doubt. She goes back to the man and stares at him. He must know she was looking at him as everyone else's attention turns to him.

Novell gives him an angry look, and the scientist hesitates, then says, "Yes, ma'am, I do have a concern."

Hellberg looks at Novell, who squirms in his seat, beads of perspiration forming on his high forehead. She returns her attention back to the scientist.

"Doctor Petrov, is it not?" she asks kindly, glad she took the time remembering all their names. Her life would soon be in their hands, so it's good to know who's who.

"Yes, Doctor Grigori Petrov. Quantum Physics department. My team is responsible for the Inabular Device. Ensuring it is compatible with Janus."

"And you have a concern about it?" she asks, leaning forward arms on the table.

Novell leans over the table to be seen. "Senator, the good doctor brought this to my attention, and I don't..."

"I wasn't talking to you, Director. I'm talking to the man who knows what the hell is going on. Are you familiar with quantum mechanics or the uncertainty principle, anything dealing with time and motion? No. You aren't. I'm no expert in these areas, either, so I will listen to what the scientists have to say, and I would appreciate you letting them talk without interruption because it's mine and my brother's ass that will be on the line," she sternly warns, giving him a hard look, then turns back to Doctor Petrov with a smile. "Please, Doctor, continue."

Petrov looks at Novell, then seems to gain confidence after Novell's berating. "Yes, as I was saying, we haven't had much time to test the compatibility of the Inabular Device with Janus. When we received the schematics and blueprints from the other scientist who worked on the Clio Project, we didn't have all of them. We only received a small portion of the blueprints needed to build your time machine. We had to bring in other experts to assist in building it from scratch. We have tested the machine, and we know you are anxious to get moving on this, but I'm still concerned about using it right now. We don't know how the Inabular Device works, only that it does," Petrov finishes and leans his forearms on the table. "Of course, the final decision is yours to make."

Hellberg looks at Doctor Petrov for a few seconds. "Do you think it will work, though?" she asks with a warning smile.

Petrov hesitates, then says, "Yes, I do believe it will work, but it still bothers me. The creator installed very sophisticated failsafe's. Without further testing…" he fades off under the senator's stare.

"I'll take your warning under advisement, good doctor. With that said, is there anything else?' Hellberg asks it in a tone indicating there will be nothing else. "Good. I just wanted to see all of you and thank you for all your hard work and dedication to this project. Now, please, everyone can go back to your stations and start preparing for a historical event," she finishes and stands, indicating the meeting is over.

The technicians and scientists file out of the conference room, leaving Hellberg, her brother, and Novell behind. Hellberg turns to Novell, "That will be all director," she says to Novell, who nods and leaves the room. Hellberg looks at her brother. "You look concerned, Aeson. What is it?" she asks him.

"This is a big step we're taking. Shouldn't we wait until we're absolutely certain everything will go as planned? I wasn't trained to jump into something blindly. We train and plan each mission and rehearse it before going in," he tells his sister.

"Aeson, listen. I trust these people, and I know they have concerns, but that's their jobs. I haven't met a scientist who isn't worried about something. This is all new to them, so they're going to fret over every little detail. They would want to run simulations and tests for years if we let them. Sometimes, you just got to go for it. If I sat around and waited for everybody else to make my decisions for me, I wouldn't be a US Senator, now would I?" she says, walking over to her brother and placing her hand on his arm. "It's all good. I'm going. You can stay if you want, but I would rather you come with me."

Aeson looks down at her, and a slight smile grows across his face, and he slowly shakes his head. "I'm not letting you have all the fun. If you say we go, we go."

"Fine, that's what I like to hear. Shall we go change and ensure Janus is ready?" Hellberg says, and they leave the room.

CHAPTER 19

Colonel Gorman is on the phone with Colonel Rhodes not five minutes after he's told the news. One of the new drones they are using caught a picture of a person physically disappearing near an abandoned mining town north of Area 51.

"What do you mean *disappearing*?" Rhodes asks.

"Strangest thing. A satellite was just coming into range in an area the Pentagon has been keeping an eye on, and it snapped a picture of a person riding an ATV. It snapped several pictures in a row, and in one of the pictures it shows only half of the person and ATV, then the next picture there is nothing. First, we thought it was a glitch with the satellite or an optical illusion, but experts have studied it, and they agree, the person on the ATV just vanished."

"You mean like an *Invisible Man* vanish?" Rhodes asks.

"No, No, nothing so outlandish," Gorman says.

"Outlandish. This coming from a man who works at Area 51 and talks with a man who oversees a time machine program," Rhodes tells him, chuckling softly.

"Not what I meant. We think that he went under some type of canopy. Something covering the desert to throw us off. The pictures were enlarged and enhanced. If you look closely, you can see a straight shadow and what looks like an outline of some sort. That's what we believe is an edge to some type of cover."

He explains that a joint team of Special Operators and Special Forces are being formed up as they speak. The team is to be flown in and dropped off several kilometers from the area where they will hike the rest of the way in to see what is going in on the supposedly deserted town.

"Sounds good," Rhodes answers. "Well, good luck, and keep me posted."

"You know it," Gorman replies and disconnects the call.

~ ~ ~

The Blackhawk flies low over the desert floor, under the radar, if there happens to be any. The pilot and co-pilot's faces light up a bright green under their helmets' visors. The glow is from the night vision equipment they are using to operate the multimillion-dollar aircraft.

"One minute out," the pilot announces to the leader of the joint task force.

The Green Beret captain gets the others' attention and signals one minute by holding up his index finger. The rest of the team becomes more active and double-checks their equipment and weapons. The helicopter slows, flares, and drops to hover just a foot off the ground. The captain jumps down, and the team members follow behind him.

Every man flips down their NODs, night observation devices, which turn the desert into an eerie green landscape. The captain drops down to one knee, and the team follows suit, each man facing outwards covering a 360-degree area. The Blackhawk rises a few feet, turns, and heads back towards the base. Once the sand has settled, the captain stands and runs in the direction of the ghost town.

It takes the team about thirty minutes to reach their objective. The captain raises a fist indicating the team should stop. He drops down and crawls up to the crest of a small berm that looks down onto where a deserted town should be. He lifts his NOD and brings a pair of night vision binoculars to his eyes to scan the surrounding area. Not seeing any movement, he waves the team to rally around him.

"I don't see the town," he whispers, then points to two men. "Barnes, Wells," he whispers to the two USAF Special Operations Reconnaissance team members, "you're up. I want to know if there are any underground listening devices, pressure plates, laser trips, whatever you can find. Go," he says, and the two men crawl over the berm and down towards the missing town.

It takes them a few minutes to get to the area and conduct the sweeps, which prove vital.

"Wolf, this is Hawk, over," the leader of the two-man team calls over his headset.

"Hawk, Wolf, go with traffic," the captain answers.

"Contact and squashed."

"Copy that, stand one," the captain tells them and turns towards the rest of the team. "Alright, we go down low and slow. Set up overwatch and let the electro boys do their job." He pushes the talk button. "Hawk, Wolf."

"Go, Wolf."

"On our way down," he says and hears a double click indicating they heard him, and he begins crawling down the slope. Once the entire team is in position, the captain saddles up next to the two airmen.

"Only motion detection sensors here and here," the NCO says, showing the captain where they are located on his small computer screen. "We need to move slowly and scan for any other devices they might have set up. This is definitely our objective. No reason for this type of equipment being used for anything but security. Of course, it could be a meth lab operation," he says with a grin.

The captain grins, white teeth showing. "Yeah, you know them meth-heads, security savvy,"

The two-man team moves ahead and conducts sweeps. Getting closer to the objective, they notice something peculiar and call for the captain. In a few seconds, the captain slides up beside the USAF men.

"What's up?"

"Check this out. It's no wonder we didn't have reconnaissance photos." He shows him the computer screen."

The screen shows what looks like a bridge or archway. It's huge and covers the entire town.

"I'll bet you drinks at the club that is one giant camouflaged canopy stretching across the entire town. A life-sized painting of the town on top so when a drone or satellite flies over they get a picture of a ghost town, while underneath, people can work with no worries of being spotted. Heard of something like this, but first time seeing it."

The captain calls his team forward, and they move toward where the town should be located. It doesn't take them long to come upon a section of canopy that stretches as far as they can see. It's painted to look like the desert and blends in superbly. As they cautiously get closer, they can see openings at different intervals to allow access underneath the canopy.

Team members leapfrog towards the opening, some running while the others provide security, then they alternate. Stacking up alongside the canopy openings, they peer in. The two Air Force NCOs scan the area with their equipment and give the captain the all-clear signal. The team enters and trot to the closet building.

They are vigilant the entire way. Too many variables, too many places for a person to hide, lots of ambush sites. They hope whoever oversees security for this place is so overconfident in their electronic detection systems and camouflage that they have grown complacent. They must be because they haven't seen a sentry yet. So far, so good.

The team stacks up along a building that looks like it was once a hotel. The captain points to the lieutenant and three of the sergeants, and with a hand signal, informs them they are to move to the rear and check for possible entry. The rest of the team takes up overwatch positions covering the front, rear, sides, and upper floors of the other buildings, to include the one they are against.

A few seconds go by, and the captain hears a double *click* in his earpiece and knows the lieutenant has found a way into the building. They all move around the rear, and the Air Force sergeants check the building for more electronic alarms. They find one and disarm it.

Once it's disabled, the entire team enters the abandoned hotel. A four-man fire team goes up the stairs to ensure the second floor is clear, then return to join the others.

The captain pulls his binoculars out, and standing back from the window, he scans the street and the other buildings. He takes his time, and as his view passes what looks like an old livery stable, he stops. Zooming, he adjusts the focus until he thinks he spots something noteworthy.

"Phil?" he calls for the lieutenant. "Take a look." The lieutenant moves up beside him. "Tell me what you see. Scan the livery stable." He hands the binocs to the other officer.

The man takes the glasses and scans the area for a few seconds. "I see it," he announces to the captain. "Someone's using that building. Tried to cover any tracks and did too good of a job. Too perfect. The doors are too straight, and the ground has been swept. Very subtle, but it's there," he says.

"Yup, what I was thinking," the captain replies, then goes back to the team where he tells the RTO (Radio, Telephone Operator) to set up

COMSEC (Communication Security) line with home base. Once communication is established, the captain informs Area 51 and the Bank of the situation.

"Any idea what is inside?" Gorman asks.

"No, sir. In the process of scanning the interior now, but we won't actually know until we get inside. We are sure to run into some problems, as well as resistance. We will try to find out what is going on and be back in contact when we do," the captain explains.

"Captain?" Rhodes asks.

"Sir."

"We don't know what they are up to, but when they took the device you are looking for, it is not for the good of America or the world. Since this isn't a sanctioned experiment, and the fact that MILES personnel are involved, we can only assume it is being run by a rogue government agency. We can't have that, and we can't have the device in any other hands. Get it back no matter what you have to do. We can only assume they have a time machine of some type. That's the only reason for stealing the device that we know of. It won't do them any good, but we can't have it just floating around out there. Get it back, or destroy it if you must, but get it done. Got it."

"Loud and clear."

"Good luck. Come back in one piece and with the device or evidence of its destruction."

"Yes, sir. Wolf out," the captain says, ending the transmission. He turns towards the team. "The man says it time to go play." He looks at the two Air Force sergeants, who are just finishing setting up their surveillance equipment. It only takes them a few minutes to get what information the captain needs.

"Sir, there are four heat signatures moving around inside. The walls are covered in a heat-reducing signature material, an attempt to block any heat source from being detected. This is no drug manufacturing building, this is high tech stuff being used. Only military, CIA, NSA would have access to this type of equipment."

"MILES?" the captain asks.

"Possible, I guess. They do have military personnel working for them," the USAF NCO explains. "There is also a vehicle inside. This building contains an elevator against the back wall, probably built into the mountain that the rear of the building butts against. I can't tell where it goes. Scanners won't go that far from here. We would need to get inside. Sorry."

The captain shakes his head. "Don't be, good work. Besides, once we're in, we'll figure out where it goes," he tells them and looks again through the binocs. "Cameras?" he asks no one in particular.

"There are two in front of the building. Look up and to your left, in the corner of the eave. The other is directly opposite," one of the SpecOps sergeants says, pointing.

The captain scans and finally spots the tiny devices. "Got 'em. You boys got something for that?" he asks, turning to look at them. Both men smirk. "I say something funny?"

"No, sir. We just thought that was a rhetorical question." And they again rummage through their packs and come up with two small black contraptions that look like rifle scopes. Each man unfolds a tripod, and they each move to a separate side of the windows and place the scopes onto the tripods. They squat and stare through the scopes for a few seconds, then look at each other.

"Ready?" one NCO asks.

"Good to go," the other NCO answers, and they both flip a switch on the scope. The two NCOs go back to their packs and load up the equipment.

The other team members and the captain just watch the airmen until the captain can't stand it.

"Okay, what did you guys just do?"

Still packing, one NCO answers, "We sent a frequency that scrambles the camera equipment. They'll think it just a simple camera malfunction. We will be able to approach and enter without anyone seeing us. Not until we get inside the building, then there could be other cameras."

The captain grins. "Hooah, Air Force," he says and receives an, "Aim high Army," reply from one of the Air Force sergeants. The captain smirks, then returns to the group. "Alright, let's go," he says, leading the way out the back door.

The captain takes point, and the others fall into the procession line and rush across the dusty street, then splitting off with different teams setting up on both sides of the livery stable doors. One SpecOps NCO watches a computer screen, which shows the four personnel inside. He directs the screen to the rest of the team and the captain points to himself and three others and informs them of who they will take out when entering.

The four-man team checks their weapons as they line up for entry. The captain moves in front of the door and tries to open it, smiling to himself when he sees it's unlocked. Nodding three times, he pulls the door open, and the four men rush in.

The four guards are startled as the group of men, yelling and screaming orders, barge into the building. The inside of the building is nothing like what is seen from outside. The dilapidated looking livery stable is actually a well-maintained garage with an elevator located in the back. A Suburban is on a rotating rack that turns the car 180 degrees so it faces the door for easy egress.

The Special Forces team doesn't have time to take in what the building looks like as their attention is on the four guards inside. Two of the guards immediately drop their weapons as they see weapons pointed at them and raise their hands. The third makes the mistake of raising his rifle towards the military group, and his life is ended with a small *pfooft* sound from the sound suppressed weapon, followed by the *thwack* the round makes striking the guard in the face.

The fourth guard stands behind the vehicle and makes a dash for the rear of the building. There is an alarm button located against the wall, and he almost makes it to the panel before a 9mm Parabellum round strikes him in the back of the skull, dropping him like a wet sack of cement onto the ground, where a pool of red forms from the spurts of blood coming out of his head.

Team members are quick to grab the two remaining guards and duct tape their mouths and Zip-Tie their hands behind their backs, then search them for weapons. They march one of them over to the elevator, while the other is given an injection that puts him to sleep in an instant. Seeing this, the other guard starts to struggle.

"Calm down, Crusty. It's only a sedative. We're not here to kill people, well not unless they do stupid things like try to kill us or make our presence known," he tells the man, then grabs the guard and drags him to the elevator. He removes the identification badge, swipes it, then pushes the guard's face against the scanner. The light turns red above the door, as a *ding* sounds, then the door opens. The guard's usefulness is over, so one the team comes over with a syringe.

"Time for nighty-night." He injects the guard, who passes out within a couple of seconds and is left propped against the wall next to his partner. The bodies of the two other guards are collected and dragged over and also propped against the wall.

While the special forces team handles the guards and elevator, the SpecOps NCOs work their magic and disable the alarm, cameras, and they sweep the inside of the building for any other gadgets that could disrupt their mission. Once all is declared clear, the entire team makes their way to the elevator. Time to enter the devil's lair.

CHAPTER 20

Senator Helen Hellberg and her brother, Aeson Minten are each in their quarters changing clothes. They each dress in clothing befitting the era they intend to travel to, thus fitting in. The plan is to go back and intercept their father and warn him of the mistakes he will make concerning the Clio Project. If it goes as planned, they will arrive in a time before everything was set into motion that led him to make the wrong decisions, mostly relying on inept personnel, ultimately leading to his embarrassing banishment from the Senate and his eventual death.

After changing, they meet in the hallway outside their quarters, where Novell and a couple of MILES SF members wait to escort them down to the Janus room.

"Well, Novell, come here to get in the last of the ass-kissing before we're off?" Aeson asks with a sneer and a snort.

Novell gives him a hard stare that turns into a smile. "You know, Mr. Minten, unlike one of my predecessors who worked for your father, I am competent. Something your sister did right, unlike the choosing of my predecessor," he finishes, the corner of his mouth turn up into a smile.

It takes Aeson a second or two to realize Novell just insulted his father. Aeson moves towards Novell, his hands turning into fists. Before he can do anything, his sister steps in between them and places a hand on her brother's chest.

"Not now, Aeson. I still need this man. He is right in that he is competent, and I did pick him to run MILES. Now, calm down, and let's just concentrate on the mission. I'll handle this. Now, go on down to see how things are coming along with Janus. Okay?" she says softly to him looking into his eyes, which are still glued to Novell. She turns and looks at the guards, "Please, escort Colonel Minten to the disembarkation room."

The guards nod and approach warily. She turns her attention back to Aeson and pats his chest, then reaches for his face, gently touching it. "Aeson, time for that later. Think. We have got a job to do," and she gently pats his face.

Minten looks down at his sister and smiles, then looks back at Novell and gives him a different smile, one that doesn't seem to faze Novell in the least. Novell might be a sycophant, but he is good at his job and did not get where he was backing down from anyone. He cocks his head almost imperceptibly and stares back at Minten. Minten sees it and knows it's a challenge, so he nods his understanding. They both know this isn't over. Well, at least one of them knows it isn't.

Minten looks back down at his sister again, smiles, and walks away. When he turns the corner, Hellberg rounds on Novell.

"Just what the fuck was that?" she demands in a strong voice but one not so loud as to carry down the corridor. Her face reddens as she moves into Novell's personal space. "Huh? You know we've got a mission using an untested time machine, and here you are trying to rile up my brother. Good God, man, he could have killed you, and then what would we be doing. The mission could have been scrubbed, and even if he didn't kill you, Aeson would be so upset I couldn't use him. God damn you, Novell. I ought to fire you right now, but you're needed. You are a good leader and get things done. Now, try to cool it with my brother. Better yet, stay away from him, and if you do see him, keep your goddamn remarks to yourself. Got it?"

Novell keeps a straight face and nods. "Yes, ma'am. Got it."

She doesn't believe him but doesn't have time to get further into it.

"We'll finish this conversation when I return." She stalks down the hallway to the elevators with a grinning Novell at her heels.

Hellberg takes the elevator down to the level housing the Janus time machine. She exits the elevator, with Novell right behind her, and walks down the hall to the overwatch room. This room is above the level where all the computers and technicians work. Looking further into the room, she sees Janus. It is a large, cylinder shape, with opaque glass covering it from top to bottom. The glass is in sections, with bands of metal separating each, like tiers, or levels. Janus stands about thirty-five feet high and has the tubes running into it to act as a coolant.

Her brother is already in the room and staring at Janus transfixed. He doesn't even notice when his sister walks in until she places a hand on his arm. He turns and smiles, a genuine smile.

"Never ceases to amaze me," he tells her.

"Me neither," she replies. "I can't believe we actually made it this far. And just think, in a short time, we will be only the second group of people sent back in time. Only it's planned, and we have a pre-prepared mission to accomplish. You ready?" she asks.

"It'll be great to see dad again. And to finally reset the course of history the way it should have been in the first place," he answers and looks at his watch, then looks back over his shoulder to see Novell standing near the door. Aeson smirks, and then looks back at his sister. "I guess we all need our pets."

Hellberg slaps him on the arm. "Forget that. Let's head on down. It's time," she tells Aeson and turns to leave with him in tow.

As they walk through the door, Aeson bumps into Novell sharply and walks down the hall. Novell just shakes his head and follows.

The small group makes their way to where Doctor Petrov runs around checking readings and talking with technicians. He sees Hellberg, smiles broadly, and runs over to her.

"Ah, Senator, you're right on time. We are ready for you," he says, his body shaking with excitement.

"Hellberg smiles. "Doctor Petrov, please, call me Helen."

"Ah, yes, good. Helen. As I say, we are ready for you, and you, too, Mr. Minten," he tells them. "Come with me, please." He walks away without even looking to see if he is being followed. He takes them to a door that, when opened, leads into a large room covered in a type of material that resembles a recording studio room. The doctor notices Aeson running his hand along the wall. "That's to reduce the amount of static electricity when the time transference happens. It also reduces any noise."

Aeson stops and looks at the doctor with a grin on his face. "Static, huh? Hope that's all."

The doctor waves his hand in a dismissive manner. "No, nothing to worry about, all part of the process. You don't even see it; you'll already be gone. This is just a byproduct of the time displacement, like a sonic boom where there was something there, then it's gone, and a void must be filled. Nothing for you to concern yourself about. All quite natural."

"Well, let hope so, Doc." Aeson snorts.

The doctor turns towards Hellberg, the previous conversation already gone from his mind. "Whenever you are ready, let me know. Remember, there will be some motion sickness when you arrive. The pills we gave you should help, but since no one has done this since that debacle seventeen years ago, we just don't know. Please, try and remember what you see and feel immediately after you arrive. It will help us in future endeavors."

Hellberg takes a deep breath and looks at Aeson, who seems at home in the room like he's patiently waiting his turn on the next amusement ride. She shakes her head. *How can he do that?* she thinks, then turns back towards the doctor.

"We're in your hands, Doctor Petrov. Let's get the show on the road, as they say."

The doctor smiles, and using both his hands, shakes her hand, then walks over and shakes Aeson's hand.

"Good luck," he says and exits the room. Helen and Aeson stand, facing each other. When the door slams shut, she jumps a little, and Aeson chuckles.

"Come on, Sis. You've been through raging typhoons on a ship, scuba diving with sharks, this is just another adventure," he tells her.

"Sure, but this is something a lot scarier. If this screws up, we could end up in a wall or get eaten by a dinosaur."

This causes Aeson to laugh, especially with the look on Helen's face. She slaps him hard on the arm, and he laughs even harder, feigning like he is hurt. Watching him, she laughs. Before they can say anything else, the doctor's heavily-accented voice sounds in the room.

"Senator, Mr. Minten, we are ready to proceed. As a precaution, I would suggest maybe squatting, or even better, sitting on the ground. We wouldn't want you to rematerialize with the possibility of being extremely dizzy and fainting or losing your balance and falling, now would we?"

"Thank you, Doctor, good advice," she says, looking at the ceiling, then sits on the floor. Minten hunkers down in a manner that almost looks like a track runner's starting position. Both breathe a little faster as the room seems to move.

~ ~ ~

Doctor Petrov leaves the room, where the senator and Minten prepare for their send-off. He walks over to the phone when he sees Novell peering into the room. He picks up the receiver and watches Novell look around for the other phone. Novell picks it up.

"Is everything ready, Doctor?" he asks as soon as he answers it.

"Yes, sir. We are ready to proceed," Petrov answers.

"Then let's get on with it," he says and disconnects the call.

Petrov places the handset back in the cradle and nods to one of the technicians. The tech picks up a box and walks over to Petrov. He opens it, then hands it to the scientist. Petrov looks in the box, reaches in, and removes the Inabular Device. He takes one final look at Novell, smiles, raises the Inabular Device so Novell can see it, and then walks over to Janus's main panel.

The doctor places the Inabular Device into an open slot. He calls out to each technician, asking their status. Once he is satisfied everyone is ready, he flips the switch that initiates the countdown for sixty seconds.

"*What is that strange noise?*" he asks himself, hearing something as he watches the countdown clock. "*Is that someone yelling?*" He turns and looks around the room, searching for the noise. "*Janus isn't making that noise. It's coming from outside the room.*"

He notices that others in the room are also looking around. He looks up but doesn't see Novell any longer. He looks at the clock. Twenty-five seconds have expired. Janus is revving up and making its own sound, almost drowning out yelling, but not quite. The yelling is getting louder, and t getting closer.

Then, without warning, the doors leading into the control room bursts open, and several men rush into the room. The men, all dressed in military garb, carry what looks like weapons, pointing them at his technicians and scientists. They are screaming and shouting orders. He doesn't understand what is happening.

He sees a MILES guard come from around one of the panels where he watched the technician work, and he raises his hand with something in it. One of the military men turns towards the guard and raises a weapon. Petrov sees a flash from the weapon's muzzle but doesn't hear a gun report. The guard is flung backwards like being struck by an invisible fist. Petrov realizes the man was just shot, but why, and by who? Who are these men? What do they want?

Then Petrov sees that one of the men looks at him as another points. This terrifies Petrov because he knows he is about to be shot but, instead, the man runs at him. The other men spread out amongst the others in the room and hold weapons on them. They herd the technicians and scientists away from their stations and into a corner of the room.

Janus is still charging and is about to transfer the two people in the debarkation room to another time. Petrov looks again at the clock: fifteen seconds left. The man with the weapon pointing at him stops inches from Petrov's face. Petrov can smell the man's sweat and see the coldness in his eyes.

"Where's the Inabular Device?" the man yells.

Petrov's eyes are open wide. Beads of perspiration pop out on his forehead as he shakes his head. "W-what?" he stammers.

"Where is the Goddamn Inabular Device, Doctor?" the man screams and comes even closer.

Petrov is shaking but finally understands what the scary man wants and points to Janus's main console. The warrior sees the panel and the device and reaches for it. Petrov comes out of his daze when he sees what the man is about to do and lunges at him, screaming at the same time.

"Nooooo! You can't, that will disrupt the time transference sequence." He tries to grab at the man. A second man has moved in behind the doctor and holds him. Petrov looks around wildly. "You don't understand, Janus is active. It's going to transmit now," he screams, again trying to get to the man reaching for the Inabular Device. Petrov looks at the clock, 3…2…1, and there is a crescendo from Janus that shuts off instantly when the man yanks the Inabular Device from the console.

Janus shuts down so fast that the room goes into a deafening silence. That silence is short-lived as the military men yell for everyone to get out of the room. The terrified technicians and scientists do as they are told, Petrov included.

"What have you done? What have you done?" he asks the men while being pushed out the door and into the hallway, all the while looking over his shoulder trying to see the debarkation room. His questions go unanswered as he is ushered into a room across the hallway. Once everyone is safely inside, one of the men orders them down on the floor and yells at them to stay there.

Once down, the man shuts the door as he leaves, and the room is silent. Suddenly, explosions shake the room. There are quite a few, and the people in the room yelp from fright. Someone can be heard praying, and another sobbing. Only a few minutes have passed but it seems like hours before the door is opened and Novell enters. Petrov looks up, not comprehending what he is seeing until Novell spots Petrov.

"Doctor Petrov, come here. All of you, get up. Let's go," Novell yells.

Petrov stands, as do the others, and heads for the door. When he gets into the corridor, Novell grabs him by the arm.

"What the fuck happened in there?" he asks, his voice loud.

"I-I don't know," Petrov says, looking around as if for an answer, then his eyes widen. "Janus!" he shouts and breaks from Novell's grasp and runs into the control room. What he sees shocks him.

The entire room is destroyed. The control panels are sparking and burning, releasing an acidic odor into the room. Smoke makes it hard to see but it is already clearing as the overhead exhaust fans are running on full. Petrov picks his way around the debris strewn about the room and locates the main control panel, or what is left of it. The panel is torn open, the sides split apart like a metal banana peel, with the insides smoldering. Completely destroyed.

Petrov stares at the panel for a few seconds, then looks at the disembarkation room where Senator Hellberg and her brother were waiting to be transported back in time.

Oh, my God," he utters and stumbles his way towards the room, with Novell right behind him.

He reaches the door, which has been damaged by the explosions and attempts to open it. The door frame is warped so the door won't budge for him. He pulls and yanks and yells, but it won't open. Novell pushes him aside and tries his luck to no avail. He releases the handle and tells a couple of MILES guards to get something to open the door. Both guards run from the room, and Novell again tries to force the door open with brute strength.

Two minutes pass, and a MILES quick reaction team comes into the room carrying what looks like Jaws of Life equipment. Two of the men move past Novell and Petrov and place the contraption in a small gap and activate it. A groaning sound can be heard as the door is forced away from the frame, and after a few seconds, it pops free and swings open. The men step back, and Petrov and Novell rush into an empty room.

CHAPTER 21

When Colonel Black completes the story, both men have finished their drinks. Rees shakes his head and stands and stretches.

"That's was quite a tale, Colonel," he says and takes the empty glass from Black and walks into the kitchen area to make another drink.

"I do have a few questions first?" Rees says over his shoulder but is cut off by Black.

"What happened to Senator Hellberg and Aeson Minten?" the colonel says before Rees can ask. "Nobody knows. Nothing in the timeline seems to have been affected, so we assume they were killed. That or they may be in limbo, like you and your team were."

Rees looks down, thinking. "If they are in limbo, couldn't you find them? I mean, you found us," he asks after a few seconds, walking back into the living room and handing the drink to Black and setting down a bowl of pretzels.

"Difference is, we knew how to find you. Dad still had you located in the quantum realm or something like that. I was told they didn't know where to start looking for them. Once the team grabbed the Inabular Device, the time machine was blown to bits, so there was no tracing where they were sent, if they were sent at all."

"Christ, that's got to suck. No one should go out that way," Rees replies, walking back into the kitchen to retrieve his drink. Coming back, he sits on the couch.

"Could they have been sent further back, or even forward?" Rees asks.

Black shakes his head. "No one knows. No one has seen or heard from them, so we don't know."

"I assume you've tried? I mean, after you got Clio back up," Rees asks.

"Oh, of course, but the Janus machine was different from Clio. Basically the same process, but it was... I don't know, just built differently. It wasn't an exact duplicate of Clio. We tried using Clio, but as I said, Janus was different. Also, Janus was too severely damaged by the Special Forces team, and before we could take complete control of Olympus..."

"Olympus?" Rees asks.

"Yes, that's the name Senator Hellberg gave it, something to do with her and her brother's Greek names. Funny, though, from what I understand, her brother called it the Dragon Lair. I find that more fitting for what we believe they intended to use the time machine for. Anyway, before we could take control of the facility, most of the personnel had fled. We rounded up a few, but most of the lead scientists, to include Doctor Petrov, vanished into thin air. We assume they had altered passports and are all living abroad, incognito. It's taken years to rebuild Janus, and it was only used once, in an attempt to find Senator Hellberg and her brother. We didn't have any luck locating them with either time machines, so we basically mothballed Janus."

"So, Olympus is still there?" Rees asks.

"Yes, of course. We rebuilt the base, made some changes, updates. Janus is used mostly as a training device. But is also there in case we need a backup. You never know if Clio III goes down for whatever reason."

"Clio Three? That's what you call it?"

"Officially, yes, but we just call her Clio."

"Can we go see Janus?" Scott asks.

"Maybe later. You've a mission to go on first. When that's over, we'll see about taking you and your team out there to see it. Never know, some of your guys might want to be assigned there. But for now, let's just work on the Clio Project as it has finally been granted full operation and backing."

"You're right, of course. Just get excited thinking of all the advances that have been made since 1980. There is still so much for me to learn, for all of us to learn," Scott says. Then he changes the subject. "Going back to the story, what happened to the group known as MILES?"

"Oh, them? Disbanded, just like their forerunner MISS back in your time. These rogue units are getting out of hand. They still exist, some even going private, sort of like Black Water. Private contracting security companies hired by the governments to fill in where they don't want active duty military going. Since they're private, they get away with more. I don't agree with it, but it's the nature of the beast."

"I see. I was simply curious. Seems like these groups will always be around."

"You're probably right, Scott," Black says, "but you don't have to worry about that now. We don't use anything like that, and after MILES was disbanded, a bill was passed by the Senate that forbids any senator or congressman from forming their own police force, or intelligence organization, or private military. I think they learned their lesson after allowing it in the first place, especially after two senators were allowed to run amok using them."

"Sounds good to me, sir." Rees raises his glass.

The colonel takes a sip and sets the glass on the table, interlaces his fingers, and leans forwards, forearms resting on his knees. He looks at Rees. "You ready to go?"

Rees is caught off guard by the question.

"Ah, yes, sir, I am at that. Actually, I'm anxious to get going. If I hang around here much longer, I think I'll go stir crazy. Also, I want to get back into the action. For some reason, ever since I returned and finally got over the shock of what had happened to us, I've been itching to go back. Don't ask me why. The shrink can probably come up with some good psychobabble why I want to, but I don't know. I just… I'm ready. Plus, it's the right thing to do for Andy."

This time, Colonel Black lifts his drink, and the two men clink glasses.

Here's to past events, may they always be in our favor," the colonel toasts, and they drink.

Before they even set their glasses back down, the door chime sounds, and Rees asks the computer who it is. She announces that Chief Black is at the door.

"Well, let the man in," he tells the computer, and a second later the door opens. Chief Black looks at the door while shaking his head and walks in. He sees his son in the room and walks over to the two men, who have risen as he entered.

"Chief, how are you? You're late for the little story the colonel just told me. Quite a tale," Rees says, shaking the man's hand.

"I'm good. Hi, John."

"Dad."

"I hope I'm not intruding. Thought this might be a good time to have that talk," the chief says to Rees.

"Ah, yes, sure it is. Have a seat. Can I get you a drink?"

The chief sits in a chair across from the couch. "Yes, water please."

Rees goes into the kitchen, and Colonel Black makes to leave, "Since you two have something to talk about, I'll let you get to it."

The chief raises his hand to stop the colonel. "No, stay. This involves you as well. I just haven't had time to discuss it with you."

The colonel looks at his father quizzically and sits back down. Rees comes back into the room and hands the chief a glass of chilled water. Chief Black thanks Rees, then has a sip and sets the glass down.

"Okay, down to brass tacks, as they say."

CHAPTER 22

Captain Brunell is in the Bank's lab, watching over technicians operating DNA sequencing equipment. The lab was set up to check all Bank personnel ancestry backgrounds. This was not a case of security requirements but used to determine if anyone may have an ancestor who somehow is vital to the course of history. In cases where there is a match, it will be used to ensure that anyone involved in the Clio Project, anyone sent back in time, will not interfere with that person's life. Interference cannot be allowed, or a possible space-time continuum displacement could occur, and no one wants that.

Just as Captain Brunell walks past Lieutenant Perkins, she calls out to him, "Captain Brunell?"

Brunell stops and walks backwards to her work area.

"What, Perkins? What is it?" he asks.

"Sir, I was running my assigned DNA sequences, and this came up as a result," she tells him, pointing to a screen.

Brunell leans over and reads the screen, then stands back up.

"Are you sure that's correct?"

"Yes, sir. I ran it three times just to be sure," the lieutenant responds.

"Okay," Brunell says. "Print me a copy." He walks back to the area of the lab where the copier is located and waits for the printout. Once it slides out, he picks it up and studies the page for a few seconds while shaking his head. Brunell takes the page and walks into his office, shutting the door behind him. He grabs his phone and calls Colonel Michelle Thompson, Chief Medical Officer.

"Col0nel Thompson," she says when she answers the phone.

"Ma'am, Captain Brunell. I just wanted to see if you were in your office. I've got something here I think you need to see," he tells her.

"What is it?" she asks.

"I would rather show you if you don't mind."

"Sure, come on down," she tells him and disconnects. A few minutes later, he walks into her office and hands her the sheet of paper. She reads it and smiles, looking up at the captain. "Thanks for bringing this to my attention. I'll get it to him right now," she tells Brunell, who dutifully departs.

Colonel Thompson calls the office she wants to go to and finds who she wants to talk to. She then asks for a meeting, and after a few minutes is told she can come in anytime. Thompson goes to the elevator and gets off on the floor where she needs to go and walks into the receptionist's office to be greeted by Sam.

"Good afternoon, Colonel. How are you today?" Sam asks.

"Just fine, Sam. Yourself? And how's your pursuit of a certain young NCO going?"

Sam gives her a sideways glance. "How does everyone in the building seem to know my business, ma'am?" she says good-naturedly.

"You know, Sam, this is just like a small town, gossip everywhere," the colonel replies with a grin, then changes the subject. "Colonel Black is in I assume?"

"Yes, ma'am, go on in," Sam says, and the colonel knocks and enters. When she walks into the office, she sees that Chief Black sits in a chair across from Colonel Black's desk.

"Well, this makes it convenient for me," she says, walking over to the two men. Chief Black stands and shakes the colonel's hand, and she receives a nod from Colonel Black.

"This is a little unexpected, Colonel Thompson. A house call, I mean," Colonel Black says, and Thompson chuckles.

"Not at all, Colonel. I'm here to ask you some questions about your ancestry if I may be so bold. Both of yours, in fact. That is why I was glad to see the chief here as well," she tells the men.

"Sure, but what's this about?" Colonel Black asks.

"Well, the DNA lab was running their sequencers and came up with something, something we weren't expecting, but that's why we run the tests in the first place," she says.

"Okay, but again, what's this about?" Colonel Back asks again.

"Sir, how far back do either of you know your family history?" Thompson asks, looking at first one then the other man.

Colonel Black has a questioning look and turns towards his father. "Not too far back. Dad?" he asks.

Chief Black thinks back. "Well, not too far, I guess. I knew my great-grandfather, barely. Seen pictures of his father, but I've never really thought about it. I know our families moved around some, from up north, until settling in North Carolina. No, not really a lot. Why, what's wrong," he asks, squinting, his eyes boring into the doctor's. "We got some kind of exotic genetic disease or something?"

Thompson smiles. "No, nothing like that," she tells him, then walks over to the desk and places the paper in front of the colonel. "The lab discovered this. Just thought it quite the coincidence," she finishes and steps back.

Colonel Black picks up the paper and reads it for a minute, then looks up at the doctor, then back at the paper. He turns towards his father and hands the paper to him. Chief Black also reads it, then holds it down by his side while shaking his head. "Didn't see this coming," he says and turns to look at Thompson, "Are you sure?"

"The lab said they ran it three times to make sure, Chief."

Chief Black places the paper on the desk where the DNA comparison shows the one name in bold print: O'Toole.

~ ~ ~

Once Colonel Thompson leaves the office, Colonel Black picks the paper back up and glances at it again. "I had no idea, Dad."

"Neither did I," the chief says with a faraway look on his face. "You know what this means, don't you?" he asks his son.

"That I do," Colonel Black replies. "We stay the course and send him back," he says. "Another question is, do we tell him?"

Chief Black shakes his head. "No, definitely not. Not that I wouldn't mind telling him, but if he knows, he might do something that would cause some change in him. Make him do something different. No, I think we just send him back and let nature run its course."

"Yes, I agree. That makes sense. What about Rees and Farnsworth. Think we should let them know?" Colonel Black asks.

Chief Black again looks thoughtful, then stands and walks over to the window looking down into the Clio Project control room. He stands there for a minute, then turns back to face his son. "Rees, yes, Farnsworth, no," he finally says. "Sorry, but I don't know Farnsworth. Not that I don't trust him, but he's an outsider."

"Agreed. As much as I like the senator and appreciate his backing us on the project, I don't really care for him picking our team members," the colonel replies to his father. "I'll have Sam contact Sergeant Rees and ask him up. He'll get a kick out of this."

~ ~ ~

Rees bounds up the stairs leading to the colonel's office. He opens the door to Sam's office and smiles. Sam smiles back solicitously, and Rees gets flustered.

"Will you stop doing that?" he tells her.

"Doing what?" Sam asks in a sweet tone of voice, then laughs.

"That!" he says, pointing to her. "You know what. Damn, I don't have time for this. That's harassment you know?" he asks, pointing a finger while squinting at her, but not meaning it.

"Oh, I'm sorry, good sergeant, but who's the one who kissed whom?" she asks in a seemingly serious manner, which makes Rees pause. She grins. "I think *that's* called harassment."

Rees stands still, not sure what to do next, which is usual for him around Sam.

Sam shakes her head. "You are too easy, Scott. Now, get in there and see the colonel and chief. Shoo now, get," she says, flapping her hand in a dismissive wave, then returning to her work. Completely unnerved, Rees heads into the colonel's office.

Upon entering, he conducts the proper protocol, and the colonel tells him to sit, noticing the flush look on Rees' face.

"She at it again, Scott?" he asks, and Rees gets more flustered.

The chief looks at him. "My God, man, you alright, need a doctor?" he asks with a straight face, but with a knowing twinkle in his eyes.

"I'm fine, sir. Thanks for asking," Rees responds, face flushing.

The colonel is still chuckling. "I'm going to talk to her. I can't have my senior NCO all out of sorts, especially right before a mission."

"No!" Rees blurts with a quick shake of his head, then remembering who he talking to, "Sir! Please, don't. You know that'll just make it worse. Please, sir. I'll handle it. Like I said before, I have just got to catch up with the times. Just when I think I have her figured out, bam! She does a 180 on me and comes back with something else. I can't win for losing. Too bad she's still not in the Air Force, at least then I could pull rank."

The other two men laugh at Rees' predicament. Rees watches them, then laughs, too. "Sorry, I'll get the hang of it," he says, then he changes the subject. "You ask to see me, sir?"

The colonel chuckles once more and sits in his chair, then points to his father. "I'll give you the honors, Dad."

Chief Black looks at Rees. "Well, to make it simple, we just found out from the DNA lab that we are descendants of Corporal O'Toole."

Rees stares at the chief for a few seconds, then laughs. "Get out of here, sir." Then he looks at the colonel, who raises his hand in the air. He stops laughing. "You're serious?"

"That is what we were told," the colonel says and hands Rees the piece of paper from the lab. Rees takes it and reads. Once finished, he hands it back. "I don't know what to say. Does O'Toole know?"

"No. And he won't," the colonel says. "We thought it best he not be made aware. Since we're sending him back, we don't want him dwelling on it. May cause him to second guess himself. Maybe do something different than he would normally do."

Rees thinks for a second. "But, sir, I don't think it would matter. Things are fine now, nothing has changed," Rees says.

"That we know of."

"Yes, sir. That we know of. But if we are here, and you and the chief are here, doesn't that mean everything is as it should be? I don't believe that anything O'Toole does will change anything. No matter what he does, things will be as they should be, as they are. It's kind of a paradox. It's like history abhors a vacuum. No matter what, it will try to remedy itself, correct itself so that no matter what we do in the past, everything stays the same. Sorry, I'm rambling."

The colonel and chief look at each other then, the chief looks at Rees. "No, Son, that's pretty profound thinking. You're getting into this surprisingly good."

"Oh, no, I just read a lot of science fiction. I'm probably plagiarizing from someone. Not sure who, but that's something I probably read."

"Well, it makes sense no matter who said it," Chief Black says, "but humor us. Let's just keep it between us. Okay?"

Rees looks to one, then the other man. "That's fine by me. What about Farnsworth?" Rees asks.

Colonel Black answers, "We think it best that only you know."

Sir?" Rees asks, brow furrowed. "He still going?"

"Yes, he is, but being brought in from another squadron and not having been here that long, well, let's just keep it amongst us. Okay?"

"Yes, sir. If you don't mind my asking, is it something I should be concerned about? About Farnsworth, I mean."

Colonel Black shakes his head. "No, no, nothing like that. I'm sure he's going to do well, and you two seem to get along, but we think the fewer who know about this the better."

"Yes, sir. I understand."

"Good. Now, I know you have some things to do before the mission, so we won't keep you."

Rees stands and salutes, nods to the chief, and walks towards the door.

"And, Sergeant Rees..."

Rees stops, hand on the door handle. "Yes, sir?"

"Good luck running back through the gauntlet," Colonel Black says with a smile, and the chief chuckles.

CHAPTER 23

The next day, Rees is in his office going over some last-minute details before his mission. Earlier in the day, he had made his way to the Staff Judge Advocates Office (SJAG) to set up a will. He had never been sure if he needed one before but decided he did. He set it up so that in case of his demise, he would leave everything to Nora. He had spoken with her, and she informed him she didn't need anything, but he insisted. Scott told her to give it to charity, or her children, or throw the world's biggest Irish wake in his honor.

The idea of him leaving her everything in the will bothered Nora.

"Why are you doing this? Making a will, I mean? What's going on?" she asks with concern in her voice.

"Nothing. It's just a good idea to have a will. Just something I thought of after coming back. I didn't have one when the incident occurred, and even though I didn't have much, what I did have would have gone to the government. No one wants that. Since I have no immediate family, I thought you should have it," he tells her, hoping it's a good reason. She accepts it and agrees it is probably a good idea. One never knows.

"I didn't know the Welsh had an Irish wake," she says to him. Rees takes it in stride.

"You ever been to a Welsh wake?" he asks.

"No, I can't say that I have," Nora replies.

"Neither have I, but I'm sure they're boring and solemn as hell. Crying, wailing, shitty music. Naw, Irish wake is the way to go."

"But you're not Irish," Nora tells him.

"Hey, my ancestors are just across the pond from there. I'm sure some Irish lad snuck over and got some Welsh lass to give it up. So, there might be some Irish in me somewhere, never know," Rees says good-naturedly.

"You're incorrigible, Scott," Nora answers with a laugh. He still likes her laugh.

They talk a bit more, catching up since they last saw each other, without Rees telling her what he is preparing to do. After hanging up, he turns back around in his chair to find Kriger leaning on the door frame peering in.

"Nora?" he asks.

"Yup. I put her in my will. Just letting her know."

Kriger looks offended and grabs at his chest and makes a look of shock on his face.

"What? You aren't leaving me all your worldly possessions? Not to mention that small fortune you've acquired?"

That only got him the middle finger salute from Rees.

"You're IQ?" Kriger asks.

"No," Rees answers, "how long your dick is in inches."

"Ouch. Gonna give me a complex," Kriger replies, again feigning being hurt.

"Other than busting my balls, I'm sure you have a good reason for lurking around my office door, Sergeant."

"Yeah, we're needed at Q's office. He's got a few more things for your little journey."

"Really? What more could he come up with that we need?" Rees asks as he stands to follow Dave out the door.

A few minutes later, they enter the lab where Captain Epstein works and find him running around checking other technicians' work like a crazed mad scientist. Standing in the corner, Captain Farnsworth speaks with Sergeant Bouvier. Rees sees them and walks over.

"Morning," he says.

"Back at ya," Bouvier says.

"Morning, Sergeant Rees," Farnsworth says with a grin. "Captain Epstein says he got more gadgets for us. Can't wait."

And as if on cue, Epstein turns and sees the four men watching him, and a grin breaks across his face.

"Good, you're here. Come on, got some more things for you. Actually, some of these are from our friend in Services," he says as they follow him into another area of the lab. He approaches a table, and the men can see an array of what looks like food.

"MREs?" Rees asks.

Epstein look sat Rees for a few seconds, not comprehending why he would ask that.

"No. Well. Yes. Well. Sort of," Epstein stammers, now understanding what Rees was asking. Then he picks up a stack of what looks like thick crackers.

"Looks like hard tack," Farnsworth says and sees the others look at him. "It was a staple of what both armies ate back then, easy to make, carry. They still make it and sell it today.

"Very good, Captain. Basically, it's just cooked dough and salt with extraordinarily little flavor and no nutritional value." Epstein picks a piece up, and he hands it to Rees. Rees takes the hard tack, sniffs it, and hands it over to Farnsworth. Epstein grins.

The thing is, this isn't like the stuff they ate. This has been modified. It has nutrients, vitamins, minerals, and flavor. Try a piece," he tells them, and each man snaps a piece off, and they take a bite.

"Wow, not bad, sir," Rees says while still chewing.

"We thought it best you had rations that looked like everyone else's so as not to draw too much attention to yourselves if you had to eat amongst soldiers."

"Good thinking. I'll just make sure we don't share," Farnsworth says with a wry smile.

"Anything else?" he adds.

"For food, not really. You will be given plenty of that, some dried fruit, beef jerky, and some tinned food. Mostly beef and pork stew. You also have some freeze-dried stuff you should keep to yourselves, and that includes the coffee. You will have some already ground if you do decide to share." He looks at Farnsworth, who shrugs.

Epstein moves over to another table and picks up a small syrette. "Morphine," he says, holding it up for the others to see. "We do have the auto-injectors but thought it best you have these smaller syrettes rather than a larger injector. Easier to conceal. You each will have a small medical kit that can be hidden in compartments located in your saddlebags. Sergeant Kriger will go over all its contents with you. Bandages, of course, antibiotic ointments, standard stuff. Let's just hope you don't need them."

"Roger that," Bouvier says, looking at the others.

Captain Epstein moves along to another table. "Here we have what looks like standard USA buttons. Something you might have extra of, especially an officer. To replace any lost on your uniform. But these are not real buttons," he says, picking one up. "This one is an officer's button, C for cavalry in the center and an eagle." Epstein looks up and smiles. "In case you're wondering. But on the back is a small tab. See it'?" the captain asks, showing it to the men, who squint and lean over each other to examine the button.

Satisfied everyone has seen it, he turns it back over. Epstein pushes the small tab and attaches it to a post located on the table. He does the same with another button and places it on another post opposite the first. He adjusts them so they are at the same level. He hands each man a third button and tells them to hold it near their ear. Once they have complied, he waves his hand between the button, and each man jumps and pulls the button from their ears. The captain smiles.

"Sensors," he says proudly. "You can put these up anywhere, up to fifteen feet apart. Anyone or anything breaks the beam, and you'll hear an alarm as long as the receiver is close to your ear."

Captain Epstein picks up a different button, this one smooth with just a C in the middle, indicating cavalry, and shows the men. "We have them with small flares that will blind a person at night, and this one here, pewter, is a small explosive." He grabs a white bar of what looks like soap wrapped in a waxy paper. "This is a newly developed explosive, similar to EPX-1, but much more powerful, so don't try bathing with it," he says with a self-appreciating chuckle.

"What is EPX-1? Never heard of it." Rees asks.

Epstein's grin widens. "EPX-1 explosive contains pentaerythritol tetranitrate with a different particle size as explosive filler bonded by non-energetic thermoplastic binder plasticized by dibutyl phthalate. Thus, making it really powerful."

Rees raises his hands in surrender. "Sorry I asked."

Non-plussed, the Captain continues. "You can use the explosive button as a detonator," he explains while he grabs one of the buttons and moves into the weapons range, holding it out for them to see. He turns the small base of the button and throws it. It explodes with so much force the men are shocked. The force was loud, and the concussive wave was strongly felt.

"Wouldn't want that going off on my jacket," Farnsworth says.

Epstein turns to look at him. "No worries, Captain. You really have to work it to get one to explode. They won't arm themselves by a little jostling. Must be intentionally set to explode. I want you to work with these. Each turn gives the explosive more time. The more you turn the base, the longer it takes to go off. I have some practice charges for you to, well, to practice with. Not to worry, they only pop when they explode, won't even hurt if it goes off in your hand, not that you would be holding it when it explodes."

"Good to hear. We'll practice with them later," Farnsworth replies.

"Anything else, Captain?" Rees asks.

Shaking his head, the captain informs him that's all he has for them. He adds that he hopes it does the job for them. Rees says he does, too, and appreciates all he has done.

Rees turns back to the others and looks at his watch.

"Jack, Dave, want to go get the others, including O'Toole?"

Kriger and Bouvier nod. "Sure, what's up?"

Time for some horseback riding. Gotta keep up the training," Rees says with a smile. Farnsworth claps his hands together and rubs them briskly. The other two men groan and sloop their shoulders as they follow Rees out the door.

CHAPTER 24

Two days until the men leave, and all three are in the doctor's office receiving a final examination. Rees and Farnsworth are given booster shots to help protect them from all the diseases that ran rampant during the Civil War. Pneumonia, typhoid, diarrhea/dysentery, measles, malaria ran throughout both armies, killing an estimated two-thirds of the soldiers. This meant that out of approximately 700,000 deaths attributed to the war, most died of disease.

The doctors want to ensure these two men are given as much of a chance to survive as possible. O'Toole will have to hope for the best since he did not have any of these shots available to him in his time period. He will return just as when he came. Since he is an ancestor of the Blacks, it is reasonable enough to assume he will be alright.

O'Toole becomes more adjusted to his environment but still wishes to return to his own time. To get back to his people. Who could blame him?

The three men pass their final exams with good results and are declared fit for duty. They leave the medical facility and go for lunch. After lunch, O'Toole is escorted back to his quarters, and Farnsworth has a meeting to attend. Rees decides to go the Sergeant Shepard's office just to see what no good he is probably up to.

~ ~ ~

Chief Black is in the colonel's office, reading some daily reports from different sections of the Clio Project. Most of them are routine and nothing of great importance as far as he is concerned. Not being in charge, he doesn't have to be as informed as his son now does, but it's good to keep up with some of the activities. After all, he did create the project and is still working in an advisory capacity, limited as he believes it is.

Sighing, he sets the reports down and looks at his son, who diligently pores over reports of his own. Hearing his father sigh, he looks up from his current report.

"Something wrong?" he asks, thinking his father found something in one of the reports.

Chief Black purses his lips while looking out the window, seemingly to watch one of the large screens set against the wall in the control room. He looks back at the colonel.

"Something's not right," he begins, then stops.

Colonel Black waits patiently for him to continue, and when he doesn't, the colonel prompts him. "And?" he asks.

The chief stands and drops the report onto the chair. "I know the senator has become a personal friend of yours, and I know he has been incredibly supportive of this project since it was allowed to come back online. And I appreciate all that he has done for us..." he says and pauses.

"I feel a *but* coming in here somewhere, Dad," Colonel Black says.

Chief Black smiles. "*But...*" he says, "something is off. I can't put my finger on it, but there is."

"Does it have to do with Captain Farnsworth?" Colonel Black asks. "You know he was vetted. He checks out. Seven years in service, right out of the Air Force Academy, served in Iraq and Afghanistan. Right number of accommodations, citations. It's no wonder he popped up on Olsen's radar. That and the fact he's an amateur Civil War historian. I don't see the problem."

"The problem is that's it's too much of a coincidence. The program is being reinstated, and this officer is dropped in our laps with instructions for us to have him tag along. For what reason, Son? Why does the good senator want him along? This is wrong, I'm telling you," Chief Black says angrily.

"All right, Dad, calm down. Blood pressure," the colonel tells his father. The chief gives his son a sardonic look.

"Please," he says sarcastically, "my blood pressure is just fine, thank you. I can still probably outrun you." This time with a sardonic smile.

"Okay, okay, but the mission is set. There is no reason to postpone it," Colonel Black says.

"I didn't say anything about postponing it. But we will bring Scott in here and talk with him about it," the chief says.

"You think that's a good idea? I mean, they seem to work well together and get along. Do you really want to plant a seed of doubt into Scott's head before a mission?"

Chief Black thinks for a minute. "Yes," he answers. "Listen, I'm not wanting to worry him. I may be way off base here, and I'm willing to tell him so. I just want him to be aware of his surroundings. Take all precautions to ensure the mission is a success."

Colonel Black, who stood in front of his desk while listening to his father, walks over to the door and opens it. Sam looks up and smiles.

"Sam, can you get in touch with Sergeant Rees and ask him to come to my office?" he asks and sees the smile change from a warm friendly smile to something else before she answers.

"Yes, sir."

He shakes his head. "Sam?"

She stops with the phone halfway to her head. "Sir?"

"Please, leave enough of the young man for us to be able to send him on a mission."

"No promises, sir, but I'll do my best to make sure he's left in one piece. Just for you, Colonel."

"That's all I ask, Sam. Thank you," he replies and shuts the door.

~ ~ ~

Rees is in Shepard's office, along with Nionee, Harris, and Tosseti. They are having a laugh about Tosseti and his horse. Seems that Tosseti's horse doesn't like him, and the feeling is mutual. The horse runs in circles when he tries to mount, won't obey when he pulls the reins, stops when it wants, and attempts to bite him whenever it gets a chance, which is often.

Tosseti reacts to the barbs with his usual curses and threats, always with a heavy accent and red face. This just makes it worse as the guys all laugh more until he finally storms out of the room.

"I'm from the city, not supposed to be riding no dumb animal. Air Force, my ass," he grumbles amongst more laughter.

Shepard's phone rings, and he picks it up. Rees moves towards the door to head back to his office when Shepard stops him.

"Sergeant Rees?" he calls out, and Rees stops. "Colonel wants to see you," he finishes as he hangs up.

"Thanks," Rees says and walks out the door.

"And I'm sure a certain assistant wants to see you, too," Shepard yells loud enough for Rees, as well as anyone within earshot, to hear. Rees continues on his way as people passing look at him and grin.

~ ~ ~

Rees enters Sam's office and is ready for her comments.

"Well, took you long enough to get here, Sergeant. You know when the colonel calls, you need to get here ASAP."

Rees stands by her desk. "This is ASAP, thank you very much."

"Oh, I thought you would have gotten here a little sooner so we could spend some quality time together. I guess I'm not worth a little extra time. Well, that's okay. Go on in," Sam says to him with a fake hurt look on her face. "Go on now, he's waiting."

Rees opens his mouth to say something, then decides against it. As usual, he's at a loss for words, so he knocks on the colonel's door and enters.

Rees conducts the proper protocol, and after taking a seat, he is briefed on their concerns.

"Sirs, I'm not seeing it. Captain Farnsworth has been steadfast in assuring this mission goes as planned. He has been thorough with the training and mission preparedness. He is liked by everyone, good sense of humor, dedicated. And we seemed to have hit it off. Sorry, I just don't see it," Rees tells the two men. "But…" he continues before they can say anything, "I will be alert."

The colonel and chief nod.

"Also, if it makes you feel any better. I was going to keep an eye out anyway. You can never really trust a person who you haven't known for very long or been under fire with, or seen the elephant with, as they say back then. So, you have no worries there."

The chief smiles and nods in understanding. Colonel Black looks at the countdown clock on the wall in the control room. Twenty-three hours until the mission.

CHAPTER 25

All three men are issued their blue uniforms, which are trimmed with yellow, indicating they're US Cavalrymen. It was determined that the ranks for Rees and Farnsworth would be significantly different than their official ranks for the USAF. Farnsworth will wear the eagles of a colonel, and Rees the twin silver bars of a captain. This will allow them easier access and movement among the units they may run across. O'Toole, of course, will retain his rank of corporal.

Both Rees and Farnsworth receive a small surprise in the form of a letter. The letter reads that these men are on special assignment and are to be allowed thoroughfare anywhere they wish, as well as being assisted with any task they require. They are to be granted access to men, supplies, and equipment, which will assist them with their assigned duties. Both letters are signed by the President of the United States, Abraham Lincoln, and the Secretary of War, Edwin M. Stanton.

Both men were astonished at the details of the forgery. It stands to reason that some of the troops they are likely to run across will be dubious of the letter, but it can't hurt. The letters are each rolled up in a water-resistant leather pouch to hopefully keep them in good shape.

After the men don their uniforms and gather their gear, they make their way topside. They take an elevator to the top level and are meet by Rees' team, the colonel, chief, Sam, and a few other technicians.

Everyone wishes them good luck, and Sam walks over to Rees and whispers in his ear. He jerks his head back, eyes wide as he stares at her, his face flush, much to the enjoyment and snickers of some of the others.

A Humvee waits for them, and the men move towards it and enter. It takes them to the secluded destination, and when they arrive, they climb out and shade their eyes from the sun and scan the area.

"Sure wish I had those glasses you gave me before," O'Toole says as he pulls the brim of his Kepi down over his eyes.

They walk over to the area where three horses wait for them. The saddles and other gear are on the ground next to them. The horses have been somewhat sedated, just enough to keep them from becoming too skittish after they arrive, or so the men are told.

Rees, Farnsworth, and O'Toole each grab the reins of their assigned horse and force them to lay on the ground, and each man lies across the animals' necks to keep them calm. A few minutes pass, and they hear in their earpieces that they are ready to go.

The entire area is open space, and the sun is high in the sky. There is no sound except that of the insects and an occasional chirping of a bird. The heat makes Rees sweat, and the horses start getting antsy. O'Toole's horse whinnies, snorts, and attempt to get up. O'Toole being a consummate horseman calms the animal, and it lies its head back on the ground as O'Toole gently talks to it. He sees Rees watching him and smiles.

"I know how she feels. Believe me, I want to get up and run me self."

Rees nods his understanding and notices the insects and birds have suddenly gone silent. Looking up, he sees the blue sky has turned a hazy color, and he can feel the hairs on his arm rising. He snorts and looks at Farnsworth, who glances around, gripping the reins of his horse so tightly his knuckles are showing white. Rees smiles himself.

"Here we go, Captain. See you on the other side,"

The air electrifies. Rees swears he can see it move, shimmer, warp. He shakes his head, then closes his eyes. A pain welts up in him, pressure in his ears. His horse kicks and tries to stand, Rees concentrates putting all his weight on the animal, but he's getting dizzy, and the pain is becoming extreme. Finally, he yells, and he can see Farnsworth's horse fighting him, breaking free from Farnsworth's grasp, but it doesn't have time to bolt as darkness overcomes them all.

Before Rees accepts the darkness that takes away the pain, he hears Bob Seger singing "Midnight Rider," and he mentally shakes his head. He starts to ask Bob why he is always singing to him on these occasions, but then he listens to the lyrics and doesn't know if it's a good thing or a bad before the nothingness envelopes him.

Operation Ameliorate begins.

CHAPTER 26

"Well, get it back up!" Chief Black sternly tells one of the junior officers operating the control system for the cameras. Rees' team, code-named Saber, are being monitored from a distance, and everyone watches in fascination as they completely disappear. The cameras Rees and Farnsworth wear flicker for a few seconds, then clear, revealing a shot from two different angles. One camera shows the brown hide of one of the horses, and the other shows grass and trees at a low angle. There is no movement to be seen, then there is nothing. Blank. The cameras shut down.

"What the hell happened, Lieutenant?" Colonel Black asks, his voice lower in volume than his father's.

"Sir, not sure. The camera's all show operational, but we are not receiving a signal."

"What about audio? Can we hear anything?" the chief asks.

The lieutenant looks over at his counterpart wearing headphones. Looking like a submarine sonar operator, his hands are over the headphones, pressing them close to his ears. While everyone watches, he adjusts a frequency dial and concentrates. Finally, he looks up and shakes his head. Removing the headphones, he tells them he cannot hear a thing.

"Well, that's just great. Almost forty years have gone by since we sent anyone into the past, and we still can't get audio or visual equipment to work correctly," Chief Black grumbles and storms over to another station, where a civilian scientist works. "Doctor Cole? Renee?" he calls to her as he approaches. "Did you get any abnormality readings when the team jumped?"

"Ah, yes I did, as a matter of fact. Thought it might be a slight power fluctuation, screen distortion. It was minor and very quick," she tells the chief.

"Okay, go back and start a diagnostic test on the entire system. Try to find what caused the fluctuation and let me know the second you do. Okay?"

"Sure, not a problem, sir."

Chief Black turns to his son. "John, not to take over, but if you don't mind, can you tell each technician operating an independent system to run diagnostics. I might just be a paranoid old man, but I've got a feeling we're going to find something fishy has happened."

Colonel Black looks at his father for a few seconds, processing what he was just told.

"So, you think we've been sabotaged?" he asks, watching his father as the chief slowly nods. Colonel Black sighs, nods, then taps his father's elbow as he passes him, walking over to a public address system. He picks the handset up and clicks the talk button to ensure it is on. Hearing the *click* over the loudspeaker, he again presses the talk button.

"May I have your attention, please?" he asks and waits for the noise in the room to quiet down. Once it does, he continues, "Thank you. As you all know, we are having an issue with the visual and audible from Clio. We hope from what little information we have so far is that the Saber team made it safely to their destination. But we won't know until we can get the video feed back up and running. While teams work on that problem, I want everyone else who has a system designated just for Clio to run diagnostic tests. We want to know of any malfunction, glitches, or abnormalities that may have occurred during the transfer. I don't care how minute it is, even if you think it's anything I might not want to know, I *do* want to know. Thank you," he finishes and replaces the microphone on its hook.

He watches the room and sees that everyone immediately goes to work on the tasks placed upon them. He turns towards his father, who looks solemn, then leaves the control room A few seconds later, his father does the same. Both men walk up the stairs and go back into the colonel's office.

"Okay, Dad," the colonel says as soon as the door is shut, "what gives? I mean, what do you think we'll find?" he asks and walks behind his desk and sits.

"I'm not sure, John, but I had a feeling something would happen. I've got a feeling we've been infiltrated, and like I said before, I had a bad feeling since Farnsworth came on board."

Colonel Black sighs. "We went over this already. Captain Farnsworth checks out. The senator vouches for him. What more do you want, Dad?" he asks, frustrated. "Why can't this just be a technical hang-up? Happens all the time, even with sophisticated equipment as this. Hell, especially with sophisticated equipment like this. An electrode burns out, power surge trips a switch. It doesn't have to be a conspiracy all the time."

"I know that, and you're probably right. It's just that the first time we used Clio..." Black trails off.

"Dad, that was a long time ago, a different time. Things have changed a lot since then. We have more security in place, better people in office, more rules and regulations."

Chief Black snorts. "Yeah, more rules and regulations. Look where that's gotten us."

Colonel Black chuckles. "You got me on that one," he agrees, "but let's just see what the good folks operating Clio find out, okay? Until then, how about a refreshment?"

~ ~ ~

Rees wakes lying on his side, one of his arms still wrapped around his horse. The horse is moving, but barely, eyes open staring around, still groggy from the time jump. He releases his grip and rolls over onto his back. His head reels, but nothing compared to what he felt like the first time he time traveled. He blinks his eyes and takes several deep breaths, which helps clear his head. *The pills worked,* he thinks, then rolls again, this time onto his front side, and attempts to rise.

Taking more deep breaths, he makes his way into a standing position, wobbly, but able to do so without getting sick. His horse kicks and snorts and tries to stand but only falls before it raises its head. It lies on the ground and looks at Rees with what looks like to him is fear or confusion or an accusation. He goes to the animal and kneels, gently caressing and talking calmly to it.

He looks over at where O'Toole lays and sees him stirring, then looks to Farnsworth. The man is on his back, taking large gulps of air, then he suddenly rolls over and vomits. Rees shakes his head and chuckles.

"Welcome to the world of time jumping, sir," he tells him with a half-smile. This gets him a middle finger raised in the air, causing Rees to chuckle more.

Rees works with his horse, finally getting him to his feet, and he leaves him standing as he goes over to Farnsworth, who has made it into a seated position.

"You alright, sir?" Rees asks, and Farnsworth gives him a glazed-eye look and nods. Satisfied the captain, or colonel now, is going to make it, he walks over to O'Toole, who is already standing and tending to his horse.

"Andy, good to go?" Rees asks, and O'Toole gives him a grin.

"I'm fine, Sergeant. I do not want to be doing that all the time now, though. Still a little squeamish. Kinda like the day after a night of drinking hot stuff, you know?"

"I hear you. Don't know what you said, but I hear you. And remember, Andy, I'm a captain now, alright?"

Rees goes back to Farnsworth, who seems to have gotten over his little bout of time travel sickness, and looks around.

"Where are we?" he asks.

"Should be where I was sent the first time one-hundred-fifty years or so earlier. Need to take a reading and get our bearings," Rees answers, reaching into his pocket for the GPS pocket watch. He turns it on and receives…nothing. He checks the mechanism over and finds that everything is working, except there are no coordinates showing.

"Well, this isn't working. Try yours," He tells Farnsworth. Farnsworth pulls his watch out and gets the same results.

"Nope, not working," he says. "The good captain did say it might not."

Rees clicks his camouflaged whisper mic and calls out to the control room, "Saber 2 to Clio," and waits. He hears nothing, not even static. He tries again, "Saber 2 to Clio, come in." Still nothing.

Farnsworth tries and gets the same results.

"Well, this sucks," Rees says. "No GPS, no comms."

Farnsworth shakes his head. "We knew this could happen, so we'll do it the old-fashioned way." He pulls out a map and compass.

"Not needed yet, sir. If we're near where we should be, we can move east and hopefully run into the river, then we'll have a better idea of where we are and move on from there," Rees says.

O'Toole walks over, leading his horse. "Why don't we just go in that direction," he suggests, pointing in a northerly direction.

"We could," Rees says, "but we would be traveling blind, could run into Rebel patrols. No, it's better we try to reach the river.

"We could just as easily run into Johnny Reb going that way as well, sir," O'Toole says.

"Man's got a point, but I agree. We should make our way east first and find the river," Farnsworth adds.

"Okay, let's do this," Rees says, and they all check the condition of their animals and mount up. It takes them all a few minutes to get their bearings and stop the vertigo they feel once in the saddle. They head off in an easterly direction, looking like drunken cowboys riding drunken horses.

Rees is again fascinated by the serene calmness of the area in this time period. No traffic noise, no aircraft flying overhead leaving contrails, no smog, none of the sounds of modern civilization. Only the rustling of the trees from the wind and the sound of the horses trotting along occasionally shaking their head causing the bridles to jingle. Rees looks to his right when he catches movement out of the corner of his eye and sees a red fox staring at them before running off in a different direction. Rees smiles and sees Farnsworth looking all around, either enjoying the scenery or checking for danger.

"This is amazing," Farnsworth finally says. "Haven't had this much quiet since I was backpacking in Yosemite. Beautiful area when it's not disturbed."

That answers Rees' question.

The men travel on in quiet, each enjoying the scenery and calmness of the expanse. They are about to ride into a heavily wooded area when they feel, more than hear, movement in the woods and are quickly confronted by several men wearing the gray and butternut clothing of Confederate soldiers. The Rebels quickly surround the horsemen pointing long-barreled muskets at them.

"Damn it," Farnsworth blurts under his breath. "Let myself get distracted."

"Told ya," O'Toole says under his breath, which only gets him a sidelong look from the two others.

One of the soldiers, a sergeant, waves a pistol at the Union-clad horse soldiers. Rees and the others stop and raise their hands so as not to get shot.

"Well, well, lookie what we got here, boys. Three blue bellies traipsing in our territory. Not your lucky day, Yanks," he says to the laughter of the others. "Now, why don't ya'll climb on down off them fine animals, which by the way I thank you for." He waves his pistol, indicating they should remove themselves from the saddles. The men comply.

Farnsworth and Rees each count the number of men surrounding them, noting only five. Farnsworth turns toward Rees and whispers, "Deserters."

Rees nods his understanding, angry with himself as well for not paying attention to their surroundings. Situational awareness.

These men left whatever their unit was and are now deserters. Gone rogue, they are little more than highwaymen. Wandering the countryside and, more likely than not, robbing whomever they come across. They are probably only used to robbing civilians. Poor souls trying to flee the war only to be robbed and probably killed.

Once the men dismount, the Rebels take their pistols and search them, taking whatever they can find, to include their watches. They don't do a great search, more of a pat-down, and poorly at that. They rummage through the haversacks, yelping, and whooping at the bounty they have found, but missing the more vital items hidden in the sacks, as well as the saddlebags. Two of the Rebels push the men towards the woods. Farnsworth and Rees know they are going to be shot. O'Toole looks scared, as Rees is, but he tries to look more defiant.

The sergeant falls in behind the other two and follows them into the woods. The last two men stay behind and look over their spoils.

"Whatcha wanna do with 'em, boss?" one of the older men asks, showing rotten and missing teeth, a sickly grin on his face.

"You don't floss much do you?" Farnsworth asks the man with a look of disgust on his face.

One corner of the man's upper lip curls upward, and he tilts his head like a puppy. "What?" he asks.

Farnsworth mimics flossing his teeth, and the three men each glance at each other. The toothless man becomes agitated and moves towards Farnsworth. "You making fun at me, Billy Yank?" The deserter snarls.

"Naw, I wouldn't do that to such a Nancy Boy as you. Hey, you and your possum over there maybe…" Farnsworth says, making a fist with one hand and sticking his finger in and out of it in a sexual manner. This is all it takes for the Reb to lose it.

"Why, you Mudsill Yellow Dog son of a whore." He makes a move as if to attack Farnsworth, which is his mistake.

Farnsworth grasps the man's musket with one hand, and using his other, he drives an open hand into the man's throat. The Reb's eyes go wide, and he releases the musket to grab for his throat. Farnsworth holds onto the musket and whips it around and strikes the sergeant in the head with the barrel of the weapon. As the sergeant goes down, Farnsworth is on top of him in a heartbeat and wrestles the pistol way.

As soon as Farnsworth makes his first move, Rees rushes the third soldier, who is distracted, and tackles him to the ground. The Rebel drops his rifle as he tries to fend off Rees. Rees uses all his weight when he falls on the man, causing the deserter to let out a *whoosh* of air. Rees swiftly reaches into the collar of his uniform and pulls out a small knife and jabs it into his ear, causing the man to scream in pain.

Rees turns and sees the first soldier, who has dropped to his knees, while still holding his throat with one hand and attempting to draw his pistol with the other. Rees looks at O'Toole. "Andy!" he shouts, and O'Toole sees what is happening.

He runs over and kicks the man in the face with his boot. Blood sprays across the ground as the deserter is flung over from the blow, releasing the pistol, and grabbing his broken nose. Rees scurries over and finishes the man off with his knife. O'Toole just stares as Rees withdraws the knife and wipes the blood on the dead man's pants.

Rees and O'Toole turn to watch as Farnsworth takes the sergeant's head, and with one swift move, breaks the man's neck. O'Toole looks astonished.

"I ain't ne'r seen that before," looking at Rees. "Did you have to kill them?"

Farnsworth doesn't respond but looks to see if the other two are incapacitated. Seeing they are, he reaches down for the sergeant's pistol, and lucky he did. Just as he squats to retrieve the weapon, they hear the report of a musket rifle being discharged. A split second later, a Minnie ball strikes a tree right where Farnsworth was just standing, covering him with splinters.

Rees and O'Toole each return fire at the man holding the musket, who attempts to reload. Both Rees' and O'Toole's shots strike the man in the chest and stomach. He falls dead before he hits the ground.

The three men race out of the woods in time to see the fifth man riding off on O'Toole's horse while holding the reins of Rees' horse, pulling it behind him. Farnsworth goes to his horse and retrieves his Spencer rifle. In a flash, it is out of the scabbard, and he is on one knee, aiming in the direction of the fleeing Rebel. A shot is heard, and a split second later, the man falls from the horse.

Rees' horse stops running and walks over to eat grass. O'Toole's horse continues to run as if not knowing his rider is missing. Farnsworth jumps onto his horse and rides off after O'Toole's horse as Rees runs to grab his before it wanders off.

A few minutes later, Farnsworth returns with the horse.

"We had better get out of here. No telling who may have heard this racket."

"What about them?" O'Toole asks.

"What about them?" Farnsworth asks.

"We gotta bury 'em."

"You're kidding, right?"

"No, sir, it's the Christian thing to do. No matter that they are Rebs or robbers, they are still men."

Farnsworth climbs down off his horse and approaches O'Toole.

"Listen, Andy. I get it. And I agree. But this is war, and we are in enemy territory. We don't have time to dig five graves. There could be enemy soldiers in the area heading this way as we speak. We don't have the luxury of being civilized. Okay?"

O'Toole looks at Rees for support but sees he is not paying attention.

"Scott? You okay?" Farnsworth asks, noticing that Rees is staring back at where they just escaped. "Rees!" Farnsworth exclaims. "Are you alright?"

Rees lifts his head and takes a deep breath, then looks at the two men. "I'm fine. Just never killed a man close up before. Different than shooting from a distance."

"Yes, it is. And it's something that will be with you for the rest of your life, so don't try to forget it, but don't dwell on it, either. You've been trained to fight and survive, and what you did covered the first basic instinct of man. Survive. And you did. As the grunts say, 'Welcome to the suck.' Now, let's get moving."

O'Toole moves towards Farnsworth. "Again, sir, what about these men?"

Farnsworth climbs back onto his horse and shakes his head. "Critters gotta eat, too." He rides off.

O'Toole stands open-mouthed, and Rees pats him on the back. "Just got to get used to the Special Forces mentality, Andy. Whole different breed. I think General Sherman would like him," he tells him, then climbs on his horse and looks down at O'Toole. "Listen, if it makes you feel any better, someone more likely than not heard the ruckus we made and will be along any minute. When they do, I'm sure they'll take care of them," Rees says, then turns his horse and follows Farnsworth, leaving O'Toole looking at the dead men. A few seconds later, O'Toole catches up to them.

CHAPTER 27

The three cavalrymen continue traveling east for several hours until they reach the river just before sunset. The men dismount, remove the saddles from the horses, and let them graze. Rees and Farnsworth set up camp, with O'Toole tending to the horses. Rees grabs the intrusion detection devices and places them among the trees, ensuring a completely secure perimeter. He also intermittingly dispersed some of the flares, just in case.

They each fill their canteens and add the purification tablets, as well as place water into a pot to make dinner. O'Toole is still amazed at how they can take dried pieces of food and make a delicious meal. This time, they make a beef stew, and he is grateful for it.

"I wish I could take some of this stuff home with me," he tells the other two.

"Now, Andy, you know we can't let you do that," Rees says, stirring the stew.

"I know, I know. I just wished, is all."

"Sorry, troop, but we can't take a chance you invent something that didn't get invented for years after you're gone," Farnsworth adds.

"Think we'll find his unit tomorrow?" Rees asks, spooning out the stew onto metal plates.

"Now that I know where we are and where they should be, maybe. We lost most of a day getting here to get our bearings."

"Damn it," Rees blurts.

"What?" Farnsworth asks.

"We could have just gone towards the town of Hendricks Hill. That would have saved us some time. I'm not thinking straight," Rees complains, then eats a spoonful of stew, followed by a bite of his hard tack.

Farnsworth pulls out his map and studies it until he finds the town Rees speaks of.

"Yep, we could have. I didn't think of checking the map for a town before we headed this way. We were closer to it than here. And the Union Forces are probably already there. Could have gotten directions to the Maryland Brigades location. Oh, well, spilled milk, my friend. Besides, we're three cavalrymen with better horses and can probably catch up to an army who is mostly marching on foot."

O'Toole watches the men while he eats, listening.

"You already know what going to happen with this war, don't ya? I mean, who dies and who lives?" he asks.

"Yeah, sure. But we don't know what happened to every person fighting it. Oh, sure, mostly the politicians and generals made history, but there were several enlisted men whose names are remembered, as well as junior officers, they're just not as well known, but many are mentioned in several of the history books as well. Those who made an impact on the war itself. There are letters that were passed down from generation to generation, and a lot of them were preserved, so we know what happened to a lot of the soldiers, but not all of them," Farnsworth explains to Andy, who just nods staring at the ground.

Farnsworth looks to Rees, not sure where to go with this, so Rees continues, "Andy, are you asking about the war or you?"

Andy eyes Rees. "I guess about me mostly."

Rees only shakes his head. "As far as the history book goes, you are mentioned. When we returned to our time and brought you along, the people we work for checked you out during the battle we fought, and you were listed as missing. Nothing else is said about you. You were presumed captured or killed, and that's all we know," Rees lies.

Andy looks at the ground again and shakes his head, and when he looks up, he's smiling. "I guess it don't matter. I am here now, ain't I?"

"That you are, and we're getting you back to where you belong. You've got things to do, a girl to marry, and babies to make," Farnsworth adds and looks around. "Guess we should get some sleep. I'll take first watch. Wake you up in two, Rees."

"Sounds good," Rees replies, eyeing Farnsworth. *Why would he say that?* Rees thinks.

"What about me?" Andy asks. "I can pull picket duty. Besides, can't have you officers doing that and me just sluffing off now, can I?"

"You got it. Rees will wake you after his shift. Okay?"

Andy agrees, and he and Rees settle down for some rest, with Rees again wondering why Farnsworth mentioned babies.

~　~　~

The night goes by without incident. Rees and Farnsworth swapped out sentry duties, and both men exchanged small talk. They especially like how quiet it is in these woods, but it is a little off-putting with all the wildlife scurrying about. None of the alarms were triggered, and the men got enough sleep even in between sentry duties.

When peach hues of color begin showing in the east, announcing the beginning of a new day, the three men are already eating breakfast and drinking coffee. As they start breaking camp, Rees stops and walks closer to the river, watching the water flow and listening to the quiet lapping it makes on the shore's edge. Squinting in thought, he looks up the river then back down, a slight smile forming on his lips.

"What's the matter, Rees?" Farnsworth asks, noticing him staring along the riverbank.

Rees' smile widens. "If you two don't mind, I'd like to take a little side jaunt up the river."

Farnsworth looks at Andy, who shrugs. "Can I ask what for?"

"Just humor me, if you don't mind. It's not that far off course and shouldn't take more than a couple of hours. It'll help get something off my mind that's been bugging me for a while now. We'll be able to find Andy's unit, don't worry. Besides, time is on our side, isn't it?"

"Speaking of time," Farnsworth adds and clicks his microphone. "Saber One to Clio," he calls, then waits a few seconds, "Saber One to Clio, come in." He looks at Rees, who tries his mic. "Saber Two to Clio." He waits, repeating, "Saber Two to Clio," and shakes his head. I can hear you fine but can't get Clio. I just hope something hasn't gone wrong. I wouldn't want a repeat of what happened forty years ago," he says, then thinks out loud, "Or is that over one hundred years from now?"

"Don't start that shit," Farnsworth warns while cinching his horse's saddle. "They may have had a glitch or something. I'm sure everything is fine. Besides, nothing we can do about it anyway, so we might as well go on with the mission."

The three Union-clad time travelers finish stowing their gear and climb onto their horses. Rees takes lead, with Andy behind him and Farnsworth in the rear. They are more diligent this time around, and each man keeps an eye out for any movement. Rees and Farnsworth, having more modern military training and experience, also watch for shapes that don't belong and sounds that are manmade.

About an hour into their ride, Rees raises his hand, stops, and looks around. He stands in his saddle, looking further up the river, and then sits, turns to look at Andy and Farnsworth, then smiles. "Found it." He then moves up the river.

A few minutes later, the three men approach an area where there are three mounds of dirt, and at the head of each is an M-16 rifle, with the bayonet in the ground and a steel pot helmet on each. Scott climbs down and approaches the graves, then ties his horse's reins off on a tree limb.

Andy and Farnsworth sit on their horses and look on.

"I take it this is where you buried your comrades," Farnsworth finally says.

"Yes," Rees answers. "I was thinking about it last night. When we buried them, we left the weapons and helmets here. Not a smart thing to do on our part. When we returned to our timeline and located the graves, the weapons and helmet were in the ground with the…with my friends' remains. I didn't think anything of it at the time, but now I know how they got there," he says and looks up at the two men. "We buried them."

"Un-uh, no," Andy says. "That's sacrilege. We ain't digging up no dead men. I ain't havin' none of it."

"No, Andy, we're not digging them up. We just bury the weapons in a hole next to them. It was always in the back of my head. You know, how come these items weren't found. Even though it was a desolate place back then…now, civilization moved here eventually, and nothing was ever said about the modern weapons and helmets," Rees looks at the graves for a few more seconds, then walks over to his saddlebag and retrieves a small shovel.

Farnsworth and O'Toole climb off their animals, grabbing shovels as well, and walk over to assist Rees, who has already begun digging.

An hour later, the weapons and helmets are buried beside the three men who had lost their lives on the first time travel experiment. Rees wipes the sweat from his brow and looks at the graves. "Sorry, guys. I wish there was something we could have done better." He gives the graves a knowing smile.

Farnsworth and Andy stand by their horses and watch Rees, with Andy giving the sign of the cross over his chest. Rees gives a half-salute and grabs his jacket. "See you soon," he says to himself, donning his jacket, buckling his gun belt, and adjusting his gear. He climbs back onto his horse and looks at his watch; still no GPS coordinates. Farnsworth pulls out the map, and after conferring with the compass, they decide on a direction.

"Okay, how about we get Andy back to where he belongs," Rees says, pulling the horse's reins and galloping off.

CHAPTER 28

Colonel Black and the chief are in the colonel's office. The colonel has his desk chair turned, facing the large window, and looking down into the control room, watching the many technicians and scientists scrambling about, running their diagnostics, checking equipment for malfunctions, and everything else they can think of to get visual or audio.

The chief paces the office, snapping his fingers and tapping the side of his leg, not only because another glitch has happened to his project, but for not being able to help right now.

"Dad, can you stop? I know you want to help, but these people have it under control," Colonel Black tells his father and turns his chair around to watch the older man pace.

"Can't help it, John. Waiting is not something I like doing anymore. Was a time I had the patience of a cat. Now, waiting drives me crazy," he tells his son, then walks over to look down into the control room.

The phone buzzes, and Colonel Black snatches it up and looks into the control room to see Major Washington on the other end.

"Tell me some good news, Major," Black demands.

"That depends on what you consider good to be, sir," the major answers.

"Major Washington, I'm in no mood..." Black starts to say before the major shakes his head.

"No, sir. We believe we have found the problem. You and the chief may want to come down."

"On our way," the colonel replies and hangs up before hearing anything else from the major. He turns towards his father. "They think they found the problem." He heads towards the door, with the chief right behind him.

Once in the control room, they make their way to Major Washington, OIC of the current shift.

"Okay, Major, sitrep," the colonel demands when within earshot.

Major Washington stands with one of the lieutenants who works the comms.

"Sir, the lieutenant's diagnostic found a breach in the computer," he says and nods at the lieutenant, who takes her cue.

"Yes, sir. Colonel Black, a virus was introduced into the system. From what we found, it looks like the virus was introduced not long ago. It was designed to wait until Clio was activated, then start interfering with the system. From what little we know as of now, it seems it was meant to disrupt communications, then when completed, it would self-destruct by wiping the system clean, to include itself.

"Okay, so comms are disrupted, to what ends. The mission would continue, and we could just bring the men back."

The lieutenant stares for a few seconds. "Sorry, sir, maybe I wasn't clear. The communication disruption was only the beginning. That was just to throw us off. While we were looking into why the comms were down, the virus would continue to run its course until it took over the entire system.

"So, someone has sabotaged the mission?" Chief Black asks.

"No, Chief, not exactly," the lieutenant tells him.

"Well then, what?" Colonel Black asks, tension in his voice.

"Sir, the virus only jammed up the system, it didn't get fully functional. When we ran test programs earlier this week, the virus was already there. We only ran partial tests, but the virus didn't know that. It thought we were running a full mission, so it tried to initiate its programming. When Clio didn't fully activate, the virus became confused and couldn't complete its full programming. Part of the programming thought it had done its job, so it partially self-destructed, leaving only part of the virus active. Just enough to interfere with comms, but not enough to destroy the entire system."

"Again, Lieutenant, I ask, so we were sabotaged?" Chief Black asks, this time with more force.

"Chief, it looks like someone attempted to attack the system, then made changes to the virus. We will need to do further investigation, but it looks like whoever placed the virus into the system also changed the virus to do what it did during the test run."

"I'm not following you, Lieutenant," Colonel Black says.

Major Washington jumps in, "Sir, we think that maybe someone here is a…a double agent for lack of a better term. They implanted the virus as ordered, then changed the virus before placing it, to only jam us up for a short period. The virus was initially designed to destroy Clio, but someone changed so as to only damage her. We can hopefully have her back up and running within twenty-four hours."

"So, we are blind until then. We don't know what's going on, where they are, or if they even made it to where they were supposed to be, and if they did, are they are still alive? We don't know jack shit. That's great!" the colonel replies, almost shouting.

"That's not the only problem we have. We have been infiltrated. Someone attempted to destroy Clio and interfere with the mission. We need to find out who and why," the chief says, looking at the colonel. "Before anything worse happens."

"I want everyone involved with this project re-vetted. I want to know when the virus was introduced. I want to know who was working the shifts when it happened. I want some goddamn answers, Major. I want someone's ass, too. Most importantly, I want Clio up and running. Mission Ameliorate is still on, and those men might need our help. We need to know what is going on, and running blind is not acceptable. Get Clio up and running ASAP, got it?"

"Yes, sir! We're on it," Washington replies and points in the direction of the control panels, indicating the lieutenant is dismissed and should get on with it.

Colonel Black and Chief Black look at the screen, both men willing it to show something.

"We need to get OSI involved right now. I suggest we have them go over all video footage from the last few days and see if they can find anything that may be useful," the chief says.

"Already thought of that, Dad." He looks at his father. "Great minds think alike." He walks out of the control room to make a call to Colonel Gorman.

CHAPTER 29

Rees, Farnsworth, and O'Toole make their way towards the town of Hendricks Hill. They stop well short of the town and continue on foot, careful to not run into any Confederate patrols. They stop just on the outskirts and see a large contingency of Union troops milling around. The three men mount their horses and trot their way into town. They are completely ignored by most of the other soldiers and townsfolk. Just more troops wandering about.

Rees looks over to his left and sees the store he had visited the first time here. The window has been replaced, and he can see inside. Mr. Olsen stands behind the counter, working. Sarah, his daughter, comes out the front door. She stands on the stoop with her arms across her chest, staring at the passing soldiers as if daring them to speak to her. As Rees passes, he smiles and tips his hat.

Sarah just sets her jaw and lifts it in a challenge, then suddenly she relaxes somewhat, and her face relaxes as she tilts her head, studying Rees. Realization dawns on her as her mouth drops open and her arms fall to her side. Rees turns his head back around so as not to face her as she stares at him. Rees bites his lip to keep from laughing.

They ride on through the town until they find what they believe is a Union headquarters tent. The tent is large and has two sentries out front. The three men stop in front and dismount.

Farnsworth approaches one of the sentries, who salutes. Farnsworth returns the salute.

"Might I ask if you are part of the General Burnside expedition?"

"Yes, sir, we are," the sentry answers, staring at the large officer.

"Is this Brigadier General John Foster's tent?"

"Yes, sir, it is."

"With my compliments to the general, would you be so obliged to give him this letter and tell him Colonel Farnsworth and company would like to speak with him," Farnsworth asks the sentry and gives him a copy of the letter addressed by Lincoln and Stanton.

The sentry takes the letter and goes into the tent. Farnsworth can hear the murmur of conversation but can't make out what is said. Suddenly, the tent flap is thrown open, and a heavily sideburned man with a thick mustache wearing Union blue pants and a dingy white shirt with suspenders comes outside. Farnsworth recognizes the man from old photographs but doesn't let on he knows this is General Foster. The man looks Farnsworth over, then looks at Rees and O'Toole.

Farnsworth snaps off a salute, and the general gives a half-hearted salute in return. The general looks at the letter and holds it up.

"What in the blazes is this? Who are you, and what do you want?" the general asks gruffly.

"Begging you're pardon, General. We're not needing much of anything, just some information if you have a few minutes to spare?" Farnsworth asks.

The general looks at the letter again, then back at Farnsworth.

"Well, I wouldn't want to be impolite to an officer who is apparently working for the President of these United State and the Secretary of War. Come on in," he tells the men and goes back into the tent.

Rees and O'Toole dismount and follow Farnsworth into the tent, and Rees notices the surprised looks on the sentry's faces as he passes. He knows there's going to be some rumors flying around the camp tonight.

Once they enter the tent, they are introduced to two other officers, who are there regarding other matters. The general dismisses them and tells them to come back later. They both salute and walk out of the tent, eyeing the three newcomers as they pass.

"Can I offer you men a drink or coffee?" the general asks, then looks at O'Toole and his rank. He doesn't say anything but raises his eyebrows. Farnsworth and Rees both notice, and Farnsworth assures the general that O'Toole is also working directly for the president and declines his offer of a drink.

"General Foster, we are trying to catch up to a Maryland brigade we assumed passed through here."

The general looks at Farnsworth, tapping a finger to his lips, looking upwards, then nods. "Yes, a Maryland brigade was here, but they are on their way to Alabama or Mississippi, I believe. They helped us out a bit with a battle a few days ago, then went on their way. I do know that some of their cavalry units were separated and sent on a different mission towards Fayetteville. I'm assuming you're looking for the cavalry since you are cavalry yourself?" the general asks, trying to get some information out of the men.

Farnsworth smiles. "I can assure you, General, we are cavalry. Just on a special mission we can't talk about. But be assured, we won't be bothering you or your men. We just need the information you gave us."

The general eyes Farnsworth. "You talk like a Reb, Colonel."

Rees looks at Farnsworth, who is still smiling. "Yes, sir, I probably do. I was born in Kentucky but moved north when I was young. Spent most of my time in New York. Went to West Point, engineering. War broke out, I stayed with the Union."

The general breaks into a smile. "Well, I'll be. I'm an engineer myself. Good to see another. I think we make better officers, don't you?" he asks with his smile growing wider.

"Yes, sir, I do at that," Farnsworth replies.

"Well, if there is anything else I can do for you men, just let me know."

"I thank you, General, but information is all we require at this time," Farnsworth answers.

The general nods and reaches his hand out and shakes Farnsworth's. "Well, good luck, and I hope your mission is a success. And I hope it's something that will help end this damnable war."

"I do, too, sir. Thank you for the help."

The general laughs. "Hell, I didn't do much, but you're welcome. If you happen to see those two officers who were here earlier, would you send them to me?"

"Yes, sir, we will," Farnsworth answers and turns to leaves. Rees and O'Toole salute and exit the tent. The three men saddle up and make their way to the west through the Union encampment outside the town.

"You really from Kentucky?" Rees asks once they are out of earshot from everyone else.

Farnsworth chuckles. "Hell no. I was born in Fort Benning, Georgia. My dad was US Army stationed there. I ain't never been to New York, much less West Point. Really, West Point? Yuck."

Rees laughs, and O'Toole just looks at the two men, not quite sure what is going on.

CHAPTER 30

Colonel Gorman, OSI commander Area 51, is on video conference with Colonel Black and Chief Black.

"The lab technician went over the video frame by frame. I have sent you a section of video you may find interesting. Call me if you need anything else, John," he says and disconnects.

The face of Colonel Gorman is replaced with the emblem of OSI for a few seconds, then begins running a section of the security video. Both men watch for a few minutes. Chief Black stands up and shakes his head.

"Goddammit, I knew it. That sneaky little captain planted the virus. I'll kick his Special Ops ass all the way back to MacDill!" he cries out.

Colonel Black is silent, watching the rest of the video until it cuts out, then watches it again.

"But why would he implant a virus in the first place, to what end, other than to destroy the project. If that was his intent, then why didn't it work? I mean, the lieutenant said the virus had been reprogrammed to only fuss with the system, not destroy it. I can't see him doing this on his own. It would have been almost impossible for him to be assigned to this project in the first place unless he had help. So, it stands to reason that he is working for someone else," the colonel says, still studying the video. I also want to know what he and that NCO were talking about."

"I'll tell you who he's working for. That damn senator we trust so much. He's the one who put the man inside here, so it's reasonable to think he had him plant the virus."

The colonel looks up. "But why?"

The chief raises his hands in surrender, "I have no clue. Maybe he's bat-shit crazy. Maybe he's running some type of scam to get himself moved on up in Washington. He could be telling the president that this project is just spending too much money, and a failure would give him a reason to shut us down and save some taxpayer dimes. I don't know, John, I'm just spit-balling here."

The colonel stops watching the video and stands up. "No, Dad, that makes sense, but I would be more comfortable having some facts first. We're just starting this investigation, and I intend to get to the bottom of it. I just hope the senator is not involved. He has been a strong advocate of this project for years. Makes no sense that he would want to jeopardize it now."

"I agree. Like I said, I was spit-balling an idea of why. It could be a number of things, and you're right. Facts. But right now, our main concern is getting Clio fully operational. I'm confident the team is okay. I don't know why, but I am. They are probably having the time of their lives. Or at least I hope they are," the chief says, looking at the colonel, who is again watching the video.

~   ~   ~

"Yaa! Faster horse! Faster!" Rees screams as he leans forward in the saddle, urging the animal to run faster. He chances a glance behind him and sees Farnsworth and O'Toole both galloping as fast as he is and hears them urging their steeds on as well. He can also hear the yells and screams of the Confederate cavalry giving chase.

"Get to the trees!" Farnsworth yells, and Rees turns back around and sees a large grove of trees several hundred feet just to the right of him. He pulls the reins slightly, and the animal moves in the right direction as smooth as driving a car.

Before he can get to cover, he hears Farnsworth scream a curse behind him, "Arrrrghh! Motherfucker!" and takes a quick glance to see Farnsworth leaning forward in the saddle, gritting his teeth in obvious pain.

As Rees faces forward, Farnsworth aims his pistol to his rear and hears the report of the weapon discharging, as well as the popping sound of weapons fire from the Rebel cavalry giving chase.

Rees reaches the trees and pulls up on the reins, causing the horse to skid, throwing up dirt and grass as it tries to stop. Before the animal is completely still, Rees dismounts and reaches for his rifle in the scabbard at the same time. He gets his hand on the rifle and gets his boot caught in the stirrup, causing him to lose his balance. He lands on his backside, cursing the entire time. Still cursing himself, he manages to hang onto his weapon and yanks it out of the scabbard. Now mumbling to himself, he rolls over and scrambles for a tree to use as cover.

He aims at the lead Reb even before Farnsworth and O'Toole are inside the tree line. Using the tree to steady himself, Rees takes a deep breath, relaxes, and squeezes the trigger. The rifle shoots the 5.56 round true and straight, striking the lead cavalryman in the throat. The man careens backwards out of the saddle, grabbing his throat as bright red blood spurts between his fingers and splays through the air and onto the soldiers following him.

The rest of the Rebel cavalry continues the charge. By now, Farnsworth and O'Toole are in the tree line and quickly and smoothly dismount their horses. Taking similar positions behind trees, they aim at the charging men and their mounts.

Farnsworth and Rees have the modified rifles, O'Toole doesn't, and his first shot misses. He quickly pulls down the lever, and another round is injected. Though not as fast a weapon as the other two men have, it's still better than a musket. Rees and Farnsworth fire semi-auto with thirty-round magazines, making quick work of the galloping enemy.

The Confederate cavalrymen are no match. Rees and Farnsworth's shots almost always hit a target, and before they know it, eight more dead soldiers lie on the ground, along with one horse. The rest of the soldiers stop, turn, and flee, taking potshot into the trees as they retreat. One more soldier falls as O'Toole takes a shot and sees an impact in the back of the gray uniform and watches as the man falls forward in the saddle as he is carried away by his horse. Even though the man still maintains his balance, he is more than likely dead.

Rees and Farnsworth switch out their modified magazines and watch and wait for the cavalry to return. Rees snorts with laughter.

"Bet they weren't expecting that. Three Union troops taking out eight or more of their men."

O'Toole looks over at the two men, shaking his head.

"How in the world did you reload that fast? There's no way I can shoot that many times in that short of time, Spencer or not. You two ain't natural," he says, shaking his head.

Farnsworth looks back around the tree he uses as cover and grimaces, then grins at O'Toole. "It's okay, Andy. We're cheating. Some of the future stuff we have that you don't. Still, you got a righteous kill with that last shot."

O'Toole continues shaking his head and whispers, "Damn Devil work there."

"Naw, Andy, God's on our side." Farnsworth replies with a grin

Rees pulls out his binoculars, then looks at Farnsworth, studying him. "You going to be okay?"

Farnsworth nods, throwing his shoulders back. "I'm fine. Just hurts like hell. But I bet it doesn't hurt as much as your pride does right now from falling off your horse."

"I didn't fall off my horse," Rees says, flinching with a snort.

"I would say you took a tumble off that horse, sir, cannot be denying it," O'Toole chimes in.

Rees looks at one man, and then the other, trying to say something, "Well. Well. Just shut up, both of you," he says, waving his hand at them before scanning the area where the Reb cavalry rode off to.

"I don't see any sign of them. They probably think there are more than three of us in these woods. I don't believe we'll be seeing them again.

Farnsworth stands and walks to the edge of the tree line, rotating his left arm. One of the Rebel soldier's rounds struck him in the upper left shoulder. The bullet-resistant uniform did its job and stopped the ball from penetrating, but the force of the round was still enough to cause severe pain, like being hit with a hammer.

"I think you're right. We're good for now, but I don't want to hang around in case they decide to come back with friends and bigger guns if you know what I mean?" he says, the corner of his mouth turning up in a half-smile, eyebrows raised

Rees nods. "I hear ya." He takes a sip of water from his canteen. "Let me take a look at your shoulder," he tells Farnsworth.

"Naw, I'm okay. Gonna have a bruise, I'm sure," he replies, removing his coat and looking where the round struck. There is a small indentation, but the material held. He holds it up for the others to see and smiles. "One for Captain Epstein. Gonna have to buy the man a beer when we get back," he says as he slips the coat back on, wincing.

Rees walks over to his horse and pours some water into his hat so it can have a drink. Farnsworth and O'Toole follow suit. Once the animals have had enough water, they mount up.

"You need some help getting on the horse, Rees?" Farnsworth asks and hears O'Toole snort.

Rees gives Farnsworth the middle finger. "Sir." He points at O'Toole. "That's insubordination, trooper," he says and climbs on his horse hiding his grin. O'Toole snorts again but restrains himself when he sees the stern look Rees give him.

The team begins a slow gait deeper into the forest, away from any other trouble, they hope.

CHAPTER 31

Senator Olsen sits in his jet, wondering what is going on at the Bank. He knows that Operation Ameliorate was initiated, and he is hoping he isn't being asked to come there because something went wrong.

Olsen decided long ago that he would help the Clio Project in any way he could, but when it came time for the missions to begin, he would stay away. Not because he wanted to distance himself in case something went wrong, but because he always felt it was best to let those who know what they're doing run the show without interference from him. His job is to get the funding, backing, and support of the government. The personnel at the Bank are responsible for Clio and her operation. They don't need a senator standing over their shoulders micromanaging them.

His jet lands, and he is quickly escorted to the Bank. He passes through the checkpoints and makes his way to Colonel Black's office. One of the escorts opens the door leading into Sam's office, and he walks in with a mirthless smile.

"Good morning, Sam," he says when he sees her.

"Good morning, Senator," Sam says back with a humorless smile.

The senator stops in front of her desk, and Sam announces he is there. The colonel responds, and Sam informs the senator he may go in. He thanks Sam and opens the office door.

"Please, tell me I'm here because you have had a successful mission and you both want to thank me personally for my support," a smiling Olsen says, walking over to shake hands.

Both the chief and colonel shake his hand, but not warmly. The colonel points to a chair, which Olsen adjusts then sits. He leans back and crosses his legs, trying to act relaxed but not feeling it. Colonel Black goes back behind his desk, which is not a good indicator as the senator sees it. This is official. The colonel sits and leans his elbows on the desk. The chief sits in a chair next to Olsen and scoots it a little so he can face the man. Olsen doesn't care for the vibes in the room.

"Okay, gentlemen, I'm not getting a warm fuzzy feeling from either of you. Spill it. What's wrong?"

The colonel looks first at his father, then to the senator.

"Sir, how well do you know Captain Farnsworth?"

The senator wasn't expecting this question. To be honest, he didn't know what he expected.

"Let me see, my wife introduced him to me about a year ago. She said she knew his father a long ago, a Special Forces type, I believe. We were in Florida, at MacDill Air Force Base on an inspection, and she introduced him to me. She seemed quite taken by the young man, as was I. He's very personable, bright, in great shape, had the right amount of citations and medals to ensure he moves up in rank quickly. He's the type who could even make it in politics, I'm sure. I spoke with his CO, and he was highly qualified for this assignment. All his test scores are superb, exemplary evaluations. I don't know. What are you looking for?" Olsen finishes with a question.

"No, sir. I want to know how well you *really* know him," the colonel asks more sternly than he wanted it to come across.

The senator notices and cocks his head.

"Why, Colonel? Why the third degree? What is going on? I have always backed you and this project and, for some reason, I'm getting the feeling I'm being placed under the spotlight. You get my meaning, sir?" he asks, his face becoming slightly red, his body tensing.

Chief Black jumps in.

"Senator, we have a problem," he begins, and the colonel interrupts.

"Dad."

Chief Black raises his hand at his son. "No, let's give the good senator the benefit of the doubt here," he says to the surprise of Colonel Black.

The senator squints his eyes at the chief, yanking on his suit jacket as he squares his shoulders.

"Alright, Colonel, Chief, out with it. Apparently, you two think I've done something, and it must involve Captain Farnsworth."

The colonel sighs. "Yes, it does," he says, then pushes a button that opens the blinds so they can look into the control room. The senator stands, walks to the large window, and looks at the blank screen.

"I thought you ran a mission with Rees, Farnsworth, and O'Toole?"

"We did, Senator. And as far as we can guess, they are where they should be. But we don't know for certain," the colonel says to his back as he, too, stands.

"Okay, what? Why isn't it showing on screen?" the senator asks, turning to look at the colonel, who has moved beside him, then the chief, who is still seated.

"We were sabotaged," the chief answers, and this causes the senator to turn in surprise.

He's either genuinely surprised or he the greatest actor I ever saw, the chief thinks.

"Sabotage? Who? When. What happened?" the senator rapidly blurts out the questions.

The colonel turns on the large screen television on the wall in his office.

"Senator, you need to see this," he says and types a few strokes into his computer keyboard, and the OSI emblem appears on the screen, then is swiftly replaced by a video showing the control room. It flashes a date from a few days' past, 0136 hours.

The video shows the third shift of scientists and technicians working. People moving about, talking, watching monitors, checking readouts. The picture has the door to the corridor in view, and you can see when Captain Farnsworth enters. He walks in, looking around saying hello to everyone he comes across, and makes his way to one of the control stations. The technician, a Master Sergeant, turns in his chair and talks with the captain.

They have what seems to be a tense conversation for a few minutes. The captain says something the sergeant doesn't seem to care for as his hand grips the chair handle. His back goes rigid, as well as his jaw, and he stares at the captain, unflinching. The sergeant abruptly stands and looks at his watch while shaking his head. The captain says something else, and the sergeant storms away from his station out of view of the camera.

Captain Farnsworth quickly pulls a flash drive from his pocket. Inserting it into the computer and typing in a command. A few seconds later, he removes the drive and pockets it. The sergeant returns with a sheet of paper and shows it to the captain. They seem to argue, then the captain raises his hands in surrender, backing away. The NCO stares at the captain's back until the officer is out of the room, then he returns to his station.

"Okay. What did I just see?" the senator asks, turning back to the two men, looking for an answer.

The chief walks back to his chair and sits, watching the two men. Colonel Black faces the senator.

"Senator Olsen, when Operation Ameliorate was initiated, a virus was introduced into the programming, causing a major disruption of the communications. No visual, no audio. Further, it was discovered the virus was originally intended to destroy Clio. Completely. But for some unknown reason, the virus was altered. It was made to only disable Clio for a short time, at least until we can complete repairs. The virus is being wiped as we speak, and Clio should be up and running today."

The senator looks relieved, and the more the chief watches, the more he thinks the man has nothing to do with the sabotage.

"So, that's a good thing?" he asks, tilting his head at the colonel.

"Yes, sir, that's the good news. The bad news is you just saw who we think implanted the virus into the system in the first place," the colonel says, pointing to the screen, which repeats the scene.

The senator looks and points at the television screen. "You're telling me Captain Farnsworth is the saboteur? Bullshit," he states, rolling his eyes and turning away.

"Yes, sir. As of right now, the man we think attempted to destroy Clio is out there on a mission with Sergeant Rees and Corporal O'Toole doing God knows what."

The senator snorts and walks away. "That makes no sense. Why? For what purpose? He must have known he was on camera."

"No idea. We don't have enough to go by, but from what we know so far, he's the number one suspect. We talked with Sergeant Danner, the NCO at the console. He said Captain Farnsworth wanted some interworking information on Clio that he couldn't give him. He said they argued, and he told Farnsworth to get authorization for the information, then printed a copy of an authorization form for him.”

The chief, who has been silent during the exchange, breaks in, “Senator, you said your wife introduced you to him?”

The senator nods. “Yes, like I said, about a year ago. Why?”

The chief shakes his head. “Nothing, sir, just wanted to clarify.”

The senator’s face goes red. “Don’t fucking involve my wife in this, Chief. You don’t want to do that,” he says and takes a step towards the chief.

“And you, sir, don’t want to take another step towards me,” the chief says, his eyes narrowed in warning.

The senator thinks better of it, knowing the chief, even at his age, would probably kick his ass, even though he is in good shape himself.

“Your wife’s not involved, Senator. That’s not why we asked. We just wanted to know how you know him. That’s all. Right, Dad?” the colonel asks, looking at his father with a hard smile.

The chief nods. “That’s all, Senator.”

“Okay, well then, what is the next step?”

The colonel walks back to the window. “We get Clio back up and running, see what the team is up to. If they are still on mission, we will monitor them and, hopefully, make contact. We will let the scenario play out and keep an eye on Captain Farnsworth. I’m sure the team is wondering what has happened, but Rees has no idea Farnsworth sabotaged the system. He is aware, though, we had doubts about Farnsworth.”

This causes the senator to look sharply at the colonel. “What?”

“We had some misgivings about the captain, so we instructed Rees to be wary of him. Keep vigilant,” the colonel says reassuringly.

The senator takes everything in and decides he has had enough of this meeting. "Okay, we good here? I hope I'm off the hook. I have done nothing but support this endeavor for years. And I sure as hell would not put a saboteur in the works to fuck it up. Good God," he quips then looks at his watch. "I've got to get back. But, please, keep me posted. If you need anything, let me know, day or night. This project is too important to fail," the senator says, looking at each man. He shakes the colonel's hand and moves to the chief, who stands and shakes his hand. They lock eyes for a second, then the senator releases his grip and walks towards the door, turning back toward them before opening it.

"Again, gentlemen, my wife is off-limits," he warns as he leaves.

The colonel and chief look at each other, and the chief smirks. "Yeah, right."

CHAPTER 32

The large screen flickers, trying to come back online, occasionally showing a picture, then disappearing. The technicians and programmers work frantically, adjusting controls, and watching monitors. People talk all at the same time, voices overlapping until it is just white noise coming over the speakers in the colonel's office.

The colonel and chief watch the activity going on below, growing inpatient. Finally, the colonel grabs the phone, which is immediately picked up in the control room.

"Major Donnelly, what the hell is going on? I was told the virus had been cleaned out and that the system would be up and running. I'm not seeing that."

The major looks up at the colonel. "Sorry, sir. I was told that the virus was thought to be gone, but somehow it managed to hide a subroutine that is trying to foul up the works again. The technicians tell me they can correct it, but the damn thing is being elusive. Once they think they have it cornered, it pops up somewhere else. They say it's like playing Whack-A-Mole. That's why we're only getting glimpses from a camera."

"Okay, Major, just keep at it, and let me know the minute they get rid of that damn thing and can get my comms back up," the colonel tells the man and hangs up the phone, not even listening to the major. He shakes his head, and the chief just watches him.

"John, they are doing what they can. Look at the bright side, at least we know the men are alive."

The chief refers to the intermediate shots they received from the flickering screen. They can't make out great details, but they can tell from the quick glimpses allowed them that the team is alive and riding their horses through the woods. Where, exactly, is still a mystery.

"Yes, that's true, thankfully. But you're right, we have some of the best people in the world working on this," the colonel says, staring at the flickering, flashing screen.

He walks over to get a cup of coffee and attempt to relax. Fretting about this isn't doing anyone any good, even though it goes against his nature.

His intercom buzzes, and he answers, "Yes, Sam?"

"Sir, Sergeant Rees' flight members are here to see you," she informs the colonel.

The chief smiles, and the colonel tells her to have them come in. The door opens, and Rees' entire squad of flight members file into the office.

"Well, good afternoon," the colonel says. "To what do we owe the pleasure?"

MSgt Bouvier salutes and walks further into the room. The chief shakes his hand and says hello to the rest of the men, as does the colonel.

"Just wanted to see if there is anything we can do to help, sir. We're naturally worried and want you to know we're available."

The colonel eyes the group of first time-travelers and nods. "I understand the frustration, believe me, I do. We're working on it as fast as possible," he says, then points to the screen. "As you can see, it's wanting to come online but, so far, this is all we're getting. I was told they're still having problems with the virus. Shouldn't be too much longer, and then we will know more."

"What about Captain Farnsworth?" Kriger asks.

This takes the colonel and chief by surprise.

"What do you mean?" the colonel asks, but he and the chief gave away their poker faces when the question was asked.

"Sorry, sir, we weren't sure, but we just didn't trust the man since he was brought on board, and by both of your reactions to the question, I think you aren't, either. We should have been the ones going with Sergeant Rees if anyone was going to," he explains, then adds, "sir."

The colonel and chief look at each other, and the chief scratches his cheek.

"Yes, we're not in the trusting mood right now ourselves, Sergeant Kriger, men. This stays in this room, got it?" the chief asks, looking at each man in turn. They all agree. "We have evidence that shows the captain placing a flash drive into one of the computers. We believe he inserted a virus, which is what has caused these problems."

"That sonofabitch!" Shepard grumbles loudly.

"We don't know why he did it, and we don't believe he acted alone. We're investigating as we speak, and we have OSI coming in to interview every person involved with the project," he says and looks at each of the men again. "That includes you guys as well."

"Well, fuck that, sir," Tosseti says in a loud, accented voice. "That's our sergeant out there, our friend, and you know we didn't do anything to jep…jep… What the hell?" he stumbles.

"Jeopardize," Green tells him.

"Yeah, that. Jeopardize the mission or him and Andy, or the captain for that matter, though if I get my hands on that…" Tosseti complains without finishing.

"Just a formality, Sergeant. You aren't under suspicion, but they have to talk with everyone," the chief says, watching Tosseti's face turn red.

Colonel Black steps towards the men. "Listen, just keep monitoring your channels. You men are the only ones who have access to what we have. When we know something, you will know something. Just keep watching. If you need anything, let Sam know. She will ensure you get it, or she will contact us, and we will make sure you get it. Okay?"

The small group of men nod and acknowledge what the colonel just said.

"Now, guys, if you don't mind, we're busy, and I'm sure there are things you have to do," he says, ending the conversation and watching as the men file back out of the office.

"Master Sergeant Bouvier, Tech Sergeant Kriger, please, stay behind. There's something we would like to discuss with you," the colonel tells the two men before they can leave.

Once the last man has left and closes the door, the colonel looks at the two men, and the chief walks over.

"You guys are ready to help? Okay, here's what I need from you two."

~ ~ ~

When Bouvier and Kriger leave the room, Colonel Black goes behind his desk and sits. The chief finds his chair, doing the same.

"Contingency?" the chief asks.

"Contingency," the colonel answers. "Plus, that'll give them something constructive to do to get their minds off this. To a point, anyway."

"Good idea. I should have thought about it," the chief says, grinning.

"That's why they made me a colonel. Just wait until I make general, then you'll really be impressed."

Both men chuckle, and the phone on the colonel's desk buzzes. He picks it up and turns in his chair to look at whoever called him. He doesn't get that far as his eye catches sight of the control room screen. The chief sees it also, quickly standing and moving to the window to get a better view.

The screen shows a full-color picture of two Union-clad men on horseback. They can tell the person directly in front of the camera is Corporal O'Toole but can't see in front of him. At least they know all three men are alive.

"Talk to me, Major," the colonel says into the phone.

"Sir, as you can see, we have visual, but no audio. Yet. We're still working on it. The virus is almost gone, and when they finish, we hope to have audio."

"Okay, Major. Good work. Tell your team good job, and let me know as soon as it is up. This is good, though, very good."

"Thank you, sir, we'll get it done," the major answers.

"Major, please split the screen so we can get a camera shot from Rees and Farnsworth, please."

"Yes, sir," the major answers and covers the mouthpiece as he tells a technician something Colonel Black can't hear. A second later, the screen is split in two, and on one half is the same picture they were watching before, and the second screen shows the back of a horse's head. While they watch, the camera from the second screen moves as the rider turns in his saddle to look back. The screen shows Corporal O'Toole and Captain Farnsworth. Then the rider turns back forward.

"Okay, that's Rees in front. Now, we have some clarity on who is who," the chief says.

"Okay, thank God they are alive. Now, we need to know where they are. Any Idea?" the colonel asks his father, who just shakes his head and studies the video. "I'm going down," the colonel says and heads for the door, with his father in tow.

Both men enter the control room and walk directly to Major Donnelly's station.

"Any idea where they are, Major," Colonel Black asks as he approaches.

"Yes, sir," the major answers. "We believe they are about fifteen miles west of the Town of Hendricks Hill. The GPS isn't working, but we can get a good idea from the camera reception. Triangulation of a sort."

The room is abuzz with activity as technicians, scientists, and other military personnel go about their assigned job. The colonel and chief watch the people working, and both think the same thing, about how proud they are of the team they have assembled. Except for Captain Farnsworth, of course.

Watching the screen, they can tell the men are conversing with each other, and they wish they could hear what they were saying.

~ ~ ~

"You're telling me you haven't seen *Stargate SG-1,* yet?" Farnsworth asks.

"No, I haven't had time. Damn, you know how many movies, TV shows, books, news programs I haven't had time to catch up on?" Rees replies. "I do have a job, as well as classes and training. Not to mention I've been busy getting ready for this little adventure."

Farnsworth laughs. "Ah, man, you got to watch it. It beats *Star Trek* hands down, and it's Air Force! Too bad it went off the air."

"I won't allow blasphemy in my presence, Colonel," Rees tells him, grinning.

"I do not know what you two are jawing about? I never know what you two are jawing about. I cannot wait to get back to people I know so I can carry on a decent conversation about something I know about," O'Toole cuts in.

Rees and Farnsworth chuckle at the man's statement, then Rees starts singing, "Free Bird," to the groans of Farnsworth.

"Can't you a least sing something from the 21ˢᵗ Century?"

O'Toole looks back at Farnsworth, and in his slight brogue accent, says, "Colonel, I kinda like the tune."

~ ~ ~

"What is that?" a lieutenant says, holding his headphones close to his ear. Another lieutenant grabs his headset and listens in.

"Oh, shit!" he exclaims and types a few strokes on his keyboard, and the screen speakers come to life.

The colonel, major, and chief turn as one to look at the screen. The entire room follows suit, and they all listen as a not very pleasant voice is heard singing an off-key version of "Free Bird" over the speakers.

"Hot damn, we have audio," the chief announces to the small group around him.

"Good job, everyone. Now, get in contact with them. I want to speak with them right now!" the colonel demands of the lieutenants manning the audio stations.

The two men work feverishly to find a frequency that will allow them to contact the time travelers. After several minutes go by, the colonel shakes his head.

"Gentlemen, what's the problem?" he asks, tension in his voice.

"Sorry, sir," the young 1st Lieutenant says. "We can hear them, but for some reason, they can't hear us."

"Why not?" the colonel asks, moving to stand over the seated officers.

"I'm not sure, Colonel. We have open airwaves, and the frequencies are correct. We should be able to talk with them, but…but there's nothing." The lieutenant's eyebrows draw together as he stares at his console.

The colonel takes a breath and pats the younger man on the shoulder. "Just keep at it," he tells the men in a softer tone and moves back to the chief and major.

"John," the chief says, looking in thought. The colonel moves closer to him, as does the major. "We had this same problem forty years ago. We could see and hear them perfectly, but they couldn't hear us. If you remember from my reports, we had to send a cassette tape recording through Clio to them so we could explain what we were doing. Maybe there is some time fluctuation that doesn't allow us to send radio signals to them. I don't know. When we rebuilt Clio, we didn't do any experiments or real research into the matter. My fault. Should have thought about that," he says, staring off in the distance.

"No, not your fault. We all should have done more research into this aspect of the project. One of those we *assume* situations. We'll figure something out," the colonel says to the group, then picks up a phone at the major's station and presses a button that turns on the loudspeakers.

"May I have your attention, please? Thank you. As you can see, we have a picture, and we can hear the team. We are having a problem contacting them, though. I ask that everyone try to think of a solution to this problem. I don't care if it's a short-term solution or not. We need to contact the team and inform them we are here. If anyone has any ideas, I don't care how dumb you think it may be or how insignificant it may seem, you contact me or the chief directly. Thank you again." The colonel hangs the phone up and turns towards the major. "Major, if anyone has anything, I mean anything, I want to know. We will decide what is important or not, understood?"

"Yes, sir, understood," the major answers.

The colonel and chief head back up to the colonel's office. When they get to the outer office door, the colonel opens it for the chief to enter.

"Contingency time?" the chief asks as he passes his son.

"Contingency time," the colonel replies.

CHAPTER 33

Rees raises his hand for the team to stop. Farnsworth and O'Toole ride up beside Rees. Before either can ask what is going on, they understand. Off in the distance, the sound of artillery rumbles.

"Let go look for some trouble," Farnsworth says.

"That's not really why we're here now, is it?" Rees questions. "We're to get Andy back to his unit."

Farnsworth smiles. "Well, who's to say his unit isn't where that battle is."

O'Toole looks from one man to the other. "Could be, sir. The general did say part of my brigade broke off to help some other company, didn't he?"

"You're the colonel, Captain," Rees responds, throwing a hand up in resignation.

Farnsworth laughs. "That's the spirit. A little adventure is good for the soul. Plus, now I'll get to see a real battle." He urges his horse to a trot towards the sound of rolling thunder.

Rees shakes his head. "Not what you expect," he says to himself and follows.

They go at a fast pace and come to two small hills and stop short of them. The men dismount, and Rees and Farnsworth grab their binoculars and walk towards the saddle between the hills. When in position, they drop and crawl the rest of the way. Once cresting the saddle, they remove their hats, then using their elbows for support, they steady the binoculars and scope then begin scanning the area in front of them. Farnsworth winces at the pain in his shoulder. Rees watches him.

"You okay?"

"Yeah, just hurts like the devil."

"Would have hurt a lot more if you weren't wearing that specialized uniform," Rees says, binoculars up to his eyes.

Farnsworth snorts, then watches the activity below them.

What they witness takes Farnsworth's breath away and still amazes Rees. Though Rees has seen the magnitude of the armies fighting, he didn't get a chance to watch from a safe distance as the two armies attacked. He was too busy trying to keep him and his men alive.

A line of Union cannon is poised for battle, aligned side by side with men holding lanyards taut with one hand while covering their ear nearest the pieces with the other. Behind them are sergeants watching a commander on horseback. The commander looks downrange, and Farnsworth turns his binoculars to follow his line of sight. He stops when he sees what the Union commander looks at.

A Confederate brigade of cannon points towards the commander's cannon, all placed behind barricades. They, too, have a commander on horseback, galloping up and down the ranks. Farnsworth can't hear the man, but he can see he is yelling something. He draws his attention back to the Union side and watches as the commander yells in response and points his saber towards the enemy. A second later, all the cannon spew fire from the barrels, and a brief moment later, he feels and hears the concussion from the blast of each Napoleon.

Farnsworth is enthralled by the sheer power of the older weapons. He again turns his attention towards the Rebel lines and watches as the ground around the barricaded artillery erupts. Geysers of earth fly upwards, obscuring most of the line. He sees one or two explosions behind the barricade and assumes either cannons or caisson have been hit. *Probably fired bolts,* he thinks.

Still watching the Rebel battery, the air clears enough so they can see them fire their cannon in retaliation. The air is filled with screaming shot and rumbling explosions that roll across the landscape. The ground underneath the men shakes and vibrates.

The Union lines are struck by the Confederate shells, and the results are devastating. Several cannons are struck and destroyed, along with their crew. Farnsworth can see men writhing on the ground in obvious pain, many missing limbs. Horses are not spared, either, as a caisson exploded from a direct hit, ripping the carriage apart as well as the animal attached to it. All up and down the line, men scramble to replace their downed comrades.

Rammers swab out cannons, powder and shell are rammed down the barrel as lanyards are inserted and pulled tight, the men awaiting orders to fire again. No one can see the commander, so the sergeants take it upon themselves to fire once a cannon is ready.

The first time the cannons let loose, they were a single blast, now it is a sporadic roar as each crew fires at will.

This continues for some time, both sides killing and being killed with each volley fired.

Rees watches the carnage and shakes his head. He takes his eyes away from the binoculars and gives them to Corporal O'Toole. Rees just watches the scene in front of him without focusing on a single event.

Farnsworth turns and looks at Rees. "My God. What devastation. I've seen battles, but not like this. They are so close. They can't be more than two thousand yards away from each other! With the weapons we have now, we would have wiped them out in about thirty seconds. How could men just stand there like that, what bravery," he says, his voice loud, senses heightened as he quickly returns his attention to the onslaught.

Rees just watches Farnsworth for a few seconds, amazed at the man's excitement. "We need to get around this. I don't see any cavalry around here. This line must go further northwest. This wasn't the artillery we heard coming up here."

Farnsworth nods. "Yeah, you're right." He adjusts his telescope to look northwest. "I just make out smoke in that direction, maybe another battle."

"We don't want to get caught up in that mess down there," Rees says. "Can't go in that direction, of course," Rees says, gesturing in the direction of the southern lines.

Farnsworth snorts. "You think?" Then looks back at Rees. "Sorry, just kidding."

The men scoot back from the crest, then stand. When they do, they hear a commotion coming from the bottom of the hill. They see Confederate cavalrymen approaching rapidly. The three men race down the hill, trying to get to their horses before the gray-clad horse soldiers get to them. Just when they reach their mounts, they hear gunfire, and dirt flies up in front of them where the round strikes. Before they can get on their horses, they are surrounded. Pistols are aimed at them from several Rebel soldiers. A captain trots up and looks at the men. He sees the rank on Farnsworth's uniform and salutes.

"Colonel, I'm captain Schneider, 1st North Carolina Cavalry Regiment, Company H, and you, sir, and your men are my prisoners. Now, if'n you would be so kind as to unbuckle them belts and drop your hog legs to the ground, I would be much obliged," the bearded officer says, leaning on his saddle horn and staring at Farnsworth.

O'Toole has his Spencer rifle in his hands and tries to bring it up. Rees sees this and places his hand on the barrel and shakes his head. The Rebel captain smiles.

"That's right smart of you, Captain. No sense in dying today. Now, do as I ask and unarm. That includes you, too, Corporal."

One of the Rebel cavalrymen climbs off his horse and walks over to O'Toole, snatching the rifle from him. Admiring the weapon, he grins, then uses the butt to slam it into O'Toole's midsection. O'Toole *grumps* and bends over, clutching his stomach, then drops to his knees. Rees and Farnsworth both instinctively attempt to defend the fallen man.

"Ah, ah, ah, ah, Colonel. Stay where you are," the captain tells them, then looks at the soldier still holding the Spencer.

"Corporal Clancy. These men are our prisoners. You do something like that again, and I will make you an infantryman and send you packing. Act like a civilized person," he berates the corporal, who acknowledges the reprimand and apologizes to the captain.

"I'm sorry, Colonel. We don't treat our prisoners like that," he tells Farnsworth, then orders a couple of his troopers to tie the prisoner's hands and get them on their horses. Two men dismount and grab ropes, then proceed to tie the hands of the Union-clad soldiers. Once bound, each man is helped into their saddles, and the procession moves south towards the Confederate lines and towards what awaits them, they do not know.

~ ~ ~

Colonel Black and the chief watch the scene unfold on the screen. They get a full view of the carnage the bodycams showed between the north and south artillery blasting each other. They then watch in shock and dismay as the three men are captured by Rebel troopers. This is not good, not at all, and there is nothing they can do to help. The team is on its own.

Chief Black stands next to his son.

"I'm not worried, John. Think about it, we got a Special Operations officer and a Security Forces sergeant being captured by 19th Century soldiers. I feel sorry for them."

The colonel looks at his father. "I do, too. There's no telling where they will take them, or what they will do with them. Down to Andersonville? I hope not."

The chief snorts. "No, Son, I feel sorry for the Confederate troops who just took them. They are in for a world of hurt."

The colonel turns to look at his smiling father.

"You're joking, right?"

~   ~   ~

A half an hour later, the troopers arrive at their cavalry camp headquarters. The prisoners are taken off their horses and searched. The search is nothing compared to modern-day police searches, just a preliminary search for maps, papers, other weapons. The letters from Lincoln and Stewart are of particular interest to the captain. He reads the letters and looks at the three Union cavalrymen.

"Well, I be damned. We got us some important people here. Special orders from that tyrant Abraham Lincoln himself, and what is this? Secretary of War, Stanton? You boys are *real* important now, ain't cha?" the captain asks, looking at each prisoner one at a time.

He turns to his troopers and tells them to keep an eye on them as he walks off towards a large tent. Rees presumes it belongs to the commander of this unit, and the captain can't wait to tell him who he captured.

A few minutes pass, and the captain and a colonel come out of the tent and walk over. The colonel comes up to Farnsworth and studies him, having to look up into his face as Farnsworth towers over the man. Hell, he *and* Rees both practically tower over everyone.

"Colonel, my name is Colonel James Gordon. To whom do I have the pleasure of speaking with?" the man asks.

Farnsworth looks down at the bearded man.

"Colonel Gabriel Farnsworth," Farnsworth replies, then nods towards the other two. "And this is Captain Scott Rees and Corporal Andy O'Toole."

Colonel Gordon looks at the two other men and strokes his beard as he walks around, studying them.

"And what outfit are you with, Colonel?" he asks when standing behind the men. "I don't see any regimental emblem or anything that says who you are with. If not for the uniforms, I would say you are spies. What with this letter," Gordon says, holding it up in front of Farnsworth's face, "indicating you are on special assignment for your government?" More of a question than a statement.

"No, Colonel, we are not spies," Farnsworth answers and has to stifle a smirk, thinking *Name, rank, and serial number.*

"Well, just what were you doing on that hill my men found you on? You were apparently doing something up there, watching? Signaling? Just what now, Colonel?" Gordon asks.

"Well, Colonel Gordon, we were looking for a way to get around the battle so we could be on our way," Farnsworth tells him.

"And just where were you going, good sir?"

"Well, Colonel. You want the truth?"

Colonel Gordon moves around in front of Farnsworth and throws out his chest and attempts to stand taller as he moves into Farnsworth's personal space.

"No, Colonel Farnsworth, lie to me. I expect that, anyway."

"Okay, we are trying to get corporal O'Toole back to his home so he can marry his girl before a draft-dodging scoundrel can take her away from him. See, he has to get married so he can make some babies who are vital to the security of this nation."

Rees and O'Toole stare wide-eyed at Farnsworth. Rees is shocked as to the answer, wondering why Farnsworth would say something like that. Not about O'Toole getting back, but about the babies and the future of the nation. What does Farnsworth know, and how?

"Are you mocking me, sir?"

"Not at all, Colonel. But you have to know we can't be telling you what we are doing, just as it would be if our side caught some of your men. You wouldn't want them talking now, would you? Sorry," Farnsworth explains.

The colonel eyes him, then slowly shakes his head. "Alright, be that way, Colonel. I do not have time for this, anyway. I have got a battle to prepare for," he says and turns towards the Reb captain.

"Captain, please have these men taken away and place them in the cage. When you are finished, come to my tent for further orders. We'll be heading to battle as soon as our artillery finishes softening up the Yanks," the colonel orders, then turns back to Farnsworth and Rees. "I'm sorry, Colonel, Captain, but I must place you in captivity with an enlisted man. I do not have the manpower to watch over you separately. I do apologize."

Farnsworth's smiles. "Ain't nothing but a thing," he says and watches as the Rebels squint and look around at each other, Colonel Gordon as well.

Shaking his head, the colonel leaves, and two enlisted men escort the three Union-clad men to a wagon that contains a large iron cage.

"Get on up in there, Yanks," one of the enlisted men tells them. Well, not a man, more of a boy. Small, ragged clothes, bad teeth, peach fuzz on his face.

"How old are you?" Rees asks.

"Old enough to put a bullet in ya, Yank," he gets as an answer. "Now, get on up in there. We ain't get all day now. Go on now. Get!"

The three men climb into the back of the wagon and enter the cage. The young soldier shuts the door behind them and locks it with a large padlock. After securing the cage, the two soldiers turn to walk away. Farnsworth leans against the bars and watches them.

"Ya'll come on now, ya hear!" he says and smiles. The two soldiers turn and stare for a few seconds, then leave.

"Just had to get the last word in, didn't you?" Rees asks, chuckling. Then he notices O'Toole looking around quickly, wiping the palms of his hands on his pants and eyes wide. Farnsworth sees it, too.

"Hey, cheer up. It's not that bad."

O'Toole looks at Farnsworth and Rees.

"Not that bad. We have been captured, now inside a cage in a Rebel camp. You know where they take Union prisoners? Andersonville, that is where. If we even get that far. They might just as well shoot us."

"Hey, Andy, calm down. We're fine. We'll be out of here and on our way soon enough. Just wait until dark. You'll see," Rees tells him.

O'Toole looks at Rees, then at Farnsworth, who is grinning.

"Captain Rees is right, Corporal. Just wait, we'll be out of here and on our way in a few hours." Then he sits down in a corner and lowers his hat over his eyes. Rees pats Andy on the shoulder and winks. Besides, they'd take us to Salisbury, not Andersonville.

"Oh, thank you, Captain, that makes it much better."

Rees looks at O'Toole with his mouth open and starts to ask him if that was a smart ass comeback but decides against it. Instead, he chuckles, then moves into one of the other corners of the cage and sits. Still smiling, he looks at Farnsworth.

"Gabriel? Really?"

CHAPTER 34

Captain Brunell is again walking through the lab, watching personnel working on sequencing DNA strains when he passes Lieutenant Perkins. He stops and notices she is studiously reading her screen.

"Perkins?" he asks. "You got something? You seem intently engrossed with whatever it is on your screen."

The lieutenant jumps when the captain speaks, so engrossed in what she was reading she didn't notice him standing over her.

"Sorry, Perkins, didn't mean to startle you."

"No, sir, that's alright. I was about to call you over, anyway," she replies, "You're not going to believe this?" She points at her screen.

Brunell leans over and reads.

"Lieutenant, what is it with you and these surprises?" the captain asks, shaking his head. He stands up, sighs, and then looks at her. "Print it out for me."

Captain Brunell walks to the room with the printer and waits for the DNA report to print. Once it does, he collects it, reads it, and then shakes his head. He goes into his office and calls Colonel Thompson.

The colonel picks up on the first ring. "Colonel Thompson."

"Colonel, Captain Brunell. If you've got a minute, I have something to show you."

There is a silence on her end for a few seconds. "Another surprise, Captain?" she finally asks.

"Yes, ma'am," Brunell answers.

"Bring it, Captain," she tells him and disconnects.

It only takes a couple of minutes before the captain enters the colonel's office and hands her the sheet of paper. She reads it and looks up at him.

"How long have you had this?" she asks.

"Just a few minutes, ma'am. Lieutenant Perkins just discovered it not more than ten minutes ago."

The colonel is already on the phone and talking to Sam, explaining she needs to see Colonel Black. Hanging up, she stands and heads for the door. "Come with me, Captain," she orders, and he follows her.

A few minutes later, they are standing in front of the colonel's desk. She watches as he reads the DNA report.

The colonel shakes his head and looks at the two officers.

"When it rains it pours?" he says. "Not much we can do about it right now. Thanks for bringing this to me, Colonel, Captain. Good job. I just wish we'd done this sooner."

"I apologize, sir. The tests are generally run for a different reason, so we don't run them as a priority. This was unexpected. I know it's a little late, but I think we will change our SOPs to begin prioritizing anyone brought into the Bank immediately."

Colonel Black looks at Colonel Thompson. "Good idea. Not your fault. Or yours, Captain," he adds, "I should have known to do this after what you discovered earlier about Corporal O'Toole. Thank you, you're dismissed. Oh, and tell Lieutenant Perkins good job if you will, Captain Brunell. Might have to make her a captain and give her your job," he says with a grin.

"Yes, sir. Will do," the captain answers back with a nervous chuckle, but not sure if the colonel is joking or not. Once they depart, the colonel calls down to the control room, and Major Washington picks up.

"Yes, sir?" he answers, looking up.

"Major, the chief down there?"

"Yes, sir. I believe he's over by the Inabular panel helping some of the techs," the major says, straining to look in the direction of the console. "I don't see him, but that's where he was a few minutes ago."

"Okay, Major. I'm coming down, I need to speak with him. If you see him, tell him I'm on my way. Thanks."

He disconnects the call and grabs the sheet of paper and makes his way down to the control room. Once in the room, he stares at the screen and the two pictures there. One frame shows Farnsworth, who looks to be sleeping, and glimpses of O'Toole, who seems to be pacing. The other picture is of Rees sitting in the corner of the cage. Black continues until he finds his father kneeling in front of the Inabular Device console, with a side panel open and a screwdriver in his hand.

"Just can't help yourself, can you, Chief?" the colonel asks as he approaches.

The chief looks up and grins. "Got to keep her in tip-top shape. I just wished they could figure out what was wrong with the audio. Makes no sense to me, virus or no virus." He stands.

The colonel hands him the paper. "Well, here's another nut in the works," he says.

The chief takes the paper, reads it, and smiles. "And the hits just keep on coming. Why is it we didn't know about this beforehand?"

"Just something we didn't think about, but that doesn't matter. We need to get the senator in here right now. He's got some explaining to do."

Suddenly, the screen goes blank. There is a commotion among the technicians, and the colonel and chief turn to see what is happening. It takes them a second to realize there is no longer a picture on the screen.

"Major Washington, what is happening?" Colonel Black shouts from across the room and makes his way towards his station.

The major doesn't answer, as he is already making his way to Lieutenant Lopez's station to find the problem.

"Lieutenant?" he asks calmly, watching her fingers as they fly over her keyboard.

"I think the virus has reactivated, sir. Give me a second, and I should be able to let you know," she says and looks over at Sergeant Coles' monitor. "Kirk, what's it look like?"

The master sergeant also types away, and then stops. He looks at the lieutenant, who stops typing, and he stares at her screen. The major moves closer to Lopez.

"Lieutenant?" he asks again just as Colonel Black and the chief approach.

"What do we have?" the colonel asks, walking up and looking over the lieutenant's shoulder.

Lieutenant Lopez turns in her chair. "Sirs, I've confirmed the virus reactivated and is spreading again. It is playing havoc with our communications. It's not disrupting any of the other systems, just comms. We placed some additional firewalls to prevent it from going into other systems, but the virus just seems intent on disrupting comms, nothing else."

"Dammit. We take one step forward and two steps back. Now, we are completely blind again," the colonel says bitterly. "I'm in a good mind just to terminate the mission and bring them back right now."

This brings a stern look from the chief and worried looks from some of the others. The colonel sees them and shakes his head. "No, I'm not. Just venting," he says and looks at everyone in the immediate area. "Okay, suggestions? Ideas?"

"We can make another attempt at killing the virus," the sergeant says.

"What about a complete wipe of the system?" the major suggests.

The lieutenant shakes her head. "No, sir. That would disrupt the entire systems, and it would take time to recalibrate."

The chief nods in agreement. "She's right. The men could be stranded there for no telling how long waiting for us to bring them back. Anything could happen during that time frame. They might think we abandoned them."

The colonel looks at the lieutenant. "Go ahead and start working on isolating the virus. Again. We can start with that and work from there."

The chief scratches his face and walks away. He goes over to the Inabular Device console and stares at it.

"Chief, what is it?" the colonel asks.

"We have personnel here who can isolate the virus and purge Clio of it. So now, we do what we talked about before. We go to Janus and start it up. You've already sent a team out to Olympus, so it should be ready to go."

The colonel nods. "Sounds good. Get your things together. We'll get you on a flight out of here ASAP," he says and turns to walk away, then stops and hands the DNA report to the chief. "If it's not one thing, it's another. This makes it more important we get communications up and running. No telling what will happen unless we can get a warning out to Rees."

"I agree," replies the chief.

"When you're ready to go, let me know," the colonel says and starts walking away.

"What are going to do about this?" the chief asks, holding the paper up and following the colonel.

The colonel looks over his shoulder at his father. "Time I had a little heart to heart video chat with the good senator."

CHAPTER 35

Rees watches the sun as it makes its way into the horizon, turning the sky red, then orange, and working down from a light purple into almost darkness. He glances over at Farnsworth, who has lifted his hat off his head and stares back at him. O'Toole has quit pacing and sits in another corner of the cage, arms resting on his knees with his head down.

Farnsworth grins and looks at Rees.

"Ready?"

Rees returns the grin, then pushes himself up and stands. He lifts his leg so he can get to the heel of his boot. He turns the bottom and removes a piece of the plastic explosive Captain Epstein created. Farnsworth removes a piece of his uniform that is actually a fuse.

O'Toole hears the two men rustling around and looks up to see what they are up to. Rees looks at O'Toole and wiggles his eyebrows, then shows him the explosive as he pushes a small amount into the cage lock. Farnsworth inserts the fuse, which contains a tiny blasting cap, into the small bomb. Rees taps O'Toole on the shoulder and indicates he should move away from the door and come with him to the back of the cage.

"What you doing?" O'Toole asks.

"Something I learned from Robert Conrad," Rees tells him and removes his belt buckle, humming the theme song from *Wild, Wild West*

Rees opens the heel of his other boot and retrieves some other items, then removes his belt buckle. Farnsworth's mirror's his actions, and within a couple of minutes, both men are armed with small .22 caliber pistols. O'Toole just watches, eyes darting from one man to the other.

The two men ensure the weapons are operational, then Farnsworth pulls a match from a pocket. Rees grins and starts singing Thin Lizzy's "Jailbreak." Farnsworth looks at him and shakes his head. "You have got to learn some modern songs, bro," he says and strikes the match.

In only a couple of seconds, the Semtex goes off with a louder bang than what they would have liked, but the results are what they want. The lock disengages from the cage, and the door swings open.

The three men waste no time exiting and making their way to the tent where they last saw their weapons and equipment being taken, watching to see if anyone reacts to the small explosion. They approach the rear of the tent, and Rees peeks under the tent. He can see their belongings and gives Farnsworth a thumbs up.

Farnsworth pulls the knife from his jacket collar and cuts a large enough slit in the back of the tent for the men to get inside. Once there, Rees goes to the front of the tent and peers through a crack in the flap. He sees two Rebels standing about three feet from him, talking. He hand-signals to Farnsworth what he sees. Once Farnsworth and O'Toole have their equipment, Rees and Farnsworth switch places. Rees gathers his belongings and puts on his weapon belt. Once all three are done, they head for the rear of the tent to make good their escape, but not before the two Rebels enter the front of the tent.

All three Union-clad men turn as one and stare at the Confederate soldiers who stand in the tent opening, staring back, mouths hanging slack. Both Rebels clumsily attempt to bring their muskets to bear on the team, but before they do, Rees and Farnsworth fire their .22 caliber pistols, two shots each. The small hollow point rounds strike the soldiers, who drop their rifles to grab at the small but deadly holes in their bodies. They don't go down fast enough to suit Farnsworth, so he rushes at them and stabs one in the neck with his knife.

The other Rebel hollers' and stumbles out of the tent, falling to the ground. Rees makes for the front of the tent and opens it up with the intent of pulling the wounded man back inside. Too late. The man's cries alert the small detachment of soldiers left behind to guard the encampment.

Rees watches as a small group of soldiers head their way, and he back peddles into the tent, no longer worried about stealth as he yells for O'Toole and Farnsworth to get out. All three scramble out the rear of the tent, pulling their pistols again as they do. They hear shouts and curses. Rees turns and sees a Rebel sergeant enter the tent. Rees raises his pistol and fires, hitting the man in the face, spraying blood, bone, and brain through the back of the man's head, and driving him back through the opening.

They are far enough away they can turn and head to where the horses are being kept, hoping they are still there. Before they can get far enough away, they hear gunshots and instinctively crouch down as Minnie balls and shotgun pellets rip through the tent as the Rebels take no chances in entering and possibly receiving the same fate as their sergeant.

A few of the rounds strike trees all around the team as they continue to run. Rees stops and removes a couple of button charges and sets them quickly between two trees. Farnsworth slows and watches. In a hoarse whisper, tells Rees, "Move your ass." Rees nods and finishes up.

The men run as fast as they can and find where the horses are corralled on the far side of the camp. Two guards watch the animals, and Farnsworth and Rees dispatch them quickly with single shots to each man. O'Toole sees their horses and yells to the others. The horses are bare, but the saddles are stacked on a fallen tree. O'Toole grabs his saddle and throws it on his horse, tightening the straps and placing the bit and bridle. Farnsworth and Rees grab the rifles from their saddles and instruct O'Toole to saddle their horses while they cover. O'Toole doesn't hesitate and gets to it.

Farnsworth and Rees each take up a position that lets them see a wide area in front of them, allowing for good fields of fire when the Rebels come at them. Suddenly, there is a small explosion and screams of pain as the small mines explode in the distance.

"Goddamn!" exclaims Farnsworth. "What the hell did Epstein put in those?"

They continue to hear yelling and cursing and finally see Confederate soldiers coming towards them.

"Hurry the hell up, O'Toole, we got company!" Rees yells at the corporal and raises his rifle and fires.

Farnsworth follows suit and opens up on the advancing soldiers. It isn't much of a fight. The Rebels fire off a couple of shots, most going wild, except for one round that hits a horse causing it to jump around, nearly slamming into O'Toole, then falling over.

Rees and Farnsworth's shots are more accurate. The first few who die from being shot causes the others to hesitate and fall back, seeking cover. That's all the time the team needs. O'Toole yells that the horses are ready, and the three men leap into the saddles and turn their steeds to gallop out of the camp.

Before they do, Rees grabs two more of the buttons and turns the rings, throwing them in the direction the Rebel soldiers will be coming from. He turns his horse and starts after the other two men. When he catches up to them, he hears two more explosions.

Farnsworth looks over at him as they race away. "I think Captain Epstein created a monster."

Rees flashes him a wolfish grin.

CHAPTER 36

Chief Black stands on the tarmac dressed in a flight suit, G-suit, parachute harness, and clutching a flight helmet. He and Colonel Black stare at the F-15D Eagle fighter with the Air National Guard markings on the tail.

Before coming here, he was transported to Life Support, where technicians briefed him on what to expect when he climbs into the F-15 fighter, including the uncomfortable ACES II ejection seat.

It was decided a fighter would get him to Nellis more rapidly than if they waited on a private jet or took a slower C-17, so Colonel Black contacted Air Combat Command (ACC) and requested a *special mission*. Not as comfortable a flight, but the chief didn't mind and even joked that all it took for him to get a ride in a fighter after all his years of service was to invent a time machine and have someone screw it up.

The transient services ground crew work around the aircraft, making last-minute adjustments. The pilot, a major, exits base operations after filing his flight plan and walks to the aircraft, where the crew chief hands him the 781, aircraft records binder. The pilot scans the forms looking for any major discrepancies that may scrub the flight. Finding none, the pilot conducts a walk around of the fighter as the crew chief observes.

The colonel looks at his father and laughs.

Chief Black turns and squints at his son.

"What's so funny?"

"Sorry, Dad, just never saw you in a flight suit before. I'm used to you in your fatigues or blues."

"And again, I ask, what's so funny/"

The colonel looks at the sky, pressing his lips together with a smile.

"Let's just say I don't think you'll be getting any requests to audition for a *Top Gun* sequel or *Iron Eagle 15.*"

A remark forms on the chief's lips, but he is interrupted by the crew chief approaching and asking if he is ready. The chief nods and turns towards the colonel and releases a breath.

"Hope this works."

The colonel nods and shouts to be heard as another fighter takes off on the nearby runway, afterburner blasting so loud that it's almost impossible to hear.

"It will. You invented Clio, and they basically stole your ideas and made Janus, so it should operate the same. I'll talk with you when you get there." He smiles and nods towards the F-15. "Have fun."

Chief Black looks over his shoulder at the plane and smiles. The crew chief waves at him, so Black walks over and climbs the ladder, handing his helmet to the crew chief. He scrambles into the back seat settling in and the helmet is returned. He dons it, then the crew chief assists him in tightening his seatbelt harness and ensuring his oxygen mask and G-suit hose are connected. While Chief Black looks around, the crew chief taps him on the shoulder and hands him two *barf bags*.

"Just in case, Chief," the crew chief advises with an eyebrow arched. "The Nellis crew chief will appreciate it if you use these."

Chief Black looks at the bags, then the crew chief, snorts, then places them in a pocket for easy access. Just in case.

The pilot's voice comes over the helmet's communication system, and he asks if the chief is settled in. Black acknowledges he is, and the plane vibrates, and the sound of whines, rumbles, and other mechanical noise is heard as the engines come to life and various hydraulics come online.

The pilot gets his flight clearance, then signals the crew chief to remove the chocks. Once accomplished, the crew chief gives the pilot a thumbs up and a salute. Returning the salute, the pilot maneuvers the aircraft to the end of the taxi as the canopy closes. Black watches the canopy drop, then looks to his left and sees the colonel and a few others watching him. He waves, and they wave back. He turns his attention forward taking everything in.

"Chief, we are going to climb to 46,000 feet and use military power to cruise just under the speed of sound, about .98 Mach, or about 750 miles per hour for dirt lovers. We will rendezvous with a KC-135 tanker for air refuel and be at Nellis before you know it. Oh, by the way, I'll be using the afterburner for your enjoyment."

The Chief is not concerned but thinks about the two plastic bags in his pocket.

He can hear the pilot and control tower talking through his headset, and the pilot comes back over the intercom.

"Hang on, Chief."

Then the chief is thrown back into his seat as the powerful engines roar, afterburner kicking in as the plane plunges forward. In just a few seconds, the front of the aircraft lifts upwards, then the plane is in the air and climbing at an almost vertical angle. Before Chief Black has time to regain his composure, the jet rolls and levels out at 21,000 feet. The major requests a climb to Flight Level 46,000 feet and banks towards Oklahoma.

"How we doing, Chief?"

The chief laughs. "I should have done this a long time ago. I didn't know what I was missing."

"I hear you. This is the best job in the Air Force."

The chief looks all around him and remembers the barf bags. He shoves them further in his pocket and zips it up.

"Ha!" he says, grinning.

"What was that Chief?"

"Nothing, sir, just thinking aloud."

The major smiles under his mask.

"You want to take a try at flying?"

The rear seat has a duplicate set of flight controls, which the chief studies. Stick, throttles, and rudder paddles. Shaking his head, the chief remembers being warned by the life support techs that he was not to touch any of the controls.

"Oh, ah, no, thank you. I would at some point in my life, but right now, I need to concentrate on the job ahead of me. You handle the flying, Major, I'll enjoy the scenery," he tells him, moving his butt in a futile attempt to get comfortable.

The flight is over before the chief knows it as the fighter descends for the approach to Nellis Air Force Base. Within a couple of minutes, they are on the ground and taxing to a position in front of a hanger. Before the engines shut down, the captain comes over the comms.

"Thank you for flying Eagle Airlines. I hope your flight was a pleasant one, and I look forward to serving you again."

The chief smiles under his mask.

Hearing a commotion around him he looks to see a crew chief coming to assist him. Black climbs out and makes his way down the ladder. Once on the ground, he thanks the crew chief and pilot. He turns and spots Colonel Gorman and a Security Forces master sergeant dressed in full battle rattle, rifle resting across his chest, waiting for him.

"Chief, how was the flight?" Gorman asks, shaking hands with the man.

"It was fun. Always wanted to do that," he answers, ending the small talk. "We have transportation, I take it?"

"Yes, Chief, right over there," the colonel says and points to a Blackhawk helicopter about fifty feet away with the propeller turning, ready for take-off.

"The sergeant will escort you the rest of the way. I'll be heading back to the branch office. If you need anything, let me know," he says and shakes the chief's hand again.

Black indicates that the NCO should lead the way, which he does. Once at the open door of the aircraft, the chopper's crew chief is standing by and assists both men as they board. The crew chief follows them in and ensures they are seated and belted. He hands both men headphones, which they don. Chief Black can hear the tinny voices of the pilot, co-pilot, and crew chief through the set. The crew chief tells the pilot the passengers are on board and secure.

Black listens as the crew converse and the tower tells them they are cleared. He feels the sensation of movement as the chopper lifts and banks sharply in the direction of Olympus, he assumes.

He watches the Joshua Trees and sagebrush passing below him in blurs, then he looks ahead as the mountain range comes closer into view with each passing second. In just a short time, the helicopter loses altitude and flies between the mountains. Within a few more minutes, Black can see the small area that is the ground-level portion of the base known as Olympus. The helicopter dips, and the chief looks up as the craft flies under the domed canopy built as camouflage years before.

The pilot announces their arrival and comes in slower, then hovers, landing the flying machine gently on the ground.

Black unbuckles his seatbelt and heads for the doorway. The crew chief is already out of the aircraft and assists both men down. They nod their thanks and walk towards the new building, where the elevator waits. The chief looks up again at the canopy hundreds of feet above him, marveling at the ingenuity and engineering feat to build it.

The old town had been torn down years ago once the military took over the facility that houses Janus. The old livery stable is now a large steel and concrete building that not only leads to the elevators but is where the small Security Forces squadron is maintained. The base is small, as far as buildings go, though the area itself encompasses about 700,000 acres, give or take a few hundred acres.

Chief Black and the master sergeant walk to the main door, and the SF NCO goes through quick security identification procedures, and the door opens into a sally port. Both men enter and work their way through more security check procedures and are allowed entry into the facility. Black thanks the master sergeant for the escort and proceeds to the bank of elevators. He has been here a few times and knows his way around.

He places his ID card against the reader and waits for it to turn amber. Once it does, he types in his security code, and the panel turns green, and one of the elevators opens. He steps inside and tells the elevator, "Janus," as the door closes. In a few seconds, he is on the Janus floor, and the door opens to reveal a large room full of activity.

"Hey, Chief," he hears a familiar voice call to him. He turns slightly to his left to see MSgt Bouvier and TSgt Kriger approaching.

"Sergeants," he says and shakes their hands. "Colonel Black had a feeling something might go wrong. Good idea to send you two here and make sure everything is in order. Everything is ready to go?"

"Yes, sir. Colonel Weiss says everything checks out, and he's just waiting for you to arrive," Kriger says.

"Well, let's go see the man."

The room where Janus is maintained is not unlike the control room for Clio. A slightly larger room, same rectangle shape, full of consoles, computers, monitors. There are some minor differences with the Janus control room. One is that the time machine itself is located in the control room instead of in another room, not out of sight like Clio.

The second difference is that the observation room is the central command room, or Command & Control (C&C). The OIC has his station located here instead of on the ground floor. The idea is that the command structure can observe what is transpiring in the room below them and make decisions more readily than being eye level with all the stations spread throughout the room.

The commander's office is also located above the control room, but next to the C&C room. The colonel can watch from his office but can also get to the OIC's station quicker than having to go downstairs or call.

The observation room is split into two rooms, one for C&C and the other for just observation.

Another difference is the screens. This room has three separate large screens and multiple smaller screens dispersed in between the larger, as well as other areas throughout the room. Multiple shots can be monitored without having to split one screen into different shots.

"Tomayto-Tomahto," says the chief when he was told about the screens.

The large debarkation room has been changed also. It is bigger and has a large Plexiglas window so one can see inside.

Chief Black and the two NCOs make their way up the stairs and into the command room. The colonel watches a major as he converses with the C&C staff who are monitoring their stations. Weiss had seen the chief come into the building and is awaiting his arrival. Once the door opens, he greets the retired NCO and the two active-duty NCOs with him.

"Hello, Chief. That's was quick," he says, referring to Black arriving after only a few hours.

"Yes, Colonel Weiss, it was," Black answers and gets on with the subject at hand. "Where are we are as far as preparations?" he asks.

"Just waiting on you. Everything is green. You can go over the systems if you like, it is your show after all."

Black looks around. He has to trust that these people know what they are doing and doesn't want to insult them by rechecking everything himself. He does want to take a look at the Inabular Device beforehand and tells the major so. "Nothing against you or your people, Major, but I want to take a look at the device before a jump," he says and tells the colonel since everything is green, then they can initiate pre-launch procedures, and once he has looked at the Inabular Device, they can proceed.

"Very good, Chief," the colonel answers and tells the major to announce over the public address system that all stations should initiate pre-launch checks.

Black, Bouvier, and Kriger walk down to the main control room and to the Inabular Device console. The technician in charge of the console sees the chief and moves from the console to allow him access. Black asks for the device, and the technician opens the box and shows him. Chief Black takes the device out of the box and examines it. He walks over to another console and runs a quick diagnostic on the device. Satisfied it is in good shape, he returns it to the technician.

"Good to go, Captain," he tells the man, smiling.

The three walk back into the C&C, and the chief informs the colonel he can begin when he wants. The colonel stands and opens the comms channel for the entire building.

"This is Colonel Weiss. All systems are green. Begin," he says without flourish, something Black admires.

Even though he has seen this procedure before, he still gets a thrill. After all, he invented the time machine. Not this one, but the original. This is a cheap knock off in the chiefs' opinion.

Static electricity fills the rooms as the Inabular Device talks to Janus, letting it know it can go to work, which it does. The lights dim slightly from the amount of power being drawn to run the machine. The humming sound can still be heard in the C&C through the thick glass and soundproof walls.

There is a hazy look in the rooms as well as a shimmering of light becomes steady and slightly brighter, then all is quiet again, except the voices of the personnel talking amongst themselves on headsets. Everyone watches the flickering screens.

Suddenly, one of the techs in the C&C shouts, "Look!" and raises half out of her seat, pointing towards the disembarkation room.

Everyone in the control room turns to look into the other room, not understanding what they are seeing. There are two people inside, a man and a woman. Both look like ghosts as they fade in, then fade out of view. One second, they are perfectly solid and staring out the window, their mouths open and eyes squinting, next they fade out, and you can see through them. They are moving, looking at each other, at the people in the room. The woman takes step towards the window, and then as suddenly as they appear, they are gone.

"What the hell was that?" Bouvier asks, moving to get a better look. The room buzzes with everyone talking at once.

"Quiet, everyone, and get back to work on comms," the colonel says, taking charge and getting the focus back to what they are there for. "Time to worry about what you just saw later. Our mission is contacting the team."

The chief likes this colonel more and more. He turns towards Bouvier and Kriger.

"I do believe that was the lost senator and her brother."

Everyone settles down and gets back to their jobs, and within just a few seconds, the screens begin to flutter, then they are on. The clear picture shows two different views of two Union soldiers staring up at Rees and Farnsworth.

"Thank God for small miracles," the chief mutters and allows just a second to rejoice before he asks the next question. "Sound? Do we have sound? Communication?" he asks, walking over to where the colonel stands.

"Lieutenant, status of comms?" the colonel asks.

"Nothing yet, sir," he replies. "Wait one, sir," he says a moment later and raises his right hand to his headset, eyes squinting as he listens. "Okay, we have sound," he announces.

The static sound on the overhead speakers clear, and they hear Farnsworth talking.

"We came from the town of Hendricks Hill two days ago. Was going west when we got picked up by some Rebel Cavalry about twenty-five miles back," he says, pointing over his shoulder. "Managed to escape, lost them, and now we're heading up north. Trying to locate a Maryland cavalry unit that may be up that way. You seen any Maryland troopers around?"

CHAPTER 37

Senator Minten hates the United States Air Force. Well, not so much the branch itself, just the people who make up that branch of service. He has a son in the Army and a daughter in the Navy. Both were groomed to serve him, if need be, in whatever capacity he can find for them in their branches of service.

He figured any major projects awarded to the military would be given to the Army or Navy, not the damn Air Force. But it seems the Air Force gets all the good projects, all the time. Area 51 for one, Edwards Air Force Base for another, where all the cool gadgets are tested. He assumes the laws of probability would favor the other branches of service and they were due to receive their share of intriguing new projects.

Now, the Air Force has been granted the Clio project. He can't really blame them, considering the man responsible for creating Clio is an Air Force enlisted man. A goddamn enlisted man, for all the nerve. Not even an officer. Why couldn't he have been Army and an officer?

This means Minten now must rely on his nephew to be the inside man. Captain Randall Henries is assigned to the Clio project, and Minten is hoping his nephew can provide some inside information he can use to take over the project.

Henries has lapsed in reporting so far, and seldom does he have anything useful to contribute when he does report.

Minten is an ambitious, power-hungry man. Standing six-feet-five inches tall and muscular, he towers over most men and uses his physical presence as an intimidation factor. His dark, wavy hair and perfect white teeth disarm other politicians and cause their wives to swoon. He is the poster child for a perfect politician: handsome, conniving, and not averse to playing dirty. Most of his peers are afraid of him, and he seems to always get his way, usually by bullying and making threats.

Minten became acquainted with the Clio project while serving on the House Committee on Armed Services. Since then, he has kept his ear to the ground, listening for any news about the project. He also made sure he became a member of the Bank Council, an unofficial group of powerful politicians for whom he feels nothing but contempt. These narrow-minded individuals don't know what they have in their control.

The Clio project is the greatest achievement in human history, and they have yet to understand its potential. They just want to play with a new toy and look back at history like a television program. Minten wants to use it to make history, reshape history, or even bend history to his will until he has the world in his grasp.

Taking control of the Clio project would almost guarantee Minten an enormous step toward the presidency. But why stop there? He figures that's peanuts compared to what he can do with that type of power. He could become king, no, emperor of the entire world. A god amongst men. He doesn't care who he must crush to get there and will go to any lengths to ensure his legacy. He has had his fingers in the Clio pie since witnessing the first demonstration, ensuring he was always in the loop. Now, he wants the whole pie. Hell, he wants the recipe, bakers, and the entire kitchen.

One of the first steps Minten took as a congressman was to create the Military Intelligence Security Services, or MISS, under the guise of national security. This secret organization provides him with a vehicle he can use to throw the weight of his power around the military and gather information he can't get through regular channels. He also made sure the clandestine organization operates under black ops guidelines. It is known, but not known, in political and military circles.

Minten placed John Clayborn in the role as MISS director. Clayborn was a CIA agent in another life and has slowly worked his way up the food chain, but not as quickly as his colleagues. He didn't fit the profile the higher-ups thought a leader should look or act like. Minten found Clayborn to be somewhat desperate and easily manipulated. He had enough drive to succeed but was expendable if necessary. If Minten needs to throw someone under the bus, Clayborn would be available to take the brunt of the punishment.

Clayborn has some good qualities in that he is moderately intelligent, knows how to take orders, and as loyal as a puppy dog. Clayborn reminds Minten of a pig rather than a dog. Short in stature, slightly overweight, with a receding hairline and pencil-thin mustache, he is known to tilt the bottle on more than one occasion. He is the perfect tool for Minten's cause.

Minten stands at his desk, staring at his wall of pictures, and thinking about his next move for Clio when his assistant informs him that Clayborn is in the outer office. He closes his eyes in exasperation, lets out a deep breath through his nose, and is about to tell his secretary to send Clayborn in when there is a sudden change in the room temperature, as well as an electric discharge, unseen, mild, filling the room. Minten turns from facing the wall to look around the room.

"What the …?" he asks himself out loud, not finishing the question. The room seems to be moving, warbling, warping, moving without moving. He believes he is hallucinating, becomes disoriented, and his breathing becomes shallow. Now, it seems he's having an anxiety attack or maybe a heart attack.

Am I dying? Is this what it feels like? he thinks.

Then the room goes back to normal, except now there are two people in it with him. A man and woman who appeared out of thin air. They both look around the room, turning, eyes blinking rapidly, and it would almost be comical if he wasn't standing there with his mouth hanging open.

He drops into his high-backed chair, his eyes growing wide. The woman looks at him, and it causes him to take a breath. He knows her. He just stares. The woman looks to be in her late fifties, maybe, attractive, and awfully familiar looking. The man who stands beside her seems to gather his thoughts as well and looks at Minten, and the senator also knows this person, but it can't be. His heart beats hard in his chest. Looking from one to the other, he believes them to be siblings. His children?

The woman stands and tries to take a step towards the senator, then stops as she wavers, almost as if intoxicated

"Senator, Dad, please, wait," she pleads.

Minten stands up so fast his chair slams back into the wall. He knows that voice as well.

"Who the hell are you? What…what just happened? How did you get in here? What did you do to me?" he asks, eyes bulging, taking a step back.

The intercom on his desk buzzes, and a voice comes over, "Sir, are you alright? I heard a loud bang in there. Do you need help with something?"

He looks at the two strangers in the room with him and reaches for the button.

The woman takes another step towards Minten. Minten pushes the button, and the man and woman give almost identical pleading looks.

The woman approaches cautiously and holds her hands up in a non-threatening manner.

"Dad, please, listen," she implores.

Breathing heavily, Minten takes a step closer to his desk, his eyes never leaving hers, eyes he knows, and that voice. Did she say *Dad*? It can't be.

He presses the intercom button after regaining some normalcy. "Everything is fine. Just knocked the chair against the wall when trying to move a picture."

"Okay, sir," the voice answers. "Director Clayborn is still waiting."

Senator Minten had completely forgotten about him.

"I'm sorry, but something has come up. Tell the director I will see him tomorrow."

Before he can turn his attention back to the two visitors from who knows where, his secretary is back on the intercom.

"Sir, Director Clayborn says it's important."

Senator Minten has now regained enough composure to not want to be questioned. He slams his hand on the intercom. "Tell that goddamned sycophant I don't give a damn. I'll deal with him tomorrow!" he yells and releases the intercom button.

"Okay, you've got my undivided attention. Who are you, and what do you want?" he asks in what he hopes is a confident tone of voice, even though he is actually shaking inside. "Wait, are you part of the Clio Project?"

The woman moves towards him some more. "Don't you recognize us, Father?"

"You can't be my children. You can't be. You're...old!" he says, voice rising.

She laughs and looks at her brother. "No, Dad, it's us, and yes, we are older. We came from the future. We're here to warn you."

"The future. I don't understand?" he asks, frowning, eyes darting at each of them.

The room fills with static once again. Alarmed, Hellberg and Aeson look at each other. The room bends again and warbles, and the two figures disappear, then re-appear.

"Now what?" the senator cries out.

"No!" Hellberg screams, watching as her brother fades, she turns towards her father. "Dad, don't go through…" is all that she has time to say before she disappears.

The senator stares at the empty spot where just a second ago stood a woman and man who claim to be his children. He doesn't know what to think. The door to his office opens, and his secretary and two security personnel run into the room.

"Sir, are you alright? I heard a woman scream," his secretary says, looking around the room.

Senator Minten is still staring at the spot in front of his desk where just a second ago an older version of his daughter stood. He slowly looks up and realizes there are other people now in his office. He comes back to the here and now and focuses on his secretary, then regains his composure, his face turning red.

"I thought I said I didn't want to be interrupted!" he yells.

The secretary looks aghast. "I'm sorry, Senator, I swear I heard a woman yelling."

The senator stands and straightens his clothing. He looks disdainfully at the three people in the room, "Do you see a goddamned woman in the room? Huh? When I say I don't want to be bothered, I'm not whistling Dixie. Now, get the fuck out of my office and don't bother me unless I call for you. Is that clear?" he says in an angry tone.

"Yes, sir. I'm sorry, sir," she replies in a scared voice, then swiftly leaves the room, with the two security personnel following. They shut the door behind them.

Minten takes a deep breath and sits back down. He looks around the room and promptly stands back up. He heads for the bar and pours himself a Scotch. Downing it in one gulp, he pours another and turns and leans on the bar table, holding the drink in front of his lips. He starts to drink then sits the glass down.

"What did the woman say? Don't go through… Yes, that was it. But don't go through with what? Don't go through the…time machine? No, that can't be it. Don't go through. Don't go through…" he repeats while staring at the floor.

The senator returns to his desk and sits. He leans back in his chair, thinking, then leans forward and presses his intercom button.

"Is Clayborn still here?" he asks.

"No, sir. He left when you said you didn't want to see him."

"Well, now I want to see him. Get his ass back in here," he says irritably.

"Yes, sir. Right away."

Minten sits in his chair, sipping his Scotch. "I don't have time for this shit. People from the future giving me cryptic messages. I've got bigger fish to fry," he says aloud, then leans back, thinking about how he *is* going to go through with taking over the Clio Project, time-traveling children from the future forgotten.

CHAPTER 38

Rees, Farnsworth, and O'Toole ride for a few hours and decide to stop for the rest of the night. They doubled back earlier to see if they had been followed. Once they were satisfied no one was coming after them, they headed back in a southwesterly direction towards Fayetteville.

They climb off the horses and remove the saddles. O'Toole brushes the horses as Rees and Farnsworth set up camp, to include the early warning devices. Rees looks around, and Farnsworth watches him.

"What's the matter?"

"They took our haversacks. Those lousy bastards took out haversacks."

Farnsworth and O'Toole look around and see Rees is right.

"Well, at least they left everything else. We're fine. All they got was most of the food," Farnsworth tells Rees, "We have extra in our saddlebags."

"I had most of my hard tack in the haversack. I like my hard tack," Rees whines with a mock look of hurt on his face. He then starts feeling around his body, then goes to look in his saddlebags.

"Now what?" Farnsworth asks.

"The letters, they still have the letters!" Rees exclaims.

Farnsworth smiles. "Hey," he says and holds up a letter.

Rees comes over and takes the letter, opening it. "How did you get them back? I thought the colonel took them."

Farnsworth nods. "He did. These are extras. I had them made just in case something like this happened."

Rees harrumphs. "Good thinking. Guess that's why you're a colonel and why you left that little bit of information out," he says aloud, then thinks, *And what else are you keeping from me?*

The men settle down, eat, and then set up watch as the others sleep.

Before dawn, the three men are up and breaking camp. They saddle the horses and move out, heading north.

"Still nothing from the Bank. I hope everything is okay with them. I don't relish the idea of staying in the 1860s for the rest of my life," Rees says.

"Look at it this way, with what we know, we could become millionaires, live a life of luxury," Farnsworth answers.

"Oh, and I'm sure that wouldn't play havoc with the space-time continuum at all," Rees says back. "Not to mention I don't think luxury in this time period means much compared to what we are used to."

"HALT!" a voice shouts, and the three men stop, looking around for who yelled.

"Dammit, wasn't paying attention," Farnsworth says to Rees.

They spot movement up the road about twenty to thirty feet away. Two Union-clad men come from around a clump of pines rifles, held in front of them, not pointing at the travelers but close enough.

"Advance and be recognized one of the privates tells them. Keeping their hands away from their pistols and on the reins, the three faux Yankees trod up to the sentries.

"Colonel Farnsworth, Captain Rees, and Corporal O'Toole, 1st Cavalry."

Both privates salute, and the one who seems to be in charge asks where they came from and where they are going.

"We came from the town of Hendricks Hill two days ago. Was going west when we got picked up by some Rebel Cavalry about twenty-five miles back. Managed to escape, lost them, and now we're heading up north. Trying to locate a Maryland cavalry unit that may be up that way. You seen any Maryland troopers around?" Farnsworth asks.

The private shakes his head.

"I cannot say as we have. Lots of activity here, sir. All sorts of people running all over the place. Really do not pay attention to who is coming and who is going. You might want to ask Major Connors," the private says and points up the road. "He is in charge for right now. The colonel went and got himself killed last battle. You can find the major in camp about half a mile up the road, sir."

Farnsworth, Rees, and O'Toole all look to where the soldier points. Farnsworth thanks the sentry, returns the salute, and the team heads up the road towards the Union camp. They find the camp just as the sentry said, full of activity. The team stops, looking for where the major might be located.

"Sergeant!" Rees calls out to an NCO barking orders at his men. The sergeant turns a beefy red face, a tightness in his expression, towards Rees, then sees the rank and changes his demeanor. He runs over to Rees, saluting.

"Sorry, Captain. Beg your pardon, sir. We are in somewhat of a rush, got orders to pull out and help some of our boys west of here."

"That's fine, Sergeant, won't keep you. Looking for Major Connors, he around here?"

The NCO looks towards a large tent being taken down and points. "That is the colonel's tent. Sorry, major's tent since the colonel got killed. He should be over there, sir."

Rees thanks the sergeant, salutes, and watches as he turns and starts cursing and screaming at his men. Rees smiles. Even back in this day and time, you can tell a career NCO from regular soldiers, and they haven't changed.

The team makes their way to where the tent is being dismantled, and they see a major huddled over a table, looking at a map, surrounded by captains and lieutenants. The major looks up as the three troopers climb off their horses and approach. The major salutes Farnsworth as he noticeably takes in the size of the man, and with a weak smile, asks, "I do not suppose you're here to replace Colonel Dyer, are you, sir?"

Farnsworth shakes his head. "Sorry, Major. We're on a different mission."

The major sadly shakes his head. "Oh, well. It could not hurt to ask. What can I do for you, Colonel…?"

"Oh, sorry, Colonel Farnsworth," he says and introduces Rees and O'Toole. "We're on special assignment." He brings out the letter and hands it to the major. Connor reads it and looks at Farnsworth.

"I'll do what I can, sir, but as you can see, we're packing up. Got to move west to support a regiment that has run into some resistance. I cannot spare men or equipment."

"Not needed, Major. Just information. Have you seen a Maryland cavalry unit around here? Last couple of day's maybe?"

The major thinks for a minute. "Sorry, sir, I cannot recall seeing any, but then again, units are coming and going all the time. Could be I just missed them if they came through."

A captain who stands nearby clears his throat. The other looks at him. "Sir, there was a cavalry unit that passed through here a couple of days ago."

The major nods. "That is right, thank you, Captain," and turns to Farnsworth. "Yes, one did, but they seemed in a hurry and did not stop. I did not get a look at them," he finishes and turns towards the captain. "Did you see who they were?"

The captain shakes his head. "No, sir, too busy, and they rode straight on through. I did not pay them any mind."

The major looks around the table, and the other officers shake their heads. He turns back to Farnsworth.

"Sorry, Colonel. That is all we can tell you."

Farnsworth nods and thanks the major for his help and wishes them Godspeed. The major thanks the colonel, salutes, and turns back to his map.

The three climb onto their horses.

"I guess we just keep heading the way we were. Hopefully, we can catch up to them," Rees says.

"*If* that was them," Farnsworth adds.

Just as the men are about to leave, there is a commotion from the direction they need to go. A general and a couple of officers on horseback, followed by a group of infantry, comes down the road. The general comes in fast, watching the three cavalrymen. He approaches the men and reins in his horse. The three men salute as the general stops in front of them.

"Colonel, you in charge here?" the general demands more than asks.

"No, sir. That would be Major Connors over there by the table." He points him out. The general looks in the direction Farnsworth points and sees the major and a group of officers staring back at him. He turns back to Farnsworth. "And why in the blazes is a major in charge when a colonel is on his horse right in front of me?" he demands.

"We are passing through, General, on special assignment from Washington," Farnsworth explains and pulls out the letter, handing it to the general. The general takes the letter and reads it, then hands it back.

"Not anymore you're not, Colonel. We have Confederate troops not fifteen miles from here, and they are heading this way. I need every able-bodied man to help fend off those gray-backs or we are going to lose all the ground we have gained. Now, I want you to gather some men and get out there and do some scouting. I need to know the size of the enemy and their location. I need information, and that is what the cavalry is here for. So do your duty, Colonel, and get me some information!"

"Sir, first I have to finish my mission. Second, we don't have any cavalry here. It's just us."

The general's eyes flash fire, and his face turns red under his thick salt and pepper beard.

"I do not give a damn about your orders, Colonel. You are now under my command. You will do as I say, or I will have you arrested, or shot. You do what I say, then you may go on and finish your mission. If President Lincoln has a problem with that, then so be it. I will handle the repercussions. He is in the White House not out here. As far as cavalry is concerned…" the general begins to say, then calls out to the three officers on horseback who arrived with him. Then he calls Major Connors over. He tells the major to release any horses he can spare and get him as many soldiers that have riding experience or prior cavalry training. He intends to make a cavalry unit with Farnsworth in charge. The major salutes, then calls over to his officers barking orders.

Rees turns his horse to face away from the general and comes up to Farnsworth. "Ah, shit. This isn't good. Not why we're here."

Farnsworth's mouth is set in a stern look. "I know, dammit, but what can we do? We just go along, get what the general wants, then hightail it out of here before he gets any more bright ideas of what to do with us."

O'Toole comes up beside the men. "For what it's worth, I am here to fight. I know I want to get back to where I belong, but if I have to fight, I'm not one to run."

Rees and Farnsworth grin at the man.

"I guess that settles it. We are now officially cavalrymen," Farnsworth says, "but once we get the information the general wants, we are out of here and getting you back to your unit, okay?"

O'Toole nods, turns his horse, and gallops away.

"For the record, I disagree. I think we should just take off as soon as we can and head on up north," Rees says.

"Not a good idea. Think about it. We take off. The general finds out and sends word that two officers and an enlisted man disobeyed orders and deserted. Once it's out that we are deserters and we're caught, then we're either arrested or shot. Not only that, but someone is also likely to contact Washington and find out that neither Lincoln nor Stanton signed a special order for us. With my southern accent, we'd be hung as spies. No, we do as the general asks, and then we go on our way," Farnsworth explains.

"Yeah, you're right. I just don't like it. Wasn't planning on getting into combat."

"Hey, come on. Where's your sense of adventure. Just think, you might even qualify for an army Combat Action Badge when we get back," Farnsworth jokes.

CHAPTER 39

The Mount Olympus personnel in the C&C watch as the three blue-clad time travelers make their way into a Union camp and talk with the acting commander. They are not happy with what the Civil War general has ordered the team to do.

"This isn't good," Black says out loud to no one in particular.

"We knew they may run into some problems, but we weren't expecting them to be involved in any ground warfare. Those orders should have given them free access through all the lines without interference. Damn general wanting to make a name for himself. He could have just sent out skirmishers and let them get his information. I just think he's one of those who wants to show others who's in charge," the chief says, then looks at the major. "Major, can we talk with them yet?"

"No, chief," he replies. "Same thing as before. We can hear and see them, but we can't communicate."

"Dammit!" Chief Black says. "What in blue blazes is causing this problem?" he says again out loud, but nobody answers as they know it's a rhetorical question, one the chief has asked before.

The chief thinks for a few minutes, then nods. "I need to talk with the Bank, Colonel Black specifically. Where can I do this?"

The major leads the chief into the second observation room and quickly shows him how to use the video conference equipment and leaves him alone, shutting the door behind him.

"How's it going so far, Dad?" the colonel asks as soon as he is on screen.

"Still not good. We are in the same boat as before, got visual and audio, and only receiving. We know what they're doing, but we can't contact them, and they have no way of knowing we're watching and listening. We can't tell Rees what's going on, but I have an idea. Before I get into it, have you contacted the senator yet?" the chief inquires.

Nodding. "Yes, went as well as expected," the colonel says and tells him what transpired.

~   ~   ~

Colonel Black left the control room after showing his father the DNA results that Captain Brunell's team discovered. He went back to his office and instructed Sam to get a flight ready for Chief Black, and then to contact Senator Olsen and request a tele-meeting in his office.

Fifteen minutes later, Sam comes over the intercom and says a flight is being prepped for the chief, and that Senator Olsen will be contacting the colonel shortly. A half an hour later, Sam tells the colonel the senator is on the line.

Colonel Black types a few strokes on his computer, and the large screen hanging on his office wall reveals Senator Olsen's face.

The senator smiles. "Colonel Black, what can I do for you?" he asks cheerily. "Hope everything is going well with the project?"

The colonel is not smiling. "No, sir, the project has some hiccups, but we're working on that. Nothing we can't handle. But that's not why I wanted to talk with you. I'm sending you a secure email that contains a DNA match I would like you to see," he tells the senator and sends the information.

The senator, still smiling looks at his computer, and the smile fades. He continues to read, then looks at the colonel.

"Colonel, what is this? Where did you get it? I don't understand?"

The colonel shakes his head slightly. "That, Senator, is evidence your wife planted a spy in our midst."

The senator looks surprised. "She never told me about having a child. She was never married. I know that much from the background I ran on her," the senator exclaims, ignoring the part about a spy. "And yes, before you ask, I did run a background on her. Both her parents are dead, she went to college, joined the Air Force, did four years, honorable discharge, went into government work, and that's where I met her. Nothing about her having a child. When I met her, her last name was Newton."

The colonel stares at the screen.

"You're going to tell me you had no idea Captain Farnsworth is your wife's son? Or that you never knew she is a Minten?"

The senator looks up disbelievingly.

"I had no idea, Colonel. I-I don't know what to say. There has to be a mix-up. You got the wrong DNA, something."

"No, Senator, we've got the right information, and apparently your background check was doctored or flawed, or she knew you were going to do one and somehow intercepted it, then had someone change it and give you false information. There are a number of things that could have happened. If you're telling me the truth, then your wife has lied to you. She had you gain her access to this facility and has manipulated you into granting her son, her son you claim no knowledge about, entry into this project. Her son who is now under suspicion of sabotage, espionage, and is in command of a mission that could possibly allow him to alter the course of history."

The senator's face grows ashen, and he looks into the camera, then closes his eyes. The colonel almost believes him. The senator actually looks like he is in shock from what was just revealed to him.

"What do you want me to do, Colonel Black?" the senator asks in a more subdued tone, face slack.

"Right now, Senator, nothing. Just go about your business as usual. If you're not involved in this, I want reports on what your wife's activities are."

"You want me to spy on my wife?" the senator asks, his face draining of color.

"Call it what you may, Senator. I can have you arrested right now, and we can see how that plays out. But if you had nothing to do with this subterfuge, then you will monitor your wife's activities and inform us of everything she does."

The senator presses his lip tightly and slowly shakes his head, again becoming more subdued. He looks back into the camera, sighing. "What did Captain Farnsworth do that makes him a liability?"

The colonel looks back at the senator, wondering how much he should say, then decides to tell the senator some of the truth.

"We think he planted a virus into Clio, which disrupted communications. We are cleaning that up, but for right now, we don't have contact with the team, so we don't know what they are doing," he says, not revealing everything but not lying.

"But how can you be sure my wife is involved?" Olsen asks almost pleadingly.

"Senator," Black starts, then stops to think, "we don't have direct evidence linking your wife to what is going on right now, but there is enough circumstantial evidence that makes us believe she's involved. She doesn't tell you about her son, then introduces him as an acquaintance. She talks him up to you, plants a bug in your ear, suggesting he be involved in the Clio Project. She knows we want to re-initiate the program and you are backing us. Rees comes up with a plan to take O'Toole back to his time period, and that gives you an excuse to get Farnsworth involved. Come on, Senator, you didn't get where you are being that naïve. Not unless you were involved in this from the start."

The senator, who looked down, listening, jerks his head up at the statement.

"Now, hold on there, Colonel," he says, his voice rising.

"No, goddammit, Senator, you hold on!" the colonel shouts back. "You're in no position to do anything but listen to what I say and do what I say. We don't know what your wife's endgame is here, but I've got a good idea. And if it's what I think it is, then I take it personally."

"And just what do you think she wants?" Olsen asks, trying to regain some composure and control.

"That's not you're concern, Senator. If you're part of this, then you already know. If you're not, then you'll help us get to the bottom of it. But be aware, sir, we will now be watching you, and I expect reports on your wife's activities."

The senator tries to look dignified but fails miserably. The colonel believes the man has no idea what is going on but will not let his guard down until he is absolutely certain.

"If there's nothing else, Colonel, I need to get on with other matters," the senator says, releasing a breath, standing taller, pulling at the bottom of his suit coat.

"No, Senator, nothing else. I expect to hear from you soon. Good day," the colonel says and disconnects the call. He presses his intercom.

"Yes, sir?"

"Sam, please get in contact with Colonel Gorman. Tell him I need some security checks run on a few people, and I'll need some of his agents, too."

CHAPTER 40

Having accepted their orders, the team goes to Major Connors and asks if any of his men are good horsemen. The major isn't happy about giving up some of his men, but orders are orders, so he tells a lieutenant to take them around and collect those men who can handle horses and assign them as cavalry. For the time being. He tells Farnsworth that once they are through to please return them so they can rejoin their units.

The officer walks around and assembles several men from different areas of the camp. Once they find about twelve good men, Farnsworth explains to them what the general wants. Most of the men are glad to get out of whatever it was they were doing and get a chance to ride a horse.

They follow Farnsworth and Rees to where O'Toole has amassed horses and equipment. The soldiers find saddles and put them on horses and check equipment, weapons then gather around Farnsworth.

"Okay, men. I don't have time to go over even the basics of being a cavalryman. Just stay in single file behind me. If we need to go into battle, I will need you to peel off and make a line starting from my right or left. Whichever way I point my sword. I hope we don't run into any problems out there, but you never know. You men are being given Spencer rifles. Anyone here not know how to use one?" he asks, and no one raises their hands. "Well, that's a good start right there. We are a reconnaissance patrol, not a fighting patrol. We are to locate the enemy, gather what information we can, then return with that information. Hopefully without being seen or having to fight," he tells the group while looking at each man. "Captain Rees is next in charge, then Corporal O'Toole."

Farnsworth sees a sergeant raises his hand. "Sir, I should be next as I'm the ranking man," the NCO says with a heavy Scottish accent.

Farnsworth shakes his head. "Sorry, Sergeant, but you aren't cavalry, O'Toole is, he knows how we operate, so he will be in charge. Nothing against you, as I'm sure you're quite qualified as an infantryman, but on horses, we rule. Tell you what, you will be fourth and ride up front next to O'Toole as we can still use your expertise," he says, hoping to appease the older NCO. "What is your name, Sergeant?"

"Yes, sir, thank you, sir, McGregor, sir," the sergeant says, lifting his chin and puffing his chest out.

"Of course, it is," Farnsworth says softly so that only Rees can hear him. "Scottish, I take it?" Farnsworth asks louder.

"Aye, sir," the man replies with a grin.

Farnsworth turns to Rees. "We've got a Welshman, an Irishman, and a Scotsman. All we need now is an Englishman and the entire British Isles will be represented."

When he says that, O'Toole, the sergeant, and a few others spit. Farnsworth's eyebrows go up, as does Rees'.

"Beg your pardon, sir, but we don't be needing any Englishman amongst us now. Present company accepted, of course," the sergeant tells him.

"Okay, of course, Sergeant, good," Farnsworth says, his face blushing, not realizing his last name is English. He looks at Rees, who chuckles. "Really, you're going to go there?"

A soldier whispers a little too loudly to another soldier, "He sure talks funny."

"That's because I'm from the south, and I'm very well educated. That's why I'm an officer and in charge of this unit. You have a problem with that, soldier?" Farnsworth says, coming in front of the man and towering over him.

"No. no, sir. Don't mean nothing by it, sir," the startled soldier sputters.

"Good, now get on your horses and let's move out," Farnsworth barks and watches as the men scramble to their animals. Rees and Farnsworth share a grin. "This might be fun after all," Rees says, climbing into his saddle.

Farnsworth and Rees take lead, with O'Toole and Sergeant McGregor behind them, followed by the rest of the troopers.

They ride along the road that leads them out of the encampment and are flagged by the general.

"You men take care and get me what I need to stop those damn Rebs. They got us running circles all over this damned state. Godspeed, Colonel."

"Thank you, General. We'll get what we can and rendezvous in a day," Farnsworth says and salutes.

They continue on their way. Once outside of the camp they pick up the pace and make their way towards the Confederate lines. Farnsworth explains to Rees he intends to flank the Rebels, then move in, reconnoiter, and then get the hell out and back to the general.

Riding a little further, Rees begins singing a song from the Marshall Tucker Band, about a woman doing him wrong." and notices that Farnsworth hasn't made any smart-ass comment about his singing or choice of songs.

"Okay, what's the problem?"

Farnsworth huffs and looks back at the soldiers behind them, wanting to ensure they can't hear what he is about to say. Satisfied that O'Toole and the sergeant aren't within earshot, he turns back to Rees.

"We're heading towards Fayetteville."

Rees shrugs. "Yeah, so what?"

"If I remember my history, that's where a great cavalry battle was fought."

Rees just looks at him. "Again, yeah, so what?"

"There were two divisions of Confederate cavalry that beat one division of Union cavalry, and if you haven't noticed, we're Union cavalry."

Rees shakes his head. "But we're not going to get into the battle, plus, do we look like a division? Like you said, we're going to flank and get info and get back. This is simple. Since you know the strength and where the Rebs are, why are we even going there? Just stop along the way. You, me, and O'Toole go on ahead, stop for a while, then come back. We tell the rest we found the Rebs and head on back to camp, give the info to the general, then we're on our way. Easy-Peasy."

"I'm not so sure. I'm not certain of the dates of the battle, and I don't want to get wrong info. Might cause some time malady or some such time travel thingy."

Rees laughs. "That's real scientific of you, time malady, time travel thingy?"

"You know what I mean," Farnsworth says, looking over his shoulder again. "We can't afford not getting O'Toole back. Plus, I don't want to get into a fight." Then he laughs. "Know what's in the area the battle was fought?"

Rees shakes his head. "No idea."

"Fort Bragg."

Rees looks surprised. "No shit?"

"No shit. There are even some unknown Union soldier graves there. We'll go look when we get back," Farnsworth adds.

"Just what I need to see, more Civil War stuff," Rees mumbles loud enough for Farnsworth to hear.

They ride for about two hours and stop. Farnsworth takes his telescope and stands in his saddle. He looks west and sees dust rising. Rees uses his binocs and watches also.

"Tell me what you see."

Rees still scans the area in front of him. "I see dust," he replies after a few seconds of searching.

"That means either heavy infantry or cavalry coming down a dirt road," Farnsworth says.

"You sure?" Rees asks.

Farnsworth turns to O'Toole and McGregor. "Corporal, Sergeant, up here," he orders, and both men ride up to him. Farnsworth hands the scope to O'Toole, and he has him to look west and tell him what he sees.

"Dust," O'Toole says and gives the scope to Sergeant McGregor. He watches for them to remove the scope from his eye and looks at it in astonishment. Shaking his head, he places the scope back up to his eye. Farnsworth cringes when he remembers these are newer telescopes and binoculars than what McGregor is used to. McGregor doesn't make any comment as he continues scanning.

"Yes, sir. More likely a lot of Rebs walking this way," he replies after a few more seconds.

Farnsworth and Rees look behind them and see they haven't caused a dust storm with their horses as they have been riding on the side of the roads in the grass. The two men stare at a large section of Pine trees to the northwest. Rees points it out.

"That looks like a good place to lay low and possibly get a good look at what's coming."

Farnsworth agrees, "Good cover, and we can get out fast if need be," then he looks at O'Toole and McGregor. "Go back and tell the men we're going into that tree line. Go slowly and spread out once there. I want a skirmish line inside the woods. We are only here to get information not get into a firefight," he says, and Rees clears his throat as O'Toole and McGregor face each other, one with a frown the other turning the corner of his mouth upwards. Farnsworth doesn't understand he used a modern term for combat.

Rees interjects, "He means a fight, and we're not looking for a fight."

Farnsworth then understands what he said and tells the men to carry on with his orders.

Rees smiles. "Hey, want to get artillery on the comms so we can call in a fire support mission and maybe send out an LP/OP?"

"Fuck you," Farnsworth says, snorting. "Hey, so I didn't study up on my Civil War combat slang, okay?"

"That's fine. Let's just get what we need and get back," Rees says and starts towards the tree line. Farnsworth signals the rest to follow, and he heads towards the trees also.

There, everyone dismounts and takes cover. Rees and Farnsworth pull out their eyepieces. They watch and see a regimental size Confederate infantry unit heading on a road and in the direction of the Union forces.

"That's a lot of infantry, but I don't think it's enough to do any damage to the Union boys," Farnsworth notes, "unless there are more coming. I don't see any artillery, nor cavalry. Of course, the Cav's probably running all over the countryside looking for us."

"You think we should go further, see what else is out there?" Rees asks.

"You're kidding, right?"

"Yup," Rees says and grins at Farnsworth. "This is enough and doesn't make any difference, anyway. Outcome will still be the same."

"You're probably right. Okay, let's go," Farnsworth says and signals the troops to mount up.

CHAPTER 41

"**M**Sgt Danner was detained about half an hour ago and is being transported to the Bank as we speak. Two OSI agents, along with Sergeants Tucker and McGuire went to his home and found him packing. He said he had leave coming and was just getting ready for when the mission was over. Of course, we checked, and he wasn't scheduled for any leave. Should be available for questioning shortly," Colonel Gorman tells Colonel Black.

"That's good. Seems like he is more involved in this than we would like. I'm sure your agents can get what we need from him," Black says.

Gorman looks down at his paperwork. "We checked his phones, both landline and cell. He received several calls from a Washington DC area code. The numbers were not available for trace, but we'll find out who they're from any minute now."

Colonel Black snorts. "I can take two guesses who it'll come back to. Either Senator Olsen or his wife."

Gorman looks surprised. "Why do you say that?"

Colonel Black explains what has been going on with the senator and his wife and about the talk he had earlier with the senator.

"I'll be damned. So, you think the senator and his wife are somehow involved in what's happening to the project?" Gorman asks.

"I wholeheartedly believe his wife is involved, being a Minten, and supposedly hiding her true identity from the senator. The more I talk with the senator, the more I believe he really is being duped by her. He has always been the wind to our backs and has done everything in his power to ensure Clio would become viable again."

"I hope that's true, but don't let your guard down."

"Oh, believe me, I won't. We'll see if he comes through with the task I gave him."

Gorman nods. "Well, back to Sergeant Danner. He was assigned in Washington for five years, worked at the Pentagon, and had contact with Olsen during his time there. When the assignment came up for the Clio Project, guess who recommended him for posting?"

"You're kidding?" Black asks, a muscle in his jaw twitching.

"Nope, our friend Senator Olsen."

"Goddammit," Blacks spits the word. "This just keeps getting better and better."

The intercom on Black's desk buzzes.

"Yeah, Sam?"

"Your guest is in the interrogation room, sir," she announces.

"Okay, tell the agents I'll be down shortly and not to start the interview before I get there." He turns back to the television screen and Gorman.

"They're here. I want to be down there when they talk with him. Let me know if your surveillance team finds anything useful."

Gorman nods and starts to disconnect, then stops.

"John? Hang on a second, I just received an email, and it says…" Gorman trails off, reading the message. "Okay. Hey, you're right. Some of those numbers come back to a phone for Mrs. Olsen and some from the senator and their home. All different hours of the day and night.

More frequently when the mission was announced. Could be something you can use."

Colonel Black nods, thanks Gorman, then disconnects the call. Leaving his office, he tells Sam he will be in the observation room watching the interview. He walks down the hallway and goes to the elevator, taking it to the security section of the Bank, where he is met by Tucker and McGuire.

"Sergeants, how'd it go?" he asks, coming out of the elevator.

"He is scared, I can tell you that. He's not talking, but he's scared," Tucker says. "The OSI team wants to let him wait for an hour or so before questioning him. Give him time to think. They say it makes a person jumpy wondering why it's taking so long to talk with them."

Colonel Black looks at his watch. "Well, we will do as the experts ask, but I want to get a look at him." He heads towards the observation room. When he opens the door, he sees two agents inside observing Danner. They see Colonel Black and straighten. Even though they are wearing civilian clothes, they are still military and respect for higher rank is embedded in their core.

"Colonel, I'm Special agent Nguyen, and this is Special Agent Torres."

The colonel shakes their hands and asks what is going on so far.

Agent Nguyen shakes his head.

"Nothing right now, sir. We're letting him sweat. When we see him getting fidgety, we'll go in."

"Then what?" Black asks.

"Oh, we'll get what you want out of him, Colonel. He's scared and knows we already caught him in one lie."

"The supposed leave?"

Nguyen looks at the colonel. "Yes, sir. I see Colonel Gorman has already filled you in."

Black nods. "Yes, and he also just found out that Sergeant Danner has been corresponding with the Olsens quite a bit, even more so lately. Not sure if it's just one of them or both, but all the numbers come back to their home and her cell phone. I'm no Sherlock Holmes, but after speaking with the senator, I would put my money on the wife."

The agents don't respond and turn their attention back to Danner, who looks around the room, occasionally stealing a glance at the room where everyone watches. The men and one woman in the room carry on some small talk for almost an hour. When Danner puts his head down on the table, Nguyen says it's time to go in.

When the door to the interview room opens, Danner lifts his head and sits back in his chair, his demeanor changing in a heartbeat. First, his shoulders were slack, now they're thrown back; his eyes were droopy and his face slack, now they are squinting, and his jaw is set as he grinds his teeth. He watches Nguyen pull up a chair, sit, and place a laptop on the table. His eyes follow Torres as she walks to the other side of the room and leans against the wall, staring back at him.

"Oh, good cop, bad cop routine, I take it?" Danner asks, crossing his arms over his chest. "When do I get a lawyer?"

Nguyen looks at Torres, then back at Danner. He types a command into the computer and turns it towards Danner. Danner looks at Nguyen, then the computer. "What's this?" he asks, shrugging.

Nguyen ignores him. The screen comes on and shows the control room where Danner sits, and the scene unfolds where he and Farnsworth have a chat. Once it's over, Nguyen closes the laptop and moves it to one side.

"Naw, we don't have to play that game, and you don't get a lawyer. See, you're going to help us out because you're in the Air Force, and you know it's the right thing to do. It's not like in the civilian world where they have to play by the rules. You're a hundred feet underground, in a secure facility, in a locked room, and you're never leaving until we get what we want from you. You're going to tell us what you and Captain Farnsworth were having an argument about and what he put into the computer."

Danner leans back in his chair, his face not showing any emotion, but the vein in his neck is visible and pulsing fast. Sweat forms on his brow, and there is a slight tic on his cheek.

"Bullshit. You can't do that," he says with false bravado. "I know my rights, and you can't do anything to me. The UCMJ (Uniform Code of Military Justice) doesn't allow what you're suggesting, so don't bullshit me."

Torres walks over and leans on the table, next to Danner's head, and whispers, "No, Sergeant, you're wrong. Think about where you are. We can throw you in a cell and leave you there until you rot, and no one will know you're here except us," she waggles a finger between herself and Nguyen, "and a select few. Once we leave, you will be screwed royally, and not a good screwing, unless you tell us what we want to know."

Torres looks him in the eye and smiles. "Ah, that's the look I like," she says, then straightens and walks back to the wall, resuming her position.

Danner's eyes widen and dart from one agent to the other. Nguyen smiles now. "You see, one thing about being in these top-secret super facilities is that, when you mess up, you can disappear. Happens all the time. Kind of like being a friend of the Clintons, you just don't know what's going to happen. Wait, I'm sorry," Nguyen corrects himself, raising a finger, "*you* will know." He then leans closer, "Do yourself a favor, and us, answer our questions, and you might get out of this more or less intact. I can tell you right now, you won't be in the Air Force much longer, you can kiss your rank, oh, hell, your retirement goodbye. Would you rather spend time in Fort Leavenworth, with a chance to get out, or do you prefer to disappear?"

Nguyen leans back and watches Danner, who is visibly trembling and sweating, looking down at his feet and shaking his head.

"Okay, I fucked up. But you got to help me. I can't go to prison, please," he begs.

Nguyen shakes his head. "That's not up to us, Sergeant. You cooperate, and it'll show good faith on your part, and the powers that be may show some mercy. That's not our call."

"No, you tell whoever is behind that mirror," he points, "that I want some kind of protection and no jail. I won't last one day there. They would get to me somehow. I'll talk with you, but I want out and relocated. Not in this country, either. You talk to them, and then I'll talk."

Nguyen stares at Danner, glances over at Torres, and signals they should leave. Once in the observation room, they look at the colonel questioningly. Black watches Danner, who seems deep in thought.

"Okay, tell him I can get him discharged without prison time. I can get him out of the country, wherever he wants to go, but that's it. No money, no more help from us. He's on his own."

"Yes, sir," Nguyen replies, and the agents head towards the door. Before exiting, the colonel stops them.

"And I want a word with him when you're through."

"Yes, sir," Nguyen says, and the two agents go back into the room and explain the offer. Danner has a blank look on his face as he listens, then nods.

"Okay, ask your questions."

An hour later, they have what they need. They leave Danner in the room and return to the colonel.

"I wasn't expecting that," the colonel says, "but I guess it's the oldest tale around. That's why we have training about contact with the opposite sex in a foreign country. Not the exact same thing but close. I hope she was worth it because his life is over as he knows it."

Danner told the agents that Joyce Olsen met him years ago when he had temporary duty at MacDill Air Force Base, Florida. She was there on some senator wives' duties, and she introduced Captain Farnsworth to him. Nothing unusual there, but then, one day, she happens to be in the same area he works in at the Pentagon. She made a fuss about meeting him, very friendly, overfriendly he thought at the time. Then she would drop little hints to him that she would like to see him. Danner blew it off. No way would a beautiful woman like her want to be with him. Besides, she was married to a US senator.

Time went by, and she kept up her pursuit until he finally relinquished, and they met at a hotel in New York City. He was smitten after that first encounter, and she had him. They would meet whenever they could until the day he told her he would be going to another assignment.

Lying in bed one afternoon, she cuddled up against him, rubbing her hand across his chest, and told him she knew about his new posting. He asked her how, and she told him she made sure he got the job. Danner didn't care how, but he wanted this. It would be the highlight of his career, and he could write his own ticket after this plush assignment.

She had told him she loved him, and that they could still see each other whenever he could get away or she could get down his way. He asked about her husband, and she just laughed, telling Danner that the senator was stupid as well as blind. He spent most of his time working and not paying attention to her, except as eye candy when he went to a party or on a campaign trail.

Once Danner was assigned to the Bank and had been working for about a year, he asked Joyce to leave the senator, and she said she would, but that he had to do something for her first. She wanted him to place a program into Clio. At first, he laughed. He didn't believe her, thought she was joking. She was adamant and finally convinced him she was serious. She wouldn't tell him what it was but assured him it wouldn't cause any damage, and no one would get hurt.

He pressed her on it, but she refused to get into details, other than to say it would give her an opportunity to make enough money that she could leave her husband and be with Danner, and they could go anywhere, do anything they wanted. She told him that when the program was planted, Captain Farnsworth would contact him. Once he did what she asked and everything was in place, she would ask her husband for a divorce, and she would be his.

Danner fell for it and regretted it as soon as he did it. He knew it wasn't right, but she had him believing she would leave her rich and powerful husband to be with him, an enlisted man. He knew better but didn't think it through before it was too late. He had already committed sabotage. When Captain Farnsworth came to see him, Danner wasn't happy about it. He let the captain know and even threatened to turn himself in. Farnsworth dismissed that idea when he was told that it wouldn't end pretty for him if he did.

Danner swore he didn't know what she had him placed into the Clio computers, nor did he have any knowledge Farnsworth had also placed something into the computers.

When they questioned him about why he was packing his bags, he said that Joyce told him to do so. She said that he would be questioned once the military figured out that the Clio Project had been infiltrated. They would be questioning everyone and, sooner or later, he would become a prime suspect, so he had to be prepared to leave. She told him she would let him know where to go, and she would join him later.

Agent Nguyen and Torres finish their interview and head back into the observation room. Colonel Black walks into the room to have a chat with Danner.

Danner immediately stands to attention.

"Sit your ass down, Danner. I don't want you standing for me as I don't recognize you as an NCO in my Air Force."

Danner swallows, his features going blank, and his shoulders slumping, then he drops back in place. Black pulls out the chair that Nguyen used and sits. He leans back, glaring at the disgraced NCO.

"So, you let a woman talk you into ruining your life?" he asks, and when Danner starts to speak, the colonel stops him. "Don't answer that, it was rhetorical. My God, man, what were you thinking?"

"I'm sorry, sir, I really am. I don't know. She's a witch, cast a spell over me," Danner says as a feeble excuse, head down in shame.

"Can it, Danner. Not buying it," Black says and leans on the table towards the man. Danner looks up and sits back, distancing himself from his commander. "Here's what's going to happen. You're going to go home and call your mistress and tell her you have been granted leave. She'll ask you how, and you tell her that the project is over and it's time to go."

"She won't buy into that, sir. She has eyes and ears in this place. I know it. She'll figure out that I've been discovered, compromised. She's smart, that one," Danner tells the colonel.

Black shakes his head, his lip curled in a snarl. "I don't give two shits, Danner. You do what I say, and maybe, just maybe, I'll see about getting you out of the country. Don't do what I say, and the deal you made with the two OSI agents is off. You fuck with me, and you'll never even see the inside of Fort Leavenworth because you'll be left here in a cell for the rest of your miserable life. Got it?" he asks, staring daggers at Danner.

Danner nods frantically, and Black leans further forward.

"That's not a rhetorical question, shit for brains. That one requires an answer."

Danner's eyes widen. "Yes, sir. Perfectly clear, sir. I will do as you say, Colonel."

"Damn right you will," Black says with a quick, disgusted snort and leaves the room.

When he enters the observation room, Tucker and McGuire are grinning.

"Damn, sir. You should have been a cop. You made these two yahoos look like rookies." McGuire says, pointing over his shoulder at Nguyen and Torres, neither smiling at the jest. He looks over his shoulder at them. "Hey, guys, lighten up, it was a joke."

Nguyen looks straight at McGuire. "We're OSI, we don't joke." Then, after a few seconds, and seeing the look on McGuire's face change from a smile to worry, Nguyen breaks out into a smile. "Gotcha, Sergeant." He fist-bumps Torres.

"All right, people, that's enough. Get that piece of trash out of my facility and back to his home. Before he goes, I want all his phones tapped, twenty-four-hour surveillance, the works. I want to know if and when any of the Olsens contact him. I'll let Colonel Gorman know, so you shouldn't have any problems getting what you need. Thank you for your help," the colonel tells the group and leaves.

He goes back into his office and calls Gorman, then sends him a copy of the session with Danner. He does some paperwork, trying to get his mind off Danner. After a couple of hours, he decides to contact Olympus to update his father.

"You think it's a good idea to let him go? I don't mean just to his home, but when this is over? He committed treason, after all," Chief Black asks his son.

"I'm not real satisfied with the deal, but we got him to talk, and I think it'll work out. I'm more concerned about getting my hands on the senator's wife, and the senator, if he's involved."

The chief stares into the screen at his son, "Okay. Hey, that's your call to make."

"That's right, the power of command. Enough on that right now. How's the team doing? Farnsworth doing anything suspicious, anything to help us figure what he is up to?"

The chief shakes his head. "No. They had some Union general order them to deviate from their written orders and gathers some troopers and go on a scouting mission."

The colonel frowns. "What?"

"Yes, they are now actually a part of a real cavalry unit out on a real mission. The general overrode Lincoln and Stanton. I kind of find that ballsy, but hey, you officer types just do what you want," the chief says with mirth in his voice.

"Not now, Dad," the colonel admonishes. "Okay, what's the plan?"

"We just keep working on a solution to our comms problem and monitor our boys. As I said, I don't know what Farnsworth is up to, and he hasn't shown his hand. He's been the consummate officer and really seems to get along with Rees. He's either a great actor, or maybe there's something else going on here. We'll just keep monitoring them and see what happens."

"Chief, if you think something is off, I want them brought back."

"You sure? What about *our* timeline?"

"We'll worry about that later. We're still here, so everything must be good. I don't know. Just do whatever is necessary to keep O'Toole alive. That means if he has to come back here, he does. We can always try again, right?"

"You're in charge, remember. I'm just here as a consultant. But it'll get done."

"Good, I'll contact you later. Keep that feed you have coming into the Bank."

"Will do," the chief answers and disconnects the call.

As soon as the colonel and the chief end their conversation, Sam comes over the intercom and says that the senator is on another line for him. The colonel thanks her and snatches the phone up.

"What is it, Senator? You got something for me?" The phone is silent. "Senator? You there?"

Still silence, then breathing, then the senator's voice slurred comes through.

"I'm sorry, John. I fucked up."

Colonel Black rolls his eyes and sighs. "What, Senator?"

"I confronted Joyce about Farnsworth and her lying to me for all these years."

Colonel Black's face turns a dark red, "You what?! What were you thinking? I told you to just keep an eye on her and let me know what she is up to. Now she knows we're on to her. This doesn't look good for you, Senator. Did you plan this so you could wiggle out of being under suspicion yourself because, from where I'm standing, it sure looks like it?"

"No, Colonel, I did not plan on it. I don't care if you think I had something to do with this or not, because I didn't. That's not my worry. She told me about her plans, and that she has been sleeping with some NCO assigned to your facility. She said his name was Tanner, I think. I wasn't paying attention after she told me of the affair. She said I was the one who recommended him to you. I don't remember, just another person she talked me into backing for one thing or another. She said she talked him into doing something to the Clio Project, something that would cause some great changes. She didn't say what. She said that in a short time, history would be re-written, and all would return as it should have been. I don't know what she was going on about," the senator utters in a dazed voice.

"Where is she now, Olsen?" Colonel Black asks, ignoring the senator's title.

"I-I don't know. There was an argument, and she just up and left. I don't know where. I just watched her leave, then sat down and started drinking."

"How long ago?" Black demands.

"I don't know. An hour, maybe two. I don't—" the senator starts to say, but Colonel Black has already hung up. He opens the door to Sam's office in such a way her hand reaches for the pistol. The colonel doesn't even notice.

"Get me in touch with those two agents and the Security Forces with them."

~ ~ ~

Special Agent Torres drives a Chevrolet Suburban towards Danner's home. Agent Nguyen is in the front passenger seat, with Danner sandwiched between Sergeants Tucker and McGuire. Following behind them are Sergeants Tosseti and Nionee in an unmarked police unit.

It takes them almost half an hour to get to Danner's home, located far north of the base. When they are nearby, the unmarked unit turns right onto another street, goes one block, then left. They drive through the backside of the neighborhood with both sergeants watching for any unusual activity. They circle around two blocks, then park about a block away facing the opposite direction from where the other vehicle is coming. They radio the agents their position.

Torres stops the Suburban half a block from Danner's home. Tucker un-cuffs Danner, opens the door, and steps out, allowing Danner to do the same. No one says a word to Danner as he walks away. Everyone watches him slowly approach his home, fumble with his keys, and enter the home, shutting the door behind him.

The laptop screen in the Suburban flashes that someone wants to talk. Nguyen types in the command to answer, and Sam's face appears.

"Agent, please stand by for Colonel Black," she says and the screen goes blank for a split second then comes back on showing Colonel Black's face.

"Agent Nguyen, where are you?" the colonel blurts out.

"We're parked outside Danner's home, sir."

"Where's Danner?"

"He just went inside his house, sir. What's going on?"

"Get him out of there, now! I believe his life is in danger and…"

The colonel is still speaking, but he is interrupted when Torres blurts out, "Did you see that?"

Nguyen and the others look towards the house and see a flash of light, followed by another.

"Oh, shit," Nguyen shouts and opens the SUV's door, as do the sergeant's in back, as well as Torres. Colonel Black is still on the screen asking what is going on but is ignored. All he hears is someone shouting, "Shots fired."

Across the street, Nionee and Tosseti run towards the house. Nguyen sees them and waves his pistol towards the back of the house. Nionee and Tosseti turn and run the direction indicated.

Nguyen and Torres crouch and run to the front porch of the house, with Tucker right behind them. McGuire runs towards the back yard to help Tosseti and Nionee.

The porch light is off, a plus for them as they cautiously walk up the three front steps onto the porch and work their way to the front door. Tucker stays off the porch and covers a window with his weapon.

Nguyen tries the front door and finds it locked. He then steps back and kicks it several times, not able to get it open. He curses and aims his pistol and fires into the door frame by the lock area. Torres has just enough time to move around him as he does.

Before he can shoot, Nguyen is flung backwards when rounds permeate the door. Four holes appear diagonally in the door as the rounds travel through, with two of them striking Nguyen square in the chest. The vest he wears does nothing to stop the rounds.

He tumbles off the porch and lies on the ground at the base of the steps, where he is opening and closing his mouth, trying to sit up. His hands are covered in blood as he feels around the wounds. He tries to speak, with only a gurgle emitted, then blood spews from his mouth as he chokes and coughs.

Tucker runs to him while still watching the home. He grabs Nguyen's jacket and drags the man closer to the house, out of sight of the door.

"Goddammit, you motherfuckers!" Torres screams at whoever is in the house and is answered by another round of shots through the door.

Tucker grabs his radio and yells that Agent Nguyen is down and asks for medical help and back-up. Already, he can hear the distant wailing of sirens. *Neighbors must have called,* he thinks while trying to stanch the flow of blood pouring out of Nguyen, wondering why he wasn't wearing a vest. He stands far enough to look over the porch and sees Torres breathing hard, staring at the locked door. She tenses, raising her weapon.

"Torres!" he shouts, realizing what she is about to do. She turns and looks at him. Tucker shakes his head. "Stay where you are. Help is coming."

She stares at him, then grimaces and turns to face the door, firing several rounds through it. Kicking it open, she disappears inside the dark interior.

Tucker scrambles to the porch. "Fuck," he says as he moves to follow her in. Before he can get to the door, he sees flashes and hears the faint muffled sound of suppressed weapons' fire. Automatic weapons' fire, two weapons. He also hears the slapping of rounds striking something soft and the wood splintering around the door area where he stands.

Crouching down, he peeks around the corner. The house is too dark to see, but he can make out a part of Agent Torres' body faintly illuminated by the streetlights shining through the open door. There is dark fluid pooling around her.

"Torres?" he asks, already knowing he'll get no answer. "Torres?"

He grabs his radio and again asks for help and informs the security desk another agent is down. The sound of the sirens grow closer, but help won't be here soon enough. He is about to take another look into the house when he hears shouting and gunfire from the rear of the home.

~ ~ ~

Tosseti and Nionee take up positions that allow them the watch the rear of the home and affords them good cover. They both have weapons out and at the ready. The two men are startled when McGuire comes running around the corner at a crouch, looking around, apparently for them.

"Dammit, Sean, over here," Nionee whispers loud enough for McGuire to hear.

Sean sees them and hurries over. He crouches down beside them.

"What the fuck, Mac, we could have shot you," Tosseti tells him.

"Naw, Tosseti, you forget, I've seen you shoot. You can't hit the side of a barn, so I wasn't in any danger."

"Fuck youse," Tosseti answers and lightly punches McGuire in the shoulder,

"Shut up, both of you, watch the house," Nionee orders, and they both do.

They hear noise coming from the front of the house, then barely hear muffled weapons' fire, each knowing its suppressed automatic weapons. Not good for anybody, except those welding those weapons. Becoming focused, they aim their pistols at the back door.

They hear Tucker on the radio alerting the desk that an OSI agent is down and they need help. The three NCOs look at each other, and Nionee points to the corner of the house, then at McGuire, then points at the other side and to himself. Both men scramble out of cover and to the corners of the rear of the home.

As soon as they arrive at the corners, they hear louder gunfire coming from the front of the house, then what sounds like the door being kicked. Then more muffled gunfire. Quiet, then Tucker yelling.

Suddenly, the back door opens, and two figures cautiously come out, each person looking in opposite directions, scanning for trouble as they walk into the rear yard. The figures are dressed completely in dark clothing, with balaclavas covering their heads.

McGuire whistles and both figures turn, weapons up and firing. McGuire is already moving from the corner of the house as a spray of bullets shatters the rear and corner of the home. The two figures don't even have time to turn back around before Tosseti and Nionee return fire, not even giving them a chance to turn their weapons on them. Tosseti and Nionee know the unidentified people in front of them are probably wearing Kevlar, so they shoot at the lower extremities, and then at their heads.

Tosseti's first round is too high and strikes the person standing to the left of him in the chest. Tosseti curses himself as he watches the person recoil, taking one step back, recovering and bringing their weapon up to shoot. Tosseti's second round hits the person in the left kneecap. This brings them down, but they still attempt to bring their weapon to bear on Tosseti. They get a short burst off before Tosseti's third round takes the top of their head off, blood, bone, and brain spraying the air. The weapon goes silent. The rounds harmlessly slapping into the ground.

Nionee fires at the same time as Tosseti, and his first round hits its target under the armpit. A luckily timed shot, as he aims for the arm, but the figure is in the process of raising their weapon to fire at Tosseti when the round struck. The figure screams and turns the barrel of their weapon towards Nionee. They attempt to raise the weapon and fire one-handed. The weapon doesn't even move before a second round strikes the individual in the temple, and they drop like a bag of wet sand, blood spewing from the head wound with each beat of a dying heart.

McGuire comes back around the corner when he hears the military 9MM weapons being fired. By the time he glances around the corner, both assailants are dropping from their mortal injuries. He covers the door as Tosseti and Nionee check the two figures for any signs of life. Finding none, they lift the masks off and see one female and one male.

Nionee calls for Tucker, who answers by asking if they are all right. Nionee informs him they are, and that they have two bad guys down and are going into the house from the rear. Tucker acknowledges and says he's got the front covered.

The three men hear the screeching of tires and see blue and red flashing lights from the front of the house. They cautiously approach and move to the sides of the open door. Nionee does a quick peek. Not seeing anything, he enters with Tosseti and McGuire behind him. They spread out, and each man covers an opening. Nionee walks to the door leading from the kitchen area to the living room. He can see the open front door and the police and rescue vehicles in the street.

"Tucker?" he yells.

"I'm here. You see Torres?"

Yeah, she's not moving, we're in the kitchen, all clear. I've got the living room covered and turning on the living room lights," he announces and reaches around the corner and locates a switch. Nothing happens. He reaches for his flashlight and turns it on, seeing Torres more clearly, lying on the floor, bleeding from wounds. He also sees Danner's bullet-riddled body sprawled across the couch, his mouth open, sightless eyes staring at the ceiling as if frozen in the middle of a prayer to the heavens, or a curse.

Nionee enters the living room, keeping his weapon pointed on the next open door. Tosseti and McGuire move down the hallway from another door leading from the kitchen. Tosseti peeks around the corner of the hallway door that leads into the living room and sees Nionee. Nionee lowers his weapon just as Tucker comes into the home with his light on. Tosseti and McGuire move further down the hallway.

Tucker and Nionee turn their attention to Torres. Tucker feels her neck. "She's still alive!" he declares loudly and jumps up and runs to the door, screaming for a medic. Local police officers rush up, and Tucker asks them to stand by and not go into the home. He tells them there are two bodies in the back that need securing and that OSI is on their way. One patrol sergeant says that his crime scene units are also on the way.

Two medics rush in with their cases and immediately begin to work on Torres. Tucker watches for a second, then walks down the stairs to see another team of medics hovering over Nguyen. His shirt is ripped open, the vest lying on the ground next to him. Tucker sees the vest and realizes the assassins must have been using armor-piercing rounds. The two holes in the agent have stopped bleeding. Tucker knows the man is dead.

Tosseti and McGuire continue down the hallway and ensure the remainder of the house is clear. Satisfied everything is secure, they go through the living room towards the front door, passing the medics as they work on Torres.

"What the hell was that all about?" McGuire asks once outside. "A dead NCO, a dead OSI agent, and a critically injured one. Two dead bad guys, whoever the hell they are. What's going on?" he asks again.

The four NCOs stand in the front yard when Major Bristol, the local OSI commander, and Colonel Black arrive. The four NCOs salute the colonel as he approaches.

"You men alright?" he asks, returning the salute.

They all acknowledge they are fine. The colonel introduces the major and asks what happened. Tucker explains his portion of the op, then Nionee finishes the report on his and the others' participation. Colonel Black nods and looks over towards the house.

"I tried to get word out to you before Sergeant Danner was released. I found out some information that led me to believe his life could have been in danger. I was going to have you all return him to the Bank for his own safety. I received the information too late."

"Sir, any idea who those two in back are?" Nionee asks.

Colonel Black shakes his head. "Who they are? No. But I got a feeling I know who they work for, or *worked* for, I should say. All indications lead to Joyce Olsen."

"What?" Tosseti asks.

"No way," McGuire says, and the others voice their opinions.

The colonel raises his hands. "Okay, men, you finish up here. You'll need to speak with the local authorities first, get that out of the way. Shouldn't be long as we've already spoken with the police chief and the DA about this and they just want the preliminary from you all. Then I want you all back at the Bank immediately after. You will need to be debriefed, and then I will sit down with all of you, to include the others at the Bank, and explain everything. There's also something I might need you all to do, so I'll see you shortly," Black finishes, ending the meeting.

Before he can leave, the paramedics come out the door with the stretcher containing Torres. Her ashen face shows but is partially obscured with an oxygen mask.

The major hurries over and asks how she's doing? They tell him she is critical, and if she makes it to the hospital, she may have a chance. They rush her to the open doors of the waiting vehicle and place the stretcher inside. The major tells the colonel he's going with her and jumps in. Colonel Black and the NCOs watch the ambulance drive away, and the colonel leaves the four men standing in the front yard, blue and red lights flashing across their faces.

CHAPTER 42

Rees and Farnsworth inform the troopers of what they found and are heading back to inform the general. McGregor clears his throat. Farnsworth looks at the man.

"You got something to say, Sergeant?"

"Ah, well, sir, that can't be all the Rebs there. There's probably more behind them, sir. Maybe some artillery, too."

"Your point, Sergeant?" Farnsworth snaps.

"Sir, don't ya think we should be going further out and see?"

Rees snorts and Farnsworth looks at him. Rees raises his palms. "Hey, I was joking earlier," He says.

Farnsworth looks at the sergeant for a few seconds. The sergeant looks back, not cowed by the officer's stare.

"Sergeant McGregor, I appreciate your candor and opinion, but our orders are to find the enemy and report it. You are right, there are probably artillery and more infantry on the way, and we can assume the soldiers are only the front of the forces. Besides that, there are probably one or more cavalry units looking for us and the Union Army. What we have is enough information for the general. That will give him a start, and if he needs more information, then he can send out skirmishers. If we go gallivanting further, those soldiers back there will get even closer to the Union lines, thus giving the general less time to prepare.

The sergeant's shoulders droop just slightly, and he slowly nods his understanding. "Yes, sir. Of course, you're right, sir."

Farnsworth catches the subtle change in the older NCO. "No, Sergeant, you did what a sergeant is supposed to do. You see something and you let the officer know. It's up to the officer whether he takes the information and uses it or not, but you are doing your job. Besides looking out for your men, you are to keep me on my toes. Good job."

The sergeant nods. "Yes, sir, I will do that, Colonel, and thank you."

"Now, let's move out before we're spotted, and they send people after us," Farnsworth says as he turns and trots off.

Rees catches up to him,

"Damn fine speech there, Colonel. Almost brought a tear to my eye."

Farnsworth looks straight ahead. "You know, you're awfully full of it for a captain."

"Naw, that's the NCO in me. We're all smartasses."

Farnsworth chuckles. "Let's move out. Once we get this info to the man, the quicker we can get on with our mission. We've wasted enough time here. There's no telling how far away O'Toole's unit has gotten since our little sidelined jaunt," he tells Rees, then orders the column to move out.

They are moving at a slower pace than they really want, but Farnsworth and Rees agree it's best. They don't want to kick up dust from the dry roads, so they stay off the regular lanes of travel and move along open fields and as close to the wood lines as they can. They do everything they can to avoid trouble, but it comes, and no one expects it.

As the column of troopers advances up a crest of a hill, a Confederate cavalry scouting party approaches from the other side.

Neither group of soldiers knows the other is there until they both come face to face.

They each spy one another at the same time and freeze. Not expecting an enemy to be twenty feet in front of them, they are all dumbfounded. Rees and Farnsworth notice the Confederates wear black caps and hats, and it causes them to pause for a split second because they almost look like Union hats, except the officer's braid and the trooper's caps are trimmed in silver and, of course, the gray uniforms. But this only lasts a couple of seconds as Rees fires a shot from his pistol at the captain leading the Rebel troopers. The round misses but strikes the flag bearer, who tumbles out of his saddle and lands heavily on the ground, wounded.

Now, the fight is on. Both sides reach for weapons. The Rebel captain pulls his saber and charges towards Farnsworth. Farnsworth pulls his saber and advances towards the captain.

Rees' horse jumps from the shot and turns in a circle. He can't get a second shot off. The rest of the Union troopers are raising their rifles and pistols at the same time as the Rebel troopers. Everyone fires from horseback and only a couple of shots strike anyone. One Union trooper's round strikes a Rebel horse, and the animal rears back, causing his rider to fall off and land on his neck, snapping it with a sickening *crunch*, made worse when the large animal falls on top of him, trashing and kicking in its attempt to stand.

Smoke fills the area as each weapon is fired. There is no breeze, so the air is choked with the acidic smell of cordite and gunpowder. Men scream and curse at each other as they fire, reload, and fire again.

Some of the soldiers don't even try to reload, they just charge in and use their rifles as clubs, attempting to beat the enemy with the barrel of the weapon. Others use sabers to slash and stab.

Farnsworth and the captain clash, with their sabers clanging as each man swings with all his might at the other. The captain believes he has drawn first blood as his saber slices across the upper left arm of Farnsworth. The blade is deflected off the Kevlar-type material, causing Farnsworth a small amount of pain from the impact but no wound. The captain grimaces and thinks he can now finish off his adversary but is surprised when Farnsworth comes back at him, seemingly unfazed by the blow.

This causes the captain to hesitate for a split second, enough time for Farnsworth to feign a strike, causing the captain to react slowly and attack in the wrong direction. Farnsworth goes low after the feint and slices across the man's chest. The Gray uniform easily splits opens, and blood begins flowing from the deep gash. The captain drops his arm toward the wound, and Farnsworth finishes him off with a thrust through the man's back, the blade going through and out the front. The captain slumps, then falls from his horse.

A Rebel cavalryman sees his captain fall and takes aim with this pistol to kill Farnsworth. Farnsworth looks up and sees the weapon pointed at him but doesn't have time to reach his own gun. The Rebel jerks and fires his pistol into the ground, grabbing his side as he falls from the saddle. Farnsworth looks left, then right to see O'Toole holding his Spencer rifle up and pointing at the Rebel. O'Toole doesn't even have time to see Farnsworth looking at him as he concentrates on reloading.

Rees has taken a round square in the chest and can't catch his breath. When the round strikes him, he drops his pistol and is having trouble getting his rifle out of the scabbard. He sees a Rebel soldier charging for him, and he still can't get his rifle out and doesn't even think about his saber. Reaching into his pocket, he fumbles with a button, flipping the small switch. He removes the button and throws it at the charging cavalryman. There is a moment when he thinks he is about to die then, suddenly, the button explodes in the advancing soldier's face.

The effect is devastating and gruesome as the small charge takes most of the man's head off. Blood and gore fly through the air, some landing on Rees, as the almost headless rider gallops past Rees, then falls into the woods, horse still running. Rees doesn't have time to think about what he just witnessed as his fellow warriors need his help.

Finally catching his breath, he reaches down and removes his rifle. Steadying his horse, he aims at the closest Rebel he can see and smoothly pulls the trigger. The round is true, and another horse soldier falls from his saddle. He takes aim at another, shoots, then moves on to another. It's like the proverbial fish in a barrel.

He empties his magazine, then reloads and continues to fire. He is so engrossed in his killing spree he doesn't even feel or care when he is struck by rounds, not once, but twice. He continues firing, just as his fellow soldiers are fighting. Many men are off their horses and engaged in hand to hand combat.

O'Toole is one of those fighting hand to hand. He kills a man with his saber and turns and looks for the next soldier to fight. He doesn't see a Rebel standing about twenty feet behind, raising a pistol to aim at him, but Farnsworth does. Farnsworth pulls his pistol, then hesitates, head turning slightly away. Rees sees the Rebel soldier at the same time as Farnsworth.

Rees raises his rifle at the same time Farnsworth aims his pistol at the soldier. Rees fires his rifle, killing the soldier as three 5.56 mm rounds go into the man, the first round piercing his heart, the second and third rounds not needed. Farnsworth fires a split second after Rees, and his round hits the man in the hip as he falls from Rees' shot.

Rees wonders for a second why Farnsworth fired later than he did. Did he hesitate, and if so, why? He doesn't have time to ponder this as there is still Rebel cavalry trying to kill him, so his attention returns to firing his weapon.

Farnsworth doesn't know who kills the man as he turns to face another enemy soldier. He charges the man, who looks up just as Farnsworth brings his saber down into the man's face, slicing from the top of his skull down to his chest. The man screams and grabs his face with both hands, blood already pouring between his fingers. Blind from the blood flowing into his eyes, the soldier stumbles across the field and is trampled by soldiers on horseback fighting from the saddles. The man falls to the ground and is stomped to death by both Union and Confederate horses.

Farnsworth retrieves his rifle and picks off soldiers at an astonishing rate. With the two semi-automatic weapons being fired by expert marksmen, the Confederate soldiers' numbers dwindle quickly. The Rebel sergeant who is still alive and now in charge finally notices they are losing this battle. He calls for a retreat, and those left do not hesitate to get away from these damned Yankee berserkers.

A few more rounds are fired, then the enemy is gone. All that is left are the dead bodies of men from both sides, as well as the wounded. The men who are left look at the devastation that surrounds them. Some are still in fighting mode, adrenaline pumping and looking for someone to attack. Others rush to the aid of their fellow soldiers, ignoring the groans of pain from the Rebels left alive.

Rees and Farnsworth place their rifles back into the scabbards, and Rees gets off his horse. Rees watches Farnsworth, not sure what he had witnessed earlier. *Time to ask about that later,* he thinks.

"Get your med-kit!" Farnsworth shouts, and Rees does. The two men hand out bandages to those helping their wounded comrades.

"What about the Rebels?" Rees asks. "We can't just ignore them."

Farnsworth holds up some morphine syrettes.

"We've got quite a few of these. We can make them comfortable until help arrives. I'm sure those who retreated are going back for reinforcements, and we don't want to be here when they return."

Rees runs back to his horse and grabs some syrettes for himself and goes about injecting those Confederate soldiers with serious wounds, the cries of pain diminishing. When they are through, most of the Union wounded have been treated.

"Sergeant McGregor, Corporal O'Toole! On me," Rees shouts, and the two men look at each other as they have never heard the expression before but understand its meaning and quickly scramble over to him. "What's the status of the men?" he asks and sees that Sergeant McGregor is bleeding. "You're hurt."

Sergeant McGregor looks at the wound on his arm. "Naw, a scratch, sir," he states, grinning.

Rees shakes his head. "Get it bandaged as soon as we're finished here, Sergeant. Now, what about the men?" he asks again with concern and worry.

"Captain, we took some loses, four men dead and three seriously wounded, the rest with minor wounds," O'Toole answers.

Farnsworth walks over. "We need to get out of here now. Those Rebs will be back to collect their wounded, and we don't want another skirmish."

"Agreed," Rees says and turns and looks at the wounded. "If the seriously wounded can't ride, we'll have to leave them here. The Rebs will take care of them."

"Begging the captain's pardon," McGregor interjects, "but if we leave them, the Rebs will only take them to Andersonville or Salisbury. That is no place for any man to go to. If rumors are true about those places, we might as well shoot them now."

"Well, Sergeant, we don't have much choice. We can't take them with us, and we are not killing them. Better they get help, and hopefully live, don't you think?" Rees asks, staring at the sergeant questioningly.

"Yes, sir. I just hate thinking what will happen to them that is all," McGregor says, shaking his head.

"So do I, Sergeant, but we have to get the information back, and if we hang around here, we might just end up captured or dead ourselves. Now, get the men ready to go."

McGregor and O'Toole salute and run off as ordered.

Rees looks at the wounded and shows Farnsworth a syrette. Farnsworth nods and they go over to the men who are too injured to ride. One looks like he won't make it too much longer, and the others are going to be hit or miss, depending on when they get help and how competent that help will be. Both take a syrette and inject each man with one, watching as the drug takes almost an immediate effect as the wounded soldiers' faces relax.

After ensuring the wounded are cared for, they get on their horses and tell the troopers to move out. They go down the crest of the hill and head into the heavily wooded area towards their camp. Rees stares at Farnsworth again, wondering why the man hesitated when O'Toole was about to be shot and what he should do about it.

~ ~ ~

Sergeant Hanes, 8th Battalion, North Carolina Cavalry, rides back to his command with what is left of his company. He orders his men to re-supply and get fresh horses. Hanes jumps off his horse and rushes to the battalion HQ tent, where he is met by Lieutenant Colonel Gardner, who has come out to see what the shouting was about.

Hanes runs up to the officer, salutes, and breathlessly explains what happened.

"Colonel Gardner, sir, those damned Yankees fought like demons. Two of their officers were shooting us so fast you could not see them reload. I ain't ne'r seen anything like it. Captain Wicks even struck their colonel with the blade of his saber, and the colonel made it no never mind. The Yankee colonels' uniform didn't have a mark on it. I swear, we outnumbered them three to one, but they kilt most of us," The sergeant looks at the ground, frowning. "I thought it best we get while we still had some men left to get back here and tell ya'll."

The colonel stares at the sergeant, then claps him on the shoulder.

"Any wounded, Sergeant?" he inquires.

"Why, yes, sir," Sergeant Hanes answers. "I would like permission to go back out with more men, sir. Not only to retrieve our wounded but maybe track down those blue bellies and have a reckoning with them."

"Yes, Sergeant. You say they shot so fast that you couldn't see them reload?"

"Yes, sir. Come to think of it, I'm not even sure they did reload."

A captain standing next to the colonel leans towards him.

"Rumor going around the regiment about them northern factories working on a new type of repeater. Maybe they already got them. If so, sir, we sure could put good use to one if'n we were to capture them Yanks."

The colonel nods. "Yes, I heard that rumor as well," he says, then thinks for a minute.

"Sergeant, show me on my map where this was."

"Yes, sir," Hanes answers and follows Colonel Gardner and Captain Lewis into the tent, where a map is spread out on a table. The sergeant moves to the table and studies the map for a few seconds, then places his finger on a section.

"Right here, Colonel. We were in this area, just on the crest of this hill," he says, tapping the spot. "We were on patrol and moving in this direction," continuing to trace a line on the map with his finger, "and ran into them on the hill. After the battle, we gathered who was left and hightailed back here."

"Which direction were they coming from, Sergeant?" the colonel asks.

Sergeant Hanes points to the map again and draws a line west to east.

"They were heading east, sir. Funny thing, they were in the woods not on the roads. I took them as a scouting party, but they were not in an area that would have had anything of importance to see."

"What do you think they were doing, Sergeant?"

"Sir, I think they were trying to get back to their lines and did not want to be seen. So instead of moving quickly down a road, they were using the trees to hide them."

"It makes sense, sir. If I had that small a unit and thought I was in enemy territory and knew some information I had needed to get back and wasn't looking for a fight, I might do the same," Captain Lewis adds.

The colonel looks at the captain. "Captain Lewis, get your men together. Take Sergeant Hanes with you and go find those Union troopers. Capture them, kill them, do whatever you have to, but get those rifles. Damned if I am gonna let some Yankee cavalry kill a bunch of my boys with new weaponry and get away," he states and turns towards the sergeant. "Sergeant, did your men do any damage to the enemy?"

Hanes nods. "Oh, yes, sir. We kilt some, wounded more, but like I said, sir, those two officers were some'n fierce. No way we would have lost that many without them two shooting at us."

"Sergeant, you'll be with Captain Lewis's troop," he tells Hanes, then turns to Lewis. "Captain, take your company and move to this location," the colonel says, pointing to a spot on the map that could possibly be an area the Union cavalry would cross. "You must move with haste, Captain. Move with haste. Beat those troopers there and do your best to get me those guns," he finishes and turns to the sergeant again. "Sergeant Hanes, before you leave, get your men together, then pull some more from Captain Russell's unit and have them make their way back to the hill and gather our wounded and bury the dead. I'm sure they left their dead there, so do the Christian thing and bury them also, understand?"

"Yes, sir," the sergeant says, salutes, and hurries out of the tent.

Captain Lewis waits until the sergeant is out of the tent. "Sir, it'll be dark within the hour. We won't be able to catch up to them, and we won't be able to track them in the dark."

The colonel nods. "I understand, Captain, but time is of the essence. You must get to this point," he says, tapping the spot on the map, "before they do. You don't need to track, just get there and wait. Is that understood?"

"Yes, sir," he says, saluting and turning to leave.

"And, Captain?"

"Sir?"

"Do make haste. I want those guns."

The captain grins and nods. "Yes, sir!" Then he opens the tent flap and exits.

CHAPTER 43

Chief Black shakes his head in disgust. "I've had enough of this," he says to no one in particular after having looked at the video of the skirmish a third time. "This was supposed to be a simple insertion, take O'Toole back to his unit, drop him off, save the timeline, then come back home. Another feather in our hat for time travel, a little more history learned, an adventure for a couple of airmen, but nope, we just have to go off-mission with a little side jaunt courtesy of some glory-seeking general. Now, they get into a fight with a Rebel cavalry unit, and O'Toole almost gets killed, hell all three of them almost get killed. This has got to stop," he says, ranting, more disappointed than angry. Then he looks around the control room and sees most people smiling and acting like they're not paying attention.

"Alright. I'll be upstairs," he grumbles to the OIC and leaves the control room, his mind wandering, turning, thinking. He reaches the C&C, where Colonel Weiss watches him.

"Sorry, Chief. We're doing everything we can, as well as the Clio team," he says to the retired Chief Master Sergeant.

The chief is still lost in thought, and he doesn't pay attention to what is said. Black has a look of confusion on his face when he looks up at the colonel. It takes him a second to realize he is in the C&C, where he wanted to be.

"Damn, got to quit doing that. You will all think I'm going senile."

"No, Chief. You're just doing the absent-minded professor thing, that's all," the colonel says, with the technicians ignoring the two men, or so they act.

"Just as bad. Anyway, any word from John, I mean Colonel Black?"

"Yes, Chief. He wants you to call him. You were busy at the time, so he said to wait until you were free."

"Thanks, Colonel. May I use the observation room again?"

"Of course, Chief. You don't have to ask."

"Thank you." The chief goes into the observation room and closes the door behind him. He connects with the Bank, and soon, Colonel Black appears on the screen.

"John, what's the news on your end. Any progress with the virus or Clio?"

"Sorry, Dad. The technicians are still working on the virus. They have made progress but nothing earth-shattering. I see our boys got themselves into a little scrape while I was gone. From what I saw, those weapons and uniforms came in handy."

"Yes, they did, thank God. Did you see Rees? He got shot three times, and the material held. I just hope it doesn't degrade, and I hope they don't get shot anymore. Listen, John, maybe we should bring them back. We can regroup and try again. We've learned a lot from this go around, and with Clio being sabotaged and all, I don't know, might be time to bring them home."

"I don't think so, not yet. They got through the battle and came out okay. They are on their way back with the information the general asked for, and once he gets that, they can be on their way. Hopefully, they learned a lesson and try to stay away from units close to the fighting. Let's give them some more time. Plus, give our technicians more time to work on the virus extraction."

The chief is a professional and knows the colonel is probably right, so he consents, "Okay, you're in charge, as I have said before. I'm just giving my opinion. Anything else?"

The colonel raises his eyebrows. "Oh, yeah," then proceeds to tell him what has been going on at the Bank.

~ ~ ~

"My God, that's crazy. What is going on? What is she doing?" the chief asks, crossing his arms and frowning.

"I can hazard one guess," the colonel replies. "She's trying to somehow change the timeline back to what it was before her grandfather was killed."

"How does she think…" the chief starts to ask, then stops. "Damn, I get it," he says and shakes his head. "O'Toole. If O'Toole dies, then we cease to exist. If I don't exist, then there's no Clio Project. No Clio Project, then the senator doesn't try to overthrow the Bank because it doesn't exist, either. The senator is not booted out of office in disgrace, doesn't commit suicide, her mother doesn't steal Clio Project blueprints and build Janus, which we assume she was going to use in her attempt to alter the timeline in the same matter, or worse."

"My thoughts exactly," Colonel Black says in agreement. "But we're not out of the woods yet. Joyce Olsen is in the wind. We have people looking for her, not that she's a liability at this juncture, but we still would like a word with her. The main concern right now is Captain Farnsworth. We don't know what his end game is and won't until this plays out. It doesn't make sense to me, or OSI. Farnsworth is the daughter of Joyce Olsen and gains access to the Bank, as well as Clio. He works his way in and onto the team that takes O'Toole back. Senator Olsen is the driving force to get the project back up and running, as well as recommending Farnsworth. Once Farnsworth is inside, he plants a virus into the system," the colonel says, then stops and thinks, scratching his chin with his thumb. "Yet, there was already a virus in the system, planted by Master Sergeant Danner, so now we have another question, why two viruses?" he asks aloud, then continues, "Farnsworth is now back in time with Rees and O'Toole, to what end? I can't figure this out."

The chief shrugs, raising his arms, palms up. "Don't ask me, I'm a scientist and combat troop not an OSI investigator or psychologist. I'm worried about the time machines and the teams sent through them. We'll just keep watching Farnsworth. I've been watching footage from the bodycam's that Rees and Farnsworth are wearing. From what I see, Rees is keeping an eye on Farnsworth as well. I can tell he doesn't trust him, which is good in one way. The bad thing is I think they generally get along. Good team, except we don't trust one of them."

"That's good, Dad. Hopefully, we can get this mess sorted out. The teams here will continue to work on Clio twenty-four seven. All the video's we have are being looked over by history experts, as well as psychologists, doctors, and investigators. Everyone is involved in this. The doctors and psychologist are checking on the men's wellbeing, how they are handling the time period, any stress, being shot so many times, the usual. History guys are, well, history guys, and the investigators, profilers mostly, are watching Farnsworth, looking for any signs of what he might be up to."

"Sounds good. Well, I'll let you get back to commanding, and I'll get back to whatever it is I'm supposed to be doing."

The colonel snorts a laugh. "Alright, Dad, talk to you soon. Oh, and, Dad, get some sleep, you're not a spring chicken anymore."

"Don't push it, Son, or I'll come back there and embarrass you in front of your troops. You still ain't too big to be spanked, you know," the chief says, laughing. Then under his breath and just barely audible enough for the colonel to hear before he disconnects, "Damn smart-ass kids these days."

CHAPTER 44

Rees and Farnsworth call for a halt just as the darkening shadows in the trees make it difficult to see. They also want the troopers to rest, get some food into them, and tend to their wounds. Most of the wounds are minor, but a couple could get infected. Farnsworth and Rees agree they should use some small amount of their antibiotics on the injured.

After helping the wounded, they go about setting up the perimeter security. Rees goes out and places several of the intrusion detection devices in the wooded area. He then places a trooper on guard duty. The soldiers all look at each other, squinting, furrowing their brows, rubbing their cheeks, and scratching their chins. Rees sees the looks on their faces and assures them only one sentry is required and to trust him.

They also decide to share some of their food with the men. The soldiers' eyes widen, and small yelps can be heard as well as some backslapping. They all wonder about the hard tack because none of them have had hard tack that tasted good, and this was really good.

"Sirs?" one of the privates asks. "Where did you get this? Never had hard tack that had a taste, and the coffee is nothing I've ever had. Hell, none of us have."

Rees chuckles. "Old family recipe. Had it made for me and sent from home."

"Where is home, sir?" another trooper asks.

"I'm from Arizona," Rees replies.

"And you came all this way to fight?" the soldier asks.

"Not really," Rees says and squats by the fire and grabs the coffee pot, and pours himself a cup. "I was already in the Army in Washington when the war broke out," he tells the men a story already in place for him and Farnsworth.

"And you, Colonel?"

"Same story. I was in Washington also, working with Captain Rees," Farnsworth says, sipping his coffee. "We were working for the president."

"No shit?" another soldier says. "Honest, working for Ole Abe?"

Rees and Farnsworth both nod.

"We were on special assignment for the man, along with Corporal O'Toole, when we were grabbed by the general and asked to conduct this reconnaissance," Farnsworth adds.

The men all talk and look at O'Toole with some admiration.

Farnsworth walks closer to the fire and looks at McGregor.

"Sergeant?" he says.

McGregor stands. "Sir?"

Farnsworth shakes his head and moves his hand in a *sit down* gesture.

"No, Sergeant, sit, sit." McGregor does as he is told, still watching the colonel. Smiling, Farnsworth looks at the sergeant. "Do me a favor?"

McGregor nods. "Yes, sir."

Farnsworth looks at Rees, who is wondering what Farnsworth is up to.

"Say, good morning, Miss Moneypenny."

McGregor squints at Rees, frowning, and Rees takes a step closer, arching an eyebrow.

"Sir?"

"Say, good morning, Miss Moneypenny."

The sergeant doesn't understand why, but he does as he is asked.

"Good morning, Miss Moneypenny," he says with a Scottish accent, sounding like Sean Connery.

Farnsworth and Rees both laugh, and Rees asks him to say it again, which the sergeant does.

Farnsworth and Rees crack up laughing, with all the soldiers staring at them as if they had lost their minds. One soldier leans over to O'Toole.

"What's wrong with them? What's a money penny?" he asks.

O'Toole takes a breath, sighs, and slowly shakes his head, watching the two laughing men. "Damned if I know. I do not have a clue what these two talk about or say half the time. It's like they are from a different time, you know?" He chuckles to himself, with the soldiers scratching their heads and glancing around at one another.

After everyone is finished eating, the men attend to the horses, then settle down for the night. The sergeant asks the officers if they are sure one sentry is enough, and they reassure him it's fine. McGregor grunts a goodnight and heads for his tent. Farnsworth and Rees walk around and make sure everything is secure, then go to where they plan to bed down.

"You see the hats the Rebs wore?" Rees asks.

"Yeah, never seen black hats with silver trim before," Farnsworth responds.

"I know there are different uniforms being worn by both sides, but that was unusual. Most of the Rebs wear gray or butternut, not black. Plus, those uniforms were all gray. No mixture of color. A special unit perhaps? Guess we'll just call them the black hats."

Farnsworth grins and shakes his head. The two men settle down for the night.

~ ~ ~

Captain Lewis and his black hat troops don't stop for the night, much to the displeasure of his men, who grumble among themselves but away from the ears of the NCO and captain. Captain Lewis knows the men don't understand, but it's not their place to understand, it's their place to follow orders, and his orders were clear to him, so that should be good enough for the troopers.

They travel slowly, so as not to come upon a ditch and fall in or hit a low hanging branch. Lewis wants to get to the site in plenty of time to set up and bushwhack the damned Yankees and get their rifles. He can see a promotion already.

Even though they are riding slowly, the equipment on the men and horses makes noise. Not real loud, the jangling sound from bridles, weapons, but it is enough to bother the captain. He fears the Yankees may be near and able to hear them. This thought goes away as his mind wanders, moving back to the promotion. He is so lost in thought he doesn't even hear Sergeant Hanes talking to him.

"Sir. Captain Lewis, sir?" Hanes asks, looking at the man and wondering if something is wrong.

"Sir?" he asks again, this time getting a reaction.

"Yes, Sergeant Hanes, what is it?" he asks, annoyed because he is embarrassed being caught not paying attention.

"Over there, sir," Hanes says, pointing to his right.

Lewis turns to see where the sergeant is pointing and doesn't see anything.

"What is it, Sergeant. I don't see..." he starts to say, then understands. The captain tells the sergeant to have the men stop, and Hanes quietly rides off to halt the company.

Lewis pulls out his telescope and peers in the direction where it looks like a small campfire smolders. It's barely visible, and the captain wonders how Sergeant Hanes even spotted it. He moves the telescope around and sees tents.

No, it can't be. His luck isn't that good. The Yanks wouldn't have stopped this far back, then set up camp. That makes no sense. Why would they stop? They have to know that the Rebel army would be coming after them. This has got to be another group of soldiers, maybe even some of their own. But there shouldn't be any Confederates in this area. It's either a different group or he is one lucky son of a gun.

Sergeant Hanes comes back and stops beside the captain.

"Orders, sir?"

"Sergeant, take one man with you and move up close enough to get a better view of that encampment. Gather what information you can, then report back to me once you have it. Now, go," Lewis orders, and the sergeant salutes and climbs off his horse. He points to the closest soldier to him and signals for the trooper to come with him. Once the soldier is off his horse, the sergeant and he moves off towards the encampment.

It takes the two men several minutes to get into a good enough spot they can see into the camp. They walk as close as they can, then crouch and move in more. Finally, they lie on the ground and crawl in as close as they feel is safe.

Sergeant Hanes is confused as to why he can't see any pickets. He would expect to have come across them further back but didn't. He takes the captain's telescope out and looks around. There, he spots the lone sentry, and he is on the other side of the camp, facing away from them.

Hanes is confused. He notices movement in the camp and swings the scope back towards it. He sees two men standing and talking. As one of the men turns towards him, and he sees it's the colonel they had the encounter with earlier. His heart beats faster as he realizes they have found who they were looking for.

Hanes motions for the soldier with him to move back, and both men slide back away as quietly as possible. Once they are far enough away, they jump up and run back to their company.

~   ~   ~

The low sounding beeping of the alarm in their ears awakens Rees and Farnsworth. Both men sit up slowly and look around, then stand.

"Okay, something set it off, but I'm not seeing or hearing anything," Farnsworth says.

"Doesn't matter, we need to be ready. I'll get the men up and stand-to," Rees says and goes to each of the tents to wake the men as Farnsworth goes out to the sentry. He reaches the sentry and moves him into the camp. Once back, they join the others. Rees tells two of the men to start saddling the horses and another to put out the campfire. The others are to get dressed, grab their rifles, and set perimeter security around camp. They are to lie down, facing out, and watch and listen. Rees tells them if someone comes close to the camp, they will know it.

Once all the horses are saddled, the two soldiers join their comrades in securing the camp. Rees and Farnsworth kneel in the middle of the camp and wait.

~   ~   ~

Sergeant Hanes and the soldier return out of breath. Leaning over to catch his breath, the sergeant tells the captain the camp belongs to the Yanks they fought earlier. Captain Lewis is delighted and almost giddy.

He orders all the soldiers to dismount and form a skirmish line. Once they are formed up, Captain Lewis stands in front and points his sword in the direction they need to go.

There is just enough moonlight that the soldiers can see. They are close enough together that they can move in a line and see the soldier next to them. The thick bed of pine needles covering the ground helps silence the footfalls, but when there are three dozen men walking it can't be complete silence.

~ ~ ~

McGregor is the first to hear the faint noise out in front of him. He rolls onto his back and waves at Rees and Farnsworth. They move to him, and he tells them to listen. They both hear it. Movement in front.

Rees scrambles around and moves all the men to face the area where the sound is coming from. The troopers are all ready and anxious. Rees and Farnsworth both grab their rifles and take a knee behind the prone troopers and wait.

~ ~ ~

Captain Lewis has lost sight of the campfire but knows he's heading in the right direction. The trees are sparse, and movement is not impaired as they draw closer to their objective. Moonlight comes and goes as clouds float across the sky, allowing the men quick glimpses of what lays ahead of them. Trying to work their way around trees, the men bump and jostle each other, and the occasional sounds of cursing can be heard. Captain Lewis is becoming angry, afraid the element of surprise will be lost because of noise discipline break down among the troopers.

He is about to have the men halt when he spies the shadowy outline of a white tent. He raises his hand for the men to halt, realizing they can't all see him. He opens his mouth with the intent of ordering the men to stop and set up a firing line. Before he can issue the command, he hears a loud *pop*, and then a flash of light blinds him and several of the Rebel soldiers.

The light is emitted from a trip flare Rees had set out earlier, in conjunction with the alarm system.

Some of the men raise their hands to ward off the glare but not before losing their night vision. Others just keep on going and are stopped when they, too, run into a flare. Not understanding what is going on, some of the men start firing in the direction of the camp.

~ ~ ~

Rees and Farnsworth drop down once the flares ignite and order the troopers to fire at will. The Union soldiers open fire, and most of the first round of bullets find a target. Rees and Farnsworth add their weapons' fire to the fray, and within just a couple of seconds, over a quarter of Captain Lewis' troops are dead or wounded.

Rees reaches into a pocket and grasps a half bar of explosive. It already has a detonator button attached. He turns the timer and lofts the handmade grenade towards the Rebel soldiers. "Grenade out," he yells from habit, even though the troopers probably have no idea what he is hollering about.

At first, nothing happens, and Rees thinks the button may have fallen off the bomb, but a few seconds later, there is a thunderous explosion, and a brilliance fills the darkness, turning night into day for a split second. There is enough light that the Union troopers close their eyes and cover their heads in shock from the blast. Rees and Farnsworth stand and watch as the explosion throws bodies in the air and removes limbs from several of those closest to the explosion.

"Holy shit!" Farnsworth exclaims. "Wasn't expecting that. Good one, Rees."

The two men continue firing and urge the others on.

~ ~ ~

Captain Lewis is confused and blind from the flare. He screams at his men to fire, which is not needed as the majority of them are already shooting. The majority of their shots are too high and fly over the Union soldier's heads. One round fired by a Rebel finds its mark by accident when a Rebel trooper stumbles and his rifle discharges with the barrel aimed lower. The round strikes the young private who inquired about Rees and Farnsworth's home earlier. It hits him right between the eyes, blowing the back of his head out.

Lewis shouts his men forward, and his vision is returning, as he can see the flashes of the Union soldier rifles. Knowing he has the superior forces, he yells for his men to pour fire upon the enemy. His screaming is cut off short when there is a loud explosion to his right, and he is peppered with blood, bone, and gore from men who are the recipients of the blast.

I don't understand. How is this happening? What devil's work is upon us? Lewis thinks. After the explosion, he orders his men to take cover wherever they can, and the men gratefully obey, finding trees and logs to hide behind, giving them a slight reprieve from the death being thrown at them.

Lewis knows the enemy can't hold them off, even with the devil light and the bombs. He looks and finds Sergeant Hanes screaming at the men. Hanes looks around after hearing his name and sees Lewis waving his arms frantically, signaling him over. Hanes obeys and crouches as he runs towards the captain.

"Sir?" he asks when within earshot.

Lewis kneels and grasps the sergeant's shoulder. "Sergeant Hanes, take seven or eight men and move around the other side. Flank those bastards and pour hell into them. They have already cost us a good number of my men, and they are not leaving here alive. When we take that camp, I want you to find the body of those two blue belly officers. The general wants their weapons, and I intend on fulfilling his orders. Now, go," he orders and pushes the sergeant away.

Sergeant Hanes does as he is told and grabs several men to flank his way around the Union camp.

~ ~ ~

The weapons fire is heavy, and the Union soldiers are pinned down. Even though they have inflicted heavy casualties on the Rebs, they are still outnumbered, and now the Rebs have taken cover. They are lucky so far and have only lost one man, but that leaves them with only eight men able to shoot.

Rees and Farnsworth are down on the ground with the rest of the troopers and trying to formulate a plan.

"We can't stay here, that's for sure. There's no telling how many of them there are. We killed a lot, but they just keep coming," Rees says, eyes darting.

"I agree. We are going to have to make a run for it. If I were out there, I would be sending men around either side to flank us. Classic move, and the Rebs are good at guerilla warfare."

Just as Farnsworth finishes the sentence, the perimeter alarm goes off. This time to their left flank.

"See, knew it," Farnsworth says, not boastful, but eyes glaring. As soon as he speaks, another flare pops, and they can see several Rebels plain as day. Rees and Farnsworth both roll and fire into the men they can see. They have just enough time to watch two soldiers fall before the flare burns out.

"Let's go," Farnsworth says to Rees.

"Right behind you," Rees replies.

They both low-crawl over to the men still fighting and tell them they are going to make a run for it. Rees tells them to go for the horses, and that he and Farnsworth will cover them. O'Toole and McGregor want to argue, but Rees slaps O'Toole and tells him to get the fuck on the horse, then orders McGregor to make sure O'Toole gets back to his regiment if something happens to him or Farnsworth and make sure the general gets his information.

"Now, go, damn you!" he yells and turns to fire at the cautiously approaching enemy.

O'Toole and McGregor do as they are instructed and scramble towards the waiting horses. Another Union soldier falls as he is shot in the leg. Another is killed as he and his horse are both peppered with rounds, the soldier falling to the ground and the horse screaming, running away until it falls dead.

The other soldiers all get on their horses and gallop away towards the rising sun, which is beginning to show red on the low horizon. O'Toole and McGregor both ride a few yards, then stop and look for Farnsworth and Rees until McGregor grabs O'Toole by the sleeve and pulls him away.

Rees grabs another of the grenades and flings it out towards the advancing soldiers. As soon as it explodes, he and Farnsworth are up and running. Just as they both get onto their horses, Rees is hit in the arm and drops his rifle before he can place it in the scabbard. He turns his horse around and is about to climb down when several rounds fly by him, close enough he can feel the tiny breeze the .54 caliber round makes whizzing by his face. He curses, and Farnsworth yells for him to move his ass. He looks at the rifle, then at the charging enemy soldiers, getting closer with each passing second. Cursing again, he turns his horse and chases after Farnsworth.

~ ~ ~

Captain Lewis shouts at the top of his lungs for his men to kill the two Yankee officers. He wants those rifles. Seeing both men flee on their horses, he curses as he stumbles into their deserted encampment. Swearing again, he takes one last futile shot at the receding cavalrymen. Already, his men are scrounging through whatever is left behind, tents, bedrolls, rations, cooking materials. His men are joyous, but the captain is not. He stands there fuming and watching his adversary get away with the prize he coveted most.

"Captain Lewis, sir," he hears and turns, his face a mask of rage at whoever calls for him. He sees Sergeant Hanes approaching him, carrying a rifle. He stares at the weapon as Hanes holds it up for him to see. "Can it be?" he asks himself as he reaches for the weapon. Grabbing it with both hands, he turns it over for examination. It looks like a plain Spencer rifle.

"Sergeant, this is just a Spencer."

"Yes, sir, but I saw the Yankee captain drop it when he was shot."

Lewis looks at the man. "Are you sure?"

"Oh, yes, sir. It was my ball that struck him. And again, the man shrugged it off like I had only slapped him. But it was enough for him to drop the rifle and flee. It is his for sure."

Captain Lewis turns the weapon over and examines it. When running his hands over its features, he accidentally presses the magazine release button. The bottom of the stock retracts, and he removes the magazine. He looks at it and holds it up. Sergeant Hanes is astonished.

"What in tarnation is that?" Hanes asks.

Lewis hands the rifle back to Hanes. By now, a few of the men have gained an interest in what the captain is doing and gather around him. He doesn't even notice as he tentatively removes one of the 5.56 rounds from the magazine.

"What is that?" Hanes asks brow furrowed. "Can't be a bullet, can it?"

Lewis smiles while examining the round. "Yes, Sergeant, it is, and a damned fine one, too. They have made a smaller round and encased it in brass," he answers and takes the rifle back and studies it some more.

"If'n we can make these, I think the tide of this war may change more in our favor than it already is. We need to get this back to the colonel right now," he says, looking around, a smile forming on his lips. "Gather the men, Sergeant. No time to waste, we've got to get back."

"Yes, sir," Hanes says with a grin and turns to yell at the troopers.

CHAPTER 45

Colonel Black watches the battle unfold on the split screen in the control room. Chief Black is also watching the same scene in the Olympus control room.

"I've got to give them credit, they know how to put the equipment Captain Epstein made to good use," the chief states.

"That, and they know how to fight," Colonel Black adds.

Chief Black still stares at the screen, and the colonel sees him nod his head. The chief finally turns and looks into the camera.

"This is getting a little troublesome, John. They keep getting into fights and, so far, luck has been on their side."

"Luck and good soldiering, Dad. Both of them have led their troopers out of two bad situations."

"That's the point. They weren't supposed to get into any situations in the first place. They have lost several men in two fights and, luckily, O'Toole wasn't one of those casualties. I swear, we should bring them back and try again later."

The colonel shakes his head. "No, we'll let them ride this out. They've escaped and are close to their lines. Once they get back and give the general his information, they should be able to move on out without any further delays. Couple more days of riding, and they should catch up to O'Toole's unit, then we can bring them home. As much as I want to know what Farnsworth has to say about his mother and his involvement in this conspiracy, I think it best we let them carry on."

"Speaking of Mrs. Olsen, how's that progressing?" the chief inquires.

"We have the FBI and local authorities on the lookout for her. TSA has been notified, as well as the train stations and bus depots," he says and snorts. "Like she'll take a bus. But you never know. All private flight plans are being looked at. We'll get her," the colonel tells the chief.

"What about the assassins? Find out who they were?"

Colonel Black sighs. "They were a couple of mercenaries. Seems that MILES didn't really disappear after all. Well, they did but didn't. MILES itself was disbanded, as you know, but those who evaded arrest or capture kept working in the dark. What was left of the hierarchy in 1997 regrouped and formed a shadow organization. They kept quiet and hidden, working for Joyce Olsen. When her mother disappeared, someone in MILES contacted her and, somehow, they continued hiring new recruits and placing them under her control once she gained enough power. Instead of having operatives in the open, they outsourced mercenaries in the hopes that if anything went wrong, it couldn't blow back on them. But they were wrong. OSI, NSA, CIA, and the FBI are working together to locate and track down any and all who have any ties to this organization. This includes the military. Since Danner and Farnsworth were able to infiltrate us, our security measures are being scrutinized."

The chief looks incredulous. "Hey, it's not our security that was the problem. We were duped into letting those two men in by a senator, who is either in on it or one of the dumbest senators I know. And I know a lot of them, and that's not saying much."

Colonel Black grumps, "That's not saying anything good about the company you keep, Chief."

Chief Black snorts back. "Yeah, well…" He shakes his head.

Colonel Black gets serious when he hears Rees and Farnsworth talking.

"Dad, listen," he says, pointing to the screen, and they both turn their attention to the conversation.

~   ~   ~

Rees rides as hard as he can through the woods, attempting to catch up to Farnsworth. Riding into an open field, he gallops faster. Upon passing a clump of trees, Farnsworth whistles. Rees slows and turns his horse around and makes for the trees where Farnsworth waits.

"You okay?" Farnsworth asks, looking Rees over. "Thought I saw you get hit…again."

"Yeah, no, I'm fine, jacket did its job. Bullet hit my arm. No damage, but I'm going to have another bruise to add to the others. But that's not the problem," Rees says and hesitates. "I lost my rifle."

Farnsworth's head jolts up. "You what? How?"

"I dropped it when I was shot. I tried to get it, but the Rebs were right on top of me. I didn't have time to retrieve it. I'm sure they have it by now."

"Jesus, Scott," Farnsworth says, looking in the direction from which they came. "We got to get it back."

"Oh, yeah, how?" Rees asks head tilted, eyebrows raised. "Waltz right into their camp and say, "Hey, boys, dropped my gun. Can I have it back?"

"Not helping, Rees."

"Naw, we're good," Rees replies, rubbing his eyes.

"And how do you think that?"

Rees smiles. "I thought this could happen, losing a rifle or pistol, so I brought it up to Captain Epstein. So, let's just say the Rebels are in for a surprise."

"You mean you thought this might happen and you didn't bother to tell me?" Farnsworth asks, using a controlled voice.

Rees doesn't like the captain's tone and has been waiting for an opening. Farnsworth just gave it to him.

"Listen, Captain Farnsworth, I don't know you. You come into the Bank and make nice with everyone, being everyone's buddy. Why you are here I still don't know, but being the consummate airman, I follow orders and do the best I can to get along with you. I do like you. I think you're competent and, so far, have done a good job. But there have been a couple of things bothering me since we got here."

Farnsworth's face hardens, and he just stares at Rees, waiting for him to continue. Rees sees the reaction and does just that, "Twice, you mentioned O'Toole had to get married and have babies. Why would you say that, Captain? Apparently, you know more about our mission than you were supposed to. And another thing, sir, why did you hesitate when that Reb had his pistol aimed at Andy's head? You had the Reb in your sights, yet you didn't pull the trigger, why?" Rees asks, facing Farnsworth and glaring into his eyes.

Farnsworth doesn't budge, he just sits and stares back at Rees. He fights back a wave of anger, then takes a deep breath and lowers his shoulders.

"First off, I don't know what you're talking about concerning O'Toole and getting married. If I said that, isn't that what most people do? Get married and have babies. Secondly, I hesitated because I thought I saw another Rebel in my peripheral vision, and that brought my attention away from O'Toole."

"I didn't see another Rebel," Rees adds.

"No, you didn't, and neither did I. I said I *thought* I saw a Reb. There was some movement that distracted me, that's all."

"Well, that little distraction almost cost O'Toole his life and us this mission. Luckily, I was watching," Rees says, his voice taut. "I'm sorry, Captain Farnsworth, but I don't buy any of this. There's something you're not telling me."

"Jesus, Rees. Okay, don't believe me. I don't care. I'm still going to do my job."

"Just what is your job, Captain Farnsworth? I mean, why are you here?"

"The truth, Sergeant?"

"Oh, yeah, that would be nice."

"The truth is that Senator Olsen wanted this project to proceed. It was mothballed, and he needed something that would wake congress up and get the Clio Project back up and running. You gave him that incentive when you came up with the idea to bring O'Toole back. The problem with the mission was you."

Rees draws his head back. "Me? What about me?"

Farnsworth leans on his saddle horn, looking at Rees. "The senator didn't trust you or your team. He didn't think any of you were ready to come back here, thought it too soon after what you and your men went through. The colonel and chief insisted you be allowed to lead this mission, as it was your idea. There was a compromise. None of your team could come, only you, but the senator wanted a combat-experienced officer to come along, hence, me."

"Bullshit!" Rees exclaims. "That's bullshit. Me and the entire team were cleared by multiple shrinks. Even said we were better now than before the incident. So, I call bullshit on that. There's something else going on, Captain. I can feel it, so take your little story and stick it…sir."

Farnsworth raises his hands in surrender.

"That's fine with me, Sergeant. Believe what you want, but that's the truth, take it or leave it, I don't care. What I do care about is getting back to the lines and getting our boy back so we can return him to where he belongs. Now, are you with me or not?"

"Oh, I'm with you as far as getting O'Toole back, but I'm watching you, Farnsworth. I find you a very competent officer, but there's something off, and I'll be watching.

"Fair enough. Now, can we go?"

Rees nods, and they both head out for the Union lines.

~   ~   ~

Colonel Black and the chief look at each other through the screen, each man seeing and hearing the same thing from over a thousand miles apart.

"Losing a rifle is not good, but what did he mean when he said that Captain Epstein told him about a little secret concerning the weapon?" Chief Black asks.

Colonel Black answers, "Sergeant Rees thought they could lose some of their equipment for one reason or another. Some of it doesn't matter but losing a rifle could have big repercussions on the timeline. The captain placed a self-destruct mechanism inside the rifle that will cause it to explode and burn. Phosphorous explosive, I think he said."

"Well, that was some good thinking on Rees' part," Chief Black says. "Now, to the other problem, Rees told Farnsworth he doesn't trust him."

Colonel Black stares at the split-screen, watching the two men ride back towards the Union encampment.

"Well, he didn't lie. The senator did convince us that Farnsworth was necessary to keep an eye on Rees."

The chief looks at his son. "I still disagree with it. Should have told Rees the truth. They all were cleared for active duty. Having worked and talked with the men, I know they could have handled the mission. We didn't need an outsider."

Colonel Black looks back at his father.

"You're preaching to the choir, Dad, but we had to bend some to get this project back up. In hindsight, I think we should have stuck to our guns about keeping this in house. Too late now, but lesson learned, eh?" Colonel Blacks says, then calls down to the research floor and asks Captain Epstein to come on up. Time for him to participate.

~   ~   ~

Captain Lewis has a smile that keeps coming to his face and has to turn from the men so they can't see it. He can't wait to get back with the rifle and show it to Colonel Gardner. Though thoughts of promotion are in the back of his mind, he is more excited at the prospect of the Confederate Army being able to make and match the Union Army in weaponry. They ride all morning, and when they arrive in camp, Lewis quickly climbs off his animal and runs to the colonel's tent. The colonel emerges before his arrival. Lewis snaps to attention, salutes, then brings the rifle up for the colonel to see.

"This is it, Captain Lewis?"

"Yes, sir. Don't let its looks fool ya, sir."

Colonel Gardner looks the weapon over and hands it back to Lewis.

"Show me, Captain," Gardner orders.

Lewis deftly takes the weapon and removes the magazine, then removes a bullet, giving it to the colonel. Gardner takes the bullet and turns it between his fingers, admiring the sleekness and smaller size of the round.

"Good Lord, those Yanks are a smart bunch," he says, then looks at Lewis. "Show me how it works, Captain." He hands the round back.

Lewis had taken the time earlier to get himself acquainted with the rifle. He and Sergeant Hanes broke it down as much as they could and were simply amazed. Once they figured out the working mechanisms, they fired a few rounds and could not believe what they had the good fortune of getting from the Yanks. This weapon was amazing, and they couldn't wait to get more of them into the hands of their fellow soldiers,

The colonel and a few others follow Lewis and sergeant Hanes to an open area of the camp. Hanes orders a couple of soldiers to place a bench out in the field, and he follows them, carrying empty ration cans. They place the bench about one hundred yards away, and Hanes places the cans along the top of the bench.

Lewis lies on the ground and takes aim. He squeezes the trigger, and the sharp *crack* of the weapon resounds, a shell casing flying into the air. A split second later, a can flies into the air. Colonel Gardner's eyes widen.

"Again!" he orders, grinning.

Lewis moves into a kneeling stance and fires, missing this time, but he fires a second round and hits the can. Colonel Gardner looks at Lewis, who grins like a happy child. The small group watching grows in size, and murmurs of astonishment can be heard.

"That's not all, sir," Lewis announces as he stands and aims the rifle. He quick fires five rounds in succession, five shell casings ejecting each shot and rounds striking two of the cans and the bench. He lowers the weapon and looks over at the colonel to see his reaction. As Lewis expected, the colonel just stands there, mouth open, looking at the bench.

"And…" Lewis announces, now on a roll, then raises the rifle once again and holds the trigger down long enough to make it shoot a three-round burst.

"Captain Lewis, you have just won this war for us. Once we get this rifle to Fayetteville, so they can copy and start making these in mass production. Good Lord, thank you. I do believe you may make major for this, and all your men will be in for some type of commendation. Great job, Captain, great job," Gardner says and reaches for the weapon.

While the colonel holds the rifle, there is a fizzing sound, and smoke seeps from various openings. Sergeant Hanes quickly reacts and tackles Captain Lewis just before the rifle explodes with a hot bright flash of light and flame, killing the colonel and a private standing next to them. Four others are injured from flying metal, wood, and worse. The still white-hot phosphorous particles land on several others, burning at five thousand degrees. Loud screams and curses are heard from the men, who slap at the area where the phosphorous adheres to their skin. Men shriek and run in all directions.

Sergeant Hanes rolls off Captain Lewis, and both men stare in shock at the mayhem. Finally, they come to their senses and start barking orders. Men scramble to help the wounded and see to the colonel. The camp doctor is summoned and runs out of the medical tent as fast as he can, with help following. He drops down next to the colonel and checks him for life signs. Finding none, he moves over to the private. He shakes his head at Captain Lewis. The doctor then attends to the wounded.

Well, now his dander is up as Hanes slaps his cap on the side of his legs and curses. Those damned Yankees have killed his commander. They're not even there, and yet they were still were able to kill them. Not only that, but they somehow destroyed the only repeater in their possession.

"They are gonna pay for this, and I will be the avenging angel who will come collecting!" he grumbles, fists clenched.

Captain Lewis has almost the same thoughts as sergeant Hanes. He turns to the first soldier he can find.

"Corporal Lance, get me that yank prisoner we brung with us."

"Sir, he's was being treated by the doc, so he's still in the tent," the corporal answers.

Lewis's face turns red, his jaw clenched. "I do not give a damn. Go in there and drag his blue bellied ass out here. I do not care if he dies, but not before he tells me what I want to know about those two damned Yankee officers."

CHAPTER 46

The telephone on Colonel Black's desk buzzes. He notices it's coming from the control room as he reaches for it. He looks down into the room and sees there has been a new shift rotation, and Major Washington is back on duty.

"Yes, Major Washington?"

"Sir, we've a breakthrough concerning the virus, and maybe a possible solution."

The colonel tells the man he'll be right down and hangs up. Once downstairs, he briskly walks over to Major Washington's station, where he sees the young female officer who has been working on the problem for some time.

"Talk to me, Major. Give me good news for once."

"Yes, sir," Washington says, and then looks at the lieutenant. "Lieutenant Ashford, go ahead."

"Yes, sir. Colonel, we believe we know what happened, what with the information OSI gave us and more research into the system. Sergeant Danner planted the virus into the system, which we know. What we now believe is that Captain Farnsworth planted a second virus into the system to counteract the first virus."

"What?" Black asks, grimacing. "Why?"

The lieutenant is hesitant to answer and looks to Major Washington for help.

"We don't know, Colonel. But it seems that Farnsworth was trying to stop whatever the first virus was intended to do. Maybe he thought since he was on the mission that he wouldn't be able to return if Clio was down."

Colonel Black thinks on it for a minute.

"No, I don't think so. He knows Janus could become operational. We wouldn't leave them there if Clio was down. We would just initiate Janus and get them back. That's not it," he says, still thinking, then shakes it off. "Well, good work, anyway. What else do you have?"

The lieutenant looks at the colonel. "We would like to shut Clio completely down, sir."

"You what? What for?"

"If we shut Clio down, we can purge the system and kill the virus. It would be a large-scale reboot of the system. Now that we know Janus is operational, it would be a good time to fix Clio. We can even replace some of the heavier infected areas with new systems."

"How long will it take?" Black asks.

"Once we shut Clio down, hopefully in less than a day, several hours to replace circuit boards, then make system checks, run diagnostics, sensors scans, and communication checks. I'm only estimating, sir. There could always be complications, or we could get lucky," the young officer answers.

The colonel stares at the young woman, then looks at the major.

"Major Washington?"

"I agree, sir. Only way to clean out a computer is to completely purge the system and start over."

"I take it you have called the chief and spoke with him about it."

"Yes, sir. He gave it his blessing but asked that we wait until he gets back. He assumed you would want him here, so he already made plans to return. He said that once you made the decision, he would trade places with you."

The colonel smirks. "Of course, he did. He just lets me think I'm in charge. Okay, get it done as soon as you can. I'll let Olympus know the ball is going to be in their court and that I'm on my way."

~   ~   ~

Colonel Black goes back to his office and contacts Chief Black. A few seconds pass, and the chief's face appears on the screen. The colonel shakes his head at his father when he sees the shit-eating grin on his face.

"I like the way the major went to you before me about Clio."

"Hey, Clio is still my baby. I just let you babysit her," the chief says. "No, seriously, I'll be there in a few hours. I assume you'll want to come here until Clio is back up."

"Yes, I think it best if one of us is watching over the guys at all times. So, you think this will work, shutting down Clio, I mean?"

"It should. She is a giant computer, after all. An overly-complex giant computer, but everything works on the same principles. Anyway, I'll be leaving here within the hour."

"Sounds good, but there's something else we need to discuss, not in detail right now, but we need to set up a meeting."

"About the two figures who appeared in the debarkation room," the chief says, not asking a question.

"Yes, exactly," the colonel replies.

"You know that was the senator and her brother, don't you?" the chief asks.

"We don't know that, Dad. It could have been someone picked up somehow, from some other period and brought here, then sent right back," the colonel answers, not believing it.

"You know that's crap, John. It was Helen Hellberg and Aeson Minten, and you know it as well as I, but, yes, we need to discuss it. I saw them plain as day, as did most of the control room personnel. I know what she looks like, it was her. Still wearing 1980s clothing, I might add. This just proves they're alive and still in limbo," he explains, "Again, yes, we will discuss it. I'll talk with you soon. Safe flight."

"You too," Colonel Black says, thinking about the senator as he disconnects the call.

CHAPTER 47

Rees and Farnsworth don't speak as they both ride as hard as they can to get back to the Union lines. Rees is still angry at Farnsworth as well as himself. Farnsworth for not being straight with him and himself because he lost his temper and gave away his advantage of keeping an eye on Farnsworth. Now, the man knows Rees is watching, so he'll be extra careful with whatever he does so as not to give himself away. Rees just hopes he's wrong about the man.

They make good time weaving in and out of the trees enshrouded with morning mist and fog, making it difficult to see very far. The morning sun soon rises and melts the cover away, leaving them a clear view of what lies ahead.

When they think they are close to the encampment, they slow, waiting to hear a challenge, which they get not long after slowing.

"Halt!" A voice up the road calls out. They hear the man but don't see him. "Who goes there?"

Rees looks over to Farnsworth, who looks at him.

"Colonel Farnsworth and Captain Rees. Returning from a reconnaissance mission by order of General Foster."

"Advance and be recognized," the youthful voice orders.

As the two men slowly move forward, two Union soldiers move into the road with weapons at the ready. One of the privates looks to be only about sixteen years old, and Rees shakes his head. The youth notices.

"Something the matter, sir?"

Rees smiles. "No, Private, just tired. May we proceed?"

"Yes, sir. Was told you might be coming. Some others came earlier and said you were separated. I do believe the general is waiting for you," the private says, and the guards move out of the way and let them pass.

Once inside the encampment, the two officers proceed to the area where Major Connors tent was when they left. Now, it was being used by the general. A runner was sent ahead of Rees and Farnsworth and informed the general they were back. The general tells the runner to have them come in when they arrive.

Rees and Farnsworth dismount and head for the tent, where a soldier salutes them and opens the flap for them to enter. The general and major are sitting around a table studying a map, other officers standing around different areas of the large tent and watching. It takes a second for their eyes to adjust to the dimness of the tent, and when they do, they walk directly to the general and salute.

The general doesn't look at the men but offers a wave of his hand as he studies the map. Finally, he looks up at the two fake Union soldiers and nods.

"Little bit of trouble so I hear."

"Some, sir. A small scouting patrol. Nothing too bad, though we did lose some men."

General Foster leans back in his chair, studying the men.

"Well, what did you get for me?"

"If I may, sir?" Farnsworth asks, pointing to the map. The general nods, stands, and leans over the map to see what Farnsworth has to show them.

"We took this road here, then cut over to a patch of woods here," he says, tracing a line, then stopping on a spot. We watched a battalion of infantry march up the road heading this way. They didn't seem in a great rush. I would say they were waiting for reinforcements, maybe cavalry."

"You didn't go further out to see if there may have been cavalry colonel?" the major asks, and the general gives him a look that says he asked a question when he shouldn't have.

"Yes, Colonel, why didn't you go further out?" the general asks, wanting to take back control of the conversation.

"Sir, I figured if we took the time to go further into the enemy lines, that was time wasted as the Rebs would be moving closer to you. I knew the Rebs were heading this way, and I thought it best to inform you of that small bit of information rather than spend time looking for more units we may or may not have found."

The general nods. "And you were right to do so. I had another cavalry unit show up after you left and I sent them in a different direction. They did find cavalry and artillery back behind where you were. Good call or good luck on your part. I don't care which," the general says and studies the map again. He looks up at Farnsworth, then over to Rees.

I guess you want to be getting on with that secret mission of yours?" General Foster asks.

"Yes, sir, we would. Lost a day, and we'll have to make that up," Farnsworth says, not caring if he was slamming on the general or not.

The general stiffens, then smirks.

"Got some kahunas on you, Colonel, but we need men like you if we're to win this war, and I believe I've kept you from your mission long enough," the general says, looking into Farnsworth's eyes.

"General Foster," Farnsworth says, deciding the general is alright after all, just doing his job. "Yes, sir, we will be on our way." He salutes the general, who gives an icy stare back, then returns the salute and dismisses the men.

"Oh, and, Colonel?" the general says before he can leave. "My thanks to you, Captain Rees, and the corporal, good job." He turns back to the map.

Farnsworth stares at the general for a second, then looks at the other officers, nods, and closes the tent flap as he leaves.

"Cutting that a little close, weren't you?" Rees asks. "That man could have had us arrested, you know?"

"Yeah, sorry. I just never cared for men like him. Seems like the corporate ladder climber type. Had a few of them in my squadron before, never cared for them. Looking out for themselves more so than the men, or the mission it seems. But he did thank us."

"Okay, we're free. Let's get O'Toole and get out of here. Lots of riding to do to just find his unit, and we've lost enough time."

"I thought time was irrelevant?" Rees asks, giving Farnsworth the side-eye while looking straight ahead.

Farnsworth just stares at him.

They walk through the camp, holding the reins of their horses trailing behind them. They come across two soldiers and inquire if they have seen any of the men who returned from the patrol. The first man has no idea, the second man points to the rear of the camp and says they went there to tend to the horses.

Farnsworth and Rees walk to where the horses are kept and find O'Toole and McGregor talking and rubbing their horses down.

"Corporal O'Toole," Rees yells as they approach.

"Yes, sir?"

"You ready to head on out?"

"Yes, sir!" Andy replies, eyes gleaming.

The two officers look at Sergeant McGregor, who walks over to them and salutes.

"Sirs, it's been a privilege to ride with you. Forgot what fun it is to be on one of these beasties."

Rees and Farnsworth shake the man's hand.

"The privilege was ours, Sergeant. I hope you make it through this and are able to get home," Farnsworth says.

"Aye, sir, that I hope for as well, and the same to all of you. Good luck on your mission, and I hope to see you all again one day after this fighting is over and done. Then maybe you can tell me just what it is you did and how come the both of you talk so damned funny."

Farnsworth and Rees look at each other and laugh. "Same here, Sergeant McGregor, and if we do see you again, we will," Rees tells him, shaking his hand.

The three men mount their rides. Rees calls out to McGregor and asks him to say the Moneypenny line on last time. McGregor sighs and says it. The three men head out of the encampment, turning north to look for O'Toole's unit with two of them laughing and the third shaking his head.

CHAPTER 48

Joyce Olsen exits her vehicle and walks across the tarmac to the awaiting private jet. The chauffeur retrieves her bags from the trunk and runs them over to a flight crew member to stow. Olsen rushes up the stairs and tells the pilot to get the plane in the air, now. The pilot nods and goes into the flight deck, where the co-pilot is already starting the engines. The two work their way through the checklist, and once they ensure Olsen is seated, begin taxying the plane towards the runway.

Joyce Olsen sits back and smiles. She is almost out of here, and with the death of her lover, and the impending divorce she has already started proceedings on, she will be free. Once she reaches her final destination, her son should be through with his mission. It is unfortunate he had to be left in the past, but sacrifices have to be made. Now, everything should be as it was intended to be with her mother, uncle, and grandfather all alive.

She stares out of the side window, lost in thought when flashing lights bring her back to the here and now. At first, she thinks nothing of it, as the runways and taxiways are always lit up and the servicing vehicles all have some type of flashing lights on them. She finally realizes these lights are not the typical orange or yellow lights but blue and red. Turning her head back and looking through the window as best she can, she can see one, no, two vehicles moving up fast behind the aircraft.

No, no, no, no, no! she thinks. "NO!" she yells. One vehicle accelerates and passes by the right wing and beyond her field of vision as it moves towards the front of the plane. She releases the seat restraint, then pushes her way to the flight deck and sticks her head inside. The pilots slow the aircraft in an attempt to keep from running into the vehicle in front of them.

"What do you think you're doing?" Olsen screams at the pilots, who both turn, startled at the outburst, and stare at her. "No one told you to stop. Get this thing airborne!" she demands.

"Sorry, ma'am, the control tower just informed us we are not cleared for takeoff and to shut down. So, that's what we're doing," explains the pilot, who then turns back to his control panel.

Panic overcomes Olsen, and without thinking rationally, she pushes herself further into the flight deck and shoves the pilot aside. She grabs at the control lever used to increase the engine's speed and pushes it forward, causing the small jet to accelerate quickly.

"I said get this thing airborne!" she screeches.

Before the two pilots can react, the plane lurches forwards with enough speed to overcome the vehicle in front of them. The front landing gear crashes into the rear of the vehicle, pushing it forward. The landing gear first bumps, and then snaps, bringing the nose of the plane down onto the roof of the car, killing one of the passengers in the rear seat as the vehicle roof buckles under the weight.

The driver of the vehicle turns the steering wheel to the left but is stuck under the weight of the nose of the aircraft pushing down on it. The vehicle has no control as the weight of the aircraft makes it impossible to steer. The plane still accelerates, and both the vehicle and the plane careen out of control.

Neither pilot nor co-pilot can react as the aircraft and vehicle both turn sharply to the left and straight towards the nearest object in front of them, which happens to be a refueling tanker on its way to top off another aircraft. The driver of the tanker sees the approaching aircraft with the attached vehicle and makes a split-second decision to get out of the cab.

Opening the door, he jumps and rolls along the tarmac, bruising and scratching himself until coming to a rest on his hands and knees. Survival instinct takes over as he scrambles up and stumbles from the inevitable disaster about to happen.

A few seconds later, the vehicle and plane slam into the fully loaded tanker with a sickening *crunch* of metal on metal. Nothing happens for a few more seconds until fuel begins leaking from a gash in the holding tank. It takes but a spark from metal screeching along the concrete to ignite the jet fuel. The resulting explosion is thunderous, and the heat from the fireball singes the tanker driver, who is still running as fast as he can from the death scene behind him.

The flames from the expanding fuel explosion engulfs the vehicle as well as the plane. The vehicle's gas tank as well as the plane's fuel tanks add to the fiery explosion, and soon, both the vehicles and the plane are one massive ball of flame. The occupants of the vehicle and plane are incinerated almost instantly. The entire scene looks like something out of a Michael Bay film or *Dante's Inferno*.

The second vehicle stops, and four men exit, all attempting to make their way to the first vehicle to assist. It does no good as the intense heat from the rolling flames keeps them at bay. There is nothing they can do but watch. One of the men goes back to his car to call it in, but he can already hear the sirens of the approaching rescue vehicles. He calls his office just the same to explain that four of their team are dead. After he explains the situation, he doesn't hear the response as he watches the flames. He replaces the microphone and slumps into the seat of his vehicle, shaking his head and rubbing his face.

~   ~   ~

Colonel Black is on the phone, silent, his lips pursed, staring at the floor as he listens.

"How many dead?" he asks, then hearing the response, shakes his head and rubs his eyes.

"I take it you have notified the senator?" He pauses to listen.

"No, I thank you for informing me." He hangs up the phones and sighs. Turning to look at the faces staring at him in the control room, he walks over to the intercom system.

"May I have your attention, please?" he announces and watches as most of the personnel look up to the control room.

"I've just been informed there has been a tragic accident involving Senator Olsen's wife. It seems the plane she chartered collided with a federal vehicle operated by two FBI agents, an OSI agent, and a Security Forces member. They were attempting to stop the aircraft from departing and were to apprehend Mrs. Olsen for various crimes. The plane and vehicle crashed into a tanker truck, exploding, and killing all four people in the vehicle, as well as the two pilots, a crew member, and Mrs. Olsen. Our thoughts and prayers go out to the law enforcement personnel families, the pilot's families and, of course, Senator Olsen, whom you all know is a staunch supporter of this project.

"This does not in any way change our mission, and we will continue. I just wanted everyone to hear it from me rather than on the news or secondhand from some outside source. Thank you, carry on," Black finishes and disconnects the intercom. He turns towards the OIC and tells him that he will be in the other room talking to the chief, then walks away.

Once inside, he dials up his office, which is currently being used by the chief. After two rings, the chief answers.

"You hear?" the colonel asks.

"Yes. That is quite a shame. Do they know how it happened?"

The colonel shakes his head. "Not yet. The four survivors said it looked like the plane intentionally rammed the vehicle. That makes no sense, but it's under investigation. I have spoken with NTSB (National Transportation Safety Board), and they said they will keep me in the loop. We'll see. How are things on your end? Any progress?"

"Yes, quite a lot in fact. Clio is completely down, and teams have been reprogramming her. We decided to replace all the circuit boards instead of just a few. Since we had everything we needed in supply for backup, which makes it easier. These are smart people we have here and very efficient, so it should be done sooner than we thought."

"That's great, Dad. Good to hear. Think you can figure out why we can't talk with the team?"

"That's something we're looking into. I'm not even sure it's Clio. I'm thinking it has something to do with the space-time continuum itself. Some anomalies that only allows the past to move through the causality but doesn't allow the present to move back," the chief says and shakes his head in frustration. "I don't know, but as I said, we're looking into it."

Colonel Black nods. "That's all you can do. At least we can see what they are up to. I've got the guys here, and the contingency is in place. Once we decide to use it, it's a go. So, we're good here."

"Hate to have to do that, but I have a feeling we were going to have to use it. Better safe than sorry and always have a contingency," the chief advises, then changes the subject. "You speak to the senator yet?"

"No, just got the call. He's aware, of course, but I need to get my thoughts in order first. We didn't end on a good note the last conversation we had. I was pretty abrupt with him, and he was in a bad place. He was drunk when I spoke with him last. Can't imagine what he's doing now. I just hope it's nothing rash. As much as I distrusted him, there's no need to kick a man when he's really down. For what it's worth, I do believe he had nothing to do with this whole charade, and he has always been behind us, so we still need him. I just hope he can get his shit together."

"I still don't trust him one hundred percent, John, but if you do, that's fine. I just hope he can get over this. That's a lot to process, first his wife having an affair and using that affair to gain access to our project, as well as using her husband to do it. Then leaving him, and then dying. That's a lot of shit to dump on one person in just a couple of days."

"You'll get no argument from me, Dad, but you don't need to concern yourself with that. You just need to get Clio up and running and, hopefully, figure out why we can't communicate with the team. I'm going to see how the contingency is setting up and will let you know when and if it's a go."

The chief nods and smiles. "Oh, it'll be a go."

The colonel frowns. "What makes you say that?"

"Oh, you and I are both softies when it comes to that team of men, and you just can't say no."

The colonel laughs. "You're probably right. Even if we don't need to, they're going. We wouldn't want a riot on our hands now, would we?"

Before they can continue their conversation, there is a knock on the door.

"Enter," Colonel Black commands.

The OIC opens the door halfway and sticks his head inside.

"Sorry to interrupt, sir, but you and the chief may want to see this."

Without saying a word, the colonel stands and heads for the control room. He can hear the phone from his office ringing and knows it probably the OIC calling for the chief with the same announcement.

He enters the control room, and one of the technicians turns the volume up so everyone in the room can hear.

CHAPTER 49

Having left the Union encampment mid-morning, the three time travelers move through the North Carolina woods at a steady pace, making good time. They travel north, looking for the cavalry unit, stopping a few times to avoid Rebel patrols as well as skirt any small communities or homes along the way.

Now, the sun is low on the horizon, and they have not run into any trouble, nor have they found a Union army unit to ask about the cavalry troopers they are searching for. The problem with going north is they have distanced themselves from areas of battles. This is good for them on one hand as they can avoid any confrontations, but on the other hand, it makes it more difficult to locate the cavalry troopers.

The troopers are more likely than not engaging in some of the fighting, and Rees thinks it might be better if they head more towards the east in the morning. Farnsworth disagrees, explaining that if they come upon any of the fighting, they could be caught up in it. This could get them killed or captured, or as what had happened earlier, be drafted into some unit, and given orders to do something contrary to their mission. O'Toole agrees with Rees, but they both relent.

The shadows become longer as they amble through the darkening woods. Just before losing the light, they decide to break for the night and find a good area that allows them some overhead protection, as well as cover from view by anyone passing by. They don't think they are in an area involved in the fighting, but they are still on guard. The routine is the same, O'Toole tends to the horses, Rees sets up security measures, and Farnsworth makes a fire for cooking and sets up lean-tos.

The men eat canned stew and hard tack, along with reconstituted strawberries. O'Toole still can't get over the quality of the food. Rees and Farnsworth find it edible but crave a hamburger or a slice of pizza. O'Toole asks what those are, and the two officers laugh.

"Sorry, Andy, can't tell you about hamburgers or pizza. I don't think either will be around until the next century," Rees tells him.

Farnsworth looks at Rees. "What's it gonna hurt. He didn't invent them."

Rees thinks, then nods. "Come to think about it, no one really knows who invented the hamburger." So, he proceeds to explain the delicious food to O'Toole.

O'Toole is fascinated. "I've got to try that when I get home. It sounds wonderful. Everyone will want one of those, and I'll be famous."

"Hey, hold on there, Burger Chef," Rees says.

Farnsworth smirks. "Who?"

"It's an old… Shut up," Rees tells Farnsworth, flapping his hand at him in a dismissive manner. "Sir," he adds, then turns back to O'Toole. "Just because I said they don't know who exactly invented the hamburger doesn't mean you should. If you make them, just keep it to your immediate family, okay?"

O'Toole laughs. "Nope, gonna make me some money, buy a big mansion in Baltimore, then I won't have to worry about any Tommy Walsh. Once I become rich, Emma will come a' running. You wait and see," he says, then leans towards Rees, looking serious. "Now, tell me about them things called pizzas."

Rees looks at O'Toole, opening his mouth to speak, but not finding the words "What did I just do?" he finally says, then sees the change in Andy as he breaks into a grin.

"Ah, got me one up on you there, Sarge, I mean, Captain," Andy says proudly.

Rees chuckles, relief showing in his features. "And about time."

The men finish eating and are enjoying their coffee when Rees looks at Farnsworth.

"I think we need to talk," he says aloud.

Farnsworth sips his coffee and doesn't flinch. He looks at Rees over the rim of his cup, and then lowers it as he looks at O'Toole. O'Toole looks from one to the other, eyes wide.

"I'm assuming you want to carry on the conversation from yesterday?" Farnsworth asks.

Rees nods.

"Okay, what do you want to talk about?" Farnsworth asks, taking another sip of his coffee.

"I want you to tell me the truth. Who are you really? Why are you on this mission? Like I said before, you just come waltzing into the Bank because the senator knows you. Bullshit, it's something more than that, and I want to know, or we can go our separate ways," Rees finishes, staring at Farnsworth.

O'Toole sits up straighter, eyes darting between the two men.

"What's going on?" he asks.

Neither answers. Farnsworth takes a deep breath and looks at him.

"Just listen, Corporal. Okay, Rees, you ready for a story and some answers, here it is," Farnsworth says and pours some more coffee while he thinks of what to say. He sips at his coffee, blowing on it, then looks at Rees and O'Toole. "I'm starting from the beginning, okay?" he asks and gets no reaction from the two men.

"I was born to a third-year college student whose mother and father were important people, but before I was born, her father passed, and her mother disappeared. I never knew my father, and my mother only told me that he was a military man who died on a mission somewhere in South America. My mother's last name was Newton, not her Christian name. It was changed for reasons that'll be obvious later. My father's last name was Farnsworth. I was born out of wedlock. My mother gave me my father's surname."

O'Toole shakes his head. "You poor sod. How you must have been ridiculed your entire life, and your poor mother. They must have treated her like a plague."

Rees just stares at O'Toole, and Farnsworth chuckles. "No, Andy, that stigma went away in the late 20th Century. Men and women don't always get married anymore, most do, but it's not law, and people have accepted it. A person born out of wedlock is just another person, and a woman is treated fine. But that's not important, okay?" Farnsworth says, and O'Toole closes his mouth and nods.

"Sorry, go on, please, sir."

"Anyway, I grew up and listened to my mother as she told me a story, one repeated all my life. It was a story of my great-grandfather, who was also an important figure in the government and was treated unfairly by that same government. He was in charge of a secret project that was being run by a small group of unethical men who only wanted power and glory for themselves and would do anything to get it. My grandfather tried to stop these men from conducting an experiment with the project but failed. In the meantime, these ambitious men somehow set my great-grandfather up, and he was removed from his position of importance and shamed in front of the American people he loved to serve. He left office in disgrace and retired.

"One night, he went fishing and never returned. They found his body washed up on shore days later. Official cause of death was drowning, accidental or suicide, it was not determined. Unofficially, he was assassinated by agents sent out by these evil men who proceeded with the experiment. The experiment was partially a success and partially a failure, depending on how you look at it. The men involved went on with their lives, and my family did, too, but they had suffered. My grandmother spent some time in the military, then went into politics. My grand uncle, her fraternal twin, went into the Army and became a Green Beret. He retired and went to work for my grandmother, who became a US Senator.

"My grandmother and her brother attempted to recreate the experiment invented by those corrupt men responsible for their father, my great-grandfather's, death. But before they could finish the experiment, they were set upon by a group of military personnel who destroyed the experiment while it was in use. They were sent by the same people responsible for the other problems beset upon my family. Since the experiment was in progress, my grandmother and her brother disappeared and have not been seen since."

Rees had heard enough, and he throws his coffee cup across the fire, then stands up abruptly.

"This is bullshit!" he exclaims. "Utter bullshit, and you know it!" Clenching and unclenching his fists, he stares at Farnsworth.

Farnsworth doesn't flinch but raises his one free hand at Rees.

"Hang on, Rees, hear me out. Please, let me finish, then if you still believe it's bullshit, I'll leave camp and be on my way tonight. Please, sit," he says calmly and can see the flare in Rees' eye dim somewhat. Rees doesn't reply, just takes a deep breath looks at O'Toole, then sits back down. He glares at Farnsworth.

"Go on."

"Thank you. Alright, that's the story I grew up on. My mother drove that into me my entire life. From my time as a boy, through my teenage years, all the way until adulthood. I believed my mother. Hell, who doesn't? I had no father or any other relative who could verify her story or tell me something different, so I grew up believing these stories.

"When I was nineteen and in college, I started doing research into the stories she told me. The internet is a vast source of information, and what I couldn't find there I could usually find in the library or city records. I couldn't find out as much as I wanted, mostly the same basic information about my great-grandfather's mysterious retirement and his death and the disappearance of my grandmother, but it was all so…generic, clean, almost like it was made up and repeated over and over, always sounding the same. I was beginning to think there was more to the stories my mother was telling me than she let on.

"I graduated college and joined the Air Force at the behest of my mother. I got into Special Operations, where I had access to much more information than what is on the internet, and I dug deeper into finding out what happened to my family. I found a different side to the story, and it gave me pause. I did a couple of tours in the Middle East, then was assigned to MacDill, where things started to happen.

"My mother pushed me to help her in a quest that at first sounded crazy. She told me that since I was now in the military, I was in a position to help her act revenge on those responsible for the tragedies brought onto our family. She is a zealot about this, and once she puts her mind to something, there is no stopping her. She married a US Senator and introduced him to me, but not as her son. Nice man. I thought maybe mom would be satisfied with being married and would call off her quest for vengeance, but I was wrong. Marrying this man was just part of the plan.

"By now, I had the real facts of what had happened to my relatives, and after thinking it through, I realized my mother was becoming somewhat unhinged. I tried to talk her out of her scheme, but she wouldn't listen. She became very upset with me and said if I didn't want to help that she would just do it another way. She said she already had another man inside the facility helping her because she didn't think I was up to the task.

"This scared me, so I relented and listened to her plan, ensuring her I was quite able to help out. She accepted my offer. Her plan was to have the senator vouch for me and get me attached to the secret organization called the Bank. There was going to be a time-traveling mission and that I was to be assigned to the team going. I had almost laughed in her face when she mentioned time travel but kept myself in check. She told me the commander was to be talked out of using an entire team and to send in only one man. Me.

"That didn't work because the Bank wanted at least one person with time-traveling experience along, so they added you," he says and points at Rees.

Rees stops him. "You said she had someone else inside already?"

"Yes, I'm getting to that," he explains, then continues, "She told me that once I was on the inside, I was to meet with Sergeant Danner. Danner had been given a flash drive that contained a virus that would disrupt Clio, then destroy her. I asked mom what that would mean for the time travelers sent on the mission. I remember the sad smile my mother gave me when she told me that we would not be returning."

Rees rolls his eye and tilts his head back. "Awwww, this just keeps getting better," he says. "I'm sorry, this is getting deep."

"All true, believe me. If I may?" Farnsworth asks, wanting to continue. "By now, I knew my mother's obsession had caused her to lose her perception of reality. She was so obsessed with destroying everything that had any connection to the tragedies of our family that nothing else mattered. Not even me, much less her husband."

Rees interrupts again, "What's any of this got to do with O'Toole."

"Oh, quite a lot my friend. This is where it gets good," he says and looks at O'Toole.

Rees stands up. "Whoa, we need to talk about this first. I know what you're gonna say about him," he says as the realization dawns.

O'Toole bites his lower lip, intrigued. He looks at Rees. "What about me?"

"Farnsworth, you can't," Rees warns.

"You wanted the truth, well, this is part of it. It's actually one of the main reasons I'm here, and he's got to know. *You* have to know."

Rees stares at Farnsworth, then at O'Toole. He takes the Kepi off his head, slaps his leg with it, and turns to look into the woods, thinking. He turns back around, sits, replaces his cap, and looks at O'Toole, then at Farnsworth. Taking a deep breath and raising his hands in a dismissive manner, he tells Farnsworth to continue.

"Thank you, Rees, but it's for the best," he says and looks at O'Toole. "Andy, I was sent here to kill you."

O'Toole just stares at the man, not comprehending. Rees jumps back up and places his hand on his revolver, ready to defend O'Toole if need be. Farnsworth raises his hands in surrender.

"No need for that, Scott. It's not going to happen."

"You're damn right it's not going to happen," Rees says, standing, breathing hard.

"That *was* one of my assignments, but if I may continue, it will all be explained."

Rees nods and sits but pulls out his pistol and places it across his lap. Farnsworth finds this amusing and laughs. "If you must," he says.

"I must," Rees answers.

O'Toole watches the men, then turns to Farnsworth. "Why would you want to kill me, Colonel?"

Farnsworth shakes his head. "I don't." He leans towards the man, looking him in the eye. "And I won't. I was just asked to. I told my mother I would, but I never had any intention of carrying out that request."

"Who would want me dead? Was it that Tommy Walsh?" O'Toole asks, eyes wide.

Now it's Farnsworth's turn to be confused, and Rees steps in. "That's his competition for the girl O'Toole is sweet on."

"Ahh," Farnsworth says, then to O'Toole, "No, Andy, not him."

"Who then?" Andy asks.

"My mother," Farnsworth answers.

"Your mother? But Why? I do not even know her," Andy says, rubbing his hand on his pants leg and focusing his attention on Farnsworth.

Farnsworth waves at O'Toole to calm down. "Let me finish, Andy, please. You'll see," he starts to say and looks at Rees, who is still shaking his head. "One of your descendants turns out to be Chief Master Sergeant Black. You know, the man who invented the time machine."

"Lord! You're pulling one on me now. How would you know that now? More witchery?" O'Toole asks.

"Nope, good old-fashioned science. It's called DNA. It's a hereditary gene in our body. One that can identify anyone's relationship to anyone else. So, using this DNA, scientists were able to discover that one of your great-great-great-grandchildren turns out to be the man who invented the machine that brought you back to the future, then back here."

Rees drops his head, and O'Toole just stares at Farnsworth.

"Okay," is all O'Toole can say while shaking his head and staring into the fire.

Farnsworth continues, "I was to destroy Clio, and while we were here, I was to either kill you myself or make sure you got killed."

Rees looks up. "So, that's why you hesitated before. You were going to let him get shot!"

Farnsworth shakes his head. "No, I told you the truth. There was movement to my right that caught my eye and made me hesitate. I would have been sick to my stomach if this man had been killed. I just thanked the stars you were watching out for him as well. I can't let my mother win."

Rees' brow furrows. "What?"

"This was part of my mother's plan. I was to ensure that the virus was active in Clio, thus destroying her, then I was to come here, make sure O'Toole died, ensuring Clio was never invented. She was thorough. Wanted to make sure that if one thing didn't work, something else did.

"Okay, what about this virus? The one Sergeant Danner infected Clio with?" Rees asks.

"After my mother told me about the virus, I took the liberty to sneak into her computer files and find out what it was. I copied the information and had one of my tech buddies make a virus to counteract the one she had planted. I loaded it in the computer before we left. I assume the original virus was already running when we jaunted and that it caused some of the communication problems we've been having. I made sure I was on camera when I placed my flash drive into the computer so, hopefully, by now, they have figured out what I did and are cleaning out Clio's system. Once that is accomplished, we can only hope comms come back up."

Rees and O'Toole watch Farnsworth closely, and he notices. "Hey, if I wanted O'Toole dead, he would be dead, and there wouldn't have been a thing you could have done to stop me, Rees. I'm SpecOps, remember? If I wanted to fulfill the mission my crazed mother wanted me to, I would have killed both of you. I'm sorry if you don't believe me, but that's the whole story. Once we have communication with the Bank, they can hopefully verify my story," he says, also staring into the flames.

"Listen, my life is fine as it is, things are as they should be. There's no reason we should be using this time machine for revenge. I don't believe Chief Black intended it for that use. Besides, if the time machine didn't exist, I probably wouldn't be here."

"Why would you say that?" Rees asks.

"Because of what has already happened. Think about it. Clio isn't built, my grandmother may or may not have gotten married and become pregnant with my mother. Even if my mom was born, she may or may not have taken the same path in life and met my father, but since I'm still here, the mission must be a success… I mean *our* mission. Kind of a paradox."

Rees nods. "Makes sense. I don't want to ponder on it too much, it can drive a person insane," he says, pinching the bridge of his nose. "Speaking of insane, it sounds like your mother is bat-shit crazy. Sorry, I know it's your mother but, apparently, she intended to leave us here, and I take offense at that."

"Hey, don't sweat it. I love her, but I must have gotten my father's side of the practicality gene. I have a mind of my own. I joined the Air Force because I wanted to, not because my mother had plans for me. I am a military man. Even though I have been trained, just as you have, to follow orders, I still have my own mind, and as you know the military wants people who can think for themselves as well as follow orders." Farnsworth looks to O'Toole. "Something that has taken years to change, Corporal. You just do it like you were taught."

O'Toole nods, still thinking about Farnsworth's story, and absently mutters, "Yes, sir."

Farnsworth looks at Rees. "We good?" He holds his hand out.

"For the most part. I want to believe you but still have that little voice in the back of my head telling me to be careful, seeing you hail from Minten blood. You understand?"

Farnsworth nods. "If you didn't, Rees, I would not want to work with you. I like people who are always cautious."

Rees shakes his hand. "Sir, I've learned to be cautious, but I prefer it if I don't have to be that way around my brothers. My life may be in your hands, and I don't want to have to worry about that or about that man over there."

"Nor should you, and I hear you. But to let you know, I have no worries about you. Now, how about I take first watch?"

CHAPTER 50

olonel Black listens to the whole story, as does the chief and everyone in the control rooms.

"Well, I wasn't expecting that," the chief says over the speaker system

Colonel Black watches the screen as the two views show the different images of Farnsworth going to stand guard, and Rees settling down to sleep. A blanket can be seen moving towards the camera, and the screen goes dark as the camera lens is covered.

"Turn off the sound," Colonel Black tell a technician, then turns and walks into the other room to speak privately with his father.

"Dad, what do you think? Do we believe him?"

"It does fall into line with what the lieutenant found when purging Clio of the virus. She said it looks like the second virus was introduced to counteract the first, so yes, I believe him. Besides, he is correct in that he could have killed both of them at any time. I see no reason for him having to wait. The outcome would have been the same no matter what. She intended for him to never return. She was so bent on revenge she was willing to sacrifice her son. Hell, she probably had a child with the sole purpose of planning something like this. For a family seemingly so in love with each other, they sure are willing to sacrifice each other to make a point. Hell, the entire Minten clan is institutional. Well, except for Farnsworth," the chief says.

"We still wanting to use the contingency?" Colonel Black asks.

"John, that's your call, remember? I just work here."

"That's bullshit, and you know it, Dad," the colonel says with a slight smile on his lips.

The colonel turns and looks at the screen. "It sure is quiet there, isn't it?"

"That it is, just the faint sounds of the insects can be heard," the chief replies.

The colonel stares at the screen, thinking. "Quiet. Yes, quiet!" He jolts up from his chair, knocking it over. "Quiet!" he says loudly and turns to look at the chief.

"What, John?" the chief asks, his eyes blinking.

The colonel smiles. "I've got an idea. Not sure if it'll work, but I'm going to try. Don't want to get our hopes up, but I think I can let the team know we are watching them."

"How?"

Smiling, the colonel heads for the door and says over his shoulder, "Just watch and see."

~ ~ ~

Rees isn't asleep, his mind still active, thinking about Farnsworth's story. *Can I trust him? Is he telling us the truth?* are just some of the questions circling his brain. The night is deathly quiet, except for the crickets and the whirring sound of…the whirring sound of. Rees stops thinking and listens. Yes, there it is again, a faint whirring sound.

"What the hell is that?" he asks himself and rolls over onto his back. He strains to hear it again and does. The sound is close, but he can't pinpoint it. It's like looking for the home fire detector when the battery goes dead and it *beeps,* and you can't figure out which system it is because the beeping fills the whole house. He sits up and throws off the blanket, still hearing the sound when he is still. He cocks his head downwards and realizes it's even closer, then he looks down at the camera button and turns it upwards towards his face.

He scoots closer to the fire, and using the glow of the flames, he peers into the tiny camera lens. Bringing it even closer to his eyes, he sees the tiny lens moving in, then out, then back in. The lens is focusing.

"Oh, shit," he exclaims out loud and stands.

O'Toole, who wasn't sleeping either, rolls over and looks at Rees, alarmed that they may be under attack.

"What is it, sir?" he asks, looking around and reaching for his weapon.

"They are watching, hot damn, they are watching us," he says in a quieter voice.

Farnsworth comes running into the camp. "What the hell you yelling about?"

Rees excitedly points to the camera. "Look at the camera lens, go on, look." Farnsworth comes by the fire and turns his lens and sees the eye move in and out several times.

"What the…" Farnsworth says, smiles, and looks at the two men. "How did you figure that out?"

Rees tells him.

"They must have figured since it was so quiet right now that the faint whirring could be heard. Since there's nothing else that could make that sound, they were hoping one of us would hear it."

"I wonder if they just got that portion of the comms up or if they have always been watching us?" Farnsworth asks.

"Doesn't matter. We can still communicate, well, kind of communicate," Rees says. "We can have them answer any yes or no questions by having them move the lens."

"That's right, good thinking," Farnsworth replies.

Rees looks at the lens, "Can you hear us?"

The lens moves in and out several times, and Rees' grin gets larger. He looks at Farnsworth who grins as well.

"Are you two daft? You're doing that weird act again," O'Toole says, staring at the two men holding and talking into the top button of their coats as they hold them close to their faces.

"Sorry, Andy, no we… I'll explain later," Rees says to him and returns to the camera. "Move the camera lens once for no, twice for yes, and three times for you don't know, got it?" He watches as the lens moves twice, causing another smile.

"What do we need to know?" Rees asks.

Farnsworth looks into his lens. "Can you see and hear me?" The lens moves twice. "Are you able to tell us if we're heading in the right direction?" He sees it move three times. "Shit! Was hoping they knew something we didn't."

"Have you been with us the entire time?" Rees asks, and the lens moves twice. Rees looks at Farnsworth as he asks the next question. "You heard what Captain Farnsworth told us?" again, the lens moves twice. "Is it true about the virus? I mean, did he attempt to stop the first one?" The lens moves twice. Rees arches an eyebrow. "I guess you were telling the truth."

Farnsworth looks at his camera. "Have you figured out about my mother?" The lens moves twice. "Has she been arrested?" The lens doesn't move, so he asks again. This time, it moves once. "Are you looking for her?" The lens moves once. Farnsworth looks at Rees. "I don't know why they aren't, but they must have their reasons."

Rees asks, "You are aware I lost my rifle?" Twice the lens moves. "Did you take care of it?" And the lens moves twice. "Well, that's a relief."

Farnsworth's turn. "Is there any reason we should not continue?" He gets one movement.

"I've got nothing else I can think of ask at the moment, you?" Rees asks Farnsworth, who shakes his head. Rees looks at the camera. "Okay then, I'm getting some sleep. If you think of any way to communicate two way, let us know." He gets two movements. "Oh, before I go, tell Captain Epstein thank you for these clothes, they have saved our lives more than once. I'm sorry I lost his rifle. Also, I'm sure the Rebs are enjoying the rations he made for us since the bastards took mine." He drops the front of his coat and heads back to get some sack time, a bounce in his step.

~ ~ ~

"Good thinking, John. At least now they know they are not alone," the chief says over the intercom.

"Not much else we can do right now but answer their questions," the colonel replies.

"And that's fine. It might be just a little morale booster for them knowing we are watching. They know if the shit hits the fan, at least we can bring them back."

"That's true. Well, I've been up for over twenty-four hours, time to take a nap. See you in a few hours, then we'll figure out what to do next. Night, Dad."

CHAPTER 51

The sky grows lighter in the east, and O'Toole rekindles the fire. When the coals are burning hotter, he places a pot of coffee on and throws some bacon into a pan. The smell of coffee and bacon is too much for Rees or Farnsworth to ignore, and both men sit up at almost the same time.

Farnsworth rubs the sleep from his eyes and looks at O'Toole.

"That smells great. You'll make a fine wife one day, Corporal."

O'Toole looks offended.

"Sir, that's not even funny."

"I'm afraid it is, Andy," Rees adds and yawns.

O'Toole just scowls at both of them and pours some coffee but places the cups on the ground.

"See if I be serving you officers anymore," he tells them and turns away, hiding a smile.

"I think that there is insubordination, Captain Rees."

"I agree, Colonel Farnsworth." Both men get up and retrieve their coffee.

They sit around the fire, finishing up breakfast when O'Toole stands and scrapes the remnants of his breakfast into the fire. He holds the plate down by the side of his leg and stares into the fire, lost in thought.

"Okay, Andy, what is it?" Rees asks.

"Well, sirs, I was thinking." He looks at them. "This war is not going to last much longer now, is it?"

"You know we can't tell you that, Andy," Farnsworth answers.

"I know, I know, but I listen to everyone talk, and I can hear it not only in the way you talk, but the way Dave talked about the war."

"What did blabbermouth Dave say?" Rees asks, sighing.

"Oh, no, sir. He did not tell me anything, but I just listen, as I said, and it seems this war will be one, two years. Now, I am just taking a jab at it, but am I right?"

Rees shakes his head. "Andy, the war won't last forever, but we can't give you that information. You already know too much as it is."

"Yes, sir. But what would you tell me if I asked to go home?"

This causes Farnsworth to choke on his coffee. Rees just stares, not sure how to answer.

"Uh, what do you mean? Go *home*, home? Mt. Airy home?" Rees asks.

"Yes, sir. The way I see it is, if people think I am dead, or I have been taken prisoner, there is no reason for me to keep looking for my unit. I could just go home. You two officers could tell them I had been mustered out, and you brought me home because you were heading back to Washington and thought I could use an escort because you was heading that way. Something like that. I'm not trying to shirk my responsibilities, and I ain't afraid of no fight, but if what you said is true, about Sergeant Black, then why take a chance? Besides, I miss Emma and worry that each day I am gone is another day for Tommy Walsh to be sniffing around. If she gets the word that I am dead, I just know she will marry him."

Rees and Farnsworth look at each other. Rees spreads his hands and opens his mouth but isn't sure what to say. Farnsworth does.

"That's a fine idea, Andy. And you're right. This war won't last forever, and I can't see them looking for you, so there is no reason you shouldn't go home, serenade that fine young woman and get her to marry you, then raise a family. I think it's an excellent idea," he finishes with a smile.

Rees looks unsure. "All the way to Maryland. What is that, three, four hundred miles?"

"Ah, a week, ten days, nothing we can't handle," Farnsworth says. "Besides, we won't have to get caught up in any more battles. We'll just skirt our way around any fighting and get Andy home. Mt. Airy didn't see any fighting that I know of, so we're safe there."

"It is occupied by the Union, sir. There are soldiers there watching over the railroad. Goods and soldiers are being transported from there," O'Toole tells them. "The townsfolk do not like it because they side more so with the Southern cause."

"Is that going to be a problem for you, Andy? I mean, what with you joining the Union Army instead of the Confederates?" Rees asks.

"Oh, no, sir. My folks understood my reasoning. They do not agree with it, but they understand. Besides, my brothers joined the Rebels." He looks off in the distance for a few seconds. "Hope they are alright."

Rees and Farnsworth don't answer that question, knowing the fate of the 2nd Maryland Infantry at Gettysburg. Rees thinks on it some more and pulls Farnsworth aside.

"You know that most of his regiment is in Louisiana and Alabama? Also, there are still two years left of fighting and conscription has been enacted by now."

"Yeah, so?"

"I don't know. If we take him back, won't he be considered a deserter?"

"We are officers in the Union army. We will tell anyone who asks that he was a POW, we rescued him, he was severely wounded or some other malarkey.

Rees looks at the camera. "You all hear that?" he asks and watches as the camera lens moves twice. "You good with that?' This time, the lens moves three times. Rees looks at Farnsworth.

"What did they say?"

"They gave the three-lens movement. Not sure, I guess. I think it's up to us, anyway."

"Agreed, then time's wasting," Farnsworth says, and they go back over to O'Toole with smiles on their faces.

~　~　~

Colonel Black looks into the camera at Chief Black.

"You think that's a good idea?" the colonel asks.

"Well, we never really had a set plan for what they should do, and the whole idea was to get O'Toole back into his timeline and home. I say let them. This seems to work so far. We're still here, aren't we?" the chief says with a wry smile.

"Can't argue with that logic. Okay, it's not like we can do a lot, anyway, except bring them home, and I don't want to do that. Yet."

The intercom on the colonel's desk, currently being utilized by the chief, buzzes. The colonel hears the chief answer.

"Yes, Sam."

"Chief, Major Washington is here to see you."

"Good, door's open."

"Yes, Chief," Sam says and disconnects at the same time the door opens and a smiling Major Washington enters.

"Good news, Chief," he says.

The chief points at the screen, and Washington looks over to see Colonel Black.

"Hello, sir. Good news. Clio has been restored and is ready for a test run."

Both the chief and colonel smile.

"How soon can you run tests, Major?" the colonel asks.

Washington looks at the colonel, then the chief.

"Right now, just give the word."

Colonel Black smiles. "The word is given."

The major nods at the colonel, then the chief, and leaves.

"That's some good news, at least. Speaking of news, any word on the senator?" the chief asks.

"As a matter of fact, there is. Seems he's taking a sabbatical from congress. The president wants him to get away for a while. The affair, then her death, is taking its toll on him, and the president feels it best he not be involved in politics for a while. The president assures me he would find a temporary replacement for him to act as our liaison until Olsen's return."

"That's good. I wonder who he will find for us. The senator has left some big shoes to fill. Even though I thought he was involved, and I'm glad I was wrong, we need support, so that means we need someone who can help us and not worry about their political future."

"I'm sure whoever he picks, it'll be good. I'm not concerned about that right now. I want to finish this mission on a good note."

"I hear you. When you coming back?"

"Once the first test on Clio is completed, and she's cleared to work, I'll be on my way. I want to keep Janus running since the men are here for the contingency plan. No sense in flying them back. The plans are already in place, so we might as well do it here."

"Agreed. I'll let you know as soon as the major confirms it, John. As I said before, these are smart people, and they know their stuff. Clio should be ready. And just to make sure, I'm going down there to micromanage it because you know nothing gets done unless someone is micromanaging it," the chief says with a smug grin.

"Oh, hell yeah, Dad. Why do you think I became an officer."

"Not funny, John, not funny."

~   ~   ~

Rees, Farnsworth, and O'Toole travel as fast as they can, heading in as much of a northerly direction as possible. Mt. Airy is just northwest of Washington, and the men must travel around Raleigh/Durham, bypass Charlottesville in Virginia, and step lively through the Shenandoah Valley. There is a lot of fighting, and to get to Mt. Airy safely, they will have to zigzag the countryside to avoid it or be caught by anyone from the Army of Northern Virginia. They know they will travel miles west, then turn north and travel miles east, turn north, and repeat.

They travel for a few days, making good time, even with the movements off course and once running into the Roanoke Rapids River. Traveling along its bank, they find a low enough area to cross. Rees makes a comment that the river would be a nice place to raft or kayak, and he might have to come back here one day. Once they cross over into Virginia, they have to be even more cautious as there are more battles raging throughout the state.

They travel around any towns they come across, though few and far between, but they do cross many farms consisting of corn, hay, grains, and many that raise livestock and fowl. As much as O'Toole complains that they should be grabbing a chicken for dinner, Rees and Farnsworth don't want to take a chance of being caught. It is probably bad enough that some farmers, as well as children and hunters, spot them, mostly from a distance, so they don't need to be caught stealing chickens.

They are sure someone is probably already screaming bloody murder that the whole damned Yankee army is invading. Though technically true that the Amy of the Potomac is invading, three cavalry troopers don't qualify as an army, much less an invasion. Sooner or later, someone will catch on if too many people begin reporting Union cavalry traveling through their fields or woods, and then they might send Rebel soldiers to investigate.

They move along and in between towns and areas where some of the towns aren't even on the map as of yet. They cross over future battlefields where engagements haven't been fought yet. Moving past Lawrenceville and Cool Spring, they make their way between Amelia's Courthouse and Richmond, which is the capital of the Confederates. They pass well west of Fredericksburg and work their way up towards east of Manassas.

They have to stop and hide several times as Rebel patrols or troop movements cross their paths, marching up and down the roads. They are stopped by Union soldiers asking for information on where they are heading. Occasionally, a sergeant or officer will want to know their business, and the fake papers are handed over, and they are allowed to go on their way.

Rees smells it first, wrinkling his nose and raising his gloved hand to ward off the stench to no avail. He opens his mouth to breathe. It's the putrid smell of rotting, decaying flesh that has been baking in the hot sun for days, the smell of death. They come upon an area where combat has raged. Craters from artillery strikes pockmark the trampled-upon grounds, burnt trees and grasses, and piles of corpses stacked liked macabre cords of firewood.

Dirt mounds litter the open fields, where men have been laid to rest with makeshift markers stuck into the ground. The markers are nameless, an unfitting end for men never to be known. All three men are silent as they pass these hallowed grounds, realizing death is the same no matter where you're from, place or time.

They spot a group of African American slaves digging graves for the soldiers, for both blue and gray. When the slaves see the three men, they stop what they are doing and stare.

The soldiers approach, and Rees looks down until he locates the one he believes to be in charge.

"How long you been at this?"

"Going on three days now, sir," the leader, says taking off his hat and placing it over his chest.

"Who won this battle?" Farnsworth asks.

"Can't rightly say, sir. We come on in after the fight'n through. We don't see the fight'n, just what's left after," he says, nodding his head towards the graves and bodies scattering the landscape.

Rees looks around, changing the subject. "You find any weapons lying around?"

The small group becomes concerned, and they start shuffling, looking around, eyes wide. The leader frantically shakes his head.

"We don't take no weapons, sir."

Rees stares at the man, then comprehends what is bothering them.

"No, no, I wasn't asking that. I just wanted to know if you have seen any. I lost mine, and I need a replacement. You're not in any trouble."

Hearing this, the men relax a little, and then a couple of them point to an area close to the wood line. The leader points as well.

"Any weapons we find we take over there, sir. We don't take any, and we have to be careful just moving them. Any of our mastas see us with a gun, they surely whoop us bad, or worse."

At this, all the others nod their heads.

Farnsworth leans forward in his saddle, looking at the men. "Why is it you're still here? I mean, it's only a few days journey to reach Washington. You'd be free there,"

"Oh, no, sir. We can't. Our families are back on the farms, and we can't leave them. There is no tell'n what would happen if we up and run."

Farnsworth leans back and looks at Rees and O'Toole.

Rees smiles and looks at the older man, then climbs down off his horse, handing the reins to O'Toole. Both O'Toole and Farnsworth give each other a curious glance, then watch Rees place his hand on the slave's shoulder and tells them to walk him over to the guns. He looks back at O'Toole and Farnsworth, grins, and tells them to wait, that he'll be right back.

Rees walks to the woods with all the slaves following him as they listen to what he has to say. He stops in front of weapons and searches until he locates a Henry rifle, along with a colt pistol, taking them both. Next to all the weapons, he finds ammo for both weapons and packs all he can carry.

Farnsworth and O'Toole watch from a distance, and he hears the men *ooh* and *ahh* as they listen to Rees. They hear laughing, and then see the small group walk back towards them. Once back, Rees places the Henry in the scabbard and retrieves some rations from his saddlebag, giving them to the slaves. Finished, he climbs back onto this horse. They say goodbye and wish the men luck and ride away as the slaves wave with slight smiles.

"What the hell you say to them, Rees?" Farnsworth asks when they are a few feet away and far enough away from O'Toole that he can't hear.

"Not much. Told them I could foresee the future, and that they would all be free in just a few more years. I said that where I come from, I am considered a witch doctor of sorts, and that they just need to be patient and they will see. Then I showed them a couple of magic tricks with a coin."

"Magic tricks, really? And they believed you because of that?"

"Why not? I am from the future and know the outcome of this war. This just gives them something to hope for. Besides, I am good with the coin tricks," Rees says, not making any attempt to show Farnsworth.

Farnsworth just shakes his head, and they slowly continue through the almost empty battlefield. All three men are silent for some time, each taking in the carnage and having their own thoughts about it.

"You remember what General Lee said?" Farnsworth asks as they pass by more gravesites.

"War is hell, didn't he?" Rees replies, looking around.

"No, still a good quote, though. That was Sherman. No, General Lee said, 'It is well that war is so terrible, otherwise we should grow too fond of it.'"

"Yes, that's it, I remember it now. Only those who have witnessed it could say something so profound," Rees answers.

Farnsworth continues, "Funny that Sherman and Lee had different philosophies when it came to engaging in warfare, but both men had one thing in common."

Rees looks at Farnsworth, waiting for him to continue. When Rees doesn't say anything, Farnsworth continues, "Neither of them seem to like politicians. Both made comments about how men who have never fought or seen death or heard the cries and screams of the wounded had no business making policy about war. Something to that effect."

Rees nods. "Since when did that ever change?"

"Touché," Farnsworth responds.

They pass through Clifton, where the Union Army left after the Battle of Bull Run or the battle of Manassas, depending on which side you're fighting for.

Rees looks at the sky and smiles. "Beautiful day, and we only have a couple more to go before ole Andy here gets the girl," he says, slapping Andy on the shoulder just as a shot rings out, and O'Toole's horse rears from a bullet strike, throwing him onto the ground.

~ ~ ~

Captain Lewis had taken the Union prisoner and extracted the information he sought from the injured man. He had learned the two Union officers and Corporal O'Toole were not part of their regiment. They were on some type of special assignment he was not privy to. Lewis was told the three Union troopers were on their way north and were looking for a unit of cavalrymen who were part of the corporal's regiment. But that the corporal had spoken with the trooper and told him he was wanting to go home and was working up the courage to speak to the two officers about it.

The corporal believed he could talk them into it, and the trooper believed that he could. The three men were different, especially the officers. The trooper had never met men like them. They talked funny, not just in their accents, but the way they said things. One of them said a word call *dude* and *rad,* as well as some other words none of the troopers had any idea what they were talking about. It was almost like they had a secret language between them.

"Where was this corporal from?" Lewis asks.

"He said he was from Maryland, Mount Airs, no, Mount Airy."

The prisoner did not know much else, and he was returned to the medical tent, not much worse for wear than when he was retrieved.

The captain found a map and studied it for some time. He located Mount Airy and traced a path with his finger from his current location to the town. He thought about it and decided he would go there.

Gathering his small company of troopers, he pursues the three Union cavalrymen. He knows the general direction they must be heading and decides he will take his men and travel in a direction that will cut them off. He is taking a gamble, but it is worth it if he can get his hands on another one of those rifles, as well as capture the men who wield them.

Maybe they know how to disarm it, keep it from exploding. He needs that weapon, wants that weapon, craves that weapon. He will do anything to get it and has every intention of doing so. He will kill anyone who stands in his way.

The captain tells himself he is seeking vengeance for the death of his commander and his troops, and maybe there is a little truth to it. The bigger truth is he wants what will come attached to retrieving the weapon and turning it over to General Lee. He will not bother with the chain of command, and he isn't about to let some major or lieutenant colonel take the weapon and grab all the glory. No, he will capture those Yankees, take their weapons, and march them right into the general's camp. He can just see the accolades, the recognition, maybe a promotion to major, no, full colonel, his legacy!

"Captain, sir!" is what he hears, and he thinks, *Captain?* Then he realizes his sergeant is talking to him. He had been daydreaming while waiting for the men to assemble and was lost in thought. He comes back to the here and now and looks at the sergeant, who has a concerned look on his face.

"Yes, yes, Sergeant. Good, let us move out," he finally says and moves his horse around to look at the roughly one-hundred-seven men in double columns ready to move out. The captain turns his horse back around, and raising his hand above his head, he signals the men of the Black Hats to follow.

The captain knows the area better than the Yanks do, being in his territory, his backyard, so there is hardly anyone around to stop him from moving straight through to his objective.

The other officers left in the camp are either equal to his rank or lower. There was concern about him taking so many men away on what they all thought was a foolhardy quest. He looked at the other officers and shook his head.

"Ya'll saw what that their rifle could do. We need the other ones. We need to bring those rifles back to the capital so they can make more of them for us. So, I will take those men and bring those rifles back," he announces, his eyes probing each man as if daring them to defy him.

One captain had already dispatched a rider to inform headquarters about the loss of their command leadership and needing a replacement. The captain wanted Lewis to stay until an command officer arrived to grant him permission to leave, or not. Lewis scoffed at the man and proceeded to gather his troops and make his leave. Now, he was his own commander.

Taking his troopers north, they pass the outskirts of Raleigh, then cross over the Virginia border and are making their way to Richmond. Lewis is hoping to cross paths with the Yankee interlopers soon. Luck is on his side because, when he passes some of the smaller towns, he hears rumors of a small Yankee detachment being seen riding through farms fields and the outskirts of their homes. Lewis takes his men and moves in the direction of the rumors and becomes more excited as he realizes his quarry is nearby. He decides he is going to travel towards Amelia's Courthouse. He believes the Yanks may try to get to Washington DC in as straight a line as they can. To do that, they will need to move past Amelia's Courthouse and make their way to Manassas.

Riding hard, they reach Manassas and skirt around Clifton, then stop. Lewis pulls his eyepiece and scans the distance and spots three Union cavalrymen slowly trotting along, talking like they didn't have care in the world.

"Damn Yanks think they're home free," he says aloud and hands the spyglass to the sergeant to take a look.

"Orders, sir?" Sergeant Hanes asks, handing the scope back to the captain.

Lewis takes the scope and looks around until locating an opening between groves of trees.

"There," he says, pointing to the opening. "We'll go through there, then turn back up north and set up at a spot where we can bushwhack 'em." Then he takes off at a gallop, his head tingling with the excitement that comes with chasing prey. He reaches the opening and sees his luck is still holding out as there are open fields to the north where he can move at a faster speed to get himself and his Black Hats in front of the Yankees.

The long column of soldiers follows their leader until he raises a hand to halt. Lewis orders Sergeant Hanes to move half the men forward and set up in front of the Union soldiers, but not to fire until they hear from him. The sergeant salutes and splits the force in two, explaining to the lead corporal what it is the captain wants. Half the company takes off after the corporal.

Captain Lewis dismounts and has the remaining soldiers do the same and sets up a skirmish line just inside the wood line. He can see the Union soldiers slowly advancing into his trap. He grabs his sharpshooter and tells him he wants these men alive and to only take out one of the horses.

"Which one, sir?" the rifleman asks.

"I don't give a good goddamn, soldier, just shoot one of the horses when I say to."

The soldier doesn't answer, just takes his long rifle, and aims at the closest horse. Lewis kneels behind the man, watching the cavalrymen approach. When he likes the range, he bends close to the sharpshooter's ear and whispers, "Now."

The rifle bucks when the trigger is pulled, and Lewis is satisfied to see one horse rear and throw off a Yank.

CHAPTER 52

"Colonel Black, sir?" a sergeant shouts while staring at the large screen. Colonel Black is moving away and thinking of his plans to get back to the Bank. He turns when he hears his name and locates the source. The technician, as well as most in the room, stares at the screen. The jumpy picture shows glimpses of a horse lying on the ground, then Corporal O'Toole is seen also on the ground, but only briefly. Both cameras turn, and the picture is unclear, jerky.

"What are we seeing, Sergeant?" Black asks, moving towards the man as he stares at the screen.

"Sir, there was a sound like a gunshot, then pandemonium as the cameras spun as if the horses were turning. As you saw, it looks like O'Toole's horse was possibly shot."

"Okay, get the second team going. I want Janus sending them now!" Black orders and hurries up to the control room. Once inside, he is informed everything is good to go and, on his order, the contingency team will be deployed.

"Do it!" is all he says, and Janus begins charging up, and within a few minutes, the contingency team is deployed.

Black sees his father on the communication screen.

"Chief, you seeing this?"

"Yes, I am. I also see you sent the contingency team. Hope they get there in time to help."

"As do I. I should have sent them sooner, but I was almost certain Rees' team would make it to Mt. Airy without any problems. I was sure once they were close enough to the Washington DC area, they would be home free. That's what I get for letting my guard down. Now. Who is shooting at them?"

~ ~ ~

O'Toole recovers quickly and scurries over to his saddle and retrieves his rifle and ammo, then he runs over to where Rees leans down, extending his hand. Rees and Farnsworth begin to ride away, and O'Toole grasps Rees' arm, swinging onto the back of the horse, and they gallop away. As they head towards a line of trees, they see fifty or more of the Black Hat cavalrymen emerge from the woods, rifles aimed at them.

The two horses pull up and stop, all three men looking around frantically for someplace to go. To their left, they see movement and more Black Hats coming out of the trees.

Farnsworth yells, "This way!" and turns his horse to the right as he spots a partially burned-out farmhouse several hundred yards away.

They can hear men screaming and yelling at them, with sporadic firing following. Rounds fly by, but none strike them.

No one is that bad of a shot, Rees thinks as bullets whiz by.

Cursing their bad luck, they are also thankful as they reach the relative safety of the collapsed building. It not much for cover, but it sure beats standing out in the open.

Pulling hard on the reins, the horses skid to a stop, and O'Toole pushes himself off the back while the horse is still moving and takes a defensive position before Rees or Farnsworth are out of their saddles. Once they are on the ground, they retrieve their rifles and move to cover.

The building must have been freshly burned because the wood is still warm, and there are small wisps of smoke rising from some areas. Ashes and soot cover their clothes as they take up positions using the charred planks for protection.

"Andy," Rees says, "watch our six…" he says, then remembers who he's talking to. "Watch our backsides. Make sure they don't send someone to flank us."

"Yes, sir," Andy replies and scoots over to the other side of the building's remains.

"What now?" Rees asks.

"You see who that was?" Farnsworth replies as he checks his weapon.

"You think those guys we had the first run-in with followed us?" Rees asks.

"Yep, I do. Black hats. I'm taking a guess here, but I would say they took that rifle you lost and were going to copy it, but once it was destroyed, they needed another one. You've got to admit, if the South got a hold of one and could replicate it, the outcome of this war may be different. Since we know the rifle can be destroyed, I don't think they will get their wish, it's just they don't know that."

Rees looks over to see that O'Toole guarding their rear, then turns back to Farnsworth.

"Ten to one they want us alive."

"Why's that?" Farnsworth asks, still watching the woods and the men in the distance who have stopped giving chase and mill around in front of them.

"I bet they think we can disarm the self-destruct. That's why they shot the horse and missed us when we ran. Those were intentional shots.

A good marksman would have taken any one of us out and with fifty or so men shooting. Hell, at least one round would have found its mark."

"Could be. Maybe that's why they haven't charged, wanting to wait us out. Wait until dark, try to sneak in," Farnsworth notes, removing his broad rim hat. He scratches his head and runs his fingers through his long hair, getting it out of his face while scanning the open ground in front of them. He sets the hat on the ground so he projects a smaller silhouette, less of a target.

Rees smirks. "That would be a mistake."

Farnsworth reaches down and grabs his canteen. "Only have half a canteen of water, you?"

"Same. Was hoping to come across a stream before too long, but that got interrupted."

Rees looks at O'Toole. "Andy, how much water you got?"

"Almost full. I don't drink as much water as you two officers do," he says with a grin they can't see.

"You know, just because you're almost home doesn't give you the right to be a smart-ass, Corporal," Rees tells him and turns back to watch the Rebs.

An hour passes, and nothing happens until a gray-back soldier carrying a white flag rides out into the open field. Rees and Farnsworth exchange looks.

"Hey, you're the colonel," Rees says with a grin.

"Thanks," Farnsworth replies and stands up. He waves his hand over his head then signals the horseman to approach. Keeping his weapon at the low ready, he walks around the opening on the building and towards the soldier. Farnsworth knows Rees has his weapon aimed at the Reb's head.

"That's close enough," Farnsworth announces when the man is near enough to talk without having to shout. The sergeant stops and salutes.

"My captain's compliments, Colonel. He sent me here to talk to you about surrender."

Farnsworth has to hold a laugh and turns to look at Rees, who shakes his head. This is something right out of a movie they've both seen.

"Well, tell your captain I appreciate him wanting to surrender, but I don't think we can handle all of you as prisoners."

The sergeant looks at Farnsworth, eyes squinting, then curls his lip, all respect for an officer gone. "No, ya'll fucking blue bellies. I am here to discuss ya'll's surrender."

"Oh, sorry. Well, I do not think we'll be surrendering today, Sergeant. We do have the superior force here, you just don't know it yet."

The sergeant shakes his head. "We will bring the force and the wrath of the angels down upon you if you do not surrender, Yank."

"Well, we'll just have to see whose wrath is the greatest, Sergeant. My compliments to your captain, and tell him I said," Farnsworth looks away for a second in thought, smiles, "nuts."

The sergeant's jaw tightens, and his nostrils flare. He stares at Farnsworth, his respect for the officer vanished. He doesn't even give the man a salute as he yanks the reins of his horse and gallops off towards his lines.

Farnsworth waves, then walks back to where Rees and O'Toole watch him. When he gets back behind the wall, Rees looks at him. "Really, 'Nuts?'"

Farnsworth grins. "Hey, who knows? Maybe that captain passes it down through history, and that's how General McAuliffe heard it."

~ ~ ~

"He said what?" Lewis asks, his voice rising. "That arrogant Yank. Who does he think he is? We have him outnumbered and outgunned. We have provisions, water. What does he think he's doing?"

Sergeant Hanes, who brought back the news, does not say a word, knowing the captain is ranting and really doesn't want an answer. Captain Lewis rubs his chin, thinking, then looks at the sergeant.

"We're not waiting. I do not care if they are captured or not. Ride back out there and inform them they have two hours to surrender or we will release hell upon them. Explain it to them so they understand, Sergeant." the captain orders, staring hard at the NCO to ensure he gets his meaning. "We will not take prisoners if we have to come after them."

"Yes, sir," the NCO replies, salutes, and climbs back on his horse, galloping away.

~ ~ ~

"Here comes that yahoo sergeant again," Rees says. "They want your rifle bad."

Farnsworth again stands and walks out to meet the NCO. The sergeant pulls up short of the colonel, but this time does not salute. The horse is jittery, and the sergeant turns him one way, then another. Farnsworth arches his eyebrow, wondering if this is somehow supposed to intimidate him.

"My captain has sent me again to ask you to surrender. If you do not, we will come in and kill all of you, which is what I would have done in the first place if I was in charge."

"Well, Sergeant, I guess we're just lucky you aren't in charge," Farnsworth retorts. "Sergeant, tell your captain the answer is still the same. I say bring it on, dude. We've got enough cans of whoop-ass to go around. Well, enough to take care of that half-ass ragtag group of guys you call an army."

The sergeant's eyes go wide, first because he has no idea what language the colonel is speaking. Second, because he gets the gist of what he is saying and does not like it.

So, I take it that is a no. You do understand we have over one hundred men coming for you, sir."

"Yes, Sergeant, we do, but you might want to get more men before attacking," Farnsworth tells the NCO, causing him to become angrier.

"Fine then, sir. You have two hours to surrender, and if you do not," he says with a sneer, "then I will enjoy watching ya'll die." He gallops away towards his lines.

Farnsworth turns and strolls back to the burned-out building.

"I don't think you read the book *How to Make Friends and Influence People*, did you?" Rees asks Farnsworth while watching the retreating horse and rider.

"Waiting for the movie," Farnsworth answers back, then checks his ammo. "How much ammo you have?"

"Should have enough, plus we have plenty of soap to throw at them," Rees tells him and shows a pile of plastic explosive grenades he made. He had rolled them into the shape and size of baseballs so they would be easier to throw, adding small rocks inside. "I'm going out there and place some of these along the ground in front of us. Should slow down a few of them at least. Still wish I had my rifle, but this one is better than none," he says, hefting the Henry as he heads out to plant the explosives.

Farnsworth moves over to O'Toole.

"How you holding up?"

"I'm fine, sir. Just can't believe I'm almost home and might die just shy of getting there," the corporal answers, then smiles at Farnsworth. "But it was good of you to try and get me there."

"Hey, none of that talk. We'll be fine. It might get a little dicey, but I think we'll pull through."

"There you go again, sir. Using them made-up words that don't mean a thing to me."

Farnsworth looks at O'Toole, seeing the man does not understand, then thinks back to what he just said. "Oh, dicey. It means touch and go..." he says and sees that O'Toole still doesn't know what that means. "Okay, ah, uncertain, unpredictable. That better?"

"Oh, yes, sir, much. I feel a lot more secure now."

Farnsworth slaps him on the back. "It's a good thing we're leaving once we get you home. You've been around us too long, starting to pick up our bad habits." Then he walks back to see how Rees is doing.

Farnsworth watches as Rees plants the makeshift mines, then sees him talking into the camera button. When finished, Rees walks back to the building.

"What was that all about?"

"I asked the Bank if they'd heard and saw what was going on. They did. I then asked them if they had any plans to help us out and they say, Yes." Now, what they have planned?" he says and shrugs.

~ ~ ~

"Well, if they want to die, we will oblige them, Sergeant. I want you to take your troops and charge those Yanks and bring me that rifle. We will stay here if you need re-enforcements."

Sergeant Hanes smirks. "I take it that you are jesting, sir."

"Yes, Sergeant, that was intended as humor. You should be able to handle them with forty men, shouldn't you?"

"Yes, sir. Forty troopers will do the job."

"In one hour, we will begin the attack. When you see the regimental flag dipped, that will be your signal to move out. Godspeed, Sergeant," Lewis says and turns to look across the open field towards the burned-out building. He spots Rees walking around in the field and grabs his spyglass. "What is that damned fool Yank doing?" he asks aloud.

The sergeant, who had turned to leave, turns back to see what the captain is talking about. Shielding his eyes with a hand, he stares out and can see Rees walking around and bending over occasionally but doesn't know what he is doing.

"What is he doing, Captain?"

"It looks like he placing…eggs or something. I cannot tell, but it does not matter. Damned Yanks are all a strange bunch," Lewis says and takes the telescope from his eye and gives the sergeant a look that infers he shouldn't be here.

"Yes, sir." Sergeant Hanes salutes again and walks over to his horse.

~ ~ ~

"There's something going on. Lots of movement to our flank," Rees says and grabs for his binoculars, with Farnsworth following suit. Both men watch as the flanking Rebels move back into the woods.

"Leaving?" Farnsworth asks.

"I doubt that," Rees answers.

They watch some more and see that the Rebels are getting on their horses and lining up.

"Ah, shit. They're going to charge," Farnsworth announces loud enough so O'Toole can hear him. "Andy, come on over here, I think we're about to have company.

O'Toole scrambles to where the two officers are and points his rifle towards the enemy cavalry.

The three men watch and see the Confederate battle flag being waved. Then they hear the faint sound of a bugle and watch as the cavalry advances towards them.

"Here we go!" Rees says in a calmer tone of voice than what he feels.

"You set enough explosive out there?" Farnsworth asks with a little trepidation in his voice.

Rees snorts. "We'll see. All of them have proximity charges so they should blow as soon as they cross over them."

The one real Union soldier and two acting Union soldiers spread apart and take aim at the Rebels lined up and gaining speed as they advance. The sight of forty men on horseback waving sabers and pointing pistols is awe-inspiring and terrifying at the same time.

When the Rebels are roughly two hundred yards away, Farnsworth fires, pulling the trigger as fast as he can, sending thirty 5.56 mm rounds towards the charging cavalrymen in about ten seconds. Several of the rounds strike men and horses, and five horses and nine men fall, then bounce and roll on the ground. The remaining Rebel troopers continue on at a fast pace, closing the gap quickly.

Rees fires one round from his Henry rifle, then changes to his pistol. His first round hits its mark, and he sees a trooper tumble off his horse. O'Toole fires and curses as his bullet strikes a horse. Still, the result is a Rebel soldier being thrown from a galloping animal with enough force he is no longer a threat.

When the cavalry is about seventy or so yards away, there is a series of explosions when the home-made mines ignite with devastating results. Another ten men and horses are killed or wounded. Still, the Rebels advance. By now, Farnsworth has reloaded and returns to firing in a calm manner, allowing him to take aim. His shots are on the mark, and he kills another eight men and three more horses. Rees fires the pistol, reloading, and firing again.

By just sheer luck, the Rebel sergeant makes it through and leaps his horse over the low wall the team is using for cover. He slashes down with his saber but misses Farnsworth, who falls prone to the ground. The sergeant whirls his horse around for another attack. All his attention is focused on Farnsworth, and he doesn't see Corporal O'Toole.

O'Toole stands and runs at the back of the sergeant. Just as the NCO raises his saber to take another swipe at Farnsworth, O'Toole grabs the back of the man's jacket and yanks him off his horse. The corporal pulls with all his might, and none too gently, as the sergeant slams onto the ground with a resounding *umph* emitting from him as the wind is expelled from his lungs from the impact. The sergeant is stunned and tries to stand while at the same time gasping for air.

O'Toole produces a large knife from his boot and sticks the blade under the sergeant's ribs. The blade is long as well as wide, and it slices up and into the man's heart. The Rebel doesn't even see who has stabbed him as he looks at Farnsworth with hate, but only for a couple of seconds, then he slumps to the ground one last time.

Rees and Farnsworth turn their attention back to the attacking troopers as the few remaining run back to their lines. The three men held off the initial attack and didn't even get a scratch among them.

Then they look at the dead and dying soldiers, listening as the wounded men moan and yell in pain, intermingled with the screams of the wounded horses. Farnsworth takes aim and locates the wounded animals and fires until they cannot hear them anymore. They look around to ensure they aren't being flanked but see only the bodies in front of them.

Farnsworth and Rees breathe a sigh of relief, then both pull out their eyepieces and scan the area in front of them.

They can see the captain just beyond the tree line, and he does not seem like a happy man.

~   ~   ~

"I see that they are more of a match than I previously thought. I hated sacrificing those men, but now I know the type of weaponry they have. If three men can stop forty men, then they have a slight advantage, but not one that will be able to stop over one hundred cavalry," Lewis says to a corporal, who stands next to him. "I do hate losing Sergeant Hanes, he was a good sergeant, but his death shall be avenged. Corporal, get the men formed up. We will advance upon those devil Yanks and kill them all, then we shall take all of their weapons for ourselves. Now, go," he instructs the young man, who runs off shouting at the men to mount up for a charge. Within just a few minutes, the soldiers are formed up and ready.

~   ~   ~

"Ah, shit, this isn't good," Farnsworth says, watching the one hundred plus Confederate cavalry form up. He knows this is going to be another charge. "I sure hope Colonel Black and the chief gets whatever plan they have in gear right now. If not, our asses might be grass."

Rees watches as well and looks at his camera. "You see this?" he asks the camera, seeing the lens move twice. "Please, tell us you're working on something, and real soon." Again, the lens moves twice. Rees blows out his breath and watches as the Rebel horses jerk and prances about as if they are as ready to go into combat as the riders.

O'Toole looks at the two officers. "If I get killed, I have a letter in my pocket for Emma and one for my folks. If you make it out of this, please make sure they are given to them."

Rees looks back at O'Toole and wants to say there's no need for that because he's going to make it, but in the back of his mind, he feels it might not be so and doesn't want to lie to the man. "You can be sure of it, Andy," he replies and turns back to face the enemy just as they begin to emerge from the tree line.

"Here they come," Farnsworth says in his calm voice, announcing something that Rees and O'Toole can see for themselves as the Rebel cavalry advances. Slowly at first, but all three men know their speed will increase, and they will be on top of them in no time.

To their surprise, they hear a commotion coming from the trees behind them. All three men look but don't see a thing.

"They're coming from behind us," O'Toole shouts, aiming his rifle to the rear.

"Can't be. We would have heard them or seen them before now," Farnsworth says, and then they spot Union cavalry galloping through the trees in the open area between the burned-out home and the trees. What is more amazing is there is a wagon coming in with a Gatling gun in the back, and what makes that even more amazing is Sergeant Tosseti stands in the back of the wagon, with Sergeant Tucker at the reins. Most of the team charges across the open ground on horseback, coming right towards them. Bouvier, Kriger, McGuire, Harris, Nionee, and Green.

Rees, Farnsworth, and O'Toole just stare, frozen in place. O'Toole is slack-jawed, blinking rapidly. Farnsworth's face breaks into a wide smile as he realizes what he is seeing. Rees comes out of his reverie and slaps Farnsworth's arm.

"Yeah!" Rees screams, and in response, he hears Tosseti yelling in his loud Boston accent, "Fuck Youssssse!" being directed at the Confederate cavalry approaching from the opposite direction and closing fast.

Tucker reins in the horse, slowing the wagon. He swings the side of the wagon bed towards the Confederates so Tosseti can get a better firing angle. Tosseti swings the 19th Century machine gun around and takes aim. Rees has a fleeting thought that with Tosseti standing in the back of the wagon on the Gatling gun, he looks like a Civil War version of one of the characters from an old TV show *The Rat Patrol.*

The arriving horse soldiers get to the burned-out home and dismount. Bouvier reaches into his scabbard and retrieves two rifles, throwing one to Rees.

"See if you can hold on to this one, Scott," he shouts and takes a knee behind the wall and aims at the enemy.

"And couldn't you have picked a cleaner spot to find as cover, this is a brand-new uniform?" Kriger adds.

"Good to see both of you, too," Rees answers, but with a broad grin. "Welcome to the Civil War…again."

The Rebel cavalry closes in but are suddenly brought up short as Tosseti pulls the trigger on his weapon, and it spews out round after round of 5.56 mm lead. Rees turns when he hears the weapon because it's not making the sound of a hand-cranked Gatling gun, but more so of a M-60 machine gun, no, the sound of a SAW (Squad Automatic Weapon).

"What the…?" Rees starts to say but shuts his mouth.

"Captain Epstein has been busy. Thought we could use some more firepower. He said he had this in the works before you left but didn't mention it. Like, where were you going to carry it, anyway?" Bouvier explains.

The fake Gatling gun can shoot over seven hundred rounds a minute, even though the top-loading magazine can only hold two hundred rounds, it still wreaks havoc on the Rebel soldiers as between thirty and forty men and horses are brought down under the intense firepower.

The soldiers behind the wall begin firing, adding to the devastation. Gray-clad men fall from their horses, either dead or dying. Captain Lewis screams, "Forward…don't stop…keep moving!" as he charges, waving his saber over his head and pointing it at the ruins of the home.

The remaining cavalrymen do so, also screaming the Rebel Yell and firing pistols and rifles. One Rebel gets a lucky shot in as it strikes Senior Airman Green, who is flung back from the .58 caliber round striking him in the head. The bullet-resistant Kepi he wears deflects the round, but it still has enough force to render him unconscious. Kriger stops firing and takes the time to check on Green. Seeing the man is just unconscious, he returns to the fighting.

"First, he crunches his skull from a fall, now he gets shot in the head. One thick skull he has," Kriger says between firing shots.

"Crunches. That a new medical term?" Bouvier asks, and uncharacteristically of Kriger, he doesn't have a comeback.

The machine gun ceases firing, and a couple of the airmen look back to see what is happening. Tosseti with his usual calm demeanor is banging on the gun and cursing loudly. The wagon is being peppered with round after round of Confederate shot, and the wood is shattering and sending splinters flying in all directions. Tosseti ignores the shots, even when one or two strike him. Just like his nickname "The Incredible Hulk," it only makes him madder and meaner.

Tucker sees him having problems and jumps up to help, receiving a bullet in the small of his back for his effort. The bullet-resistant jacket does its job, and the shot falls harmlessly to the ground after impact. Though not severely injured, the striking bullet causes him great pain, and the force of the impact drives him forward, where he strikes the side of the wagon.

He is just barely able to reach his hands out to stop his head from hitting the side as he falls. Cursing somewhat less than Tosseti, he scrambles up and into the back of the wagon to assist with clearing the weapon.

The rest of the men fire semi-auto, and the effect on the charging Rebels is awesome. The soldiers fall in droves, and there isn't a thing they can do to stop it. The Confederates are surprised at the voraciousness of the defending Union boys. Not all the attacking soldiers saw the rifle demonstration earlier and do not realize the weapons they face.

How can a handful of soldiers kill so many of them? How are they reloading so fast, and what is that damnable weapon in the wagon?

But still, they charge on. Several soldiers trip some of the remaining mines, which blow the legs off horses and hurl the tiny rocks embedded in the explosive like buckshot, wounding and killing everything near the explosions.

The fighting airmen hear a scream and look towards O'Toole. He takes a round in the arm and flies back from the impact.

"Andy!" Rees screams and runs over to him. "Kriger!" he yells, but it's not needed as Kriger is already there, pushing Rees away.

"I got this, get back to the fighting," he yells, and Rees hesitates for just a second, then realizes David is correct and goes back to the wall. The returning fire has dwindled down to just sporadic shots here and there. One round hits close to the top of the wall, and it sends rock chips and soot into the faces of Farnsworth and Bouvier.

Both men flinch and blink as the debris goes into their eyes. They both fall back and grab for their canteens. Nionee see what had happened and grabs Bouvier's canteen and tells both men to stop what they are doing, and he'll take care of it. It only takes a few seconds before both men are back in action.

Captain Lewis has miraculously made it to the wall, along with a few of his troopers. The men behind the wall duck as a couple of horses bound over them and travel past. The Rebel soldiers charge for the wagon, where Tucker and Tosseti try to unjam the weapon. Tucker looks up just as a Rebel saber slashes downwards at his head, along with the man calling him a derogatory name that shocks and angers Tucker at the same time.

Tucker doesn't have time to react, and just before being struck down, he is saved as Tosseti grabs him by the jacket, yanking him down in the bed of the wagon. The saber doesn't stop moving and catches Tosseti across the face, his cheek and jawline slicing open, blood instantly pouring out of the wound. Tosseti grabs his face and falls forward just as the Rebel bring the saber back up for another strike.

It doesn't come as three quick shots hit the soldier in the chest and head. One bullet enters through the right eye and exits out the back of his head with a spray of blood, brains, and bone, also sending his Kepi flying into the air. Tucker stares as the enemy horseman tumbles from the saddle, and the horse moves on. Tosseti looks up at Tucker and grins.

"Thanks, Quick Draw McGraw."

Tucker holsters his pistol. "Motherfucker, call me nigger will you, fucking cracker." He looks back at Tosseti, pointing at his face.

"What is it with you and sabers, my man? You okay?"

"I'm fine, and I know, right? Well, at least it's on the same side of my face as the first one," he says, grimacing in pain, then laughing. "Remind me not to get on your bad side, brother."

Captain Lewis turns his horse, looking for the two officers who task him. Spotting them, he raises his pistol to shoot but is struck in the back of the head with a rifle butt. He was too close to the wagon, and Tucker grabbed his rifle and swung it like a bat. The captain's eyes cross as he is struck, losing consciousness he falls from his horse, landing with a heavy thump on the ground. Before he can be secured, the men must confront the remaining Rebel soldiers who just won't give up.

The Confederates can't understand how they can be shooting these Yankees point-blank, and all they do is just jerk, yell, and then carry on as if nothing happened. The confusion amongst the Rebels is their doom as the airmen posing as Union soldiers pick them off one by one, with the last Rebel throwing down his weapons and surrendering.

The captured Rebel and his commander are secured by Zip-Ties and dragged into the burned-out building, where they are leaned against the remains of the fireplace.

Kriger patches O'Toole up as best he can. The round struck the biceps area of his arm, causing some damage to the muscle. Kriger says it's lucky he is there and that he can fix the arm good enough so the man won't lose it. If this had happened without him there, O'Toole more than likely would have to have the armed removed, or worse, he could have died. Luckily, Kriger has the knowledge, equipment, and medicine to keep him healthy.

"That reminds me," Kiger says as he reaches into his haversack, "here." He tosses Rees a package of hard tack. "Don't say I never gave you anything."

Rees laughs. "Gee, thanks, David, didn't know you cared."

Kriger grins and turns to check on Tosseti, who has walked up, holding his check in place. Kriger sees the filthy hands covering the wound.

"God, Tosseti, couldn't you wash your hands before doing that?" Kriger asks in alarm.

"No. Doing what?" he asks as dumbstruck as usual.

Kriger shakes his head and slaps Tosseti's hand away and cleans the wound so he can suture it closed. "What is it with you and sabers?"

The Rebel soldier's eyes are wide as saucers as he watches the men move about him, talking in a strange manner. He notices there are two officers, two corporals, and the rest are sergeants. *A lot of sergeants for a small group,* he thinks. He finds that strange but, of course, everything he has seen today is strange. How could this small attachment of…what, eleven, twelve men, kill a whole company of cavalry? It's not possible, yet, here he is witnessing it.

And the size of the men, most are extremely tall and muscular, well-fed, in good shape. That doesn't bode well for the confederacy if all the Yanks look like this. And their weapons? *How do we compete with that?* the soldier thinks.

The Union soldiers all move about in one fluid motion, as if they have worked together before, or have practiced. He had to admit, they were very professional.

Then the Rebel looks over at the still form of his captain. He sees that the man is breathing, so that's a good sign. A shadow falls over him, and he looks into the face of one of the Yanks. Sergeant Bouvier looks down at the Rebel.

"You hurt?" he asks.

The Rebel looks back and doesn't respond.

"I asked if you were hurt, injured in any way? We have a medic, a doctor of sort. If you're injured, I need to know so he can take a look."

The Rebel looks at his captain again. "No. I am not hurt. But my captain is."

Bouvier moves over to the motionless officer and checks on him. He raises his eyelids and checks his pupils and sees they both dilate evenly. He checks the bump on the back of the man's head and sees that the swelling is already going down. Bouvier stands back up.

"I believe he'll be fine. He'll probably have a hell of a headache when he awakens, but he'll live. When sergeant Kriger finishes with

Sergeant Tosseti, I'll have him take a look. You hungry? We've got plenty of food if you are."

"What's to be done with us? Are you going to shoot us?"

Bouvier stares at the scared soldier and smiles. "No, we don't shoot prisoners. I'm not sure what we'll do with you, that's up to the colonel and captain. But no, we're not going to shoot you. Now, you want something to eat or not?"

~   ~   ~

The chief watches the battle intently. They have several views of the area since the contingency team's arrival adding more cameras. The cameras on the wagon provide the most stable shots since it is immobile, whereas the airmen are constantly moving, causing each camera to twirl and jerk.

The entire operations room watches, and he can hear the murmurs of the people and an occasional *ohhhs* from someone after seeing the death and destruction of man and animal.

When the chief sees O'Toole get shot, he jumps and advances towards the screen as if he can somehow help the wounded man. He stares first at one screen, then a second as a camera hovers over the downed man. The shots of O'Toole are jerky, but he can see blood and can tell it's his arm that's damaged. Kriger's camera fixates on the wound as he works on it.

Knowing O'Toole is in good hands, Chief Black returns to watch the fighting. It is fierce and bloody, more so for the charging men and animals of the Rebel army. They are being mowed down from the intensity of the firepower being poured into them from the more advanced weapons.

After the final shot is heard, and the yelling and screaming ceases, he watches different views of the wounded airmen, as well as O'Toole, being cared for. He likes that Bouvier is treating the prisoners well and talking with them.

The chief is frustrated, though, because they still can't communicate with them verbally. Watching the split screens for a few more seconds, just to ensure there aren't any more surprises, he goes back to the communications station and sees that Colonel Black is still on the screen.

"That was better than I could hope for," the chief says, and Colonel Black turns and looks into the camera.

"Yes, I agree. Got a little hairy there when some of the troops got in the wire. I'm just glad the injuries are minor, or seem minor, except for O'Toole's. He could lose an arm still. I hope Kriger can prevent that from happening."

"What's the plan now?" the chief asks.

"I'm here for just a little longer, want to see what the team does next, then I'm on my way back. We'll keep Janus running, just in case something else goes wrong, but the Bank will be the main control center now that Clio is back up and running. Good job with that, by the way."

"John, you know I didn't have much to do with that. The credit all belongs to the exceptional people you found to work here, with a couple of exceptions," the chief says and watches the reaction he gets from his son. "But thanks, anyway. No, your people deserve all of the credit, I was just here for quality control. These people are smarter than me, and I'm the smartest person I know."

"How humble of you, Chief," the colonel responds without emotion. "I'll see you in a few hours, have some coffee waiting." He disconnects.

"Coffee my ass," the chief mumbles.

~　~　~

The team stands away from the burned-out home, grateful to be away from the stench. Most of the Confederate wounded have been tended to by Kriger, with help from some of the others. It mostly consists of morphine injections with an occasional bandage here and there. The prisoners have been moved up against the wagon where they can be watched.

The captain returns to consciousness a few minutes after Bouvier walks away and is none too pleased to have been captured. He swears and vows revenge against the Union invaders who killed so many of his comrades.

Tosseti shakes his head and asks the captain, "Who writes your material, man? I've heard better in comic books."

The captain spouts off some more about vengeance, wrath of God, revenge, the usual. Tosseti, flexing his muscles and hovering over the smaller man, vows to bitch slap him if he doesn't shut up. Though the captain doesn't understand what a bitch slap is, the tone of voice and the physical presence of Tosseti is enough for him to know he should remain quiet.

O'Toole is in the back of the wagon, along with Senior Airman Green, who wears corporal stripes. Something he complained about when given the uniform.

"Why the hell can't I be a sergeant?" he asked while holding his blue jacket up when it was issued to him at the Bank.

"Because you're still an airman. When you get promoted to NCO, then you can wear NCO stripes, Airman," he was told.

Green's condition is fine, but he has a large contusion and feels groggy. When he was sent back in time the last time, he fell and struck his head on a Jeep, receiving a severe concussion. One that nearly killed him. If not for Kriger doing what he could for him and being brought back to the future in time for surgery, he may well have died. Rees thought it best he rest. No sense in taking chances, not with a head injury. Tucker stretches, rubbing his back and moaning.

"Tuck, knock it off," Rees says. "Farnsworth and I have both been shot several times, and you don't see us whining. Hell, look at Tosseti, he just got sliced up, again, and you don't see him complaining."

"Yeah, well, everybody knows there something that ain't quite right with Tosseti," Tucker says, still arching his back and making faces.

"Fuck youse," is, of course, Tosseti's signature response for everything.

Farnsworth breaks in, "Thank you for coming to save our asses. I don't think we would have survived this one without the extra firepower. Nice touch with the fake Gatling gun."

McGuire snorts. "Yeah, Captain Epstein thought you would like that."

Rees interrupts, "Okay, what going on since we left. We haven't had contact with the Bank as far as two-way communication."

"Good idea using the camera lens as a communicator by the way. Anyway, as Farnsworth told you, Clio was sabotaged but is back up and running. Apparently, we still don't have voice communication, but…" Bouvier says and reaches into his haversack, "we do have these." He pulls out a small device with a screen and a tiny keyboard. "We were given a couple of these and, hopefully, we can write and receive messages."

"Do they work?" Farnsworth asks, reaching for the device.

"Don't know, sir. We didn't have time to try them out. A little busy trying to get here in time to save your asses."

Farnsworth looks at the device and raises his eyes to looks at Bouvier under the brim of his hat, seeing the grin on the sergeant's face.

"Pretty simple, just type in a message, then press…" Bouvier says and points to a small button, "that one there to send.

Farnsworth looks around, then hands it to Rees. "Go ahead. Your show, remember?"

Rees takes the device. "I thought we weren't bringing any obvious 21st Century gadgets into this time period?"

"Colonel Black and the chief were getting pretty frustrated not being able to communicate. The colonel said that since you were so close to finishing the mission, he didn't foresee any more problems with the Rebs, so he thought it wouldn't hurt to bring these. They have a self-destruction explosive inside, too."

Rees nods his understanding and thinks for a minute, then types, *Hello.*

"You take that much time to come up with *hello*?" Kriger asks, and Rees just smiles.

A few seconds pass, and *Hello back* scrawls across the tiny screen. The group of men cheer for what is taken for granted in the 21st Century. Rees begins typing again, *Welcome to the Civil War. Now, can you help us get O'Toole home?* And a few seconds later, *The Bank is here at your disposal, sir.*

"And, of course, you don't have to type, just talk, and the Bank will answer by sending back a message through that," Bouvier says, pointing at the device.

Rees nods. "Yeah, I guess that makes sense." Then says, "I take it you can hear me?" A few seconds later, *Of course, I can, o' great one,* comes across.

Rees looks at Bouvier, and both men say to the same time, "Sergeant Shepard."

"Good, well first, let's police up this area, then set up camp in those woods over there," he says, pointing to the copse north of them where the Rebels were when they charged. "We only have about sixty miles to go, but I want the wounded to get a good night's rest before we head out," he says and looks around as some of the men collect the brass from around the area. "By the way, I will assume you brought some more explosive material, as well as more buttons."

Bouvier reaches into a saddlebag. "We aim to please, and wouldn't leave home without them. Besides, Captain Epstein is getting a kick out of you using all his gadgets. He really is a Q."

He gives Rees and Farnsworth each a small bag of buttons with an exaggerated flourish, as well as several small packages of plastic explosives wrapped as soap and what looks like two-inch round wooden dowels, about eight inches in length.

"What are these?" Rees asks, grabbing one of the dowels.

"Oh, that's pretty neat," Bouvier says, removing one end of the dowel and discarding it. He twists the bottom portion, and it comes away with a string attached. Bouvier holds the dowel in his outstretched arm and pulls the string taut. He continues pulling until there is a loud *pop*, and a flare erupts from inside the dowel. It travels several hundred feet into the sky until it arches over and burns itself out. Even in the bright sunlight, it can be seen. "A signal flare," Bouvier announces with a grin.

Rees shakes his head. "Does that man ever stop making stuff? You know, instead of us using Semtex to make grenades, he should have made them look like baseballs or something similar. Would have made things easier. Oh, well, next time," Rees says, then sees the looks he's getting for even mentioning next time.

Tucker, who finally stops stretching and moaning, looks over at the two prisoners. "What are we going to do with those two, sir?"

Farnsworth and Rees give each other a glance.

"We'll figure that out in the morning. Right now, we need to set up camp, secure the perimeter, and make sure the wounded are taken care of," Rees says, and the team gets to work setting up for the night.

CHAPTER 53

Technical Sergeants Shepard and Montoya sit at a control console, typing. Both are tasked with communicating with the team. Since the loss of his leg, Shepard could not join the contingency team, so he is assigned to them in a support role. A role he is glad to have, even though he wants to be with his co-workers, his teammates, his friends.

Sergeant Montoya received a devastating head injury when he was shot during an engagement between Union and Confederate forces during the first time-travel experiment. The Minnie Ball went through his helmet, which slowed the velocity and direction of the ball, but not enough to keep it from lodging in his skull. Initially, everyone thought he had died, and no one checked due to the running battle that kept everyone on their toes trying to fend off enemies from two different directions.

When they were finally brought home, and doctors checked each of them, it was discovered that Ben Montoya was still alive. He went through several surgeries and months of rehabilitation before he was cleared fit for limited duties. He still suffers from occasional headaches, which the doctor says is to be expected, so they do not want him going on any missions until they can be sure he is completely healthy. Ben doesn't mind, he's just glad he's alive and still able to work, even if it's in a supporting role.

"Well, that's great. At least now we can talk with the team. Something going right for once," Colonel Black says from behind them, approaching the console, with the chief beside him.

"Good evening, sir. How was your flight?" TJ asks, looking over his shoulder.

"You know, Sergeant, one F-15 flight is the same as any other F-15 flight."

Shepard chuckles. "If you say so, sir."

The colonel smiles. "How are our boys doing? Everything okay for the time being?"

"Yes, sir, they seem fine. O'Toole is doing well, as is Green and Tosseti. Well, Tosseti is being Tosseti, but he'll live, Kriger stitched up his face. Hopefully, he makes it back so I can rag on his new improved ugly mug."

"Okay, Sergeant, let's keep it professional," the colonel replies with mirth in his voice.

"Got you, sir. Anyway, they are settling in for the night, and, sir?"

The colonel looks down at Shepard. "Yes."

"Um, Captain Farnsworth is asking about his mother and the senator. I didn't want to say anything to him."

The colonel presses his lips together and looks to the chief, who shrugs. "That's alright, Sergeant. I think it best if I talk with him. Can you patch him through?"

Sergeant Shepard doesn't respond but begins typing. A few seconds later, Farnsworth announces he is online. Shepard gets out of his chair, and the colonel takes his place. Sergeant Montoya also stands to allow the chief to sit.

"You want us to leave, sir?"

The colonel looks at Shepard. "No, Sergeant, this involves everyone, you're fine. Can you bring him up on this console screen so I can see him?"

Montoya leans over and makes some adjustments and brings up Farnsworth's camera, which shows a view of a campfire with some of the team sitting around eating. Shepard types to Farnsworth that he is on a single screen with the colonel. A little time passes, and the camera is moved until it is in a position showing Farnsworth's face.

Colonel Black stares at the questioning look on Farnsworth's face and begins typing.

~ ~ ~

Farnsworth finishes his conversation with the Bank and thanks them for the information. He disconnects the link and replaces his button on his uniform. After taking a few breaths, he sits. He crosses his arm on his knees and rests his head on them. McGuire happens to see Farnsworth and taps Bouvier on the arm and points in Farnsworth's direction. Bouvier gets up to locate Rees. A few minutes later, Rees walks over to Farnsworth. He stands for a few seconds, just watching.

"You okay?"

Farnsworth takes another deep breath and sighs. He looks up and stares at the fire, not even noting the men trying not to look at him.

"I'm fine. Just got off the horn with the Bank."

Rees walks closer and sits down, not asking anything further. Finally, Farnsworth tells him the tragic news he received about the death of his mother.

~ ~ ~

The next morning, while the team is breaking camp, Rees and Farnsworth talk about the prisoners and come to a decision of what to do with them. Both men walk over to the wagon and stare down at the two captives. Captain Lewis sneers at the men, but the private is content to hear what they have to say. Rees squats down and looks at them.

"We're going to leave you here. We will tie you up but will cut the rope enough that you should be able to break free by the end of the day, at least. We will leave food and water but no weapons or horses.

"But we're in Yankee territory, Captain," the private says.

"Shut up, Private!" the captain yells at him, then looks at Rees. "You can go to Hell, sir."

"Be as it may, Captain… What is your name, anyway?" he asks and only gets a hateful glare from the Rebel officer.

"Well, anyway, that's what we're doing. We aren't killing prisoners, but we can't take you with us. When you get free, you may be able to grab a stray horse. If not…" Rees shrugs his shoulders, then stands.

Rees calls for McGuire and Tucker to bring some rope. The NCOs come over, and the captain spits on the ground when Tucker grabs him. The captain calls him all sorts of names. Tucker takes it in stride, much to the surprise of the rest of the men. Tucker is none too gentle as he escorts the captain over to a tree, where he removes the Zip-Ties and uses the rope to secure him, tightly.

The corporal is also tied to the same tree, but his ropes aren't as tight, and McGuire cuts partway through to allow him to work his hands free. They place a small amount of food and water by the extinguished campfire.

The time-traveling team mount up and head off in a northerly direction. Tosseti, awkwardly riding a horse, trots by the two Rebels and stares at them with the rest of the team watching. Tosseti smiles, and with a terrible southern drawl, says, "Ya'll come back now, ya hear?" He rides away and comes up alongside Tucker.

"Geez, you took what that Rebel captain said to you pretty well," Tosseti says.

Tucker just smiles, and Tosseti squints at him.

"What?? Come on, what did you do?"

Tucker looks around to ensure no one else can hear him.

"I peed in the canteens."

"Oh, shit," is all Tosseti can say, and both men laugh.

~   ~   ~

Rees and Farnsworth are in the front of the column of men. Farnsworth is quiet, has been since receiving the word of his mother's death, just staring straight ahead. Rees doesn't want to press it. He has already said his condolences, but now he needs to know he can count on the man in a pinch.

"I can't say I know how you feel, since I don't have any family. Never knew my parents, so I won't pretend to understand. I have lost friends, but I'm sure that doesn't compare," he says and waits to see if Farnsworth responds. He doesn't, so Rees continues, "Captain, I need to know I can trust you when the time comes."

Farnsworth nods. "Yeah, Rees, I'm good to go."

Rees watches, waiting for him to continue and, eventually, he does, "I loved my mother, but I could see she was becoming someone else. She wasn't the same person who reared me. Over the years, her obsession with changing the timeline was taking its toll. All she could talk about was what had happened to her mother, uncle, and grandfather. I could see the change, but she couldn't. Every time I broached the subject or tried to persuade her to change her mind, she would turn on me. She'd call me a quitter, saying I wasn't her son, or that I didn't love her, other hurtful things.

Finally, one day, I told her I saw where she was coming from. Then she acted like nothing ever happened, like I never even brought up the subject. She was a highly intelligent woman, but overly driven, blinded by her ambitions. She just assumed that anyone involved with her was just as dedicated to achieving her mission as she was. I had a feeling that something like this was going to happen, so it didn't come as a surprise, just a disappointment. I was hoping once she found out what I had done, she would abandon her plans, but now it's too late."

Farnsworth turns his head and looks at Rees with a sad smile. "No, Rees, I'm good. We have a mission to finish. We will get that man home so he can marry his sweetheart and make babies. We will not let anyone stand in our way. I didn't become a Tier One operator letting little things like death get in my way."

"Okay, sir, that's more like it," Rees says, satisfied.

They travel for two more days without any distraction or interference. Even though they were in Maryland, they had to be on guard. The state wasn't all pro-Union, as several people still sided with the Confederacy. No one was hostile towards them, but they could feel the eyes of some townsfolk glaring. Most just nodded or waved as they passed.

The small group of soldiers trots slowly into the town of Mt. Airy. They come across a unit of Union soldiers guarding the railroad, where troops and supplies are routed through. Farnsworth speaks briefly with the commander of the detachment, showing him the letters from the president and assuring him they will not be in town long.

Corporal O'Toole becomes excited as they get closer to his home. The small group lumbers up to the front of the home just as the front door opens and a man brandishing a scattergun walks out. He stands on the front porch and keeps the weapon aimed down in a ready but non-threatening manner and ensures it is seen.

"What can I do for you?" he shouts while watching as one of the Union soldiers climbs out of the back of the wagon. He notices the soldier is wounded. Somehow knows this man.

When Andy comes around the wagon, the man recognizes his son, and his eyes go wide. He leans the shotgun against the house and turns to the open door.

"Ma, get out here, Andy's home!" He makes his way down to greet his son.

Two young girls come running out of the house, squealing and shouting Andy's name. They rush to meet him, passing their father they grab Andy's leg and waist with enough force to make him take a step back.

"Whoa, little ones, can't you see he's hurt?" their father says.

Andy smiles widely and pats his sisters on their heads when he looks up and sees his mother standing in the doorway. She is smiling and tears run down her cheeks, her one hand clutching the front of her dress, the other covering her mouth. She slowly makes her way down the steps. Andy gently pushes his sisters aside and embraces his mother with his one good arm.

"My boy, my boy. Thank the Lord, my boy is home," she says while still crying and laughing.

"Oh, my, what have they done to you?" she asks when she breaks from the embrace and stares at the wounded arm.

"I am fine, Ma. Sergeant Kriger fixed me up after I got shot. I will be okay soon enough," he tells her.

"You got shot?" a wide-eyed thirteen-year-old Kaillie asks. "Did it hurt?"

Mrs. O'Toole pulls the young girl aside and scolds her for asking a dumb question. Kaillie pouts and looks at Andy, who smiles at her.

"Yes, darling, it hurt and still does, but I will be just fine," he says, causing her pout to turn into a smile.

Arms still wrapped around his mother's shoulder, he turns around as Rees and Farnsworth approach.

"Ma, Pa, I want to introduce you to Colonel Farnsworth and Captain Rees. These men help me escape from the Rebels and escorted me back here, along with those others there as well."

Rees and Farnsworth shake Mr. O'Toole's hand and tip their hats to Mrs. O'Toole. Andy points at Sergeant Kriger. "And that's the man who patched me up. Damn fine doctor he is," to which his ma slaps him and tells him to watch his language.

Kriger, still on his horse, waves.

"You men must be hungry. I was about to start supper. You will join us, of course. Least we can do for you in gratitude for bringing my boy home."

Rees and Farnsworth look at each other, and Rees answers.

"Ma'am, that's mighty nice, but we don't want to be a bother."

Mrs. O'Toole scoffs. "Don't be silly. You are all welcome in my home."

Mr. O'Toole looks at the group and sees Tucker and Nionee. "Didn't know they allowed darkies and Injuns in the Army, Colonel."

"Ah, sir, we don't call people darkies or Indians. They are soldiers, just like the rest of us. We do not discriminate."

"I do apologize, I did not mean to offend, just not used to it, is all. Everyone is welcome here, even Yankees," he says with smiling eyes, "Sorry, but we are Southern sympathizers, as I am sure Andy has told you, but for you, we will make an exception." Still smiling. "You have done a great service by putting your lives at risk to bring my son home and, for that, I am most grateful. Please, let us get your horses to the barn. Kaillie, show the men to the barn and where they can find hay and water for their horses."

"Yes, Pa," Kaillie answers and tells the men to follow her. She skips towards the barn, with the group behind her. Rees and Farnsworth give the reins of their horses to Tucker and McGuire and ask them to look after them.

"Ada, you go help your ma," Mr. O'Toole tells her, and she scrambles back into the house.

"Gentlemen, please, come in," he tells them and claps Andy on the back as he walks up onto the porch, with the three men following.

Once inside, they are seated at a table, and a pot of coffee is brought in with cups. Each man is poured a cup by Ada, who acts as the perfect hostess. Rees and Farnsworth fawn over the young girl, making her giggle and turn red from the attention.

A cover story had been concocted way before their arrival so that everyone is on the same page as to how Andy was captured and saved by Rees' and Farnsworth's unit. The family accepts the story and really only cares that Andy is home.

After having their coffee and small talk, Rees and Farnsworth excuse themselves, informing their guests they need to check on the men. Can't leave them unsupervised for too long.

Andy asks permission to stay behind and, of course, it is granted.

"Andy, man, you're a civie now. Don't need our permission to do anything anymore. Take off the uniform if you like. This is why we brought you here," Rees says, then nods to O'Toole and walks out the door, with the parents staring at the strange talking officer.

They go to the barn and find everyone taking care of the animals, with Tosseti complaining about it.

"I joined the Air Force, not the fucking Army, and sure didn't sign up to ride some stinking horse."

Nionee looks at Tosseti. "You Heyoka, you call what you do on that animal riding? You should see your squat body bouncing around on that thing. You look like a drunk kid with a sit and bounce ball. Up and down, left to right, arms all over the place," Nionee says, flapping his arms and bouncing about. "Why do you think we put you in the wagon? We didn't want you embarrassing us in front of the Rebels."

The others snicker and laugh. Tosseti gives them the bird and his signature verbal comeback, then makes some comment about Indians and horses that causes the men to laugh even harder.

Rees and Farnsworth can hear the laughter, and they like knowing the men can find humor anywhere they go. Airman Green is up and helping out as well, though moving slower than the others. When they approach, the men ask how things are going and what the plan is. Rees shakes his head.

"Not sure yet. I'd like to stick around until O'Toole sees Emma. Curious to see her myself."

"Uh, uh," Kriger says, still brushing his horse.

Rees ignores the comment. "Once O'Toole secures his relationship with Emma, I think our job here is done, and we can be on our way," he says and looks into the camera, "Is that alright with you?" he asks, hoping the colonel gets the question.

Rees stares at the device screen, and a few seconds later, *Colonel Black here - Just tell us when and we will bring you home,* comes across the screen.

Rees informs the men they have permission to stay for a while, so they should set up camp, but stay out of the way of the O'Tooles the best they can. They have all been invited to join them for supper, so they should clean up and be on their best behavior, and remember, they are in 1862 not 1980 or 2019, so behave like it.

The meal they are served is wonderful, Chicken with mashed potatoes, carrots, green beans, corn on the cob, baked bread with home churned butter and preserves. The men bring in some of their food stores and give them to Mrs. O'Toole as a way of saying thank you. She refuses at first, then graciously accepts the gifts after much fuss.

The men eat heartily, and Mrs. O'Toole beams while watching the men enjoy her cooking. She also beams when she sees her son enjoying himself, talking and laughing with the group of young men seated around the table.

The girls are the center of attention, and they especially like Tucker and Nionee, not because they have never interacted with an African American or American Indian, but because they are friendly and funny. At first, the girls were unsure of Tosseti because of the wicked-looking scar and stitches on his face, but after getting used to him, they attempted to come near him. Tosseti would just growl as they did, but he does it good-naturedly, laughing as the girls giggle and run from him when he does.

The evening goes well, and after the men help clean up the dishes, much to the chagrin of Mrs. Farnsworth, who insists men don't wash dishes but is pleased when they do and impressed with how efficient they are. These are strange young men, and she could get used to them.

After the cleanup, everyone leaves except for Rees and Farnsworth, who are invited to stay for an after-dinner drink, cigar, and talk. A tradition when company is there. The others make fun of the officers because they get special privileges, but it's all in fun. They understand the way things were back then.

The four remaining men go to the front porch, where they light cigars and are served Irish whiskey. They talk about the war mostly, seeing that the only information the O'Toole's receive is what they read in the newspapers, which is usually days old, and they feel that, sometimes, the news isn't always correct.

Mr. Farnworth tells them of their history and about their other sons, who are fighting for the South. Rees and Farnsworth exchange looks when they receive this information, already knowing the two younger O'Tooles' fates. He tells them about the farm and the town and finally gets around to talking about Emma to Andy.

"She will be glad to see that you are still alive and have returned. She had given up hope once word got back you had either been killed or captured. We all thank the Lord it is the latter, Son," Mr. Farnsworth tells his oldest son. "She has been seeing that Thomas Walsh scallywag, though," he says with disdain. "Never cared for him or his kind. Too good for regular folks, always showing off, throwing railroad money around. That young man hasn't done a lick of hard work in his life, running around town bragging about how Emma is gonna be his wife one day. Poppy stick, I say.

"Once she sees you, ole Thomas will be long forgotten. You just wait and see, I tell you. Emma has always had her heart set on marrying you, Andy. She is a strong lass and won't be spending her time with some rich mamma's boy. She would rather be the wife of a working man, I can tell you that," he finishes his rhetoric and takes a swig of his drink, then a puff of his cigar and acts like the matter is closed as far as he is concerned.

Rees and Farnsworth are both amused at the man's antics.

"You going to go see her, Andy?" Rees asks.

"Yes, sir. Thought I would go over to her place tomorrow," he answers and looks at Farnsworth. "Colonel, I know I'm not in the Army any longer, but can I still wear my uniform?"

"Yeah, sure. It's yours, and you served, so of course," Farnsworth answers, a little surprised at the question.

"Thank you. My ma's patching and cleaning it up for me, so I look my best," he says with a broad smile.

Rees and Farnsworth smile back.

"Andy, I've got a favor to ask," Rees says.

"Yes, sir. What is it?"

"Would you mind if we escort you out to Miss Kelly's place tomorrow? Thought it might help you out if we all went as a unit. We wouldn't stay, of course, just want to help you make the best impression you can."

"Damn fine idea, Rees," Farnsworth exclaims. "Yes, Andy, you wouldn't mind, would you?"

Andy beams even more. "Why, of course not, sir. I would be honored to have you meet Emma. She would be pleased as well, I am sure. You are welcome to come along."

"Good. Well, we should call it a night, gentlemen," Farnsworth announces as he and Rees both stand.

"I want to thank you for the hospitality, and the drink, as well as these wonderful cigars," Farnsworth says.

Rees looks at Andy and points to his arm. "You might want Kriger to take a look at that in the morning before we leave."

"I will. Ma's doing pretty well with it, but I will let Sergeant Kriger take another gander."

Both men thank the O'Tooles again, then leave for the evening, taking the cigars with them, cheerily puffing on them as they make for the barn.

The next morning, the men make coffee and are surprised when the O'Toole girls and Mrs. O'Toole come out with a basket of boiled eggs and a large platter of smoked sausages.

"Ma'am, you're spoiling us. We keep eating like this, we won't be able to fit into our uniforms," Nionee says.

She waves them off and acts like it's nothing and leaves them to eat. After their meal, they clean up the area where they were staying, clean their uniforms as best they can, and break camp. Corporal O'Toole comes out wearing a newly patched, cleaned, and pressed uniform. He walks into the barn to get his horse, and Kriger smells something sweet and follows it into the barn.

"Well, I'll be. Hey, guys, our corporal here done shaved and put on some sweet-smelling Eau De Cologne or something."

At this, the other's come into the barn and harass O'Toole. He turns red from embarrassment and tries his best to ignore the hoots and whistles. Bouvier comes over and helps Andy saddle his horse after seeing he is having trouble with only one good arm.

"Come on, guys, give the guy a break. He's got a girl to see. You remember girls, don't ya?" Bouvier asks.

"Sure, we remember them, we just ain't allowed to see any," McGuire blurts out.

Rees walks over and tells the men to knock it off and that he has had a talk with the colonel about getting them off the base when they return. Once they're back, he will raise the subject again. Right now, they need to act like US Air Force Union cavalrymen and help Corporal O'Toole impress his girl. This gets a gawk from everyone. Rees grins at the made-up title, then reminds the men that a lot is at stake.

They leave the wagon hidden in the barn, securing the Gatling gun the best they can. Mr. O'Toole assures them no one will bother the wagon while they are gone.

Once they have lined up, they leave the farm and ride down towards the Kelly farm, which is just a few miles away.

Rees scratches at his beard. "Be glad to get back and shave this thing off. Always wanted one, and now that I have it, I just want it off."

Farnsworth grins. "I've always had one. You know us SpecOps guys, got to have the long hair and beards. Really aggravates the command structure."

"Well, you can keep it. Mine's coming off as soon as we get back."

About an hour later, they arrive at the Kelly farm and stop outside the open gates. O'Toole rides up beside Rees and Farnsworth, grinning like the cat that ate the canary.

"Will you look at that shit-eating grin," Farnsworth says. "You look nervous, Andy."

Andy nods. "I am. What if she doesn't recognize me or doesn't want to see me?"

Rees laughs. "Andy, you heard your pa. You don't think he would make that up, do you? Besides, we're here, and the only way you're going to find out is to go on up there and knock on the door."

Andy takes a breath and starts for the farmhouse. They travel in a column and look very professional, well, as professional as men from the future can riding horses. They stop in front of the home, and Andy climbs off his horse just as the door opens. Emma Kelly, long red hair tied in back and green eyes that Rees can see from where he sits, stands in the open door, mouth open, eyes wide in surprise at seeing Andy O'Toole standing at the bottom of the steps.

She makes a little cry in her throat and moves towards him slowly, then rushes into his open arm. She squeezes him tightly, and he makes a little sound and winces from the pain in his arm, causing Emma to release him and step back.

"My Lord, Andy, you're hurt."

"It's nothing, Emma, just a scratch," he assures her.

She squints her eyes at him in disbelief, and he laughs. "I swear, I am fine."

Emma playfully slaps him. "Do not swear, Andy O'Toole," she scolds.

Andy raises his hand in surrender and beams at the young woman.

"I was told you were missing, dead or captured. I cried my eyes out for days, but I knew you would come back to me, I just knew it," she says with happiness evident in her face and the glistening of tears starting to form at the corners of her eyes from joy. O'Toole's heart swells, and he just became the happiest man alive.

Emma finally notices the soldiers behind him, all of them smiling, happy for Andy.

"And who are your friends?" she asks and turns to see Andy staring at her. "Andy, you're staring," she scolds him, a little embarrassed.

"I'm sorry, Emma. I have had nothing on my mind except you for these long months. You are what has kept me alive, and now, I am home for good. I just hope this is not a dream."

She smiles and takes his hand in hers. "It is not, Andy. I am so happy you are home. Now, who have you brought along with you?"

Andy finally takes his eyes off Emma and turns to look at the men.

"Emma, this is Colonel Farnsworth and Captain Rees. They and these men saved my life and brought me home safely."

Rees and Farnworth touch the brim of their hats and say, "Ma'am," as the other wave and say hello or hi, tipping hats or giving half-salutes.

"Oh, please, come in, Colonel, Captain. I would so much like to hear how you brought my Andy back to me," she says with a genuine smile. Andy beams at what she said when she called him her Andy.

"Miss Kelly, we'd love to, but we need to get back to the O'Toole farm. We won't be staying long, just wanted to ensure Andy got home safely and, of course, back to you," Farnsworth tells her.

"Besides," Rees interjects, "you need to spend your time with Andy."

She turns serious for a minute and looks confused. "But doesn't Andy have to go with you?" she asks, looking at the officers, then Andy, who is still smiling.

Rees shakes his head. "No, ma'am, he's no longer in the Army. We just escorted him back here on our way to Washington. He's all yours."

Emma smiles even more, and her bright emerald eyes sparkle as she stares into Andy's deep blue ones.

Rees chuckles and leans over to Farnsworth, whispering, "These two look like something out of a soap opera or an Irish novel, 1860 style. Hey, maybe I can pitch an idea for a show like that when we get back."

They hear noise coming from behind and see a wagon… No, not a wagon, a carriage, approaching with a fancy dressed young man holding the reins. Behind him are some cowboy types but wearing nicer clothes than a cowboy would, but not looking like they belong in them. The carriage moves around the troops, and the driver stares, not kindly at them, and pulls to a stop in front of the house.

The young man climbs out of the carriage and approaches Andy and Emma. His face is set in a stern look, a look of an angry person trying not to show it. He stops short of Andy and Emma, not even looking at the soldiers. He looks Andy up and down and turns his attention to Emma, then back at Andy.

"Heard you was dead, then heard you was back," he finally says in a heavier Irish accent than Andy or Emma's.

"Well, you heard wrong and heard right, Tommy," Andy answers back, the smile gone from his face.

"What are you doing here? If you're not dead and not captured, why aren't you out there fighting?" Tommy asks with a sneer.

Rees answers for him, "He's been mustered out. Wounded in battle."

Tommy Walsh turns and looks at Rees, staring blankly at him as if he just noticed the man. He looks Rees up and down, seeming to study the man. "I do believe I was asking Corporal O'Toole, not you, good sir," he says with a pinched expression as if he just bit into something sour, then turns back to face Andy.

Rees leans back in his saddle and raises his eyebrows, then see's Farnsworth's eyes narrow. Rees can tell he's about to do something they don't need done. Reaching over, he grabs Farnsworth's arms and shakes his head. "Not worth it," he says and sees Farnsworth relax.

Emma steps between Andy and Tommy. "Tommy Walsh, you should be ashamed of yourself. Andy has been wounded and has been fighting for over a year. These kind men ensured he made it back, and you should be nicer to him."

Tommy glares at Andy, then looks at Emma. "We are to go for a ride in the country today, Emma. I have a special picnic basket all ready to go, with some of your favorites. I also have something especially important I need to speak with you about."

Emma looks at Andy, then at Tommy. "Tommy, I'm afraid I won't be going today. Maybe tomorrow. I want to talk with Andy, it's been so—"

"No, you told me it was today, and you cannot go back on your word. You need to come with me now. You can see soldier boy tomorrow. What I have to speak with you about is quite important," Tommy announces with an air of superiority.

Andy looks at Emma. "If you made a promise, Emma, I think you should keep it. I can come back tomorrow. There's plenty of time to catch up." As he starts to walk away, he leans into Tommy and tells him to enjoy his last picnic with Emma, because now that he is back, he is here to stay and intends on marrying her.

Tommy looks like he had been sucker-punched. O'Toole smiles, turns back to Emma, and promises he will be back tomorrow. Andy walks back to his horse and climbs on. With one last look at Emma, he turns the horse and rides off, with the rest of the men following.

Rees and Farnsworth are both surprised at the turn of events. They tip their hats at Emma, and then both officers give Tommy Walsh the evil eye. Farnsworth waits until the others are turned away and he is the only one facing Tommy. He stares at Tommy, then points his finger at him. Tommy just snarls back.

Rees stop when he sees that Farnsworth isn't beside him and waits for him to catch up. "What was that all about?"

"Just leaving Mr. Walsh a little message."

~ ~ ~

They make it back to the O'Toole farm, and Andy goes straight to his home. Mrs. O'Toole is surprised they are back so soon. Andy explains what transpired at the Kelly farm while Mrs. O'Toole listens, shaking her head and muttering, "Tsk-tsk," while Andy talks.

Mr. O'Toole, on the other hand, says some un-Christian like things about the Walsh family, which gets him a strong scolding from the missus.

Andy changes clothes and tells his father he'll be out in the field checking and mending some of the fences he knows are probably down. Andy knows his father is a great farmer, but fence-mending was never a strong suit for him. As Andy passes by the barn, he tells the men what he is doing and most volunteer to help. Andy says he would rather do it himself.

Andy grabs some tools, a roll of fencing wire, and some nails, and places them into a wagon. He slowly hitches up a horse and heads out into the open farmland. Everyone knows he won't be mending fences with only one good arm and assumes he just wants to be alone.

Farnsworth and Rees watch him ride out, bouncing on the seat as the wagon runs over rough spots in the field.

"I don't like him going out there alone," Rees says.

"Why not?" Farnsworth asks, coming alongside Rees and watching Andy.

"I don't know, just got a bad feeling is all. That Walsh character gave me the willies. I felt some bad vibes coming off him."

"You and me both, brother," Bouvier says from behind them.

About four hours pass, and Mr. O'Toole comes out to the barn.

"Andy should be back by now, not that much mending to be done. He knows I do not like fence-mending, but I did tend to it while he was gone. Besides, Ma's making supper."

Rees looks at the older O'Toole. "Want us to go fetch him?"

"If you would not mind, I will be grateful," Mr. O'Toole says.

"Be happy to," Rees responds and tells Farnsworth, who says he will tag along. They both saddle their horses and head out in the direction Andy was last seen traveling. They find the fence line and are amazed at how long it stretches. Turning their animals, they begin riding parallel to the fence. They enjoy the weather and make small talk as they casually make their way along the line.

Soon, they ride up a small mound and see a wagon a few hundred yards away, with Andy in the back, bent over doing something they can't see.

Andy stands up and happens to see the two men approaching. He recognizes them and waves, then he pitches forward off the wagon and lands heavily on the ground. A split-second later, Rees and Farnsworth hear the report of a rifle shot. They urge their horses into a gallop, and the hooves throw up globs of dirt with each stride.

The men reach the wagon in just a few seconds, and Rees jumps off his horse before it has stopped, stumbles, and falls. In the back of his mind, he can hear Andy making fun of him for falling, but not this time. This time, there is nothing funny.

"Andy!" he yells as he scrambles over to the downed man. Farnsworth stays in his saddle, keeping watch and searching for a gunman, his rifle already out. Rees sees a red seeping hole in Andy's back. He rolls him over and cringes when he discovers a large exit wound in the front of his chest. Whoever shot him is either an incredibly good marksman or a lucky shot, as the bullet went straight through Andy's heart, killing him before he hit the ground. Rees doesn't need to check for vital signs. Andy's lifeless eyes stare straight up into the sky like he is searching for Heaven.

Rees stands. "Son of a bitch!" he yells. "That motherfucker!" He turns towards a hill where he believes the shot was fired from.

Farnsworth still scans the area when he spots movement on the same hill not far away.

"There!" he shouts, pointing out the motion. "Someone's up there!"

Rees grabs his binoculars. Putting them to his eyes, he sees a man fleeing, then loses sight as the figure runs down the other side of the hill. Rees jumps onto his horse, and he and Farnsworth jump the fence, galloping up the hill. As they crest the top, they see two men. One is on a horse, holding the other man's mount and waiting for him to climb on. The assailants see the cavalrymen and turn to run, but Rees and Farnsworth are already heading in their direction at a full gallop.

The two figures spur their horses and, at the same time, turn to fire pistols at their pursuers. The shots are not aimed, and no one is in danger of being hit.

Anger fuels both time travelers as they quickly gain on the assassins. The two fugitives cannot shake the men coming after them. Try as they might, they aren't fast enough to get away. Rees pulls his saber and comes up quickly from behind, and he swings with all his might as the blade finds the flesh and bone of one rider.

The man screams from pain as the blade slices along his back, cutting deep into tissue, muscle, and bone. He slumps forwards, hanging onto his horse for several yards, then falls to the ground in a tumble. Rees stops his horse, turns it around, and comes back to where the man is lying, moaning from the pain. Rees slowly climbs off his steed and pulls his pistol as he approaches the injured man.

The second man turns to see Farnsworth and his mask of anger right on top of him. The man aims his pistol at point-blank range at Farnsworth. Knowing he can't miss, he pulls the trigger, and the firing pin falls on an empty chamber. He tries again with the same result. Farnworth rides up alongside the man and reaches over to grab him. The man fights him off the best he can, but Farnsworth is bigger, stronger, in better shape, and has a longer arm length. All that, and he is mad as hell.

He easily grabs ahold of the man and yanks him off his horse. The man's eyes go wide with fear as Farnsworth holds onto him, his feet dragging in the dirt. Farnsworth releases his grip, and the man rolls, flips, and bounces along the ground.

Farnsworth stops, turns back, and approaches the man, who attempts to stand. Farnsworth jumps off his horse and calmly walks over as the man stands up. He strikes him hard in the solar plexus, and the man makes a loud *oooofff* sound and falls to his knees. Farnsworth reaches down, grabs the front of the man's clothing, lifts him, and strikes him hard in the face with his fist. The man's eyes roll back as blood sprays from his now broken nose. Farnsworth hits him again and again.

Rees comes galloping up.

"Farnsworth! Stop!" he shouts, and to Farnsworth's credit, he does.

"I know, need him alive," Farnworth says and drops the man, who collapses like dead weight, though he's still breathing.

"How's the other one."

"Sorry, I don't have the self-discipline you do. He's not going to be of any help," Rees answers, then looks at the moaning man on the ground. "Recognize him?"

Farnsworth nods. "Yep, both of them. They were with that Tommy Walsh fuck back at the Kelly farm."

"Un-uh. So, that means they were sent by Walsh to kill his only rival."

Farnsworth looks up at Rees in alarm. "Oh, shit!" he exclaims. "With O'Toole dead…" he says without finishing, and Rees gets his meaning and continues his sentence.

"There are no Blacks to make a time machine. Which means, we're stuck here. But that can't be. We shouldn't even be here then. If the time machine wasn't invented, then we wouldn't be here," Rees reasons, then reaches into his jacket pocket and pulls out the device,

"Can you hear me?" he asks, then stares at the screen. There is no response, and Rees looks at Farnsworth with a worried expression. He looks back at the screen, then sees, *Yes, everything is fine. Nothing has changed. The Blacks are still here. No apparent change to the timeline. Any idea as to why?*

Farnsworth looks at Rees. "What is it?"

Rees looks up. "No change. O'Toole's death hasn't affected the timeline."

"I don't understand."

"Neither do I. We'll worry about that later. For now, we need to get this ass-wipe back and turned over to the cops, or sheriff, or whoever."

The two men round up the assassins' horses. The dead man's body is draped over one, and the savagely beaten man, Johnathan Higgins, is tied and placed onto his horse for the ride back. They reach the fence and realize they can't jump back over, so Rees climbs over, grabs wire cutters, and opens a section of fence that allows them to enter.

Just as they are getting off their horses to place Andy's body in the wagon, they hear the sound of galloping horses. In a few seconds, they spot Bouvier, Kriger, Nionee, McGuire, and Tucker riding up. They stop and all stare in shock at the sight of Andy's body.

"We heard shots. Sound carries out here. Wasn't sure, but we figured you might have run into some trouble," Bouvier says, still looking at Andy.

Kriger jumps down and goes to the body. The others climb down, and they lift Andy O'Toole's lifeless body and place it in the wagon, then cover it.

"What the hell happened?" Kriger asks.

Rees points at the beaten man and the dead man. "These two work for Walsh. They were at the Kelly farm when we were there earlier. He must have sent them to find Andy, with orders to kill him."

Kriger stares at Andy's body, then looks at the beaten man. Without even checking the bloodied man, Kriger pronounces him fit.

"Hey, I'm not a doctor, no Hippocratic Oath here. Let the bastard suffer."

Nionee climbs into the wagon and follows the others as they slowly travel back to the farm. When they arrive, Nionee takes the wagon to the back of the house. The O'Tooles come out in a hurry, eyes wide and darting around, looking for Andy.

"We saw all of you take off. What was the problem? Where is Andy?" Mrs. O'Toole asks, looking around for her son.

The men climb off their horses. Bouvier and McGuire pull the one assassin off his horse and drag walk him to the wagon.

Bouvier grabs the back of the man's hair and makes him face the wagon. Rees removes the tarp used to cover Andy's body.

Mrs. O'Toole's eyes widen in shock as she sees her son's body lying in a pool of his own blood, some of it still dripping between the floor planks.

A mournful sound wells deep from within her and erupts into a roar of grief, pain, and anger. She rushes over to the wagon, staring at Andy's body. She sobs loudly, calling Andy's name over and over.

Mr. O'Toole's face is a hardened mask. He comes over and wraps his arms around his bereaved wife, staring at the body, then at the men standing around him.

"Tell us what happened?"

Rees explains, and Mr. O'Toole stares daggers at the assassin.

The two girls stand on the back porch, not daring to approach the wagon, for if they do, the truth will be verified. As long as they stay on the porch, Andy isn't dead to them.

Mr. O'Toole suddenly releases his wife and moves for the assassin and strikes him in the face, right between the eyes and on his broken nose. The man screams in agony and tries to fall, but Bouvier and McGuire keep him upright.

"I should kill you!" Mr. O'Toole says in a low, menacing voice, "but you'll stand trial for this." He points at Andy's body. "Please, get him out of my sight or I just may take the law into my own hands."

Bouvier, McGuire, and Nionee perp-walk the man to the barn, where he will be secured for the night.

Rees and Farnsworth stand by and watch silently as the O'Toole family handles their grief. Mr. O'Toole asks the men for help in bringing Andy's body into the house for burial preparations. Once the body is inside, Mr. O'Toole thanks them, and they take it as their cue to leave.

"We'll be in the barn, interrogating…questioning the man. We'll find out what happened," Farnsworth tells Mr. O'Toole, who just looks at him and gives an almost imperceptible nod.

Rees and Farnsworth head back to the barn. "What now?" Rees asks.

"You and your men need to stay here. Mr. Higgins and I are going on a little trip."

"A trip for what?" Rees asks.

"You don't want to know. This is where my training comes in, and you don't want any part of it, believe me."

Rees nods. "I not going to preach to you about Geneva Convention or anything, but are you sure?" he says, then Farnsworth scowls. He thinks for a second, then gets what the look is for. "Yeah, okay, this coming from someone who just took a man's life instead of capturing him. Okay, I get it."

"Forget about it. Anyway, this is going to be a piece of cake compared to those I've questioned in the sandbox. I'm sure it won't be as bad as you think, which hurts my feelings," Farnsworth says, then looks at Rees. "Just saying."

Farnsworth takes Higgin, and they walk out into the night.

When Farnsworth leaves with the prisoner, the device buzzes in Rees' pocket. He removes it and reads the text. *Captain Brunell explained why O'Toole's death did not affect the timeline. We were fixated on it being one of Andy's children who leads to the births of the Blacks. The Blacks are descendants of Ava O'Toole. He finally found the bloodline, and they come from her children. Make sure the girls are secure. This is a priority.*

Rees closes his eyes. "What next?" he asks himself.

About an hour later, Farnsworth and the prisoner return. Higgins doesn't look any worse than he did when they left, but there is a look of pure horror on his face. He is terrified and tries to keep as far away from Farnsworth as possible, even though Farnsworth has a tight grip on the man's arm.

"Get what you needed?" Rees asks as Tosseti grabs Higgins, growling, taking him to the back of the barn to be secured.

"Oh, yeah, didn't take much. Man sang like a yellow bird with a yellow bill," Farnsworth replies and looks around for a cup so he can get some coffee. Finding one, he pours a cup and waits until Tosseti returns. "Just like we thought. Son of a bitch was sent here by orders of one Thomas Walsh. Said they were lucky. They didn't know when they would get a chance to kill him because we were around, and his family. Walsh said he didn't care, said that if they had to kill some of us, so be it." Taking a sip of coffee, he continues, "And if the O'Tooles got in the way, they were expendable as well, to include the little girls."

Tosseti's face turns into an angry mask, and Nionee and Tucker both become angry. Tosseti starts to walk back over to the prisoner, and Rees and Farnsworth both know what he going to do.

"Stop right there, Sergeant Tosseti," Farnsworth orders.

"Tosseti! Stop," Rees yells.

Tosseti does and turns around and looks at them, then points to the prisoner, who is even more terrified now.

"That low-lying piece of shit was going to kill little girls. Naw, he ain't living," he shouts back.

"We need him alive, Matt. Believe me, I wanted to kill him out there. Hell, I did kill the other one, and Farnsworth almost killed that one, but he knew we needed him alive. The dude will be taken to the police and turned over and will confess to what they did and tell them who sent them."

"What's to keep him from changing his story once there?" Tosseti asks.

Farnsworth snorts. "He won't. I explained to him what would happen if he did. Look at him. He's scared shitless and knows I will find him no matter where he is, in police custody or not. He does not want me to find him if he lies, because I made it clear what I could and would do to him, as well as his family if he did. He'll spill his guts to the authorities."

When the men are all in the barn, Rees calls a meeting and tells them about the message from the Bank.

"That makes sense. Problem with not looking at the big picture," Tucker says.

The next day, Farnsworth and Rees travel into town and find the sheriff. They explain the situation and are not surprised when he acts like it's not a big deal. They had a feeling the man was in the senior Walsh's pocket. The sheriff says he will be out to take custody of the prisoner and their help will no longer be needed.

Rees explains to the sheriff they only came here as a courtesy. The man killed a US Army Cavalryman and will be tried under military jurisdiction. The sheriff comes unglued and says he will have none of it and threatens them, which is pointless. He has no say in military affairs, and he knows it.

Senior Walsh, on the other hand, might have some say in the matter as it is his portion of the railroad being used to transport men and equipment to the front lines. This could get sticky if he contacts higher military authorities with whom he has had back door dealings with. No telling who he has in his pocket.

Farnsworth and Rees find the commander of the local garrison and tell them the situation. The captain is sympathetic to their plight but warns them they are right about the elder Walsh. He has friends in high places. If their prisoner is in the employ of the Walshes, then there is not much that can be done to him.

Rees looks at Farnsworth. "Sounds like the dammed mafia, like he's a made man."

Farnworth laughs. The captain doesn't.

They thank the commander for the information and go back to the O'Toole farm. They tell the men and the O'Tooles what they discovered and know there isn't much they can do. While talking with the O'Tooles, the device in Rees' pocket vibrates. He excuses himself and goes outside, away from prying eyes. Removing the device, he reads the message.

Wrap this up. Seems not much else you can do. No history on the Walsh family. Railroad owned and operated by the B&O.

Rees shakes his head. "Okay. I'll talk with the men. I don't want to just let this bastard go. We'll figure something out and complete the mission."

He returns to the house where Farnsworth is just concluding with the family. They walk out, and Rees tells him what the Bank said.

"I agree, we need to finish this up. Any ideas?"

"I say we turn him over to the garrison captain, let him make the decision. I'm sorry, but what can we do? The town is being run by some railroad tycoon, who isn't in the history books by the way, so I don't know what else to do. Of course, we could just conduct a fair trial ourselves, then shoot him."

"Not funny, Rees."

"I thought it was," Rees replies deadpan, then continues, "I can't see turning him over to the captain. He will just give him back to Walsh. No sense in making waves. Naw, we keep him for now."

They go back to the barn with the others to talk about the situation. Some of the men agree they should just leave it alone, but most don't like the idea of not finishing what was started by someone else. Andy's death needs justice, and it can't be found here. They call it a night and will make a decision in the morning.

The next day, as the men drink their coffee, they hear the sound of horses coming towards the barn. Rees, Farnsworth, and the others come around the barn and see a small cavalry unit approaching. A young lieutenant leads the men, and beside him is Sergeant McGregor.

The lieutenant salutes Farnworth and Rees, then climbs off his horse.

"With General Foster's compliments, sir," The lieutenant says, approaching the men. "He thought you might need some help on your mission after you left camp. He said that losing you a day may have an effect on the war effort, so he sent us out to try and catch up with you. You must have been moving along at a good pace. We ran into people who said they saw you, but we were always a day or two behind you. Finally, we grabbed up a couple of Rebs, a captain and private. They said they had a fight with some demon Yankees. Some balderdash story about a handful of Yankees killing a whole company of cavalry. We thought they had been hitting the bark juice until we run across a field of dead gray coats and horses. I take it, sir, that was you?"

Farnsworth and Rees just stare at the man.

"Uh, yeah, Lieutenant...?" Rees says.

"Lieutenant Holston, sir."

"Well, Lieutenant Holston, I'm afraid you've wasted your time coming here. We accomplished our mission and will be heading back to Washington shortly."

"I see. Well, if you don't mind, sir, we would like to bivouac here for the night, then we will head back to our regiment tomorrow. If that's alright with the owners."

Farnsworth sees Mr. O'Toole walking towards them.

"Here comes Mr. O'Toole now. I guess we can ask him. Also, Lieutenant, the corporal we were with, O'Toole, was shot and killed yesterday. We have one of the killers in the barn right now and are working on a plan to see that he gets a fair trial. The town is actually run by a railroad baron, and it was his son who sent the assassins."

"I'm sorry to hear that, sir," the lieutenant responds.

Mr. O'Toole arrives and looks at the soldiers.

"You planning on taking over my farm, Colonel?" the man asks, eyes narrowed but with a twinkle in them.

"I'm sorry, Mr. O'Toole, this is Lieutenant Holston. He was sent to help us but has arrived a little late. They would like to stay the night if that's all right with you. They will be heading back in the morning."

"Well, since you got that bushwhacking murderer in the barn, I got a feeling the Walshes will be coming for him, along with that no-account sheriff. Might be a good thing you have these boys here," he says and looks at the lieutenant and the others, then nods. "You're welcome to stay. We got a funeral to get ready for, so we ask we be left alone." He walks away.

"Damned war is hard on everyone. These are good people, but just to let you know, they are Southern sympathizers. Their two other boys are in the Rebel army."

The lieutenant just nods, then tells his men to dismount. When McGregor climbs down, he walks over and salutes the two officers.

"Good to see you, sirs. I'm sorry to hear about Corporal O'Toole. He was a fine lad."

"Yes, he was, Sergeant, thank you," Rees replies. "How'd you get volunteered for this?"

"Oh, that is what I did. I volunteered. I enjoyed fight'n with ya, so I thought I'd just tag along and maybe get some more in. You all have the devil inside you when it comes to kill'n."

"Yes, well, it's not something we like doing, but if we have to, we aim to win," Farnsworth tells him.

"Aye, sir. I can see that," McGregor says with a smile. "Now, if'n you'll excuse me, I'll need to get these young'uns to work or they'll go wander'n off and get lost or in trouble." He salutes, then walks away.

Rees chuckles. "Hey, Sergeant McGregor?"

The man stops and turns back around. "Sir?"

"Say it for us," Rees tells him.

The sergeant looks confused for a second, then realizes what Rees wants. He sighs. "Good morning, Miss Moneypenny." Then he shakes his head as the two officers and a few of their sergeants laugh. "Damned crazy bunch these are," he mumbles to himself.

CHAPTER 54

Joshua Walsh, the owner of the division of railroad in Mt. Airy, sits behind a large oak desk in his home office. He nurses a glass of Brandy and listens to the sniffling excuse his spoiled son gives him about how one of his men is dead and the other is in the hands of the US Army.

"Dad, please, I made a mistake. I shouldn't have sent Higgins and Selleck to take care of O'Toole. I thought it would be a simple assignment but, apparently, it was too much for them. That's the mistake I made," Tommy whines, trying to deflect the problems now confronting him onto the two assassins.

A large fist strikes the table, causing Tommy to jump. He stops talking and stares into the angry face of his father.

"You little incompetent fool. You send men out to kill a US Army soldier, my men, and without my okay. Then those men are found out, now one is dead and the other captured. What were you thinking? And do not answer that question. You were *not* thinking. You peacock about town, sparking that Kelly girl, bragging she will be your wife. Well, I have news for you, Tommy, she is not marrying you. Once word gets out about this, do you think she will have anything to do with you? And that's not even important. You have brought the attention of the Army upon us, the Army that is paying us handsomely to ensure their men and equipment get to the war. The railroad could have just as easily come in here at the beginning of the war and taken over, but I was savvy enough and had enough connections to keep my railroad and to talk them into letting us loan it to them. Now, you go and try to ruin it for us," the large man says as he walks around the room, ranting and thinking.

He turns to look at his son, then walks behind his desk, grabs pen and paper, then sits heavily into his leather-bound chair and begins writing. When he finishes the note, he folds the paper and holds it out to Tommy.

"Take this to the telegraph office and send it to my office in Baltimore," he tells his son.

Tommy walks over, takes the paper from his father, and reads it.

"Need all available men here now. Send reply."

~ ~ ~

The next day, Rees and Farnsworth ask Lieutenant Holston to stay at least until after the funeral. They all walk to the house and, after knocking, Ava opens the door and smiles at the three officers.

"Hi, Ava, is your daddy here?" Rees asks, and she scoots back into the house, yelling for her father. A few seconds later, both O'Tooles come to the door. All three men stand on the porch with their hats in their hands and smile wanly and with sympathy to the elder O'Tooles.

"Sir, ma'am," Farnsworth begins, "if you would allow us, we would be honored to attend your son's burial."

Mrs. O'Toole's eyes water, then the tears run down her face. Mr. O'Toole wraps an arm around her shoulder, pulling her towards him for comfort. He squeezes her, and with a sad smile, informs the men they are more than welcome to attend, and they both thank them.

"We will bury him early this afternoon in the family plot up on that hill yonder," he says, pointing to a hill about half a mile away with a few trees scattered on top. "I will inform you when it is time."

The men thank them and walk back to the barn.

"This sucks," Rees says a few hours later when he and Farnsworth are with their team. "Not only Andy, but soon, they'll have to bury their other sons, too."

"Wars are never easy on anyone. Whole generations were lost during most of the wars up until World War 2 when the president changed it so entire families could not join or be drafted. After the five Sullivans incident, it was just too much for the American people to bear."

"What are the five Sullivans?" Green asks.

"They were five brothers from Iowa who served on a ship during the war. The ship was attacked and sank, and all five of them died. The entire family, gone. The military changed their drafting policy so that couldn't happen again. They also changed it so that if one family member was killed, no one else could be drafted, nor could they enlist. Kind of what the movie *Saving Private Ryan* was about."

The guys all look at each other because none of them has seen the movie. Farnsworth notices and smirks. "Sorry, forgot you guys haven't caught up to all the movies, but I recommend it when you get a chance."

Rees looks around and tells the guys to get ready for the funeral. They disperse and make their separate ways. Rees asks Bouvier how the prisoner is doing.

"Oh, he's fine, bitching most of the time, that is until I send Tosseti to talk to him, then he shuts up."

"I can imagine. Just don't let Matt get carried away."

"Naw, he knows the drill. Mostly bluster."

"Just the same, you know he can lose it sometimes."

"We've got it covered, not to worry."

Rees nods, then he and Farnsworth go find Lieutenant Holston.

"Thank you for doing this, Lieutenant," Farnsworth says.

"My privilege, sir. Though I didn't know the man, some of the boys here did and said good things about him. Good things about you two as well, sir."

"Thank you, good to know."

They all turn when they notice Mr. O'Toole approaching. The men walk out to meet him. He asks if there is something the Army does for the funeral, and Rees and Farnsworth say there is something they would like to do and explain it to the grieving father, who nods his approval.

A wagon is brought to the front of the home, and members of Rees' team carry the homemade casket down the steps and place it in the back. Tucker shakes the reins, and the horses move off in a slow walk towards the hill, with the O'Toole family, the Kelly family, some townsfolk, and the US Cavalry in tow.

They arrive at the hill, and the casket is removed and placed on lumber, which has been laid across the grave opening. The priest stands at the head of the casket as everyone else stands around and listens to his sermon.

The soldiers stand at the end in formation, except for seven members of Rees' team, who are positioned further away, with their rifles across the chests. Once the priest is finished, some of the soldiers lower the casket into the ground, and on the orders of Rees, the seven men aim their rifles into the air and fire. Several members of the family and friends jump from the loud *crack* of the guns. The seven-man team fires three volley's total in a salute to a fallen comrade.

After the funeral, everyone breaks and make their way back to the O'Toole home. The people eat and talk with the family for a short time, with most folk leaving after giving condolences one last time. The soldiers mostly stay outside, with the officers, Bouvier, and Kriger inside.

Once everyone is gone, Rees, Farnsworth, and the others excuse themselves and head back to the barn. Now that the funeral is over, the lieutenant and his men will be leaving the next day, as well as Rees and his team.

About an hour later, the soldiers hear what sounds like a large group of horses coming onto the property. Rees, Farnsworth, and the lieutenant walk out of the barn and see a small militia of men coming towards them. In front is a large man who seems to be in charge.

Holston's men don't pay much attention and go about their assigned tasks but keep an eye on the newcomers. Rees' men, on the other hand, move towards their weapons and take up strategic positions. They know trouble when they see it, and they want to have the upper hand if things go south.

The large group of men stop short of the three officers and fan out in a large semi-circle, almost surrounding the barn and the soldiers. Holston's men still haven't stopped what they are doing, except McGregor, who has seen Rees' men cautiously move, grab weapons, and move into the barn. He casually makes his way to the barn and gets the attention of a couple of his men, who follow.

The large man sits high in the saddle and puffs his chest out. He looks around the area like he is taking in a view of the farm. The men hear a door slam and most look towards the house, where they see Mr. O'Toole walking towards them with his shotgun in his hands. He carries it with one hand, the barrel pointing down. He walks past several of the men on horseback, pushing through some, and makes his way to the three officers.

"What's going on, Joshua?" Mr. O'Toole asks the elder Mr. Walsh.

"Good to see you, Patrick. Aren't going to introduce me to your friends here."

"I'm Colonel Farnsworth, this is Captain Rees, and Lieutenant Holston, US Cavalry."

"Good to meet you, boys," he says, then looks at Mr. O'Toole. "Sorry to hear about your boy, Patrick. Terrible times right now."

"You come here to insult me, Joshua? You dare come here to insult me? You have the gall to bring your murdering bastard of a son onto my property the day of my son's funeral," Mr. O'Toole yells, bringing his shotgun up to the ready position across his chest. This reaction causes several of Walsh's men to reach for their pistols and bring their rifles up.

Rees moves in front of Mr. O'Toole and places his hand on the gun, looking him in the eye. "Easy there, sir. Take it easy. We don't want to start something right now."

Mr. O'Toole seethes and moves to look over Rees' shoulder, staring dagger at Walsh. He listens to Rees and relaxes his grip on the gun, lowering it.

Farnsworth takes a step forward. "Just exactly can we do for you, Mr. Walsh?"

"Ah, a man who takes charge and gets to the point. I admire that quality," Walsh replies. "I'm here to retrieve one of my men, who I believe is currently a guest of yours."

"No, sir. He's not a guest at all. He's a prisoner, being held for murder until he can get a trial. He will be taken to Baltimore, where he will be turned over to Pinkerton men so that he can get a fair trial. He did, after all, kill a soldier."

Walsh grins, and it is a nasty grin, one of warning. "You any proof he shot that man?"

"We have enough," Farnsworth answers.

Walsh leans back and takes a deep breath, again looking around.

"Colonel Farnsworth, I heard you have some letter that you been showing around saying you're on some mission for the president and Mr. Stanton, and that it allows you access almost anywhere. I did a little checking with some of my colleagues in Washington, and it seems no one has ever heard of you or your Captain Rees, for that matter. Now, I could take that at face value because you are some type of spy, but when the matter was brought up to Mr. Stanton himself, he replied he was not aware of any such letter and denounced anyone showing such a letter as a fraud. Now, tell me, Colonel, is that true?"

Farnsworth just smirks at the man. "Sir, you can believe whatever you so wish. I know our orders, and whatever someone told you is a bald-faced lie. As far as the Secretary of War goes, well, we call that plausible deniability. It doesn't matter what you think, and what we do doesn't concern you at all."

The elder Walsh just stares at Farnsworth. Tommy Walsh looks at his father. "Pa, you just gonna let this man talk to you that way. I say we just kill them all and take Higgins from them—"

The elder Walsh backhands Tommy across the face, making the younger man's head snap back. Tommy grabs his mouth, where blood trickles down from a busted lip. He pulls the hand away and looks at the blood, then stares wide-eyed at his father. Everyone's eyes are on Tommy, and he turns red from anger and embarrassment. Mr. Walsh squints while looking at Tommy.

"Shut your mouth, boy. You are the reason we are in this mess in the first place. I will handle it, and I do not need any advice from you. Now, keep quiet and let the adults talk," he finishes and turns back towards Farnsworth and Rees and acts like the display didn't even happen.

"I'll tell you what, Colonel. Why don't you just hand my man over to me and save everyone any trouble. I am sure you need to get back to the war, and I need to get back to running a railroad," he says.

"Sorry, sir, that's not going to happen," Farnsworth replies.

The elder Walsh leans forward to glower at Farnsworth. "You will give me my man, or you will regret ever seeing me. I have you outnumbered and outgunned. Give me my man, and I will be on my way, otherwise, there will be hell to pay."

Farnsworth laughs. "You are a caricature of a typical cattle baron, or I should say a railroad baron. Man, you are funny. First off, you're not getting *your* man, and second, if you try to get him, we will not leave one of you alive. Now, get your big fat ass off this good man's property or…" Farnsworth turns to look at the barn and smiles after finding what he looks for, "that man in the barn loft will put the first bullet straight into your head, and the next man over there will do the same to your son."

When Farnsworth turns back around, he sees Walsh and his men staring at the loft and the other men scattered around the property, with weapons poised at them. Mr. Walsh's face grows red, and the anger is evident in his features. He shakes, then stares at Farnsworth, points a shaking finger at him. Farnsworth raises his hand.

"I know, 'This ain't over yet,' or, 'I'll be back,' or better yet, 'You ain't seen the last of me.' Seen all the movies, know all the bad quotes."

"You're a dead man. All of you are dead men," Walsh yells, turns his horse, and gallops away, his minions following.

Farnsworth watches them leave and turns to look at Rees and O'Toole. "Shit, must not have seen that one."

Rees shakes his head and snorts. "You're one crazy SOB, Farnsworth."

~ ~ ~

Mr. O'Toole is escorted back to the home by Rees. Farnsworth stays behind to set up for what he knows is going to be a battle. He has some of the men roll the Gatling gun wagon out and place it in the doorway of the barn. Stacks of hay are thrown down from the loft and set up in a perimeter in front of the barn. Farnsworth informs the lieutenant that he and his men may leave if they so wish. He explains that it isn't their fight, and they are probably needed at their regiment. Farnsworth doesn't want to order them away, but he knows he and Rees' men can handle whatever comes at them. McGregor overhears the conversation and comes stomping over.

"Begging the colonel's pardon," he asks, then looks at the lieutenant. "Sir, if you don't mind. I know it is not my place, but me and the lads are more than willing to stay and help out. If we have any say in the matter, that is, sir." He salutes and walks away.

The lieutenant watches him leave. "Your men are rubbing off on mine, sir. I do not know what kind of Army you come from, but it seems your men are more familiar with the officers than what I am used to. I do not agree with it, but you are in charge, and it seems to work. According to the good sergeant and the general."

"We do things a little different, I agree, Lieutenant, but we get the job done," Farnsworth answers.

"I am quite aware of that, Colonel. We will stay. I am not one to run from a fight."

Farnsworth smiles. "I had a feeling you would say that. I was hoping you would leave, but I will never tell another soldier to run. I just ask that you follow mine and Captain Rees' order to the letter."

"Oh, yes, sir. That goes without saying."

"Good. Now, get your men ready."

~ ~ ~

Rees is in the house with the O'Tooles, and he listens as Mr. O'Toole tells his wife what is happening.

"I want you to take the girls and go to the Kelly farm," he says to the family.

"No, I won't go. My place is here. This is my home, and you are my husband."

"I do not have time to argue, my dear. You need to leave, now," Mr. O'Toole says, pleading with his wife.

Rees takes a step forward, clearing his throat, getting their attention.

"Ma'am, your husband is correct. You should take the children and leave. It's not a cowardly thing to do. Your children need to be away from what is coming. I'm sorry this is happening, but these men will be coming back, and there is going to be violence. You and the girls need to go where it's safe. Once it's over, I will personally bring Mr. O'Toole to retrieve you. Now, please, there isn't much time."

Mrs. O'Toole cries but is adamant about staying. She thanks Rees but claims that nothing or no one is going to make her leave her home, but the children need to go.

The two girls, who are also crying, run to their father, begging him to let them stay. Squatting down, he hugs them both, reassuring them, but sternly informs them they must go to the Kelly farm. He shoos them away to gather their belongings. Turning to Rees, he says, "Thank you for trying, Captain."

Rees nods. "I need to get back. I will send some men to take your children to the Kelly's. I would suggest you and your wife go, too, but I have a feeling that Irish temper won't allow you to, just like it won't allow the missus to leave," he says with a grin.

Mr. O'Toole smiles. "Oh, lad, you have that right. The Walsh's have been pushing us for a long time. Now, it's time we push back."

Rees agrees, then leaves the house.

Rees gets back to the barn and calls the lieutenant over. He orders him to have two of his men escort the girls to the Kelly farm. Snapping off a salute, the lieutenant does as he is told. Rees then gathers his weapons and ensures they are operational. Tucker, Green, and McGuire have been busy with the explosives and have created several mines, as well as hand grenades.

"You guys have been busy," Rees says, watching them work. "What are you telling Holston's men about the plastic explosives?"

"We told them it is an experimental type of explosive made with nitroglycerine and clay. They already think we're some kind of special unit anyway because of the letter you are carrying from the president, so they just accept it at face value and move on," McGuire explains.

"Of course, they do. Well, try to limit their exposure to our tech, even the low-end stuff," Rees warns, then asks, "Seen Farnsworth?" He is informed he was last seen walking around the perimeter, checking for best fields of fire and possible flanking areas. Rees thanks the men and heads out of the barn, looking for the colonel.

Rees searches and finally finds him standing on the hill where Andy is buried. He walks up and stands beside the man.

"Already missing him?" he asks, referring to Andy.

Farnsworth looks at Rees, then the newly covered grave. "No, I just remember the view from up here and thought I'd check out the lay of the land, look for likely avenues of approach. From what I can see, they will have to come in from the road, but that would cause a bottleneck," he says, and then points to the area behind the barn. "I would come from that direction. See that low hill over there?" he asks, pointing to the hill, and then moving his arm in a sweeping motion. "I would cut the fence, then come onto the property and stay low behind that hill, cover and concealment. Then I would have a portion of my men come at us from the front, where the road comes onto the farm. Just a small unit, enough to cause us to react, but not enough to do us any harm.

Once they have our attention, and we are focused on fighting the frontal battle, *bam*! I would come charging over the hill to our rear with the larger force, and that would be the end of that."

Rees studies the terrain and slowly nods. "Okay, so we need to send out an LP/OP, cavalry style, to watch for them."

"Yeah, exactly, but we need our men as the primaries, with one of the lieutenant's men along as back-up. I've got a feeling they'll be setting up this evening for an attack first thing in the morning. Then we will wipe them off the face of the Earth," Farnsworth says, staring across the open fields, then he feels Rees staring at him.

He turns and looks Rees in the eyes.

"That is why there's no trace of the Walshes in the future. I think we kill them all and the B&O just took over operations and nothing was ever said about a family that is probably hated so much in this area that no one cares. Seen it before."

Rees nods also, watching the countryside. "Okay, we need to get this going," he finally says. "I'll get Bouvier working on laying the mines. I think we should send McGuire to patrol the hillside over there, and Green out front to warn us when he sees Walsh's men approaching."

Back at the barn, the men are given their assignments. Each team is provided the Epstein flares, with instructions to use them when the enemy is in route, then to hightail it back to the farm ASAP. McGuire and his partner gallop off towards the low-lying hill. Green and his partner move through the front entrance, crossing under the picket head for their assigned posts. Two of the lieutenant's men bring a wagon around to the home and collect the two girls for transport to the Kelly farm.

Mr. O'Toole is grateful his wife fought to stay but more grateful his two children are out of harm's way. He thanks Farnsworth and Rees immensely. The O'Tooles help out wherever they can, to include bringing food Mrs. O'Toole insists on making for the men.

"Those boys need to have a decent meal before facing off with the Walshes," she says huffily while cooking under her husband's appraising gaze

The men work diligently, setting up defensive positions, and finishing their preparations early in the evening. Most of the men then eat and catch some sleep, while others keep guard. They all swap their posts every few hours so everyone can get some rest, even though few sleep, too pent up and anxious for the morning to arrive.

Just before dawn, all the men are up. They have eaten, taken care of personal regiments, and begin setting up in their defensive positions.

Farnsworth and Rees have sent the lieutenant out to check every position one last time. They are standing on the front porch of the O'Toole house, talking with the husband and wife, sipping coffee, when they see a wagon coming through the front entrance. A few minutes later, Emma Kelly brings a buckboard to a halt in front of the home. She climbs down and approaches the porch.

"What in blazes are you doing here, girl?" Mr. O'Toole asks. Mrs. O'Toole just smiles and shakes her head.

"I couldn't stand staying at home. I loved your son, Mr. O'Toole, and I am angry as a hornet about what they did to him, what they took from me. I plan on being here when the fighting begins, and I plan on doing some myself," she replies in a defiant tone. "Now, if you point me in the right direction, Colonel, Captain, I'll be helping," she says and holds up a Colt M 1861 Navy revolver.

Rees and Farnsworth are both at a loss for words, not sure what they should tell her. Luckily, Mrs. O'Toole saves them by stepping in.

"My dear, I am so happy you are here, foolish as it may be. You won't be doin' no fighting, child, but you will stay with me help me make bandages and boil water and make places for the wounded to rest. I will be most thankful for the help."

Emma Kelly stands there looking confused and seems ready to argue. She stares at Mrs. O'Toole, then a sad smile comes across her face. "Yes, of course, you are quite right. You will need some help. But I will be holding on to my pistol."

When she and Mrs. O'Toole enter the house, Sergeant McGuire comes riding in. He pulls up in front of them and explains there have to be at least two hundred of Walsh's men on the other side of the hill, along with two wagons. They were all packing up and getting ready to ride, so McGuire thought it prudent to come warn them.

"Just as you said, Colonel. They must have cut a large swath of fence and made their way to the hill."

"What is in the wagons, could you see?" Farnsworth asks.

"No, sir. There is a large tarp covering both of them, but they look full."

That's a lot of supplies to have for a hit and run operation like this. What do they need two full wagons of supplies for?" Rees asks.

"No time to worry about it, we need to get into position," Farnsworth tells them.

"Good job, Sean. Now, get to the barn and inform the lieutenant we are expecting company," Rees tells him and watches McGuire ride off.

Not ten minutes go by when the men see a flare lighting up the morning sky, signaling that Walsh's men are coming towards the front of the farm. Several minutes later, Green and his partner come galloping in. Rees and Farnsworth are at the barn when Green comes charging in. He informs them that about forty to fifty men are heading this way from up the road.

The stage is set, and the players are ready.

~ ~ ~

Joshua Walsh leads his men over the hill and makes their way toward the O'Toole farmhouse. They pass the fence line that has been cut, allowing them easy access to the O'Toole property. He stops and looks back over his shoulder, feeling pride looking at the two hundred or so men he has behind him. Men who are loyal, or at least loyal as long as he pays them.

Some work directly for him, others in his employ elsewhere, and the rest, he's not concerned where they came from, even though he knows some are criminals and others are hired guns. He doesn't care, as long as they wipe out the O'Tooles and those damned cavalrymen.

Walsh has coveted the O'Toole farm for years. Now, he'll be able to take it. Once the O'Tooles are dead and gone, he'll just move on in and buy it from the state at a very modest price. A price he has already worked out ahead of time with some of his backroom dealing friends.

While he thinks of what he has in store for this land, a bright stream of light races skyward in the distance and disrupts his thoughts. "What on earth is that?" he asks out loud to no one in particular.

He can hear the murmurs and whispers of bewilderment behind him but doesn't pay it any never mind. He has people to kill and land to procure. The bright light in the sky falls away, and the horizon turns a light purple as the sun seeks to come over the hills. A few more minutes pass when he hears an explosion, followed by more explosions, then gunfire. Explosions were not part of the signal, but when he hears the gunfire, he tells his civilian army to move out.

~ ~ ~

Tommy Walsh's eyes sparkle and gleam. Now is the time to make his father proud. Time to redeem himself and return to his father's good graces. The elder Walsh gave his son another chance to shine, or fall, by having him lead the frontal assault. Tommy's heart swells at the thought of glory and making his daddy love him. He has been traveling for a few hours and is close to the O'Toole farm when he sees a streak of light traveling upwards, which arches and fades away. *Strange.* It reminds him of the fireworks he saw once during a fourth of July celebration in Baltimore.

Tommy is not sure what he saw and doesn't really care. All he cares about is getting back into the good graces of his father, and to do so, he must accomplish the task given to him. He turns and yells at the men behind him to pick up the pace. The sun will be up soon, and he wants to be on the O'Toole property as soon as it is.

It only takes the men about ten minutes to reach the front of the farm. He can see the wide-open posts marking the entrance, with the large horizontal beam across the top with the name O'Toole burnt into the wood, along with a stupid looking four-leaf clover that most of the old generation adores.

Tommy sneers and hastens his pace, as do the men behind him. It is time for his vindication. He moves faster until he is at a gallop as he crosses under the wooden marker and is on the property, charging towards the barn when an explosion throws him from his horse. He lands on the ground roughly and rolls to a stop.

Before he can get his bearings, there is another explosion, and he can hear men screaming, then he hears the sound of gunfire. His ears ring, and he reaches up and pulls his hand away to see blood. He stands and wobbles, looking around. There are wounded and dead men and horses scattered all around him. He blinks and continues to turn, not understanding what has happened.

Then it dawns on him that he is in a fight, that's right, a fight, one he must win to gain absolution from his father. Still unsteady on his feet, Tommy reaches for the pistol on his hip and clumsily pulls it out. He looks up to see his men on horseback shooting towards the barn. He staggers in that direction, raising his pistol. He shuffles towards the fight, uncertainty in his gait. He gains ground as he inches closer. Time to make his father proud.

He awkwardly fires his pistol at no one in particular. He fires again and takes another few steps forward, lowering the heavy pistol. He is so close, so close. He raises his pistol again and takes aim at a blue-clad soldier, and as he pulls on the hammer of the pistol, he groggily thinks, *For you, Father, I'm doing what you asked. This is for you,* before a 5.56 mm round drills into his forehead, and he drops dead. Rees only takes a split second to watch his handiwork. Time to gloat later. Right now, there's more fighting to be done.

~ ~ ~

The mines do their job. The explosions kill or wound a large portion of the distracting element of the attackers. Their feints don't work, as the majority of Rees' soldiers are facing where they know the main force will be coming from.

Rees and his soldiers pick off the remaining attackers, using the faster shooting 21st Century Spencer rifles, accomplishing this task.

Between their marksmanship and the mines, it takes only a few minutes before every man is down, either dead or wounded, to include Tommy Walsh. Tosseti feels bad when he sees the wounded and dead horses. As much as the man doesn't like riding, it is still hard seeing such magnificent creatures suffer. The men, bah, he couldn't care less about them. They had a choice. The poor dumb animals they rode didn't.

Once Rees is sure the front is clear, they rejoin the others for the main show.

~ ~ ~

Walsh listens to the struggle going on in front of him. He smiles as his men follow. The frontal assault on the farm is working. It should keep the soldiers busy long enough for him and his men to swoop in from the rear and surprise them. Not only with an overwhelming force, but with a little extra surprise courtesy of the United States Army.

The grin on his face falters when he notices the gunfire is down to a trickle, and the explosions have ceased. As they gallop closer, the battling has completely stopped. *No, it is too soon.* The men in the front should be holding that small ragtag group of soldiers' heads down for a long time. What is that idiot son of his doing? The elder Walsh becomes angry. He knew he shouldn't have put Tommy in charge, but being his only child, he can't stay angry and just can't say no to him. Tommy begged for another chance, and the elder Walsh gave in. Well, this will be the last time. He will not give him another chance if he messes this up.

Walsh and his army move with great speed towards the O'Toole's barn. He can see the bright red building from where he sits on his horse. Having forgotten about his son and the men in the front, he concentrates on his actions for killing those left on the farm.

He turns in his saddle and signals. The men behind him fan out, making a line of horses. A group of horsemen riding side by side, two groups on each side of Joshua Walsh. His heart swells at the excitement of having such power. The men slow to allow the two wagons to catch up and move up alongside the horsemen.

The tarps covering the backs of the wagons have been thrown off, and each reveals a Gatling gun, bolted to the wood planks. Each man is being jostled around and holding on for dear life. Until they can get a little closer and slow down, or better yet, completely stop, they can't shoot.

The sun rises ever so slowly, allowing the attackers to see the barn and farmhouse more clearly. The defending soldiers can also see the attackers. Both sides ready but seemingly waiting for the other to fire first.

Joshua Walsh is giddy inside. He looks to his left and right, enjoying the sight of the long row of slayers on horseback riding alongside him. Then he looks at the pathetic group of soldiers cowering in a barn. A barn he intends to burn to the ground, along with everyone inside it. Not too much closer now, and he can begin the onslaught.

Just as he is within range of weapons' fire, he sees a flare like the one he saw earlier, except this one is off to his right and coming towards his men. The light strikes the ground and, instantly, there is a huge flash as flames erupt from the ground. The flames travel in a line directly in front of them. The fires seem to shoot out of the ground as if the Devil has opened the gates of Hell.

All his men to the right do their best to stop from rushing into the inferno. Most of the men make it, but several do not and are engulfed in the firestorm. The screams of men and horses being burned alive are horrifying, but there is nothing anyone can do about it.

The ones able to avoid the flames veer off at different angles and seek to make their way around the blazing earth. They are cut off from Walsh and now divided into two groups. Walsh and those riding to his left continue on. He can't afford to slow and wait for the others to catch up.

~ ~ ~

Tucker throws the used flare away, stands, and watches his handiwork. Earlier, the men had dug a small trench, several hundred feet long, and filled it with kerosene and oil. Tucker, one of the fastest runners, was selected to use a flare and ignite the oil when the attackers were in close enough range that it would disrupt their charge.

It worked, and Tucker watches in fascination and terror as the flames shoot up and engulf several men and horses. He is also elated to see the rest have changed course and will be in disarray long enough that the first group will be engaged in a more manageable manner. With a whoop, he turns and runs for the barn.

~　~　~

Everyone in and around the barn watches in fascination as the fire erupts in a *whoosh,* and they can almost feel the heat. Some flinch as men and horses run into the flames and exit on fire. The men and animals scream and thrash about, trying to get away from the fire consuming them. Slowly, one by one, they collapse and roll and twitch until there is no more movement, death releasing them from the agony.

The soldiers turn their attention to the large group of riders now approaching but cut in half. Even though there are fewer of the enemy attacking at once, they are still a formidable force.

Rifles are raised, and Farnsworth yells for everyone to hold fire until they hear the predetermined signal.

The men anxiously wait, fingers poised on the triggers of their weapons. They hear the signal. A series of explosions, one right after another, can be heard coming from the first row of horsemen charging them. Several of the mines have detonated, killing or maiming several of Walsh's mercenaries.

The soldiers all open fire at the approaching civilian army, who return fire at the same time. Round after round of bullets are sent out, as well as coming in. The first volley of fire does little damage to either side due to the smoke and dust from the blast and smoke obscuring everyone's sight.

Tucker makes it back to the barn and is given his rifle. He takes up a fighting position and turns to look back at the flames. He sees that, though the plan worked, and the forces are now divided into two groups, the second wave, the one he diverted, now flanks them. Not what they wanted. Oh, well, adapt, improvise, and overcome.

Sergeant Kriger also sees the problem and runs to the ladder, leading up to the loft. He yells for Bouvier.

"Jack, riders coming from the left flank!" he yells, and Bouvier disappears from the opening.

A few minutes later, the men hear the unmistakable sound of the false Gatling gun as it spews lead down and in the direction of the enemy. Tucker and the crew with him watch as rows of men and animals are brought down by the overwhelming firepower unleashed upon them. Not deterred, some of the riders break left and right, spreading out, making it harder for the soldiers to shoot them.

Even though the mines took out several of Walsh's men, those who survive continue into the fray. Between the second group that was split off and the men with Walsh, the barn and home are surrounded.

Rees, Tosseti, and Green are in the home with Emma and Mrs. O'Toole. They bring any wounded they can into the house with them. The blood is turning the floor and carpets red, and one wounded man has already succumbed to his wounds. Emma and Mrs. O'Toole treat the others as best they can.

The three soldiers take up positions to cover the side of the house facing the barn. It isn't long before they see the fire in the field, and a short time later, hear the exploding mines. They see the mercenary cavalry riding in and shooting at the barn. Rees listens as the modern-day Gatling gun shoots steadily for a few minutes, then stops. They wait.

Farnsworth runs from man to man, encouraging them to keep up the fighting. McGregor is cursing and shooting and also yelling at his men to keep up the firepower. Farnsworth really likes this old sergeant. Two of Lieutenant Holston's men are down. Though a couple of Rees' men have been hit, they are empowered with the bullet-resistant wardrobe, keeping them safe, as long as there are no shots to the face.

The fake Gatling gun jams, and Bouvier tries to clear it. While he works on the jam, he hears the indistinct sound of something else. Suddenly, there are bullets coming through the side of the barn where he stands. He is knocked back by a couple of bullets impacting him but causing no damage other than some pain and having the wind knocked out of him. *What the fuck?* he thinks and rolls over, gasping for air, trying to stand.

~   ~   ~

The two waggoneers come to a stop several hundred feet from the barns and turn the wagons so the two Gatling guns face the barn. The men in the back begin cranking the handles that turn the six barrels as each throws out a .58 caliber bullet with each turn. Both weapons firing at once is devastating, as well as a shock to the soldiers in the barn.

"What the hell?" McGuire yells. "That's what they had in those wagons. Gatling guns." He ducks as one of the guns traverses his way.

Kriger crawls to McGuire's position. "You couldn't think to maybe let us in on that little fact?"

"Hey, I didn't know, they were covered over," McGuire yells, defending himself.

Farnsworth runs over and just misses being hit, though another of the lieutenant's men isn't as lucky when he tries to change his position and is struck by a round from the Gatling gun. Farnsworth briefly looks at the man, *boy*, for a fleeting second, then continues on. He looks around and sees Tucker. Yelling his name, a couple of times, he gets his attention.

Between yelling and giving hand signals, he tells Tucker what he needs him to do. Tucker looks at Farnsworth, smiles, then nods. He grabs what he needs and climbs up the ladder. A few minutes later, there are two sharp *cracks* of a rifle, and the Gatling guns cease shooting.

Tucker climbs back down with the telescope still on his rifle. He grins as he removes the scope.

A couple of Holston's men stare in disbelief, but soon forget what they just witnessed as there are still plenty of enemies surrounding them. Everyone gets back to the business of killing.

~ ~ ~

A unit of Walsh's men breaks off from the larger group when they spot the flickering light of the lamps glowing inside the house. Hastily, they make their way to the front of the home. Rees and Tosseti run through the house to the front parlor and break out the windows. Green stays where he is, watching the side of the house.

The men get off their horses when they hear the breaking glass, which is followed by the semi-automatic fire of the upgraded Spencer rifles. One man is shot dead, and the rest scatter, using bushes, hedges, and the portions of the house as cover. They return fire and rapidly disperse around the home, trying to find an entrance.

Green spots two men climbing over the porch railing, and he kills one with a single round. The second man drops off the rail, seeking cover.

Rees yells for the women to get on the floor and make their way to his and Tosseti's location. They comply as fast as they can, just in time as bullets come flying into the home from all directions. Rees and Tosseti drop down and cover themselves as glass and wood splinters permeate the home.

The front door bursts open as two men rush through. Both Rees and Tosseti fire at the same time, killing the first intruder and sending the second scurrying back outside for safety.

They hear a voice tell the men to hold their fire, and silence ensues, except for the background sounds of the men engaging each other around the barn.

"What are they doing?" Tosseti asks.

Rees shakes his head.

They hear glass shatter and hear Green yelp. They look in the direction of Green and see flickering light, fire, then see Green crawling on his hands and knees towards them.

They threw a damned Molotov cocktail or something in the window," Green complains. "Nearly set me on fire, those assholes."

Rees crawls past Green and looks into the side room and sees the flames growing.

"Shit!" is all he says and goes back into the parlor. "We're screwed if we don't get out of here. This house will go up like a matchstick."

Crouching, Rees stands and runs towards the back of the house. He opens the rear door and is met with gunfire. He yelps, falls to the floor, and kicks the door shut. Crab-walking, he scrambles back to the parlor and informs the small group that the back way out is a no-go.

"We have a cellar, and there's a door leading out further behind the house," Mrs. O'Toole informs them.

Without thinking about it, Rees tells her to take them there. She goes to a pantry area and pulls open a door on the floor, leading into the cellar. Rees pulls out a pen and turns a switch, and a small light comes on.

Emma and Mrs. O'Toole's eyes grow wide. "What is that?" Mrs. O'Toole stammers.

"I'll explain later. Right now, get in the cellar. I will be right back," he tells the women.

"What are we doing?" Tosseti asks, his eyebrows furrowed together and his mouth open.

"We can't leave the wounded," Rees replies.

"Fuck 'em, Sarge, they tried to kill us," Tosseti answers.

"Stow that talk, Matt. We are better than that. We're not letting men who can't help themselves burn to death, now move your asses and get those men in the cellar," Rees orders.

Tosseti grumbles and curses under his breath, then shoves Green towards the wounded. The two men drag the men to the cellar, and with the help of Rees and the women, they transfer them to the dirt floor cellar. Once everyone is inside, Mrs. O'Toole leads the group to the outer cellar doors.

Rees looks around and realizes the doors are not too far from the home.

"We're going to have to go out fast, weapons ready."

"What about them?" Emma asks, referring to the wounded.

"We can't take them with us," Rees replies. "Pull them as close to the doors and, hopefully, their guys will come down and get them. Best we can do."

When they finish, Rees and Tosseti stand below the outer cellar doors. "Don't take time to aim, just run and shoot at anyone who is not one of us."

"Yeah, let's kill some damn rat fuckers," Tosseti growls.

"Tosseti!" Rees admonishes, and Tosseti looks over at the two women, barely able to see them in the dim light.

"Oh, shit, ladies, sorry."

Rees shakes his head and reaches up for one door handle and Tosseti the other.

"When we get out there, we're heading for the barn. Tosseti and I will take out any of the men we see up top. Green, you take the women and cover them. Stay with them. Be quick but stay as low and out of sight as possible. Move as quickly as the person in front of you, and do not stop," he says, then takes a deep breath, lets it out, and nods three times.

The doors fly open, and Rees and Tosseti climb out as fast as they can and take aim at the men surrounding the house. Green and the women follow and run through the opening and towards the barn.

The hired gunmen are caught off guard. Rees has a quick thought of how untrained these men are, not covering a possible escape route, standing in the open. Thought forgotten, he shoots the first man he sees as he searches the area, covering for the others to escape. Tosseti shoots two more men, then takes off after Green and the women.

Rees stands his ground and scans for any other possible threats, and when he finds none, he follows Tosseti. The house is becoming an inferno extremely fast, the old dry wood an easy fuel for the flames.

With the home ablaze, it is a backdrop for the five people running to another battle, one being engaged around them. The other mercenaries at the house run in the wrong direction after hearing the gunshots at the back of the home. Reaching the rear of the house, they see the fleeing figures of the three men and two women and begin shooting.

Green has Mrs. O'Toole by the arm, and Tosseti has Emma's. Rees turns in all directions and shoots at anyone and everyone he can. The horsemen surrounding the barn at first don't see the running people, and when they finally do, they can't believe it. Rees and his band of house survivors zigzag through and around the horses and their riders and straight towards the barn.

Some of the soldiers spot the approaching refugees at the last moment and shift their aim to cover them. By some miracle, all five of the people make it through the attackers and into the relative safety of the barn.

Mr. O'Toole, who stayed with the soldiers in the barn, is angry and elated to see his wife. She runs to him, gulping breath and trying not to cry, but she can't help it. Mr. O'Toole holds onto his wife for a brief second, then pulls her to the ground as bullets continue to fly past.

"Have you lost your mind, woman? You could have been killed," he admonishes her, not from anger but fear.

"Would have died in that house if Captain Rees and his men had not got us out of there. Just be grateful for that."

He smiles and kisses the top of her head.

Rees and the others lie on the ground, sucking in lungful's of air. Farnsworth comes to them.

"Pretty ballsy, but glad you made it. Why are you breathing so hard, though? Thought you Security Forces types were in shape?"

"Security...Police," Tosetti says between breaths. "Still can't take...being called...Security Forces, dude...I mean, sir. Sorry." More breaths. "And we are in shape. Why don't you go run through that gauntlet and back to the burning house and see if you don't get a little winded. Sir."

Farnsworth smiles and grabs Rees' hand. "Well, welcome aboard."

Rees looks around. "How's it out here?"

We're good, holding our own, but now would be a good time to get this over with and get the hell home."

"I agree wholeheartedly," Rees responds and looks into the camera.

"With a wry smile, he says, "Help me, Mr. Wizard."

~   ~   ~

The chief and colonel, as well as the whole Bank crew, watch the screen and the ensuing battles being shown. The technicians and military personnel turn and look into the control room when Rees's face fills the screen as he says, "Help me, Mr. Wizard."

Most do not have a clue to what he means, but the chief does. It's a reference to a 1960s era cartoon where a young time traveler would get into trouble and cry out for help.

The chief looks at the colonel. Colonel Black leans over and presses an intercom button. "Operation Ameliorate is concluded. Let's get our boys home."

~ ~ ~

Joshua Walsh is incensed about the outcome so far. They should have crushed this puny band of soldiers. And how in the Devil's name did they allow those five to escape from the house. Over two hundred men against a farmer, his wife, and twenty-some-odd soldiers. He is a distance away from the shooting as it continues.

Some of his men have gotten off their horses and have taken cover behind various items on the farm: hay bailers, wagons, troughs, anything they can. Others still ride theirs, trying to shoot into any opening they can find. He looks in the distance at the two men lying across the Gatling guns, which are now silent.

Why hasn't anyone gone back there and started using them again? What type of men do I have here? he thinks, his earlier pride in the men now diminished.

He is on the same hill Andy O'Toole is buried. Walsh looks down at the newly covered grave and sneers. "All because of you." He spits and turns to look back at the battle before him.

While he scans the area, he finally thinks about his son. "Where is Tommy?" he muses. Then he looks around the front of the home and yard.

His gaze comes across a lone figure sprawled across the ground in between the burning home and the barn. The clothes are right, and the hair, he knows the hair. With a lump in his throat, he makes his way down the hill, the battle forgotten. He moves slowly going down the slope, then picks up speed when he reaches level ground.

Galloping as fast as his large frame will allow the horse to go, he makes it to the downed figure and stares at the lifeless eyes of Tommy Walsh, his only son, his only child. He moans and takes a deep breath, looking at the same sky his dead son looked at earlier. He rocks back and forth in his saddle, making an angry decision to end this battle, and it is not by retreating.

~   ~   ~

The soldiers are holding their own, but the limited field of fire from the barn, as well as a moving and a dug-in enemy, keep them from total victory. The men are running low on ammo, and there are only a couple of grenades left. Bouvier announced earlier the Gatling gun was *kaput* due to a broken firing pin.

"Piece of junk," he grumbles.

Rees reminds him Epstein has done a lot of good for them, he's entitled to a mistake or two. Besides, it was probably CATM's (Combat Arms, Training, and Maintenance) fault. Always blame them.

Lieutenant Holston has lost five of his twelve men, and he is severely wounded, having been shot twice, once in the arm and once in the leg. Kriger was able to stanch the blood flow from his leg, but he knows it is only temporary. He tells Rees and Farnsworth the man's femoral artery was nicked, and he won't make it. They are sad to hear the news but now must worry about the men on their team.

While the men try to figure out how to hold on until they are jaunted back to their timeline, the two Gatling guns open up again. Three more of Holston's men are struck and killed, and everyone drops to the ground.

"Son of a…" Farnsworth exclaims. "Tucker!" he yells.

"Hey, sir, I shot them."

"I know. Now, shoot them again," he orders.

Tucker scrambles back up the ladder and falls back down as one of the Gatling gun rounds hits him, causing him to lose his grip on the top rung and fall. He strikes the ground, and his left leg lands at an odd angle. There is an audible cracking sound as a bone breaks. Tucker screams and grabs for his broken shin bone.

Kriger runs over and tries to push the man down and calls for help. Mrs. O'Toole and Emma run over to assist. He can see a protrusion under the pants leg and knows Tucker has a compound fracture. Tucker stopped screaming but moans something fierce, teeth gritted.

Kriger grabs his med bag and removes a morphine syrette, injecting it into the man's thigh. Tucker grimaces but calms. Kriger begins working on him, knowing the pain he is about to cause the man by forcing the bone back into place.

Rees looks into the camera and shouts, "Hey, guys, anytime now." He turns and finds McGuire. "McGuire, get up there and take out those damned guns."

Sean acknowledges and hurriedly climbs the ladder. Rees listens and, in a few seconds, is rewarded with the barely audible sound of the rifle firing, with first one, then the other Gatling gun going silent. Rees grins. Then there is a loud rumble, and a large section of the barn explodes.

~ ~ ~

Joshua Walsh is beyond angry. He lost his wife years ago during the birth of their daughter, who also passed away while an infant. Now, he has lost his only son. The battle is not going as planned, and he feels the repercussions of all the death may outweigh any reward. Red-faced, he finds the first man he can and gives him an order. The man nods and gallops away.

Not too long a time goes by, and the man returns with a saddlebag containing dynamite. Walsh wants the barn blown to pieces and everyone inside along with it. The hired hand rides to a safe area and gathers some others to help wrap up sticks of explosives.

~   ~   ~

Rees and Farnsworth, as well as several others, slowly come to their senses, ears ringing loudly from the deafening explosion. They look and see a large section of the barn is missing. What they don't know at this time is that the rest of Holston's troopers were killed in the blast, except for McGregor. The barn is now on fire.

Mr. Farnsworth grabs his wife and pulls her to him. They make their way to a safer area of the burning barn. Farnsworth grabs two horses and brings them to the O'Tooles. He wants them to leave the barn and go towards the area where Walsh and his men came from. He explains he and his men will be fine and will cover them until they are out of harm's way.

They protest, but Farnsworth insists, bringing up their children and reminding them they must be there for them. He looks them in the eyes and tells them he swears he and his men will survive, but they will probably never see them again. Once this is all over, they will leave immediately.

Rees comes over and gives his reassurance as well. Reluctantly, Mr. O'Toole agrees and shakes the men's hands. A stern-faced Mrs. O'Toole touches both their cheeks and offers a warm smile, thanking them for everything, then she is helped onto the bareback horse by Mr. O'Toole. He then climbs on his horse, and they gallop away. The men acting as soldiers keep up their firing and cover the O'Tooles as they ride away, passing the two abandoned wagons with the Gatling guns.

Rees looks around and has an idea, watching Tosseti cursing a blue steak and killing men left and right. Bouvier, McGuire, and Green do so as well. Rees sees Nionee and runs to him. He orders Nionee to follow him, and they take off towards the Gatling guns. Some of Walsh's men see them and give chase but are eliminated by the combined firepower from the guns of Bouvier, Green, and McGuire.

The two men reach the wagons, and Rees jumps in the back of one, and Nionee grabs the reins. Rees takes a few minutes and pulls a rope taught across the bottom planks, then slides his feet under the rope. He takes more rope and wraps it around himself and the Gatling gun, which is bolted to the plank. He is now secure from being thrown. He yells that he is set, and Nionee snaps the reins and yells, *Anagisdi*! And they're off.

The wagon comes in hard and fast, with Rees cranking the handle and aiming at every living thing outside the burning barn. Between him and the others' constant firing, they slay Walsh's army at an alarming rate. The men are as confused as the Rebels were with how they could be hitting men with their shots, and it seems to have no effect.

Walsh's men look around and don't like what they see. Too many of their small army is lying on the ground dead or dying. One by one, they begin to desert. Walsh notices and screams for them to stand their ground, to keep fighting. He threatens them. Tells them they will not be paid or will be fired or will never see work again. The men don't care, and soon, it's a rout. Finally, the battle is over, and the last man has fled the area.

As soon as the men from Rees' team see the mercenaries flee, they swiftly evacuate the burning barn, ensuring the animals are freed, retrieving as many of the dead they can before the heat overwhelms them. They gather in an open area between the two burning buildings and breathe a sigh of relief.

The men feel a familiar tingling sensation, and Rees looks at his arms to see the hairs rise. Several of the men look around and see the blue clear skies from the morning turning a hazy gray. Emma and Sergeant McGregor see the reaction the men have to the weather change and are confused.

"What is going on, Captain Rees?" McGregor asks, looking around.

Rees smiles. "You two may want to step back some. I'm sorry for what you're about to see, and I wish you didn't, but there's nothing we can do about it. It's not anything to worry about, and it's not witchcraft or sorcery or magic. I can't explain it to you, but we want you both to know we appreciate your help, and we're all sorry about Andy. But, Emma, please tell the O'Tooles we wish the best for them and the girls," he says.

"I don't understand, Captain," Emma says, her face upturned, brow wrinkling.

"Even if there was time, I couldn't really explain it."

The sky gets hazier, and the electricity becomes more prominent. While Rees talks, everyone watches him. Farnsworth comes to stand beside him as he tries to explain, very poorly, what is happening. Out of the corner of the men's eyes, they see something approaching from the smoke and ashes. A lone rider comes towards them at a full gallop, a shotgun in the rider's hands aimed directly at Emma Kelly.

The suddenness of the attack startles the men, who are a slow to react, all except for Rees, Farnsworth, and McGregor. McGregor turns his back to the rider to shield Emma at the same time Rees tackles both Emma and McGregor. They just have time to recognize the hate-filled face of Joshua Walsh before the man pulls both triggers of the shotgun, sending two barrels of buckshot in their direction.

Rees takes almost the full brunt of the small lead pellets' impact, driving him into McGregor and Emma, knocking them all to the ground. Farnsworth receives the rest of the shot, throwing him onto Rees and the others.

Rees' men have now had time to react, and every man standing shoots at Walsh. The man is riddled with bullet holes as blood flies in all directions. He is dead before he even passes the cluster of people on the ground and before he falls out of his saddle. The airmen do not even have time to see what they have done before the excruciating pain of Clio's embrace makes them drop their weapons so they can cover their ears and grimace and moan in pain, many falling to their knees.

Then they are gone, and the blue skies return to reveal only the dead.

EPILOGUE

General Richard Lucas stands in his office, staring through a large window that overlooks a room filled with military personnel, technicians, and scientists. Most are sitting behind green screen computer monitors, with others standing behind them, while still others mill about the room, checking various readouts and checking equipment.

The sound to the room is off, and even if it was on, he knew there would be little noise as most of the people whisper as if what they were about to do would be jinxed if they spoke too loud or with some reverence for the job at hand.

The general is worried. The creator of the project is not here. Chief Master Sergeant Joseph Black did not see eye to eye with the Bank Council, the group of political overseers who had pushed to have this project running before it should have been, in the chief's opinion. An argument ensued between the two powers, and Chief Black refused to be a part of the program if it was going to be greenlit before everything was ready. Again, in the chief's opinion, but one the general knew the Council should have listened to.

It doesn't matter now, as the project is about to begin, and the lives of fifteen men will hang in the balance. Fifteen men who have no idea what's in store for them. An adventure, or possibly death. The general didn't know which.

The Clio Project is the brainchild of CMSgt Black, who in the 1970s created the first working time machine, which he named Clio after the goddess of history. The general had known the chief since he was a sergeant in the Vietnam War, and the two became close as the general paved the way for Black to work on the project with government funding. It had taken years of hard work, but Clio is now operational, as far as the council is concerned.

Chief Black insisted on more trials, tests, and simulations before he would sign off on using Clio with human subjects. The Council disagreed. They had seen the tests and were pleased with the results. They felt that the government had spent enough time and money on the project, and now they wanted to see results. The council told Black and Lucas the greatest test would be to send people through time and bring them back and that they had all the confidence in the world it would work, end of discussion.

This angered the chief, who refused to be part of the project if it was to be used on human test subjects without further testing. Not only that, but sending men on a possible one-way trip and not even letting them know was diabolical. They didn't even ask for volunteers. Without the chief's knowledge, or the general's, the Council had already selected several USAF Security Policemen for the project. They picked fifteen men who had no family ties and placed them on one base, a base where the experiment would be conducted.

The chief continued to protest and, again, informed them he would not be a part of this project if they continued on the path they were taking. This fell on deaf ears, and the Council called him out on it. The chief was not bluffing, and he stormed out of the room with General Lucas excusing himself, then following the chief out the door.

"Joe. Joe, wait up," the general implores.

The chief ignores the general and continues walking down the corridor.

"Damn it, Chief, stop right there. That's an order!" Lucas commands, not wanting to do that but needing to try and talk Black out of abandoning the project.

The chief stops and turns to face the general.

"I'm sorry, sir, I will not be a part of their insane project. I built Clio, and I know how she works. She is not completely ready. It's not like I was asking for years, but we still need a few months more to ensure she is completely safe. We haven't even sent people through. I was going to volunteer myself for the first trial."

General Lucas places his hands on his hips after walking up to the chief. "Joe, listen. This project is going ahead with or without you. I believe Clio is ready, but I put stock into what you're saying. What would a couple of more months do? Would you find something else that could go wrong and postpone another mission? Listen, I'm not saying the Council is right in the way they're handling this, but it is happening. I'd prefer it happens with you in the room. If something does go wrong, who else but you should be there to fix it?"

Chief Black looks the general in the eye and holds his stare, then looks away and up at the ceiling. Sighing, he lowers his head and shakes it slowly. "Sorry, sir. No can do. They want to play with my invention, let them. You don't need me here for that. You have enough qualified personnel in there to handle any problems that arise," he says, looking back at the general. "If there's nothing else, sir, I'll leave you to it, and the best of luck. I hope I'm wrong at the Council, but I know I'm not."

The chief watches the general, who nods in defeat. The chief comes to attention and salutes the general, not that it's required in this setting but because the chief respects the general and understands the position he has been placed in. Without waiting for a return salute, the chief turns and walks down the corridor and enters an elevator. He turns and faces the general, no expression on his face as the elevator doors close.

The general stands in the corridor for a few minutes. He assumes the chief will fly back to Washington DC, where one of his apartments is located. He knows how to get in touch with him if need be, and he just hopes it doesn't come to that. The chief may calm down after the initial phase of the program begins and willingly return to ensure things run smoothly.

~ ~ ~

The next day, August 9, 1980, the general stands in his office, watching the personnel working below him. There is a knock on his door.

"Come in," he says, not turning from his view. He hears the door open, and a female voice says, "General Lucas, I've brought you some coffee and a doughnut. I know you haven't eaten anything."

Lucas turns and smiles at his secretary, Shelly, and sees she holds a small tray from the chow hall with the pastry and a mug of coffee.

"Thank you, Shelly, just set it on the desk. I promise I'll eat it," he says to her and turns back to the window.

Shelly sets the tray on the desk and turns to leave. She gets to the door and hesitates. Watching the general, Shelly wants to say something but decides against it and retreats to her office, closing the door silently behind her.

No sooner than she leaves, his desk phone rings. He picks it up.

"What have you got, Major?" he asks into the receiver, already knowing it is Major Hess from the control room.

"Sir, we're ready to proceed. All instruments indicate green across the board, and the power grid is fully charged. Just waiting on your go ahead," the major informs him.

Lucas' hand tightens on the phone as he watches the screen where he and the rest of the personnel in the control room can see the weapons munition area where the Security Policemen are assigned. The fifteen men were assigned this posting on purpose, with the sole intent of sending them back in time.

Lucas takes a deep breath and answers, "Start the procedure. And may God have mercy on all of us if we screw this up."

The major looks up at the general standing in the window. He knows what he feels because he feels the same way. Parts of him equally scared, worried, anxious, excited, and hopeful.

"Yes, sir, initiating sequence," he replies and hangs up the phone. All eyes are on him as the major tells the team, "It's a go."

The room jumps into activity as each person is assigned an individual task to start the process and monitor the course of the experiment.

The room hums as the electric power supplied from outside the control room permeates it. Anticipation fills the room as each station indicates a go. The major looks over at the scientist standing by the main control panel and nods. *The chief should be doing this,* Hess thinks. The scientist looks worried, then without further hesitation, inserts the Inabular Device into Clio.

Things happen pretty fast after that as the time machine is activated and begins the transformation of the individuals in the weapons storage area. Everyone watches in amazement.

General Lucas, still standing at the window, views the large screen mounted on the wall. After a few minutes, he sees an NCO come out of the building, looking around confused. Another picture angle shows an NCO in the control tower also looking around, and then back towards the building. There are several different camera angles, each showing different Security Policemen with each SP seemingly confused.

The hairs on several of the men rise as if static electricity fills the area. The general looks back to the first NCO, a Tech Sergeant, Rees the name on his fatigue shirt, and sees him cover his ears and watches as he falls first to his knees, then face forward onto the ground.

Lucas is concerned. "What have we done, just killed them all?" he asks himself. Before he can think of anything else, the entire area shimmers, warbles, then the SPs disappear only to be replaced by a single man wearing the blue uniform of a Civil War soldier. The soldier lies on the ground and makes his way onto his hands and knees. He pushes himself into a seated position and looks around groggily, taking deep breaths, seemingly trying to figure out where he is. He rubs his chest and grimaces in pain.

"What the hell is happening?" Lucas announces to the empty room, then reaches for the phone. Before his hand even touches it, the Union-clad soldier turns to looks directly into one of the cameras as if he knows it's there, causing the general to hesitate.

"My God," the general says, forgetting the phone and moving closer to the window. "It's that NCO who just left. What is happening?"

As if Rees hears the general, he raises his hands towards the camera and waves them back and forth in a stopping motion, and yells, "General Lucas, Chief Black sent me back. Pull the Inabular Device now! Pull it now! Stop the experiment! Do it now!"

Then Senior Master Sergeant Rees falls over unconscious.

ACKNOWLEDGMENTS

My thanks go to my editor, Tim Marquitz for all the work he put into making my words flow and to Nick Castle, the artist who created the wonderful cover.

Special thanks go out to Lieutenant Colonel Marc Van Ells (USAF Retired F-15 Pilot) for his technical input and for being a friend.

About the Author

Mark S. Roberts served in the United States Air Force for twenty years as a security policeman and is an Operational Desert Storm veteran. He holds a bachelor's degree in administration in criminal justice. Raised in Jacksonville, Florida, Mark has lived and served in locations around the world and in the United States. He currently resides in Green Bay, Wisconsin, with his wife Lori, also a USAF veteran.

www.ingramcontent.com/pod-product-compliance
Lightning Source LLC
Chambersburg PA
CBHW071932130726
47908CB00015B/125